PROPER CARE AND FEEDING OF MAGICALLY ENHANCED SIBLINGS

VAMPIRE INNOCENT
BOOK NINETEEN

MATTHEW S. COX

DIVISION ZERO PRESS

ISBN (ebook): 978-1-950738-66-3

ISBN (paperback): 978-1-950738-67-0

CONTENTS

1. A Little Too Quiet   1

2. Inconvenience is the Mother of Improvisation   17

3. Don't Panic   24

4. Nowhere Else to Hide   28

5. Two Jane Does Walk Into a Motel   34

6. Free Delivery   44

7. Friends in Unlikely Places   56

8. Movie Night   73

9. Belated   78

10. Not This Again   89

11. Another End of the World Scenario   99

12. Homework   112

13. Advanced Placement   116

14. Mildly Inconvenient   120

15. Deals, Favors, and Demons   130

16. A Collection of Irritating Inescapable Annoyances   136

17. Straight to Heck   154

18. An Alarming Development   158

19. The Sauce Miser   163

20. The Thirteenth Most Insidious Evil   167

21. Tedium   177

22. Unsporting   187

23. Nightmares of Nightmares   197

24. The Motherlode   206

25. Power of the Sacred Bean   214

26. Olmaz the Somewhat Wise   225

27. Scry Baby   228

28. Poking the Void Octopus   238

29. Merely the King of France   244

30. For Once, It Worked   260

31. The Lesser Evil is Still Evil   266

32. A Bargain of Epic Annoyance   275

33. Big Red Monster   282
34. Magical Messes Need Magical Solutions   291
35. Mission Possible: Covert Extraction   295
36. How to Reason With Fanatics   305
37. A Little Mayhem   325
38. Qualified Immunity   333
39. The Hunt: Part One   341
40. Mystic Rivalry   360
41. Holiday Spirit   377
42. Even in Death   387
43. Warning   397
44. The Darwin Awards   403
45. Vampires of Mass Destruction   421
46. The Hunt: Part Two   425
47. Fully Operational   432

Acknowledgments   439
About the Author   440
Other books by Matthew S. Cox   441

CHAPTER I
A LITTLE TOO QUIET

SUNDAY NIGHT

Happy isn't an emotion I've embraced too fully ever since my ex-boyfriend killed me.

I mean, sure. There have been moments of joy over my almost two years now of undeath, most of which involved my family or new boyfriend, Hunter. My brain went on a roller-coaster ride of weird, starting with crazy nostalgia, followed by the whole swing of emotions that made no sense. It's almost as if since I escaped the clutches of the demonic red faerie, the Universe wanted me to have *all the mood swings* at once in a few-month span.

About the only mental scar left from that time in my unlife is my unusual clinginess to home. That's probably not going anywhere soon. It's the reason I broke vampire tradition. I was scared, freaking out, and had no idea what to do... so I rushed home where I'd feel safe. They say vampires are super protective of their lairs. In my case, it seems I simply got a head start on that before actually becoming one.

As one might expect, being a vampire that's awake all night, we often have swaths of time with nothing really to do. The other night, I was watching random videos online and stumbled across one where some guy talked about a psychologist he stumbled across who did a study that confirmed it is completely normal to develop a deep longing for one's childhood home.

Of course, this psychologist was talking about adults who left the place they grew up decades ago... not teenagers, and most certainly not permanent undead teenagers who never actually went through with the whole 'leaving home' deal.

Still, it made me feel a little better about my unusual clinginess to the house. Whenever I stop to think intellectually (which I really try not to do very often) I accept that the idea we're going to live forever in that house is implausible. Aurélie, whether or not she suffers the same longing, simply cannot go back to her childhood home. The building hasn't existed for two centuries. At some point in the future, things are likely to happen that will force me, Ashley, and Chloe to find somewhere else to lair.

Whether or not any of the Littles are still going to be around at that point in time, I don't know.

Part of me kinda suspects the craziness of my life and family is only getting started. As in, two hundred years from now, Sierra, Sophia, and Sam might still be around... though I hope they grow up. Sophia said the other day she's afraid of growing up because of Dad always talking about how life was so much better as a kid. She doesn't want to deal with all the bad parts of being an adult. No, I don't mean having to get a job and work and having responsibility. I mean the sadness. My poor little sister wants to be shielded from things in life that make people sad.

Sigh.

Yeah, she's innocent and idealistic. When the day comes where the Reality Hammer™ lands on her head, it's going to be tragic.

Of course, given her unpredictable command of magic, who the hell knows what's going to happen. Sophia might stay eleven years old forever. Gonna get a little awkward, but I'm hoping she grows out of that phase. I mean, if you're going to make your siblings ageless, at least let them reach their teens first, Soph. Oh hell. Maybe it's because she's heard me talking to Ashley about how awesome it is to be free from the red faerie's grip? Vampirism isn't the only way to do that. If she never allows herself to get old enough, she, too, will escape the cruel clutches of the monthly visitor. After what happened with Sierra at the pool party, Sophia might be terrified of how her red monster is going to manifest for the first time.

Hmm. I suppose it's her life, so it should be her choice. 'Do I grow up or not' isn't the usual sort of thing one deals with. Also, maybe I'm just worrying about something that's not even an issue.

Coralie said something about Sam a while ago. His relationship with demons is going to keep him around longer than normal. An unnaturally long life is kind of like the door prize for signing up to be a demonologist or a maleficar. Neither one of those names really fits Sam since he's neither evil nor mean. Not really sure what to call him, at least in terms of his supernatural gift. I think he's closer to Sophia in that our family had some long hidden magical potential. In his case, it ended up being focused toward demons for some reason. I had a dream where my little brother looked like he'd reached his early twenties, but the background had spacecraft parked like cars in a lot. Is it weird that the idea of my brother being ageless is *more* plausible than thinking society might develop consumer-grade spaceships?

I mean, holy crap. Cars are bad enough… imagine anyone being able to go buy a spacecraft?

The insurance would be astronomical.

Anyway, sorry for the mental wanderings. I'm thinking about my siblings for two reasons. One: Ashley and I are on a long flight. Two: we stopped talking long enough that my mind latched onto my annoyance at not being home with my family.

I don't mean that Ash and I are 'not talking.' Nothing like that. We just both shut up for no particular reason at the same time.

Roaming thoughts fill the silence. Yeah, I'm annoyed. A little. It's very teenage of me. How dare an adult disturb my lounging around by sending me to do a chore. Only, this isn't taking out the trash. The adult in question who disturbed my slackerdom is not my father or mother... it's Arthur Wolent.

Technically, not him per se. He had one of his people call me. Still, it's effectively him.

There are perks to being the junior-most vampire on his... umm... payroll.

Can I call it a 'payroll' if I'm not being paid? At least not in money. Whatever. There are definitely benefits to keeping him happy and being part of official society.

Of course, there are also downsides to being the proverbial FNG. This freakin' new girl (yeah, I know that's not what the F is, but I'm not from New Jersey) just got her butt sent on a FedEx quest. This is what I get for playing *Skyrim* so damn much. My life has turned into a video game. Important NPC has sent the player on a long journey to obtain Quest Item and bring it back.

There's also some level of intrigue here, as well.

I was instructed not to bring any identifiable things with me, like my iPhone, wallet, or ID of any kind.

Normally, an instruction like that would have scared me. Like, what exactly is he expecting us to walk into? I suppose it's helpful, at least in one way. The NSA—or whoever is watching all of our cellular phones—isn't going to think their system is malfunctioning when an iPhone belonging to a teenage girl suddenly bee-lines at like 120 MPH in a straight line from Cottage Lake, Washington to East Bumblephuk, Nevada.

Yeah, Nevada.

Ugh.

So, according to Google... it's about 490 miles in a direct line. The sun set today around 4:20 p.m. Yay for December in Washington. Flying to our mission objective would take us about four hours and some minutes if we sprinted the whole way. We didn't fully sprint, but we're also not exactly taking our time. The sooner we get down there, the sooner we can get home. This job is going to eat the entire night, but we should be able to get it done in one night without having to spend the day sleeping in whatever safe spot we can find.

We also tried to be smart about things, as in not wearing any loose, flappy garments or anything wind can steal. We're both suffering uncomfortably snug sports bras, and much more comfy yoga pants. For the moment, we're barefoot. Yeah, we look like we're on the way to the beach for a California summer despite it being the first of December. Yeah, it was cold for a little while when we left the house. Eventually, we adjusted. Another neat thing about being a vampire is how after a few minutes in any climate, it all starts to feel like room temperature. Innocents, like us, suffer the shock of going between drastically different environments. Like if we walk barefoot out of a warm house into a December evening, we'll shriek and shiver for a few minutes before our bodies adjust. As far as I know, every other vampire just constantly ignores temperature. They don't even feel it at all.

This is not me complaining. I'll take a little cold shock every so often for the benefits.

Even though we're on our way to Nevada, it's still cold. We are not dressed for this weather, which isn't necessarily a problem for us personally. The problem is that running around in a sports bra and yoga pants in winter is going to make people stare at us. It's strange and weird. Strange and weird attracts attention. Things that might cause us to linger in someone's memory are bad.

So, we have sneakers, sweatshirts, and jeans tucked away in our backpacks—and an extra full change of clothes on top of that. I'm wary that a vampire job is going to end up with someone sprouting claws at some point and shredding my outfit. It's almost become a thing now. Vampire combat equals nudity. At least, if there are claws or blades involved. It almost makes being shot seem like a preferable option. The major downside to guns, though, is it only takes one lucky hit in a critical spot for the lights to go out. That's not death, mind you, but it could be. Hostile vampires could do anything they wanted to me after a bullet to the head knocks me unconscious, up to and including throwing me into a blast furnace.

Sounds weird to say, but I would much rather end up stranded naked in public than be permanently destroyed.

If anyone told me before that fateful night Scott stabbed me that I'd end up bare-assed outside in public and *not* implode into a tiny speck of mortification, I'd have laughed at them... and then promptly curled up and died at the mere thought of it. Can't say for certain if it's a vampire thing... or a being forced into the situation over and over thing, but getting stranded outside with no clothes doesn't bother me that much anymore.

Oh, sure it bothers me. Like... someone spilling coffee on my shirt would bother a normal person. I certainly don't want to do it intentionally, but if it happens, I'm not going to have a freakout. Being caught streaking is only embarrassing if witnesses live to tell about it. I'm kidding. That sounded more dramatic. If I make people forget seeing me, it's like it never happened.

Yay for vampire mind powers.

There's also a very good chance nothing will go crazy tonight. I don't know a great deal about what's going on. Neither Wolent nor his representative who gave me the job told me anything about the vampire situation in this part of Nevada, nor did they mention anything about what's on the USB stick I'm supposed to get. Ideally, this is going to be a no-contact mission. We go down there, grab the thing, go home right away without seeing a single other vampire or mortal.

The USB in question has been hidden in a motel room in a little town called Gomez, which is so damn small it's not even on the map. So, I set my navigation point to Winnemucca, which is the closest mapped town. Wolent's guy told us that Gomez is a few miles north-west of there where Google Maps just shows empty desert nothingness. A town in the middle of literal nowhere shouldn't be *that* difficult to locate. We should be able to find it flying a zigzag. Even easier if there are any lights on.

"Are we there yet?" asks Ashley in a normal tone.

I chuckle, mildly surprised she didn't put on an overly childish voice. "Not yet."

"Never been to Nevada before." Ashley gazes around at the desert zooming by under us. "Not much to see here, huh?"

"I think they compressed all the things into Las Vegas." I shrug and pull out the 'burner' phone Wolent's people provided, to check the map. They didn't want me (or Ashley) bringing our actual phones with us, both for 'government tracking' reasons as well as if anything happened to us, whoever did the bad thing could find out all sorts of information about us from our phones. Considering any such blowback could easily affect my family, I didn't protest at all. Maybe I'm too much of a child still, mentally. Stuck in that 'pleasing authority' phase or something. As soon as Wolent's people started talking about someone going through my phone for information, I should have really started asking questions about how dangerous this mission really was.

I didn't. It sounded like an easy FedEx quest to make the boss happy. Like that annoying kid who always runs to answer the door first, I took the job without asking too many questions.

Sigh.

What sucks is, right now, I'm thinking regret and trying to tell myself that next time I will ask the questions instead of doing back-flips immediately to make everyone happy and like me. But... I'm eighteen. No matter how much I tell myself I will be more method-ical and careful in the future, my brain will always be mired in teenage impulse. That whole 'acting without thinking' mess is my life forever. Thankfully, I'm not quite as bad as some people my age. A boy in my senior class, Curtis, got the bright idea to light his farts on fire. He ended up in the hospital with *internal* burns.

The mere thought of that hits me with a full-body cringe.

Yeah, I am not *that* stupid or impulsive.

Besides, I can't fart anymore.

Okay, maybe it wasn't so much my need to keep the big guy happy as much as me wanting to get it over with as fast as possible so I could go home and continue being a lazy teenager.

When I mentioned having a 'burner' phone, Dad expected this little thing he called a Nokia. Like a non-smart phone only good for making calls. This is some sort of Android device—which I am totally not used to. I've got it for two main reasons: using the map functions, and if something seriously goes wrong... I can call in some cavalry.

Granted, it would take Wolent's people a while to get down here. Not many of them can fly... at least not without the help of aircraft. Ash and I... and Chloe got really lucky. Maybe Innocents have a better chance of developing that particular power since our best option in a dangerous situation is running away. I mean, in my case, flight came immediately. The first clue that something incredibly weird happened to me was flying. Didn't even know I was a vampire at the time.

I can still see that puddle of muddy water that my subconscious mind refused to let me fall into.

The other side of that coin is that other bloodlines who get flying are almost always faster than us. Meh, whatever. Flying at all is effing amazing. I don't care if I'm slow as vampires go. Despite every-thing that's happened in my unlife, the only thing I *still* want is to be as normal as possible. That means hanging out at home, playing video games and watching anime with Ashley. Yeah, so what? I'm a boring, basic geek. Sue me... and my Uggs.

Yes, I have Uggs. They're comfortable. So what if people consider them basic? Dammit. I shouldn't have thought of them while flying through a December night barefoot. My feet briefly feel cold again until I stop thinking about the warm fuzzy interior of my ever so basic footwear.

I am a *stealth* geek, by the way.

Heh. Okay, I punned without meaning to. Dad would be so proud.

What I mean is... I'm a geek, but no one looking at me would know it. There's a stereotype look for geeky girls that I do not fit into. Sure, I'm kinda skinny and not the tallest creature in the world, but I don't *look* like a geek. Hence, my geekiness is in stealth.

I'm also a literal stealth geek thanks to Dalton. As in, if vampires were characters in D&D, I'd be a rogue. At least, the little sub-powers I seem to have inherited from him fit that. I can make locked doors open by wanting them to. That's kinda roguish, right? I can hide from security cameras and even hack into computers. Pretty sure the hacking into computers part doesn't work in D&D. There are no computers in medieval fantasy. At least there shouldn't be. If your GM starts throwing technology into their campaign, run. Run fast and never go back.

Anyway...

I look at the map on the alien Android device. "Almost. Winnemucca's about eight miles away... we should probably start looking around here."

"Kay," says Ashley.

We scan the ground, looking for any signs of civilization. Gomez, according to Wolent's people, is one of those towns that is so small it's basically a single street. They probably named it after the first guy to put a house there. Suppose it can't be *too* small if there's a motel there. That makes me suspect it's probably close-ish to Route 95. I bet someone calculated the ideal spot for motorists to get tired and want to sleep while they're on their way to Winnemucca and put a motel there.

As if Winnemucca is some tourist mecca.

Ugh. All I want to do is get this stupid USB thing and go home. I'm setting college aside for the time being so I can spend more time with my family while the Littles are still little... and now, Wolent's sending me across state lines on a Sunday night. Well, at least it's a school night and the sibs won't be up too late. It's almost nine now, so they'd only have another hour or two before Mom chases them to bed.

"Is that it?" Ashley points.

I look over at her and burst out laughing. Her fluffy red hair has entirely obscured her face thanks to the force of the wind we're flying into. She looks like some sort of crazy Muppet. My brain fills in coffee-coaster sized googly eyes in the red floof and that's it for me.

"What?" She tries unsuccessfully to look at me, then rakes her hands at her hair until she tames the wild floof. By that point, she understands why I'm laughing... and bursts out laughing, too.

"You turned into the floofbeast again." I giggle.

Ashley makes a 'yeaargh' noise somewhere between a Sesame Street monster and a pirate while fluffing her hair all over the place.

It's so dumb, it makes me cackle.

A few moments later...

The laughter subsides enough for me to finally look where she's pointing. There's obvious, and then there's this. One light bulb out in the desert at night would be a literal beacon for any flying vampire. What I am hoping is the town of Gomez has more than one light bulb. Probably like... twenty.

It looks like a hunk of the sun fell off and landed in the desert here off to my left. I can't see a damn thing but a mass of light swelling up from the earth in various shades of oranges and yellows. Kinda looks like a cartoon nuclear explosion in super slow motion. No idea how the hell I didn't see that before she pointed at it. Well, I had been focusing on the right side of the desert... and my mind was wandering.

Ironically, this lightsplosion is worse than a huge city. The light saturation from a place like Seattle is so much stronger than this little town that my eyes would already have dialed back their sensitivity. Surrounding areas aren't as dark as where we are now. So, little Gomez, Nevada is like sneaking up on someone with night vision and clicking a Maglite on in their face.

"Ouch."

Ashley cringes. "Yeah."

"And I was worried we wouldn't be able to find it."

"You worry a lot." She puts an arm around me.

"S'pose I do."

She leans her head against mine while trying to look in the direction of the glow. "Think that's Gomez?"

"I don't see any other signs of life out here anywhere close enough." I blink a few times. "That's gotta be it."

We slow to a lazy glide and veer toward the little town. As my eyes dial it back, details emerge and the super intense glow dissipates. The 'downtown' area consists of a single street running for about five blocks, plus a little development creep to either side on some crossing streets where a fast food place and gas station have cropped up off the main drag. A handful of private homes dot the desert, the closest one probably a ten-minute car trip away from the downtown area.

This town is so small it looks like a movie set. Except for the buildings being real and not just façades, that is. I spot a motel sitting by itself in the desert maybe a quarter-mile from the downtown strip, closer to Route 95 in the east. Sure enough, it's sitting alongside the road leading from 95 into Gomez.

"That's gotta be it." I point.

"Yeah. They put the motel far enough away from town so no one can hear the gunshots." Ashley makes a silly face.

I cringe a little. No idea how bad an area this is. "As if there's a cop within twenty miles anyway."

Obviously, casual normal violence doesn't terrify me anymore. It's a concern for sure, but not so bad I'd never go near a place like this now. Tiny little towns that don't appear on any maps might be full of vampires. Ordinary mortals would say Gomez, Nevada is a fictional town that doesn't really exist. That's exactly what we want them to think.

Geez, now I sound like Wolent. Heh.

We fly toward the motel, keeping ourselves high enough in the air to avoid casual observation. I don't see anyone out and about downtown. Maybe that's a warning. Maybe it's normal. Little rural towns like this tend to 'roll up the sidewalks at night' like Dad says. You know you're out in the sticks when even the McDonald's closes by sunset.

Upon finding a suitably dark spot between the little downtown area and the motel, I zip down and land. The sandy dirt is neither warm nor cold. I look around to make sure no one saw us flying. Once sure we've got about as much privacy as one can expect outside, I sling my backpack off and open it.

Ashley and I pull on our sweatshirts and jeans right over our 'flight suits,' then put sneakers on. Hopefully, we'll grab this thing and get out of here without seeing (or being seen by) anyone. Still, running around barefoot in a sports bra and yoga pants would totally attract attention on a thirty-degree night. Better safe than having to mind-wank people into forgetting us. Even sweatshirts are pushing it. This is heavy coat weather. Unfortunately, none of the coats I have would fit into my backpack.

The Gomez Motel—not sure if it's officially called that, but whatever—is a plain one-story L-shaped building with a whole bunch of doors wrapped around an attempt at a parking lot. I say attempt because it's not even paved. Honestly, it's not even named as far as I can tell. The sign only says 'motel.'

"What do we do now?" whispers Ashley.

I shrug. "We find room sixteen, grab what we need, and GTFO."

"Okay."

We walk toward the motel in a straight line through the scrub brush. Much to my surprise, an unexpected flicker of moonlight draws my attention to the right. There sits a tiny graveyard. The flash came from a marble headstone catching the moon. Oh wow. That's not creepy at all. Who builds a motel a stone's throw away from a graveyard? Even if there are only like nine tombstones, that's still a graveyard. I bet it's a bunch of prospectors or something who died here in like 1840 or something.

This is getting better and better. Not.

Yes, I'm a vampire. But mentally, I'm still 98% me. Even though it's irrational and silly, I walk faster to get away from the graveyard before anything scary jumps out at us. I really hope no other vamps are watching us now or they'd *so* make fun of me.

As we reach the flatter dirt that's pretending to be a parking lot, I realize the motel's office is all the way on the right side at the end of the longer part of the L. The rooms start at #1 right beside that, and count upward to the left. I turn on my heel and head for the opposite end of the building. The size this place is, I assume Room #16 is going to be near the end on the stubby part of the L.

We cross the lot and step up onto the little sidewalk running around the property in front of the rooms. To no one's surprise, there isn't a single car here. That's no guarantee the motel is totally empty, though. After all, *we* got here without a car.

"Man," I say just above a whisper. "We should have shotguns for this."

Ashley stops short and whirls to stare at me, eyes widening. "What? The heck are we supposed to be doing here? I thought we're just picking something up."

I chuckle. "Yeah. I'm just making a joke. You know the whole 'walking up on a motel room to do the boss's bidding thing. *Pulp Fiction?*"

"Oh." She covers her mouth to hold in a laugh.

Eyes on the wall, I keep going. Thirteen... fourteen...

"Would you give a girl a foot massage?" asks Ashley.

"Sure, why not," I mutter.

"Would you give *me* a foot massage?" She grins.

"In a completely platonic sisterly way, of course." I wink at her.

She tilts her head. "I'm not sure if you ruined my movie-quoting joke or if you're being serious."

Aha. Room# 16. I point at the door. "Bingo."

Ashley shifts her gaze to the door.

I lean close and put my ear against it, listening in case there's someone waiting for us inside. Not that I am expecting trouble… but, it's not like the motel management would be aware that vampires are using this room for a drop. Someone put a USB thing in here for us to retrieve and bring to Wolent. It's not impossible that the motel rented this room out to a random uninvolved person.

"What's on this USB anyway?" whispers Ashley.

"Don't know. Don't care."

"Seriously?" She blinks at me.

I keep listening. "Yes. Seriously."

Ashley tucks under me and also puts her head against the door. We're like a pair of tweens trying to eavesdrop on their older sister while she's on the phone with her boyfriend.

"Wow. Okay," whispers Ashley.

"Don't say it like that. I trust Mr. Wolent not to do anything bad enough I'd feel guilty over being involved. And I'm happier not knowing what's on it since no old ones can mind read it out of me."

"I don't hear anything," whispers Ashley.

"Neither do I." I reach out and grab the knob. "Let's make this quick."

Since I want to go in, the door isn't locked for me. Super handy power, that.

I turn the knob and give the door a push.

… and the next thing I know, I'm staring up at whiteness.

Okay, that's weird.

Over the next few seconds, I realize I'm flat on my back. The surface beneath me is cold, probably steel. I think I'm naked inside a plastic bag. As soon as I reach up to wipe my face, crinkling confirms that I am, in fact, inside a plastic bag.

Dammit!

I extend one claw on my right index finger and slice the bag open enough to get my head out.

Plain metal above me stretches off to either side much farther than I expected to see. I'm inside a morgue cooler, but it isn't like the other one I woke up in. This chiller is entirely open inside rather than being separated into single compartments. I've got a full view of other sliding trays to my left and right. I lift my head and peer past my feet at a square hatch. Of course, there isn't any sort of handle or latch on the inside.

"Dammit," I say out loud.

"Sarah?" asks Ashley—her voice coming from the white plastic bag immediately to my right. "What happened?"

I stare up at the metal. The last thing I remember was opening the motel room door. Or at least pushing on it. That's good. I didn't lose days of memory. When Scott killed me, I didn't even remember the party at first. The temporary amnesia had to be a side effect of the Transference, of going from mortal to undead. A vampire suffering an injury that would have been fatal to a mortal is about the same as the old Hollywood knockout blow to the head. I say Hollywood because really, hitting someone in the head hard enough to knock them out isn't something a mortal would just shrug off. It's a serious injury.

But not to a vampire.

"I dunno. Maybe snipers got us. Does your head hurt?"

She paws at the body bag, trying to get out of it. Poor Ash. She doesn't have claws. These things aren't exactly made to be opened from the inside.

"Everything kinda hurts," says Ashley.

I pull the body bag off my upper half, reach over, and slice hers open.

She starts to sit up, bonks her head on the ceiling, and lies flat again. "Ow. That was dumb."

"Heh." I sigh.

Ashley lifts her head, peering down at herself. "Crap. I'm naked."

"Yeah, that's normal. We're in a morgue."

She turns her head to stare at me. I swear it's the same 'Oh, shit are we going to get in trouble' face she always made at me whenever something we did went wrong. It's adorable.

"Well..." I sigh at the ceiling. "That's not how tonight was supposed to go."

CHAPTER 2

INCONVENIENCE IS THE MOTHER OF IMPROVISATION

PROBABLY NOT SUNDAY NIGHT

"They stole our stuff," says Ashley after a long two-minute silence.

"Not sure 'stole' is accurate, but yeah. Someone took our stuff." I fidget at the body bag, making it crinkle.

I'm kinda sore all over. The more I think about my feelings (physical that is, not emotions) the less able I am to figure out what happened. If I'd been shot in the head by a sniper, my head should hurt... or at least ache. It's confusing why my sensations of discomfort are drifting back and forth from nothing at all to a general whole-body soreness.

Ashley rolls on her side to face me, jostling her tray. All that metal-on-metal banging would totally freak the hell out of any morgue worker who happened to be in the building. "What do we do now? Fly home naked or mug someone for their clothes?"

This is simultaneously weird and normal. We have showered together a few times out of necessity. We change in front of each other all the time. Just 'casually hanging out while naked' is a new level of strange, though. Hopefully, it does not become a habit. It's only not awkward because we've been forced into the situation. Why freak out over something I have no control over?

"Something." I shrug. "We can't just chill here."

Ashley groans. "Seriously? Chill? We're in a freaking morgue cooler."

I grin. "Why do you think I said chill?"

She sighs. "Dad would be so proud."

"Sure. Once he got done being upset that we ended up in a morgue."

"Seriously though." Ashley peels herself out of the body bag and wads it up. "Am I messed up?"

"You've always been a little messed up." I grin at her.

"I mean... wounds or something."

I look over.

Ashley's covered in dirt and black marks, plus more than a little bit of dried blood. I don't see any obvious wounds, missing parts, or any clear indication of what hit us. She kinda looks like she went exploring the burned remains of a haunted house and fell through the floor into a filthy basement.

"You're kinda dirty, but I don't see any injuries."

"Your face is kinda blackened," says Ashley.

"Dammit." I sigh and extricate myself from the body bag. There isn't enough room in here to get a good look at myself, so I roll up on my side to give Ashley a view. "How about me? Anything missing?"

She studies me for a moment. "Nope. But you look like you ran naked through a coal mine."

"Fire?" I ask.

"Umm." Ashley bites her lip. "I don't think so. Wouldn't fire hurt a lot more?"

"Probably." I tap my foot on air. "Okay. I'd rather steal clothes from a store than mug someone."

Ashley nods. "Agreed. Was there a store here?"

"Good question. Gomez is pretty small." I fidget. "We might have to sneak into someone's house and steal some clothes."

"Still beats mugging someone." Ashley grins. "If we can even find someone. The town looked deserted."

"True. We could always go house to house and raid closets." I shrug. "Assuming Gomez is a real town and not just like a 'movie set' vampires around here set up to pretend they're normal."

Ashley rolls flat, glances to her right at a corpse in a body bag, then looks at me again. "Yanno... I thought it would be freakier than this to be right next to dead bodies. It's not really bothering me."

As she says this, I realize we're not the only ones in the cooler. Three other bodies are in here as well. Can't tell much about them thanks to the white body bags other than one person was more than a little overweight and all three are at least adult-sized. And yeah, it doesn't freak me out as much as I'd have thought it would.

"Yeah, that is kinda weird." I gingerly squirm around to put my head closer to the hatch door. There's not enough room overhead to get up on my hands and knees, so I lay flat on my front. As expected, the door out of here is a square of flat metal. No handles, hinges, or any obvious means to open it. "I guess we're kinda past that whole fear of death thing."

"What do you mean?" Amid the rather loud crinkling of plastic, Ashley scrambles around to face the door, lying on her stomach, her front half propped up on her elbows.

"I mean, people usually get freaked out at the idea of being around corpses because they are a reminder of mortality." I sigh hard, blowing my hair off my face. "We're kinda past that."

"Oh. Right. Yeah." She slaps her hand against the hatch door a few times. Sounds thick. "Uh oh. Are we trapped?"

"Seems that way."

"How did you escape the first time?" She folds her arms and rests her chin on them.

"Panic. I mule-kicked the door open."

"Gonna do that again?" Ashley smiles. "Or should we just wait here and scare the hell out of some poor morgue worker?"

I almost laugh. "As hilarious as that would be, it's also kinda stupid. I'd much rather get out of here without being noticed."

"Okay. So, get on with the mule-kicking."

"There's got to be an easier way that won't leave permanent damage to prove something supernatural happened here." I look around at the other trays. Seems we are on the uppermost of two levels.

Ashley squirms. "Did we get autopsied?"

"Umm." I look down at myself. Black sooty stuff is smeared all over me. Swaths of dried blood here and there remind me of road rash, but the skin is intact. I don't see a Y-scar on my chest. Everything feels like it's in the right place. No weird itchiness swarms around inside my guts.

"There's nothing in my butt," says Ashley.

"Random much?" I blush. "Why would you even say that?"

"You know, like the funeral home thing. The plastic screw they put in corpses to keep stuff from leaking out."

I shudder. "A new fear has been unlocked."

"What?" She giggles.

"Getting messed up so bad, I don't wake up in the cooler and make it all the way to the mortuary. I can't imagine that... plug is very comfortable."

"No... they screw it in. Like a legit screw." Ashley makes a screwdriver motion.

"Stop." I hold my hand out to her. "Don't make me think that."

She giggles again, in that apologetic way she laughs whenever she's sorry but only a little. "I mean, we're not in the funeral home yet. This has to be like a medical examiner's place or something. We might not still be in Gomez."

"Oh, we're definitely not. That place wasn't big enough to even have a doctor's office, much less a hospital... or whatever this is."

"Whew. No one cut us open." Ashley exhales hard, then coughs, then hacks. She makes an 'oh shit, help!' face.

"Ash?" I reach over and put a hand on her shoulder.

She coughs again and spits a small, hard object out. It bounces off my face, hits the door hatch with a *click*, then falls to the bottom.

"Ow." Ashley rubs her throat. "That was not comfortable."

"What the heck?" I try to peer down at the mystery object, but it's out of sight from this angle.

"No idea. Whatever it was had sharp edges." She grimaces.

I push at the door. Come on, you bastard. Open.

"Do you remember anything?" Ashley coughs again, clearing her throat.

"Just trying to open the door. One second, we're about to go into the motel... then we're here."

"Wow." Ashley whistles and looks around. "This had to be really scary the first time it happened to you."

I stare at the plain steel in front of my face. "Considering that I had no idea I was a vampire then? Yeah. Just a bit."

"You seem really calm." Ashley bites her lip. "Thanks. It's helping me not panic."

"I am calm. This is just annoying."

Ashley tries to swing her feet up, but they hit the ceiling. "Damn. There's no room in here. Would've been nice to have been a vampire long ago. They didn't have to worry about waking up in a cooler."

I give her side eye and deadpan, "No, they'd just have to dig themselves out of a buried coffin."

"Eep! Okay, never mind that! I like this way more."

Swear, Ashley's eyes are so big she looks like a terrified Pixar character for a second.

"You like being stuck in a cooler?" I smirk.

"No. I like it more than the idea of being buried alive... or unalive... whatever." She shudders, then goes calm again. "Oh, should we tell the 'rents that we got killed?"

"We didn't get killed. And no. 'Unexpected complications' is the phrase I'll use. Mom doesn't like thinking about the whole undead thing. Trying to keep reality as normal as possible for her."

She nods. "Yeah. Well, I'm gonna guess we won't have enough time to fly home tonight."

"Probably not." I push on the door. "But we can't stay in here. Hmm. I wonder if I can make the lock open from this side. Do I have to actually touch the knob?"

Before Ashley can say anything, the cooler hatch gives a loud mechanical click and pops open.

"You did it!" chirps Ashley. "Nice!"

I fist pump. "Yessss! Go, go, vampire rogue powers. Dalton, you are a god."

I know. Thanks, luv.

Heh. Hearing his voice in my head is kinda comforting. Wonder if he has any idea what happened to us.

Not a clue. The whole mental link to my progeny isn't like I'm watching you on camera 24/7. Most times, I don't even notice it unless you think about me or have a strong emotional outburst or some such.

Getting 'killed' wasn't a strong outburst?

Whatever put you in that cooler was enough of a surprise that you switched off before mentally processing it.

Great. I can worry about the 'what happened' later once I'm sure no one's going to catch us.

I give the door a shove, pushing it fully open, then grab the sides of the opening and pull, causing the tray I'm on to slide out into the room. I'm not too far off the ground. This tray would be about at chest level to a normal adult. Easy enough to swing myself around and jump off. The floor feels shockingly warm.

It's not. My body is refrigerated at the moment. I'm used to the cold, so I don't feel it. Normal temperature feels warm.

After hurrying around the extended tray to the adjacent hatch, I grab the handle and pull it open. Ashley slides herself out and scrambles off her tray.

Here we stand, stark naked in the middle of a highly clinical—

but small room. We are both covered in soot and dirt. Looks like we went for a bit of recreational nudist chimney diving. This is so weird.

The room's only got one door out, plus a closet and a few storage cabinets. I'm in too much of a hurry to waste time searching futilely for anything to wear in here. There won't be anything; I just know it.

So, without another second wasted, I fast-walk out the door.

CHAPTER 3
DON'T PANIC

SOMEWHEN UNKNOWN

The room with the cooler and the hallway I've entered are both empty and quiet.

There can't be anyone alive in this place or they would've heard us rattling around on those sliding trays and come running... or shit themselves and fled out into the night. A thought hits me about the last time I escaped from a cooler: I ended up on YouTube. Thankfully, the video quality was so bad no one recognized me. It was one of those paranormal ghost videos or freaky video compilations. 'Girl wakes up at a morgue – a paranormal event or an elaborate hoax? You decide' type things.

No idea if this little place has cameras, but I might as well do the thing anyway.

Ashley hurries out of the cooler room and bumps into me. She involuntarily wraps her arms around me and rests her chin on my left shoulder. "Why did you stop?"

"Security cameras," I whisper.

"What about them?"

"I got it covered... I hope?"

"Why are you whispering?" She gives me a little squeeze, then let's go.

Good question. Honestly? No idea. I brush fine debris off my left arm, sawdust, splinters, something like that. "I'm doing sneaky stuff. Just seemed appropriate to whisper."

"Makes sense." Ashley shrugs.

As best as my brain will comply, I concentrate on the desire not to be picked up on video. That is one of the things Dalton gave me, though I haven't exactly used it very often. Uh oh. There it is. I *feel* something happening. Yeah, there definitely are cameras watching us right now. Nothing to see here. We don't really exist. The desire *not* to be recorded wells up in my mind and I project it out into the world.

"Cool. I'll stay close so you can hide us both." She's no longer clinging to me, but keeps holding my hand. "Think there's any clothes in here? Scrubs maybe?"

"Maybe... I'd almost rather get out of a place full of security cameras as fast as possible before I have a lapse in concentration."

"If you want to, why not." She chuckles. "You're kinda casual about streaking."

"Gotten used to it... and I can make anyone forget." I walk forward at a deliberate, controlled pace. Not sure how I know this, but moving too fast is going to leave evidence on video. Blurs, unexplained anomalies, that sort of thing. I can't help but chuckle at the silliness. "Besides, if I'm already naked, getting into a fight with a vampire won't ruin my outfit."

She chuckles. "Ugh. Why don't morgues keep spare clothes handy in an easy-to-find place?"

"Probably for the same reason there aren't door handles *inside* the cooler. They don't expect their guests will get up and walk away."

"Fair point."

I head down the hall, walking as if I'm carrying an overfull bowl of soup I don't want to spill. We pass a little conference room, a break area, another room full of filing cabinets, small server closet, an office area with some cubicles in it... and finally reach the lobby. This facility is so small, there isn't even a reception desk... or chairs for people to wait in. Yeah, it's not exactly the kind of place people tend to go to unless they have to be here.

"Umm, Sare?" whispers Ashley, her grip on my hand tightening somewhat. "We have a serious problem."

My idea of a serious problem right now would be getting caught by anyone with a cell phone who'd take video/pictures of us. Second worst to that would be running into some hostile vampires. Wait, no. The most serious of serious problem would be if my parents were here to catch me streaking through a morgue at night.

Dad would absolutely quote *Terminator* and say, 'nice night for a walk?' at which point, I'd drop dead of embarrassment.

Still concentrating on the cameras, I slowly turn my head around to look at her. "What?"

She points.

I follow her gaze to one of those old-school analog clocks on the wall like something from the 1960s. It takes me a moment to translate the position of the hands into the time: 6:18 a.m.

Uh oh. The sun's going to be up any minute now.

"Oh, shit..." Fear almost makes me lose concentration on the camera thing, but I manage to catch myself... I hope.

"Why did we wake up so close to sunrise?" Ashley frowns. "Why not just stay asleep until the next afternoon?"

I shift my weight nervously. "Probably because we really need to get the hell out of here right away or bad things will happen to us."

"Like how vampires wake up in the middle of the day if they sense danger?" She blinks.

"Something like that, yeah."

"Eep!"

I hurry to the front door and shove it open.

Desert greets us.

What the hell? We are out in the middle of freakin' nowhere. Good thing: no one is going to see us running around with nothing on. Bad thing: the sun's about to come up and we are in the middle of nowhere.

"Uh oh," whispers Ashley. "That's not good."

I fly/float straight up... and it feels like I'm struggling to lift a weight too heavy for me. Damn. I'm exhausted, and almost certainly very low on blood. I manage to force myself up high enough to see over the building and confirm we are surrounded by miles of desert in all directions. The only thing in sight that is not desert is the dirt road leading away from the morgue facility.

Bright lights in the far distance appear to be a city of some kind, definitely not Gomez. Much too large. My guess is probably Winnemucca. I hope. If we hadn't just woken back up from a near death experience, it might be possible to fly there at full speed in time to beat the sunrise. I'm barely keeping myself in the air at a standstill hover. There is no way in hell I'm going to fly to that town before the sun comes up. In fact, I doubt I'd even make it to the city at all. I'm so low on energy, I'd 'run out of gas' halfway there and eat dirt out in the middle of the desert, and then have a nice sun bath.

Nope. That's not good.

I ease off the flying thing and drop back to my feet. Ashley has to grab me to keep me from falling over.

"Nope. We're screwed," I say. "Nothing for miles."

Ashley looks at the morgue building, at me, out into the desert, and back at the building. "Uh oh."

CHAPTER 4
NOWHERE ELSE TO HIDE

A FEW MOMENTS LATER

My mind spins with our situation.

Fortunately, it doesn't have to spin for long. An incinerating destruction in the desert is worse than whatever might happen to us if we stay in this morgue. If I'm right about the reason we woke up so soon before sunrise being some vampiric sixth sense warning us to get out of there, maybe if we aren't exactly where the Forces of Evil™ expect us to be, we'll be okay.

That means not lying on our cooler trays like helpless corpses.

"Come on. We don't have much time." I whirl around and hurry back inside.

Ashley follows.

Concentrating on the camera thing is a real pain... but I do it because, reasons.

Ashley chatters the entire way back to the cooler room, basically saying 'where are you going' 'what should we do' and that sort of thing over and over again. I'm too focused on splitting my conscious-ness and dwindling power reserves between suppressing video evidence and being able to walk and think at the same time to reply.

Once back in the cooler room, I say, "Grab the bags we woke up in and close the trays."

She gives me a look as if to ask 'while you just stand there?' but hurries to grab the discarded white plastic bundles.

"I'm keeping us off camera." I close my eyes, scraping up the reserves of power left over from putting myself back together. It occurs to me finally that I smell like burned wood and some weird sort of chemical thing I don't recognize.

"Oh hey." Ashley opens the door right below where I woke up and sticks herself halfway in, reaching down toward the bottom. "Here's that thing I coughed up."

"What is it?" I ask through a mostly clenched jaw.

"Not sure. Looks like a hunk of wood or drywall or something." She looks down at herself, realizes she has no pockets, and decides to hold onto the thing.

I wait while Ash gathers the wadded-up body bags and closes both trays. Then, we fast-creep from room to room looking for a hiding place. The file room has no good spot to stay out of view, plus it's got windows. Bad idea. The conference room is even worse. Even if we got seriously lucky and no one saw us under the table, the whole 'giant windows letting the sun in' thing would be the opposite of good.

A few minutes of increasing panic later, we're in the office area. This large room has six cubicle workstations and another door leading to a tiny office where I assume the big boss (of this place) works. There's also a supply closet in the back corner. Bingo. I hope.

I march over to it and pull the door open. Great. No windows.

"Kinda small in here." Ashley steps in behind me and closes the door. "Hope no one needs more Post-It notes today."

Hmm. Nowhere to really hide in this closet. Dammit. I sigh at the ceiling, about to curse my misfortune... and I spot a square hatch. "What's that?" I point up.

Ashley looks. "Umm. I dunno."

She floats upward, then pushes the square higher into the ceiling before sticking her head into the opening. "There's an attic up here. Sorta. It's really cramped. A crawlspace. Bunch of wires and pipes and ducts and stuff."

"Any windows?"

"Nope."

"Perfect." I grab her feet, which are floating at my eye level, and push her upward. "Hide up there."

She pulls herself into the attic. Seconds later, her face reappears, looking down at me.

I'm fairly sure they don't have a security camera *inside* the supply closet, so I relax that part of my brain. Doing so frees up enough mental resources to allow me to sorta fly straight up. This is to flying what limping with a broken leg is to walking. Ash grabs my hand and pulls me up. Wow, she's not kidding. The ceiling in here is almost as low as the cooler. Almost. There is enough room to sit upright at least.

The floor is dusty as hell, not that I care at this point. We're already filthy and covered in... something. I haul myself up into the attic crawlspace, sit on the grit-covered floor, and replace the square bit of plywood in the frame. If any of the workers happen to go into the supply closet, they shouldn't notice we went into the ceiling. Neither of us tried to climb the shelves, so no finger-slash-foot prints. Climbing the shelves wouldn't have helped anyway, since the hatch is dead center in the middle. Unless you can fly, a ladder is required to access this space.

The best part about it is no windows. It's completely dark up here, or would be if I wasn't a vampire. Hard to get comfortable sitting bare-assed on this cheap... whatever it is. Kinda looks like old kitchen linoleum but somehow, I doubt that's what it is. Obviously, the space we're in wasn't intended for frequent use, so the builders

NOWHERE ELSE TO HIDE • 31

put in the bare minimum effort. This area is not meant for storage at all. It's maintenance access. All sorts of PVC pipes, ventilation ducts, and wire bundles crisscross the room. Some are on the ceiling, the rest on the floor. Decades of dust and grit cover everything. For once, I'm glad I'm already dead or I'd be scared to breathe in here. I can practically see particles of lung cancer floating past my eyes.

Ashley tosses the body bags aside, then lets out a heavy sigh.

"Yeah. I feel that." I lower myself over sideways and stretch out on the floor.

Feels like I'm on one of those beds of nails or something. Soooo many little pebbles, sand bits and other tiny sharp things poking into me. There would be no way an ordinary person could sleep on this mess. Thankfully, once that sun comes up, I am *out*. Comfort doesn't matter at that point. I literally could sleep on a bed of nails and be just fine—for at least the unconscious portion of my day. As soon as I wake up again, the ouch would start. Considering the situation we're in right now, this is better than I could've hoped for. At least I don't have to cram myself into a tiny space and fall asleep with my head between my knees or something. For a while there, I thought we'd end up stuffing ourselves into the bottom drawer of a file cabinet.

The grit is maddening. All over my back, my butt, my legs. Feels like a million ants marching across my skin. Come on, Sun. Hurry the hell up already. Knock me out. After a minute or two in silence, the loud crinkling of plastic makes me look over at Ashley. She appears to be crawling back into one of the body bags.

"What are you doing?" I become aware of something more annoying than all the grit poking me in the lower back. Grr. I reach down and grab a four-inch scrap of wire, no doubt left on the floor from the last time someone did work up here.

"I'm cold."

"Stop thinking about it and you'll stop being cold." I shake my head slightly. "That bag is a bad idea. I wouldn't."

"Why?" She blinks.

"It's plastic. Makes a lot of noise. If we move in our sleep or wake up when people are here, they're going to hear us moving around."

Her eyes widen. "Oh. Damn. You're right." She grumbles, then re-wads the bag before chucking it safely off to the side. "Never thought we'd end up hiding naked in an attic together."

I chuckle. "Not a first for you, though."

She giggles. "I didn't know she had a boyfriend and there wasn't anywhere else to hide in that little house."

"Right."

"That was totally not my fault!" She huffs.

"Her parents would have freaked the hell out if they caught you there." I exhale. "Vicky was so deep in the closet, she's basically in Narnia."

"Valerie, not Vicky... but yeah." Ashley emits a soft sigh. "Good thing her parents were away all that week on vacation."

We laugh at the situation from like three years ago. Ash briefly dated this girl who was actually cheating on her boyfriend with her. Said boyfriend showed up unannounced at the girl's house while she and Ash were getting it on. Wow. I'm not old enough to think that being in high school was 'simpler times.' Ash has not exactly been the luckiest girl on Earth in terms of dating. Once she found out that Valerie had a boyfriend, she stopped seeing her. She didn't want to be *that* girl. If someone is dating you to cheat on someone else, that means they *will* someday cheat on you, too. It baffles me how many people out there delude themselves into thinking the cheater is choosing them... and they won't someday be the person being cheated on.

For that matter, why the hell is there a term, 'mistress' but nothing for a side guy? Like if a married woman cheats on her husband with some dude, the dude isn't a 'mistress.' Why isn't there a term for that? We could call them mister-esses. Or maybe not. That's really clumsy. Grr. I'll just sit here and be irritated.

Before I can get too annoyed at society for the double standard, the sensation of imminent sunrise crawls up my spine, about to seize my brain. Here we go.

I lie flat so I don't flop, then close my eyes. Ugh, this stupid, dirty floor. I'd never be able to sleep up here if not for being undead. Wouldn't surprise me much if this floor is so uncomfortable even vampire sleep struggles.

I whisper, "Please, don't let anyone find us up here..."

CHAPTER 5
TWO JANE DOES WALK INTO A MOTEL

THE FOLLOWING AFTERNOON

I go from cursing all the sand, grit, and bits of insulation biting into my skin to being comfortable.

Takes me a moment to process the sudden change. It no longer feels like I'm lying naked on the floor of an attic crawlspace, but rather I'm surrounded by soft fabric. Ugh. What the hell happened now? I'm comfortable, warm... covered by some sort of blankets. I reach up to check myself and discover I'm wearing a shirt of some kind, an unusually soft one.

I don't hear anything, so I decide to get it over with and open my eyes.

Of all the things to see, my bedroom wasn't even on the list of possibilities.

Stunned, I lay there in my bed and stare at my room. Warm sunlight shines in the window and hits me in the face. My small army of plush stuffies surrounds me, but I don't really pay too much attention to them as I'm too hung up on the sight of a normal window. Like... this is my old bedroom, upstairs. The one Sierra's using now.

I feel stiff and weak, but nothing hurts.

My door swings open to reveal the upper half of my dad leaning in to smile at me. "Oh, good. You're up. Cutting it close, huh? You better get moving or you'll be late for school."

"School?" I rasp, rubbing my face.

"You must've stayed up too late last night. It's Monday, kiddo." Dad drums his fingers on the door. "Oh, you'll need to take the bus today."

"Say what?" I blink and stare at him. "There's no buses to SCC."

"SCC?" Dad tilts his head. "Don't get ahead of yourself, hon. You still need to finish high school before you start thinking about college. And hey, didn't you want to go to USC? Why the sudden shift to community college? Though, your mother and I certainly wouldn't mind you staying in the area. You can still live at home then."

I'm so confused all I can say is, "Bus?"

"Sorry, kiddo." Dad grimaces at me. "Sierra's got a therapist appointment I need to drive her to. Mom's already left for work."

"Therapist? What?" I blink at him. "She didn't start seeing a therapist until after I was out of high school. And what the hell is my room doing upstairs?"

A look of concern washes over my dad's face. He steps into my room and puts a hand on my forehead as if checking me for a fever. "Are you feeling all right? Did you forget your sister had a panic attack over a school shooter?"

"It wasn't real. She just had a nightmare." I sit up. Oh, wow. I'm wearing Naruto pajamas. And my boobs are gone. Well... mostly gone. Not that they were epic to begin with, but they're noticeably smaller than they should be. "What's going on? Bus? I'm not in high school anymore. Dad, did you forget about the whole vampire thing?"

He purses his lips. "Sarah? Did you experiment with drugs last night?"

What the hell? Am I really messed up? Could all that vampire stuff have been a wild dream? I stare at my hands trying to remember what my claws look like. "No, Dad. No drugs. I thought I got turned into a vampire."

He starts to chuckle, then raises an eyebrow. "Maybe you should come with Sierra and me to the therapist."

A small pink bunny plush crawls onto my chest demanding a hug. Never mind the fact that a plush just moved by itself, I can't help myself and hug the thing. I've seen much weirder. "No one shot up Sierra's school. She just had a nightmare..." I glance at the plush bunny, which is now licking my face. "Speaking of nightmares..."

The instant I think I'm dreaming, my bedroom disappears. Once again, I'm in the attic crawlspace lying on the thousand teeth of grit. Rather than my little pink plush rabbit, I'm snuggling with a surprisingly big rat, which is presently licking my chin. Hey, at least he's friendly.

"Morning, bud," I whisper while skritching the rat on the head with one finger.

He regards me with an impossible to read rat stare for a few seconds more, then crawls off my chest and scampers away into the crawlspace in no great hurry. Undead Disney Princess me thinks animals love me, though I suppose the rat found what he thought was a dead body and might've contemplated having me for dinner.

No, I'm not too freaked out at touching a rat. Not like I can get sick anymore, and I'm already filthy. Besides, we had pet rats in my high school.

Ashley's still out cold. She's normally quite pale, so 'sleeping vampire Ashley' doesn't really look *too* much different. The biggest change is her lip color. That meme about the redhead in a bathing suit starting fires from reflected sunlight? Yeah, that's Ash.

This crawlspace has no windows, so I can't tell what time it is by looking outside.

My inventory is also completely empty. Don't even have the unremovable underwear they give video game characters. That's gotta make going to the bathroom mildly inconvenient. Alas, my 'inventory' being empty also means no phone, no watch, nothing to tell time.

I am obviously awake, and there's no one hovering over me with a stake. That means it is at least 2:30 in the afternoon. Considering I'm low on blood and we just went through a traumatic event severe enough to incapacitate us to the point mortal authorities found our bodies... it's likely I slept in.

So, the time could be anywhere from late afternoon to ten minutes before sunrise again. That's not helpful.

At least I don't feel sore anymore.

As soon as I think about how I feel, I become aware of all the dust, grit, sand, wire bits, hex nuts and probably rat turds I'm lying on top of. It's maddening. Trying to be quiet, I shift around to sit up, using my hand as a brush to clean a small 'butt-sized' area of floor that I can sit on without feeling like ten thousand tiny daggers are constantly stabbing me.

Sitting there in a ball with my chin on my knees, I stare at the square piece of plywood separating the crawlspace from the supply closet. We're not going to know if it's dark outside until one of us goes down there and looks. Suppose I should at least be happy to wake up in the same place I crashed at sunrise. That means no one found us, except for a rat. Maybe vampires smell wrong to rats, so he didn't bite us. Nah. I'd like to think animals like me. Yeah, that's it. He just wanted to be friendly.

Damn, I really want to take a long bath. I feel filthy.

Grumbling, I wipe my hand at my arm, trying to get rid of the black stuff all over me. It smells like ash from a wood fire. The odd chemical odor is all over me, too. Never smelled it before. Maybe it's something the morgue people sprayed on us. Don't feel sticky or anything. Just... covered in sand and grit and dirt and whatever this ashy crap is.

I'm pretty damn sure we weren't burned. Burns take a lot longer to heal and vampires usually wake up still partially burned and in agony. Obviously, I'm only guessing here since I haven't yet been burned to death. Hopefully, that's an experience I will never enjoy.

The squeak of hinges and the clattering of a door echoes from downstairs, along with several sets of footsteps. I reflexively cringe like a kid who's snuck into a place she doesn't belong. Yeah, it wasn't my choice to be here, but here we are. This is so stupid. I feel like I'm going to get in trouble for stealing a corpse out of a morgue even though said corpse was me. Honestly, it's less the getting in trouble and more the starting rumors of supernatural stuff that worries me. This whole situation will blow over much better for everyone if Ashley and I get out of here unseen.

"… ain't got no damn idea what the hell's going on here," says a man downstairs with a slight Spanish accent. "But it's getting' real freaky."

"There's gotta be a logical answer to this," replies another man with a deeper voice and no obvious accent.

"You saw the same video I did. *Dios nos proteja*."

Office chairs squeak. Someone slurps a drink.

"Yeah, I saw the video. A whole lot of nothing. Place was quiet all night."

The first guy mutters something in Spanish too fast and quiet for me to make out, then says, "Two Jane Does don't just disappear."

"Maybe we just imagined them," says deep voice guy.

"No, they were here. I didn't imagine helpin' Doctor Montgomery do his initial observation, then loadin' them two kids into the cooler." He sighs. "Who the hell does a thing like that to such young girls?"

I blink. A thing like what? Kill us… or did he see something we didn't? Ack. What condition were our bodies in when we got here?

"No damn idea. This world is getting worse by the day." Deep voice guy grunts in time with a chair squeak, then the clatter of computer keys fills the silence. "That detective is gonna be pissed."

"Well, she can go find the bodies then." Spanish dude makes an 'I'm done with this' kinda noise. "This is getting too weird for me. If we don't get fired over this, I may just get the hell outta here. That's like the sixth time something like this has happened."

"You just tryin' to mess with me." Deep voice guy chuckles.

"Wish I was. Bodies... they don't like to stay in this place."

That has to be one of the top ten most freaky jobs in the world: morgue worker in a town full of vampires who doesn't know that vampires exist for real.

It occurs to me that I've crawled over to the hatch without even thinking about it. I'm staring down at the plywood, damn near drooling at the scent of the two men. Oh damn. This is bad. I'm so hungry my body is doing stuff by itself.

I force myself to back away from the hatch, concentrating on the idea it's daytime. I can't go out there yet. Not only would my vampire powers shut down, leaving me a helpless mortal girl... there's a nonzero chance that I'm so weak right now my sun tolerance wouldn't work. I might open that closet door and just explode into flames.

Apparently, there's enough truth to that for my brain to relax and stop trying to force me to go down there and get all angry kitty on the two innocent morgue workers.

I sit back down on my cleared spot of floor, wrap my arms around my legs, and bury my face in my knees. Can't do anything yet. Gotta wait for at least some clue it's dark outside. The only thing I know for sure is that it has to be after 2:30 p.m. No idea how late these guys stay. This morgue must be tiny if they don't have staff here 24/7. Probably can't expect them to leave at five or five-thirty. I might be stuck here until eight or nine or even ten.

Though... once it's dark out, we won't need to keep hiding.

My body shakes from hunger. I know there's a blood meal right below me, but it's out of reach in the sunlight. Ugh. Okay, so yeah. There *are* some downsides to being a vampire, and this is one of them. I *hate* how this feels. It's terrifying being on the borderline of losing control and turning into a literal mindless monster.

Come on, Sare. Hold it together. You can do this. A couple hours is all. You stayed with Scott for six months longer than you should have. What's like three hours hiding in an attic?

Forty-seven hours later, the tedious conversation of the morgue workers goes back to being interesting. Okay, not really forty-seven hours, but it feels like it. Ashley's up, by the way. We've tried to keep quiet and still, but that works as well as two twelve-year-old girls on a sleepover who are supposed to be going to sleep... and end up talking until four in the morning.

We are whispering at least. So far, the workers downstairs haven't seemed to notice us.

Mostly, Ash is trying to keep my mind off hunger by reminiscing about hilarious or fun things from school. Hey, we're only eighteen. Of course almost everything we talk about is going to involve school. Not like we've got tons of life experience under our belts. Or even belts right now. Sigh.

Yeah, we are tragically lame. The most reckless thing we ever did in life was to sneak into an empty classroom and 'vandalize' a white-board with dry-erase markers. Oh, rebel me. We had kids in our class get caught having sex on school grounds. One boy smuggled beer in. Dumbass. Obviously, he got caught. Kevin Parker got caught with a quarter pound of weed... but he got super lucky. Mr. Hawkes, the history teacher, simply confiscated it and didn't involve the cops. Everyone knows Hawkes probably kept the pot for himself.

But yeah, the morgue workers convo has gotten interesting again. I mean, a police detective has arrived and asked about us.

"Who are you again?" asks a female voice.

"Dave Martinez," replies the worker with the faint accent.

"Kevin Jones," adds the deeper voiced guy.

"All right," says the detective. "So, you guys are telling me that two Jane Does blow up a motel and then completely disappear?"

Ashley gasps. "We didn't blow it up." She blinks. "Wait. Blow up? It exploded?"

I shrug one shoulder at her. "That explains the chunk of drywall you coughed up... and the ash all over us."

"And why we didn't feel a damn thing." Ashley cringes.

"Maybe aliens beamed them up," says Kevin.

Dave chuckles.

"This facility has surveillance video?" asks the detective.

"Yeah. We already watched it. Nothing happened." Dave's chair creaks. "Those two girls just disappeared straight out of the cooler."

"Can I see the video?"

"Sure, uhh..." Kevin hesitates. "You want to watch the entire thing right here? It's hours long of... nothing happening."

"You guys aren't too familiar with the software then, are you?" asks the detective.

"What do you mean?" Dave asks, sounding a little annoyed.

Office chairs bump around and rattle. I imagine the detective pulling a chair over to one of their desks and sitting, then sorta just taking over a workstation. Keys tap. Mouse clicks happen.

"There. See the timestamp?" asks Dave. "That video runs all the way to nine this morning when we got here with nothing happening."

The detective emits a 'hmm.' A moment later, she says, "If you go into the analyze menu here, under pixel tracking... there's a jump to next."

"What's that do?" asks Kevin.

"Well, the way these cameras work... if nothing is moving, all the pixels being recorded stay the same. Makes the video file smaller that way. As soon as there is any kind of activity or motion, some pixels change. The software can jump over all the time where nothing's happening and go right to motion. There is no reason to sit here for thirteen hours watching it directly."

Kevin whistles. "That's pretty neat."

Mouse click.

"Nothing," says Dave.

"Could be dust or something." The detective clicks again.

Everything is quiet downstairs except for intermittent mouse clicks. The fifteenth time she clicks, Kevin lets out a gasp.

"Oh, hell no," says Dave before rambling in Spanish, something about god.

I cringe. Shit. What did I miss?

"Right there. The cooler door is open for two frames," says the detective. "Then it closes again."

"*Ay Dios mio!*" whispers Dave. "Is that a face in the doorway? That girl is looking at us."

Shit. Shit. Shit. Shit. Shit.

I bonk my head into my knees repeatedly.

"I don't think so," says the detective. "That's pareidolia."

"What language is that?" asks Dave.

"English." The detective laughs. "Pareidolia is the tendency of the human mind to see faces in patterns. That looks like the foot end of a body bag with some suggestive shadows."

I raise an eyebrow. When the cooler door opened, I was absolutely on all fours right in front of it with my face at the exit. Hopefully, the security cameras here are potato quality and if my face is really captured in one or two frames, it won't be recognizable as specifically me, just some generally female shape. Maybe it isn't. The detective could be right about the pareidolia thing. More likely, they're really seeing my face, but she's not ready to believe in that stuff, so she's blaming pareidolia as a way to avoid confronting the reality that a corpse woke up.

"That's a ghost," says Kevin. "Nope. We're done. That did not happen."

"Ghosts don't steal bodies," says Dave. "Where the heck did they go? And… only one of the doors opened. Or did it? Flies open and shuts itself again? The video doesn't show anyone taking the bodies out."

"Done," repeats Kevin. "This is some weird shit."

"What are you doing?" asks Dave.

"Copying this video to add to the investigation file." The detective taps her foot with a sharp clicking noise.

I start crawling toward the hatch again. Ashley grabs me and holds me back.

"Sunlight," she whispers.

"Damn." I hang my head and stay there on my hands and knees, shaking from hunger. This is almost worse than Sam seeing a tray of cupcakes and being told not to touch them yet.

"Well, not too much left for me to do here," says the detective. "Your security system didn't show any signs of a break in. None of the interior locks are damaged. No signs of tampering at the cooler. Guess the only thing I can really do is pass around photos of the two dead girls and see if they turn up."

I snap my head up and stare at Ashley. We're nearly touching noses, eyes wide with shock. Her face totally says 'shit, they have pictures!?' and I'm sure my expression is the same.

Dammit!

CHAPTER 6
FREE DELIVERY

LATER THE SAME DAY

I
t's beyond tempting to dive through the hatch and charge into the office.

Not only am I starving, we really should stop the detective from spreading pictures of us around the area. The entire point of our mission was to get in and out without being seen or noticed. An active publicity campaign is entirely opposite to what we wanted.

Again, I stare at the hatch. The little fanged devil on my left shoulder whispers 'do it. Do it' in my ear. Maybe it's the friendly rat come back for more snuggles. I crawl forward a few inches and stop myself again.

Last night when I floated up into the air to look around, it hurt. Even that little bit of power overexerted me. Not only is it still daylight out (probably), we're both low on energy and in serious need of food.

"We can't," whispers Ashley.

"I know." I lower my head again.

"We shouldn't," whispers Ashley.

I nod.

"But it would be freaking hilarious." She snickers.

Say what? I slowly lift my head until I'm staring through my hair at her. "You're not serious."

"Those two guys are so freaked out already. Imagine what they'd do if we walked out of the supply closet."

I want to laugh but don't have the energy.

"We should totally act like zombies." She covers her mouth to hold back a real laugh. "They'd pass right out."

Okay, that is kinda hilarious. Mean, but hilarious.

Too late, though. The detective is already leaving. My chance to intercept her before she can go spreading our photo around has passed. Then again, exactly who is she going to be showing our pictures to? Is there a 'stealing bodies from morgues' industry around this area? Dave said it's happened before. My guess is we aren't the first vampires to wind up in here. Gomez is kind of a focal point for undead in this area. That's good in one respect. Our 'disappearance' might blend into the rest and become a statistic rather than a shocking single event.

"What do you want to do?" whispers Ashley, squeezing my hand.

Yeah, she's as hungry as I am. We're both shivering and not from the cold. I really don't know if it's cold or warm here. It feels like comfortable room temperature.

"Let's wait for them to leave and get out of here," I whisper.

"What about the pictures?" She winces.

"Maybe Sophia can clean that up."

Ashley smirks at me with a 'yeah right' expression. "You ask her to hide those pictures with magic and we'll be on every TV screen globally."

I chuckle. "Oh, she's not *that* bad at magic."

"The girl uses *Roger Rabbit* rules for magic." Ashley rolls her eyes. "If it's funny, embarrassing, or inconvenient, it will go wrong."

"Heh." I let out a long breath trying not to laugh and give us away. "You're not wrong. Okay, maybe Wolent's people can sanitize this."

"Hopefully."

I shrug. "Besides. Who's she going to show pictures to, anyway? It's not like this is a bar. Excuse me, have you seen these two dead girls lately?"

Ashley bites her arm to mute a laugh, then glares at me.

We sit there together, holding hands for moral support... and wait.

Dave and Kevin spend the next like two hours talking about ghosts, weird stuff, hauntings, and all sorts of theories about what happened. Kevin is a little freaked out. Dave sounds like he's on the verge of quitting. Poor guy seems majorly superstitious. He seems to think this entire town is cursed.

Honestly, he's not too far from being right. Some mortals pick up on signs of a vampire population, especially out here in the sticks. It's much easier for us to hide in a larger city or even suburbs. In a place like this, where there aren't too many people around, the weird unexplainable things start to add up and get noticed.

Kevin makes a comment about it being dark already so early.

Ashley gives me a look.

"Yeah, I am so sick of sitting on freaking pebbles or whatever the hell is everywhere up here."

I lead the way to the hatch and gingerly lift it out, revealing the supply closet below. Quiet as church mice, we glide down out of the attic crawlspace. The clean floor here feels a little warm. Guess the attic is cold. Ashley floats long enough to replace the plywood over the hole, then sinks down to land beside me.

The supply closet is less spacious than the attic, but at least we can stand up in here. We dust ourselves off as best we can with our hands. I swear, if this place wasn't full of surveillance cameras, I'd go looking for a shower and take my time leaving. At the moment, I don't think I have too much energy left to deal with hiding us from cameras. Getting out of the building as fast as possible is annoyingly the best option, even if it means venturing into the world naked.

Suppose we could feed from Dave and Kevin, take their clothes, and disappear into the night... but there are cameras on the office. No way would I be able to hide the attack. Everything would get caught on video. As hungry as I am, the instant I don't have a solid wall (or door) between me and a mortal, the primal lizard brain part of my vampire self is going to take over. I'm going to have all I can do in order to force myself not to kill the poor guy. There's no way I'll have the mental faculties to sweet talk video cameras into ignoring us. A glitchy morgue cooler door is a lot easier to dismiss as a technical problem with the camera than a full-blown vampire feeding frenzy.

Ashley pokes me. When I look at her, she silent-whispers, "What do we do if they open the door and find us?"

"Yoink them inside and try not to kill them," I reply. "No camera here."

She nods.

Sitting bare-butt on a giant cardboard box full of copier paper is not the most comfortable thing. However, compared to that damned attic crawlspace full of grit, this box of copier paper is as comfortable as a $2,000 recliner. We sit, like civilized humans, in an upright position, albeit inside a supply closet.

If that door opens, we're caught. There's nowhere to hide in here.

I find myself hoping they develop a sudden need for a new pen or something. We can't go out there to grab them, but if they come to us... game on.

So effing hungry.

When I catch myself thinking it wouldn't really be that big a deal if I overate and killed one, I realize I'm in deep shit. That's not me. That's some deep, dark, primordial ancient vampire soul inside of me. Yeah, I know. As cute and innocent as I am on the surface, a monster doth dwell within. That's true of any woman though. The monster comes out once a month. Sometimes even more often if someone steals your snacks.

The sheer ridiculousness of sitting here stark naked in a supply closet gets to me after a moment and I have to fight the urge to laugh. Oh, I wish Ashley didn't suggest we scare those two guys by pretending to be zombies. That's too damn funny, and now I can't stop thinking about it.

Yanno, if I laugh or make noise, those guys would almost certainly investigate.

No. Fight the temptation. I can't do that. Be good. What would Follows Rules Girl say?

A phantom whisper (that sounds an awful lot like my voice) says, "Eat something!"

Okay, so maybe Follows Rules Girl makes an exception for near starvation. Hell. If she's adjusting to vampire life, maybe I should, too. That doesn't mean I need to become blasé to killing mortals. Accidents happen, though. But hey, I am not *that* bad. If I was, I'd already be out of my mind and in the middle of feeding on those two guys after ripping the supply closet door down.

I'm guessing vampires kinda work like cars. The fuel needle shows empty before the tank actually *is* empty, to scare people into getting gas before they seriously run dry. My jitters now have got to be the 'you better feed damn soon or bad things will happen' warning. I'm not at the precipice of losing my mind just yet.

Eyes closed, I meditate on the promise to myself that I absolutely will feed as soon as possible—just not in this particular building where there are cameras everywhere. Well, everywhere except this supply closet. I'm going to need what little energy I have left to keep us hidden while we leave.

"Hang on," I silent-whisper. "We just need to wait a little more."

Ashley closes her eyes, then gets this wicked little smile.

"What the hell was that?" asks Kevin. "Did you hear that?"

Silence.

"Dave?"

Dave babbles in Spanish too fast for me to parse.

"Say what?" asks Kevin.

Yeah, definitely a 'say what' moment. Thanks for saying what I wanted to but can't.

Dave draws in a breath. "There's no way—"

"There it is again." Kevin's chair rolls back. "Sounds like girls giggling out in the hallway."

Ashley's grin widens.

"*A la mierda con esto. Me voy de aquí!*" yells Dave, before scrambling out of his chair and running.

Ashley's lips move without voice, saying, "We're right next to you. Please help us."

"Gaaaah!" shouts Kevin.

He, too, runs.

Ashley opens her eyes and glances at me. "Okay. We can leave now."

"What did you just do?" I blink.

"Made them think they heard giggling and ghost voices." She shrugs. "No big deal."

I whistle. "Wow. Hope they don't end up in therapy."

She grins. "They won't. They're guys. Guys don't do therapy... unless they go to see Dr. Jameson."

"Who the hell is Doctor Jameson?"

She makes a drinking gesture. "Whiskey."

"Oh..." I slap myself in the forehead.

Two cars start up outside and drive away in no small hurry. Wow. Guess she scared the absolute hell out of them. We better get lost before anyone realizes this facility has been abandoned. One of the guys mentioned a Doctor Montgomery. Maybe he's still here. Not sure. If so, he's probably in the back doing an autopsy or something. Then again, if he's a doctor, he probably shows up for two hours, two days a week.

I stand and pad over to the door, grasp the knob, and start building up the concentration to hide us from cameras.

"I don't think this one's gonna explode," whispers Ashley.

"Heh. I'm not hesitating for that. Trying to get the camera thing working."

"Oh."

After a moment, it's either working or it's not. I open the door and peek out at the empty office. Thankfully, it's dark outside. A nearby clock tells me it's only about quarter to five. Yay for daylight savings time. Hmm. Curious, I approach one of the two open work-stations. The guys ran off in such a hurry they didn't shut their computers down or even lock the screens.

I sit in the still-warm chair that smells so much like Kevin I want to bite it.

"What are you doing?" Ashley tugs on my arm. "C'mon."

"Sec. Want information."

After throwing a few minutes at poking around the computer and trying to make sense of their file system, the most useful discovery I make is that my powers also seem to work on passwords. I typed in some random stuff and it worked, letting me into their data application. No way did I just guess the dude's passcode. At least, I hope it wasn't 12345ABCD.

Alas, there's nothing in here about our situation. Someone took lots of photos of our bodies and holy cow. We look unrecognizable. I cringe away, not really wanting that memory. Let's just say that as much bone was visible as wasn't. I mash the delete button. So, apparently, that motel room exploded. The morgue computer contains no information about any investigation, nor does it offer me any clue *why* the damn motel exploded. Frustrating, but makes sense. This isn't the police department.

I'm no hacker, but I am familiar enough with computers to navi-gate them. Maybe that's why Dalton's little gift is able to adapt itself to this.

"Dammit. If I am the vampire equivalent of a D&D rogue, I totally forgot to check for traps before opening that motel door."

Ashley laughs. "I mean, it's not like we found a treasure chest in a random hallway. You had no reason to think the door would be rigged."

"True. Okay, maybe I don't feel as dumb then." I stand. "Let's get out of here."

"About time..."

A card on the desk catches my eye. I pick it up. "Detective Adriana Marquez... I should keep this so we can clean up the mess."

Ashley nods.

I start reaching to stuff the business card in my pocket, then realize I'm not wearing anything.

Sigh. Guess I hold it for now.

We scurry out of the office and into the hall. I'm focused on blotting us off video, so I'm not running as fast as I want to. Going too fast makes it hard to hide. Streaks, blurs... I don't want to leave stray pixels the detective can jump to. I bet some of those 'dust' jumps where she didn't see anything were me screwing up. Some pixels shifted as the color of the walls didn't quite match up where I failed to perfectly hide us. She didn't see anything because she'd have been looking at a 'Sarah and Ashley shaped outline' the exact same color as the background, or something like that.

Wow. The guys didn't even close the front door.

We make our way across the tiny lobby and outside.

Ashley shuts the door.

I can't help myself and do the nice thing, using my power backward to lock it. It really is our fault the guys left this place abandoned. If anyone wandered in and stole things or did damage, it would be on my conscience.

The glow of a small city far off in the distance lights up the desert. Where there's a city, there are people. I must be hungry because right now, the idea of eating is way more important than finding clothes. One is a requirement. The other is just a social norm. No one is going to end up getting shredded if I don't cover up right away. Going too much longer without blood, though... that's going to be a problem. Is this how heroin addicts feel when they're jonesing for a fix? Like, I don't care about anything right now other than feeding. Naked? Who cares. Killing someone? Ehh, hope not but if it happens, oh well.

Dammit. We gotta hurry.

I look up, then again remember how it hurt to fly last night.

"Shit. We're walking."

"Yeah. I figured." Ashley groans. "Doing that ghost voice trick kinda hurt. We really need food."

"So, we walk. City that way." I point.

"What if someone sees us?"

"Then we lie without lying." I start walking along the road away from the morgue.

She scurries to catch up and falls in stride beside me. "What? Lie without lying?"

"If someone sees two girls walking down the road naked, they are going to assume something bad happened to us. So, we say we got attacked—which we did, by a bomb. And we woke up naked in the middle of nowhere... which is technically true."

Ash makes a 'yeah, well, you kinda have a point' face.

Casual as can be, we walk along this dirt road for a while. The desert around us is silent and empty. The wind is all over us, throwing my hair about and occasionally spraying us with sand. We came down here concerned that someone seeing us in only sweatshirts without winter coats would cause a scene. I think we've gone a little past simply not having a jacket. This would be hilarious if it wasn't so damn annoying. The annoying part isn't getting stranded naked again. That's just, whatever. I'm annoyed because it's taking longer to get home. Complications suck. I wanted this to be a fast, easy errand... and it's turning into a major project.

The only good thing—so far—is that I haven't actually had to kill anyone. But I am wondering how long that's going to last. Did someone bomb us on purpose? Is this like the opening salvo of a declaration of war on Wolent's people? Or did we simply walk into a trap laid for someone else? I mean, who randomly places a bomb in a motel room? As grisly as the intake photos of us were—cringe—it's probably a good thing. No one could possibly have recognized us. Even if the detective does show photos around, they're going to be looking for horror movie zombies, not a pair of teen girls.

Ick.

The dirt road leads us to a paved highway. It's only one lane in each direction, but probably still counts as a highway around here. The lights of the city get closer, but still seem to be at least three hours of walking away. This is how it goes, right? As soon as you adjust to having a flying mount in a game, you end up in an area where you can't use it. So annoying.

"Maybe we should get used to this," says Ashley.

"Get used to what?"

"Not having clothes. Think of all the money and time we'll save never doing laundry again." She makes a goofy face at me. "It's kinda nice feeling the wind all over."

I laugh.

Of course she is not serious. She's distracting herself from hunger by being a goofball.

"We're the ultimate bait right now," I say. "Stranded out here in the middle of nowhere, helpless... no clothes."

"If a creep finds us, I'm not going to feel guilty about overfeeding." Ashley shakes her head.

"Yeah. Agreed. Not going to intentionally overfeed but... accidents happen."

We keep walking as our conversation lightens away from such morbid topics to Ashley trying to decide what anime to marathon once we get home. Yeah, spending hours outside with nothing on is definitely going to call for spending hours at home wrapped in blankets in front of a TV.

"I sense much hot cocoa in our future," I say.

"Ooh. Great idea."

Guessing about an hour after we leave the morgue, the sound of an engine rises out of the stillness behind us. I briefly contemplate hiding, then realize there's flat open nothingness all around us. Unless I could somehow shrink myself down to the size of a prairie dog, there's nowhere to hide. The scrub brush is a little tiny.

"Car," says Ashley like a kid playing wiffle ball in the road.

"I hear it."

"How do you want to play it?" she asks.

"Just like I said before. Lie without lying."

She glances over at me as the glare of headlights fall on us. "I mean, do we talk first or go right to derp hammer?"

"Oh. Umm. Let's see what happens."

"This is going to be fun." She winks.

"Fun isn't exactly the word I'd use."

The sound of the engine tells me the car is slowing down. Yeah, whoever is in the car has seen us. Hard not to. Ashley's so pale her butt's probably blinding the poor driver with the reflected glare of headlights.

A moment later, the car comes to a complete stop close behind us. Might as well look. Continuing to walk as if the car didn't exist would be too weird, I think. Right?

I stop walking and turn toward the vehicle.

For a few seconds, I see nothing but glare from the headlights. Ashley moves to stand beside me, still squeezing my hand. Hey, we're trying not to come unglued here and go full monster mode, okay? Holding hands is moral support. Maybe it's a little immature, but whatever.

My eyes gradually adjust to reveal a large, black car on the boxy side. It looks older, like something Dad's parents might've had. I make out the shapes of two men in the front, and three in the back seat. They all look Hispanic, and more than a little bit like gang members. What's the term for it? Cholo? Yeah, they look like Cholos. These are the kinds of guys girls like me from nice suburban neighborhoods are supposed to be afraid of. I'm bracing for this to escalate to exactly the place I think it's going to escalate... when my brain does a backflip.

These guys aren't thinking they just won the lottery. I'm so shocked that not a single one of them is contemplating assaulting us that I end up just gawking at them. Guess it's true what they say. Looks can be deceiving.

Both doors open. The guys all scramble out of the car.

"Hey, you girls okay?" asks one.

I'm too close to living mortals. My jaw doesn't want to work right now, at least not for speaking. I fight to hold myself back from losing control. Don't want to hurt these guys. They're actually nice.

"Ooh," whispers Ashley. "I could really go for some Five Guys right about now."

"What?" I force past my clenched jaw.

She nudges me. "There's a burger joint called Five Guys. I'm making a joke Dad would like."

"Right. Yeah. Good point."

"Umm, Sare?" She raises an eyebrow. "Does it count as DoorDash if the food comes to you on a highway in the middle of nowhere?"

"No idea." I hold back the feeding frenzy struggling to leap out of my brain and walk toward the guys. "Yeah, we've had a bad night."

"We could really use some help," adds Ashley. "I'm so glad you found us."

CHAPTER 7
FRIENDS IN UNLIKELY PLACES

FRIDAY, DECEMBER 6

W
e cruise over a small bridge past some cute boxy white street lamps.

I'm in the middle of a controlled panic attack, trying to keep this massive car under control. The steering wheel is really squirrelly and the brakes take being stepped on as more of a request than a command. Swear if I couldn't make myself stronger than my mortal self, I'd be using both feet on the brake pedal. I think this monster is a Lincoln Town Car from like 1990 or something. It's so damn big it probably has a US Navy registration number. My experience driving cars is pretty limited. Sure, I've gotten behind the wheel of Mom's Tahoe once or twice, but for the most part, I'm accustomed to my little hand-me-down Nissan Sentra.

Somehow, this Lincoln is more like a road battleship than the Tahoe, despite being a car and not a SUV. The thing is so huge it makes me feel like a child too small to get behind the wheel. I'm not at all comfortable driving it. Thankfully, I didn't need to make any turns, and we didn't pass any other cars.

At least we're not naked anymore. Ashley and I are wearing blue flannel shirts kindly donated by the guys who found us on the road. These shirts are long enough to cover everything, like short dresses, so we didn't bother stealing anyone's jeans.

This is it. We've made it to a small city. It's gotta be Winnemucca. I slow down to about twenty miles an hour. Even that crawling pace feels damn near uncontrollable in this beast of a car. We pass a place called Chihuahua's Grill & Cantina on the left down a side street. I keep going, mostly because I'm not in the mood for normal food and the idea of trying to negotiate a turn in this thing scares me.

I keep driving down the road that Route 95 became, passing Ormachea's Dinner House on the right. What, Universe? Are you trying to tell me something? A sign on the left in front of a huge building reads 'Winnemucca Convention & Visitors authority.' Say what? This place is big enough to have an 'authority' for conventions. Okay. Whatever.

Another sign up ahead at the next block tells me that 'Winners Motel' is that way along with the 'Winners Inn Casino.'

Considering how my trip to Nevada has been so far, I don't feel like doing anything involving luck right now. A motel is probably a bad idea given what happened the last time I went near a motel... but motel rooms have showers and no questions.

Gritting my teeth, I mash both feet on the brake pedal, jerking the huge car to a stop in the middle of the road. Ashley almost smacks her face into the dashboard. The five unconscious guys in the back seat half spill onto the floor.

"Hey, careful." Ashley has to lean sideways so she can reach to poke me since this car is so wide. "You're going to get us pulled over."

"Sorry. I hate this car. The brakes do absolutely nothing until they jam on too hard."

"You're just not used to it." She shrugs.

"I don't want to get used to it." I step on the gas pedal—which is bigger than my whole foot, by the way—and ease the car into a right turn.

"You are driving like a half blind grandmother." Ashley laughs.

"Whatever." I roll my eyes.

We're apparently on West Winnemucca Boulevard now. Like a block later, I spot the motel and pull into the lot. I'm still not big on maneuvering this monster of a car, so I head right for the first parking spot that requires the least amount of jockeying around. I may have parked it across two spaces because it's so freaking long. Whatever. At last, we are stopped and I can stop panicking like we're going to get into an accident at any second.

Engine off. Yes, this thing has a key that I have to physically turn to switch the engine off.

"Ash, do the thing so no one sees us."

"Okay. What's the plan?"

"We're going to borrow a shower."

"Ooh. Yes. Definitely." She nods.

I pull my hand into the flannel sleeve and do my best to wipe the steering wheel for fingerprints, then grip the door handle with my other hand covered in fabric. We get out of the Lincoln. Does it make me a wimp that I need to use some vampire boosting to shove the door closed? Good grief. Why did they ever make cars that heavy? Once the door's shut, I wipe down the handle. Another downside of being an Innocent. Unlike every other vampire bloodline, we *can* leave fingerprints. That whole being really good at faking a lifelike appearance thing means our skin has oil still.

Ashley making people not mentally process seeing us is less taxing than whatever I do to cameras. It doesn't matter if we run or creep along slowly, so we run.

My trick lets us walk right into an empty motel room and go straight to the shower. We don't hesitate at the promise of finally being clean of all this ash and dirt, and hop in together. The warm water is amazing. It's nowhere near the awesomeness of a long bath, though that luxury is one we haven't time for right now. This is all about getting clean, not about feeling better.

Maybe we don't exactly hurry, but by the time we're done, we are free of grime.

For now, we don't have much choice but to put those flannels back on. It's still not great. People will be concerned seeing us running around like that in December. However, they'd hopefully be less likely to call the police or come running over to check on us than if we continued to streak.

We sit on the bed and continue toweling our hair off. Yeah, this might be a motel bed but it's still more comfortable than a box of copier paper. Morgue tray, gritty attic floor, cardboard box, motel bed. Yes. Unlife is a series of small incremental upgrades sometimes.

"Now what?" asks Ashley.

"Food: check."

She nods.

"Clean: check."

She nods again.

"Clothes: almost." I glance down at the flannel on my thighs.

"Right. So, what's the plan there?"

I shrug. "Walmart."

"Is there one here?" Ashley scrunches her nose. "It's not a big city."

"There's a Walmart everywhere. There's gotta be one here." I stand and shake the towel out.

"Want me to drive?" She tilts her head.

"I was going to leave the car here." I head to the bathroom and put the wet towel on the bar. "There's a giant package of cocaine in the trunk. I don't want to be anywhere near it."

Ashley bites her lip. "Oh, yeah. Right. You mentioned that."

"Besides." I walk back out into the room. "We should be good to fly now."

"Think so?" Ashley rubs her stomach.

"Yeah. We ate five guys." I chuckle. "I mean we fed from five adults. That's two each plus splitting one. And I don't feel overly full."

"Neither do I." She makes a contemplating face. "I don't feel hungry either."

"Good sign. Means we ate enough." I lick my teeth. Yeah, those guys' blood tasted like when you stick French fries in your mouth while you're already chewing up a bite of burger. I blame her for making the Five Guys joke. Got me thinking about burgers.

"Will they be okay?" She tilts her head. "People don't usually pass out when we feed."

Damn. She's got a point. I'm sure we didn't kill them, but they might be in dangerous territory. I would have used one of their cell phones to call 911 already if not for the drugs in the trunk. Feels kinda bad to call the cops on them after they were so nice to us. I mean, okay sure we attacked and fed from them... but if we'd been mortals, those guys would have been nice to us. It helped they totally thought we were kids. Even criminals tend to be good to kids... except for the sorts of criminals that other criminals kill in prison.

Anyway... do we call the authorities or not?

Flashing red and blue lights up the curtains.

"Uh oh." I dart to the window and peek outside.

There's a police car now parked behind the giant black Lincoln. Two cops are shining flashlights inside. Hmm. I guess piling up five men in the back seat wasn't the most subtle thing we could've done. Someone must have spotted the car while we were in the shower and called the cops. One good thing about having been stranded out here with nothing: I'm 100% sure we didn't forget anything in the car for the police to find and trace back to us.

"Wow. Okay. That was fast." I whistle.

"Guess the police here are pretty bored." Ashley shrugs. "And we have been in here for almost an hour."

"Has it been that long?" I blink.

"At least." She fluffs her hair into the towel. Her hair is a bit thicker than mine. Takes forever to dry.

"Whenever you're ready, we can get out of here and go to Walmart."

"You left your wallet at home." She heads to the bathroom to hang the towel.

I fold my arms. "Yeah. I know. We're going to shoplift."

"Ooh, bad girls." Ashley chuckles. "What would Follows Rules Girl say?"

"She'd say something along the lines of a loss a giant corporation won't even notice is a lesser evil than us being stranded naked in the desert."

Ashley hurries back from the bathroom. "I agree with her."

Oh yeah. I have become an evil creature of the night. First, I no longer think shoplifting is a big deal. The next thing you know, I'll start putting ketchup on hotdogs. As I descend deeper into the veil of evil, I might start thinking it's acceptable to wear socks with sandals. Diabolism for sure. If I really go off the deep end, I might try pineapple on pizza.

Nah. That's just evil. If I ever start thinking it's acceptable to put fruit on pizza, I've fallen so far the only acceptable course of action would be to fling myself into the sun and end it all.

"Ready?" I ask.

"Yep." Ashley nods.

We exit the motel room and freeze—almost literally.

Going from a heated motel room to a thirty-degree December night in the desert while wearing only a stolen flannel shirt is... a brisk experience. Let's just say that the wind went right up underneath and hit sensitive places.

Ashley makes this squeaking noise. She's got one eye closed, biting her lip, and stands there in a pose that says 'I really need to pee.' I know she doesn't. We haven't consumed actual food for days. Blood meals don't send us to the bathroom, no matter how much we take.

The cops, oblivious to our presence, call for medical assistance. Oh, that's good at least. I'm almost sure the gang members are going to get busted for having such a massive quantity of drugs. Then again, maybe the police won't search the car. Yeah, right. They say no good deed goes unpunished. Would it be more evil of me to make sure the cops don't find the drugs? That would put those drugs on the street and cause all sorts of harm. Or would it be worse to 'betray' the guys who tried to help us by getting them busted? If they hadn't stopped to help us, they wouldn't have gotten caught. At least we're not the ones who called 911. Sure, we're responsible for them being unconscious in the first place.

Couldn't be helped.

There's also the worry we might've taken a bit too much blood. Getting found by the cops might save their lives. Even if it makes me feel a little guilty, I think it's best not to interfere at this point. If the cops find the drugs, so be it. If not, so be it. Either way, those men won't remember seeing us. Doesn't make me feel any less guilty but at least they won't hesitate to offer help if they ever happen to find any other girls our age in trouble—assuming they're not about to spend the next thirty years in prison for transporting a crapload of drugs.

Once we adjust to the temperature and no longer feel like our nether bits are freezing off, we hurry around behind the motel building out of sight from the parking lot... and leap into the sky.

It feels so damn nice to be flying again.

I don't care who says what about sunlight and a happy mortal life. None of that is as cool as being able to fly. Mortality is romantic, I suppose, but... aging, cancer, sickness, pain, dismemberment, death... periods. Is it really worth it? Sometimes, it makes me sad to think that Ashley technically died to join me in the 'Fang Club,' but then I think about all the bad things we're no longer vulnerable to.

No one could even say we're missing out on having children anymore, really. There's Chloe. Okay, so it's not the same. Our age gap isn't big enough for her to really feel like anything other than my kid sister that I have to watch. Still, though. Having her around is close enough to the experience of having kids. And if all that stuff about our mental state being permanent is true, I am forever a teenager. I'm never going to want to have kids because I basically still *am* one. So, yeah. I'm good. Permanent slackerdom with no real responsibilities. Sign me up.

We fly around looking for large buildings. Sure enough, there *is* a Walmart in Winnemucca. It's more or less right at the southwestern end of the built-up area. Farther south is mostly open land. Using Ashley's talents, we walk into the store—which is still open—and make our way to the clothing area. No one pays any attention to the two of us as we head to the clothing section. I keep us off the cameras while Ashley keeps us out of the minds of other shoppers and store employees.

After gathering up a few things, we do what all self-respecting shoplifters do and hit the bathrooms with our ill-gotten gains. Tee shirts, sweatshirts, jeans, socks, sneakers. We end up going commando because I'm too lazy to figure out where they put the underwear and it's not really that required in an emergency like this. One less thing to steal makes Follows Rules Girl feel a little better.

After getting dressed and throwing the tags/shoeboxes into the trash, we go back out into the store and put the flannel shirts on the rack as if they're for sale. Someone's going to be confused, but we really don't need to keep those.

"Coats?" asks Ashley.

"Nah. They're kinda expensive, and I feel bad enough as it is." I shrug.

"Okay."

Masked from cameras and living eyes, we casually walk out of the store among the shoppers. One person's service dog looks at us briefly, though their owner doesn't notice. Once safely out in the parking lot with no signs of loss prevention commandos running after us, I breathe a sigh of relief.

"Clothes: check." Ashley smiles. "Back to normal."

"Yeah, getting there." I grin. "Kinda hard to get back to normal when we were never normal to start with."

She sticks her tongue out at me. "What's the plan now?"

I shift my jaw side to side in thought. "We still didn't get the USB thing from that motel room."

"Seriously?" Ashley stares at me. "You think it's even still there?"

"No idea." I flap my arms. "How big was the bomb?"

"Umm." She makes a goofy cross-eyed face. "Big enough to knock us into next Tuesday."

"Gah! I hope that's not literal." I fidget. "What day is it, anyway?"

"Umm." Ashley looks around until she spots a man walking alone and darts toward him.

Uh oh. What is she doing? I run after her.

"Excuse me..." Ashley chirps as she skips over to the guy.

Dude looks like he's in his younger thirties. Maybe forty. He's pushing a shopping cart of groceries plus a massive package of diapers toward a silver Toyota SUV.

"Where's your coat—?" The man's eyes glaze over.

Oh boy. I facepalm and look around, hoping no one notices her derp-slapping this guy in the middle of the parking lot.

Ashley takes the cell phone off the guy's belt, swipes at the screen, then shows it to me. "We lost four days. It's Friday now. The bomb didn't knock us into next Tuesday, though we did skip over a Tuesday."

I blink. My brain chews on this data for a few seconds before I blurt, "Shit!"

"What?" She leans back, caught off guard by my reaction.

"Tuesday was the third." I gaze up at the sky. "Dammit! Why!?"

"Umm... yeah, that's how math works. The third comes between the first and the sixth. What's the big deal?"

I lower my gaze to look at her. "I missed Hunter's birthday. Grr!"

"Oof." Ashley puts the man's cell phone back in its belt holder. "Thank you." She pats the guy on the arm. "Don't mind us. You didn't see anyone in the parking lot."

Dammit. I grumble to myself and storm away from the guy. Ashley rushes to keep up.

"I'm sure he'll understand." She puts an arm around me. "It's not like you blew him off or anything. We blew up."

I sigh.

"Think of the make-up sex." She winks.

Heh. Okay, now I'm blushing.

"Hmm. It's 6:44 p.m. If we hustle, we could make it home tonight." I look up.

"Forget the USB then?"

I exhale. "I have to at least try. Wolent won't be happy if we just leave."

"I think he'd understand. He's probably freaking out that we haven't come back by now."

"Shit. The 'rents are losing their minds, I bet."

Ashley wags her head side to side. "Maybe."

"No maybe. They're definitely freaking out. I've never disappeared from home for four days at a time without any contact. What about this is a maybe?"

"Dad probably asked Sophia to scry on us to make sure we're okay."

I wipe a hand down my face. "Really hope not. If she saw us after the bomb, she's going to be having nightmares the likes of which would make Fuzzydoom seem silly."

"Fuzzydoom *is* silly," says Ashley.

"Okay, true but you know what I mean." I shiver. "For eff's sake, half of my face was gone."

"I guarantee you she didn't see that." Ashley smiles. "Or she'd have teleported here already."

That almost makes me laugh. "You are assuming the void octopus didn't object. And this is too far to mirror."

"She could've sent Klepto with a note." Ashley snaps her fingers.

"That's true." I look up again. "Okay, come on. We'll check the motel again and go home."

"Check for traps this time." She winks.

Ugh.

We fly northwest, heading for the distant spot of light that is Gomez. I wonder if something along the lines of my power to hide from cameras is at work here that keeps places like this off maps. Is it supernatural? Or do vampires with influence simply pay people off to ignore these towns? Do vampires have roving squads of mischief makers who ambush those Google cars?

It doesn't take us very long to get back to the motel where this whole mess started. Call me strange, but hurtling through the sky at over a hundred miles an hour is a lot less scary than driving that enormous Lincoln, even creeping along.

Right away, it seems the bomb wasn't *that* epic. Yellow police tape covers the area of Room 16. Looks like the windows shattered on several adjacent rooms, but the building didn't suffer visible structural damage except for the wall right at Room 16. The door is entirely gone, as is most of the wall for the width of the room. Surprisingly, rooms 17 and 15 seem more or less unscathed. The explosive couldn't have been too big.

Oh... hang on. That weird chemical smell on us. That must have been C4 or whatever they used in the bomb. My brain decided to throw that thought at me because the same smell that covered the two of us before we showered is all over this place, which rules out anything morgue workers might have sprayed on us. It's not a smell that normal people can pick up unless they're like in a factory where C4 is made... or shove the explosive up their nose. Dogs can smell explosives... and apparently, so can vampires.

"That's almost promising." Ashley gives me a surprised look. "I kinda thought the entire motel would be flattened."

"Me too. Let's check it out."

I glide down and land right by the shredded façade. There's enough of a gap in the police tape for me to slip inside the room without needing to tear any of it down. It's kinda unlikely there would be another explosive device in here, but still... I go slow and look around for any signs of a tripwire, suspicious things on the ground, or even an electric eye beam.

The inside of Room 16 looks pretty messed up. Doesn't seem like much of a fire happened. Unlike Hollywood explosions, actual bombs rarely involve fireballs, unless the bomb is attached to a container of gasoline or something equally as flammable. That I know this at my age is perhaps more disturbing than the whole vampire deal.

Everything is smashed though, no doubt from the concussion wave. That the bed and most of the furniture, albeit crushed, are still here tells me the bomb must have been right at the door. The same door Ashley and I had our freaking ears pressed into.

No wonder it was so instant. The charge went off less than two inches from my brain.

I think.

Maybe not.

Wouldn't that have vaporized me and been game over for good?

Or maybe the charge was smallish. The photos of our remains looked mauled, not blasted to tiny particles. Meh. Who cares? I still exist. I don't need to understand exactly what happened.

"The thing might actually still be here."

"Probably broken." Ashley steps over a piece of ceiling.

"That's not our fault. Try not to make too much of a mess."

"Hah." She rolls her eyes at me.

We get to searching around any of the places that might be a hiding spot for a USB memory fob. I check the bathroom first while Ash starts pulling drawers out of the smashed-up cabinet in the main room. The bathroom is small, so it doesn't take me long to feel confident no one hid a USB device in here.

Ashley holds up a drawer at me as I walk out of the bathroom. "Nothing taped to the bottom of any of the drawers. Cabinets are empty."

"Grr. It would've been nice if they told us exactly where to look." I fold my arms and stare daggers at nothing in particular.

My gaze happens to fall on the bed. Hmm. I wonder. "Check the bed."

We strip the bed, check the pillows, and look under the mattress. Right as I'm about to give up, I notice a frayed bit of fabric on the side of the mattress where it appears someone stabbed it with a knife.

"Hang on... this looks a bit sus."

"Hmm?" Ashley peers over the mattress at me. "Nothing under the bed."

"Found a hole." I stick my finger in the hole and feel around.

Bingo. There's a small plastic object stuffed in the mattress. I stick a second finger in there and pinch, then pull a USB memory stick out into view.

"Nice!" Ashley tilts her head at me. "Do you think whoever put it there knew there was going to be a bomb?"

"Dunno. Why?"

"Because they hid it inside the mattress. Cushioning." She pats the mattress. "We either got really lucky or this was a setup."

I mull that for a moment. "If we were lured here into a trap, why would they bother planting a USB for us to find at all? I think it's probably a coincidence."

"I had a feeling," says a familiar woman's voice at the door.

Like a pair of kids caught sneaking into a movie theater without paying, we both freeze. Ashley's kneeling on the other side of the bed with her back to the door... but I've got a straight on view of a woman stepping through the yellow tape. She looks professional... and she's got a detective's badge hanging on a lanyard around her neck, plus a gun on her hip. Yeah, hers is the same voice I heard talking in the morgue.

Crap. We're busted.

Oh, derp. I forgot the detective's business card in the pocket of the flannel that's now sitting in Walmart. Whoops. That's going to be fun if someone finds it.

"Umm. Hi," I say. Lamest of the lame.

Detective Marquez looks back and forth between us. "You two are vampires?"

I manage a mostly sincere sounding chuckle. "Are you serious? Those aren't real."

The detective smirks. "I'm in the know. You could say I help out the locals. And I don't recognize you two." She walks closer to us, narrowing her eyes.

Ashley stands and whirls to face her, trying to act innocent.

Hoping the detective doesn't notice, I do my best to sleight-of-hand the USB up my sweatshirt sleeve.

"You two don't really look like vampires. Thralls?"

I peek into her head. Okay, yeah. She's legit. Knows about vampires. Doesn't know what to make of us other than she's sure we are the same two mangled corpses she photographed the other day when the police found us in the middle of the parking lot. Oh, hey, she's really happy that we 'got better' and aren't actual innocent mortal kids who got caught in the crossfire. Okay, I like her.

"You were right the first time." I show my fangs. "Sorry for making a mess here. Had no idea anything was going to blow up."

"Wow." Detective Marquez walks right up to me and gives me a once over. "You're a bit young. Who approved that?"

"No one. I'm older than I look. Honestly, I was eighteen."

"Uh huh." She smirks. "Suuure you were."

I sigh. "Really. I was... my boyfriend killed me when I tried to break up with him and there just so happened to be a vampire stalking me at that moment because he thought I looked tasty."

Detective Marquez raises an eyebrow. "So, he turned you?"

"Yeah. He thought I was a kid, too. Felt bad." I hook my thumbs in my jean pockets. So nice to have pockets again.

"I see." She eyes Ashley, then looks back at me. "You two aren't from around here."

"Nope. We're... umm. Couriers? Boss sent us down here to pick up a message. Was just supposed to find it in here and go back home. But... the door exploded when I tried to open it."

The detective cringes. "Oh, bad luck then."

"What happened? Who blew us up?" Ashley puts on her best pleading look.

"You two got mixed up in a turf war going on between two local groups. One side, I'm guessing the side your boss is talking to, uses this motel room all the time. The guy who owns this motel is a vamp."

I purse my lips. "So, you think the other side planted a bomb here, hoping to randomly catch rival vampires?"

"Probably. They do that shit to each other all the time, like pranks." Detective Marquez frowns. "Makes a hell of a mess for me to clean up after the fact."

"Some prank." Ashley whistles.

"Hey, I've seen vamps play 'laser tag' with real guns for fun." I shiver.

"Yeah, they do that here, too." Detective Marquez smiles at us. "You two planning on sticking around?"

"Nope. We're going right home," I say. "Oh, speaking of cleaning up messes... would you mind not showing our pictures around?"

She nods at me. "Don't sweat it. I wasn't going to do that. Just said it for the morgue workers' benefit."

"Cool." I smile.

Detective Marquez pauses, giving me a quizzical stare. "How the hell do you know that?"

Ashley giggles.

"We were hiding in the supply closet the whole time you were talking with those two guys." I twirl some of my hair around my finger. "Woke up too close to sunrise to go anywhere, so we had to spend another day there."

For a moment, the detective just stands there looking at us, then she bursts out laughing.

Ashley and I exchange a glance but keep quiet.

"Oh, man. Whatever you two did to those boys... Martinez quit and Jones is convinced it's haunted." She shakes her head. "You should be a little more careful."

"We didn't do that much." I nudge Ashley. "Just made them think they heard a couple of girls' giggling in the distance. They didn't see us."

"Yeah." Ashley smiles. "We needed to get out of there and those guys weren't leaving."

"It was either scare them off or lure them into a closet and feed." I manage a weak smile. "In the state we were in, I didn't really trust that we'd be able to control ourselves."

The detective stops smiling. "Hmm. All right. Makes sense. Those two won't ever know how lucky they got hearing ghosts." She gives me a side eye glance. "You guys wouldn't happen to know anything about a black Lincoln Town Car full of half-dead Cholos would you?"

"Umm, yeah. About that..." I offer a quick explanation. "Go easy on them if you can. They were going to be nice to us."

"Why would we need to go easy on them?" She asks.

"Guess you didn't look in the trunk," I blurt. "Oops."

The detective raises both eyebrows. "What's in the trunk? A body?"

"No. Drugs." I fidget, feeling like a narc.

Weird thing... in life, I'd have had zero problem telling on someone for having *eeeevil* drugs. You know. The whole good girl thing. Drugs are bad, mmmmkay? Now, I kinda feel a bit crappy about it. Though, I don't feel bad if the police stop those drugs from hitting the streets.

"Oh, is that all?" She shakes her head dismissively. "One of the local groups financing their activities."

"Seriously?" I blink.

"Yeah. Almost all the drugs in this part of the state are managed by the undead. At least anything worth more than a few hundred bucks." She chuckles. "Those guys work for the vamps, even if they don't know it."

"They didn't know it." I fidget. "Hope no one's mad at us."

"We didn't kill them," says Ashley. "Did we?"

"Close. One of them was borderline. If we hadn't found them when we did…"

Ashley looks guilty. "Sorry."

"Not your fault." I nudge her. "Don't know which guy it was. Might have been me that drank a little too much."

The detective keeps looking at me expectantly.

"We got blown up and put ourselves back together. Left us a bit hungry. That's all." I exhale. "Not looking to retaliate for the bomb or cause trouble here."

She nods. "I understand. You guys get a little manic if you take too much of a beating. I've seen some messes. You might want to disappear for a little while, just in case."

"Yeah. Thanks. We're leaving right now…" I start for the door.

"So, what's on the memory stick?" asks the detective.

"I have no idea. I'm just a courier." I pause, turning to look at her.

She raises her hands in a 'hey, easy' manner. "I know there's nothing I can do to stop you from taking it. I'm just a mortal. Only asking for curiosity."

"I honestly don't know. They never told us." I shrug. "I'm very, very, very low on the totem pole. Basically, the intern."

Detective Marquez laughs. "All right. Stay out of trouble."

"Will try…" I shake my head.

Staying out of trouble seems to be getting more and more difficult as time goes by.

I head outside, look around to make sure no one is watching, then zip into the air. Ashley pulls up alongside and we start zooming northward.

"Hope whatever's on that thing was worth it," says Ashley.

"Honestly? I don't care." I shrug. "The mess is already done. I just want to get home."

CHAPTER 8

MOVIE NIGHT

FRIDAY

Not having a phone makes finding our way home a little more annoying.

We end up following an airplane to SEA-TAC. Yeah, jets are significantly faster than us, but we can still see them at a distance. I suppose it would be more accurate to say we followed *several* airplanes. It's not like we literally chased one down and tailed it. We just kinda went in the same direction all the planes were going after we thought we'd made it back to Washington State.

Once we spotted the airport, making it back to Cottage Lake wasn't too difficult. Having a phone would've shaved about half an hour off our trip time as it would've eliminated all guesswork and looking around for landmarks.

Anyway, we get home. Wolent can wait one more night for this stupid memory thing.

The TV is on when we enter the kitchen via the patio door. The Littles are talking, which means it's probably not *too* late yet. I glance at the stove clock and nearly gasp when I see it's a few minutes before ten. Wow. We really must have wanted to be home. Without even thinking about it, we hauled serious ass. That might explain why I'm feeling a little tired, like I just ran a small marathon.

It's so good to be home. I stand there taking in the smells and ambiance of the place. There's got to be something wrong with me since no one my age should be *this* clingy to home, but it is what it is. Oh, it has to be the vampire stuff making my feelings of security here more intense. Home always was kinda my security blanket. Now it's my *lair* too. Vampires get very touchy about their lairs.

The somewhat dull voice coming from the living room sounds like a nature documentary. That means the TV is on to no particular channel while Dad hunts for a movie. It's Friday night after all.

"I don't really want to watch a movie," grumps Sierra. "Not until Sarah gets home."

Damn. Feeling guilty already.

I never really did anything that bad to get in trouble. So why is it that I feel like I snuck out to go to a party that I was forbidden to go to… and they're catching me trying to sneak back inside after my bedtime? Might as well get it over with.

Trying to be casual, I walk down the hall to the living room. Mom and Dad are in their usual spots. Sierra's sprawled on the rug in a pile of pillows, giving off an 'okay I'll watch the movie but I won't like it' energy. Sam and Sophia are on the couch near Mom.

As soon as I walk in, you'd think Justin Bieber just entered a classroom full of eighth grade girls. All three Littles practically jump on me, cheering. Even the normally reserved Sam has surrendered to his need for a cling hug. The cheering is deafening for a moment.

"Sorry… sorry. I didn't mean to be away this long. Stuff got complicated."

Sierra gives me a look that demands to know details.

Sophia's crying. I think she's just too happy to handle it. The other two let go of me, but she keeps clinging, which is fine.

Sam simply smiles once he gets the hugging out of his system.

Mom glances over at me. "Is disappearing for days at a time going to become a common thing?"

I cringe. "No. Shouldn't. We had an uhh, unexpected complication."

Dad nods once. "Did you two at least have fun in Nevada?"

"Oh, yeah. Sure." Ashley grins. "We had a real blast."

"Oof," I whisper.

"Uh oh." Sierra cringes. "She's being literal, isn't she?"

Mom flicks her gaze between us. "What happened?"

Sophia whispers, "Coralie said they'd be fine," over and over to herself.

"Umm, what do you mean?" I attempt (and fail) at Innocent Smile™.

"I don't recognize those outfits." Mom fixes me with her lawyer stare. "You're both wearing entirely new clothing. Something bad must have happened."

"The girls probably got into a fight with another vampire," says Dad, sounding awfully casual. "Claws don't play nice with fabric."

Mom's barely controlled worry gets under my skin. She doesn't have to say anything else, merely look at me with this 'how can you do this to us' expression.

"It wasn't our fault..." I move around the sofa end and sit next to her, with Sophia in my lap. "We were supposed to go down there to a motel room, find a hidden memory stick and bring it back."

Ashley flops beside me. Sophia grabs Ash's arm and clings to it while leaning against me. Aww. She's upset. I wonder how much she knows? She's not freaking out *too* much, so I am hopeful she didn't see our exploded state.

"That sounds simple enough." Dad pushes his glasses up. "Which means it went wildly wrong."

"Yeah. I forgot to check the door for traps." I fold my arms. "There was a bomb."

"Oh my god..." Mom starts fussing over me like I'm five years old and just fell off my bike. "Are you okay? Does it hurt anywhere?"

"Mom, she set off a bomb, she didn't wipe out on a skateboard," says Sierra.

"Not helping," deadpans Sam.

Dad clucks his tongue. "You know what happens when you rush the door without checking for traps."

"Checking for traps takes too long." Sierra kicks the air like a barbarian battering down a door. "Grog smash."

Ashley blinks at him. He's being *way* too casual about this news. I'm guessing he's just not processing it. Or he's intentionally ignoring the meaning of the words and focusing on me still being here. He doesn't have to—or want to—think about what happened. Yeah. Dad is disassociating. Okay, I swear. If anyone ever shows him the pictures of our post-explosion remains, I will kill them.

I tolerate Mom's fussing. Eventually, she appears satisfied I'm intact and not bleeding.

"Well, you two made it home just in time for movie night." Dad smiles, holding up a DVD of *The Last Starfighter*. "Care to join us?"

"I wouldn't miss it for anything." I smile. "Mind if I go change first? Never quite managed to get my shoes off."

"Ack!" says Mom, as if I'd just admitted to spilling dog poop on the rug.

That time, she's obviously overacting on purpose… for humor. She's too happy that I'm home in one piece to really be upset at me for violating her 'no shoes in the house' rule.

Dad nods. "Of course."

I get up. Sophia doesn't let go. In fact, she insists on staying with me as I go downstairs. Maybe this is a worrisome level of clingy… but I don't mind. Soon, I've traded the stolen clothes for a comfy over-sized T-shirt. One of the extra-long ones that's down past my knees. They're great for sleeping in. Basically, my PJs. Ashley puts on actual PJs. Yes, they are pink and covered in unicorns.

We head back up out of the basement to the living room. I'm basically carrying Sophia like a baby. I'd be more worried but she's not crying anymore, so that's good. Once we settle on the couch,

Sierra unceremoniously adds herself to the sofa, leaning into me from the side. It's subtle, but for her, it's an obvious show of affection and worry. I put an arm around her, too. She doesn't protest. I do see her giving the 'rents the look, hoping they don't notice her being 'mega clingy.' It's not really mega clingy for any normal person. Seems like the parents either didn't notice or are doing a good job of not reacting. Sam sits on the floor, leaning back into the sofa between me and Ashley. Chloe's relaxing on a pile of small pillows in front of the TV, swishing her feet back and forth in the air.

It's good to be home again.

CHAPTER 9
BELATED

SATURDAY NIGHT

Dropping the mystery USB off at Wolent's manor didn't take too long.

Naturally, I had to explain why it took me so long to get back with it. The boss didn't seem upset at the delay, only curious. I'm sure if we didn't have a good reason for being so late, he'd have been angry. Not like I treated this job like Sierra getting a writing assignment from school and kept putting it off.

I still didn't ask what was on it, nor was any information offered. There didn't seem to be any point to me knowing. What would I do, refuse to go get it if I knew it contained information that would be used to do something Follows Rules Girl would have an anxiety attack over? I mean, sure. There are some things that I would refuse to do even if Wolent ordered me to... but they're drastic and the kind of things I'd be willing to get kicked out of vampire society over. Fortunately, I really doubt the big guy is ever going to order me to kill my family or go around murdering innocent children or something vile like that. Really, I don't think he has it in him. After all, he's let

Chloe stick around. I've heard a few whispers during the soirees that vampires in other parts of the world wouldn't tolerate the existence of a child vampire at all.

No, it's not out of any sort of moral issue with the idea. Permanent children are a risk to vampire existence staying secret. I suppose there's also the worry about what happens if one of them grows old and powerful and still has the temperament of a kid. Tantrums and meltdowns aren't so cute when the kid having a freakout can knock down walls.

Thankfully, Chloe isn't the tantruming sort of kid. So far, she hasn't really ever gotten upset about anything. I'm sure the day will come when she has a fit about *something*. Here's hoping I handle it well enough.

So, yeah. Project Gomez is done... at least as far as my involvement goes.

After leaving the manor, I swing over to downtown Seattle. It's a bit challenging to find a secluded spot to land without being seen near the mall. Eventually, an opportunity arrives and I surreptitiously change modes from UFO to pedestrian. I'm on another mission, only this one's personal and not from Mr. Wolent.

Hunter's birthday happened while I was in a C4 induced coma. Yes, I have already called him and explained why I didn't call or visit him on the third. Over the phone, I didn't give any details beyond saying I had a 'very weird day', leaning heavily on the word weird. He knows that's code for vampire related things I don't want to talk about on the phone. My mission right now is to find something to get him as a birthday gift.

Thanks to a certain incident with a leprechaun, I could really get him anything up to and including a new truck. Yeah, that might be a bit excessive, and it would upset him. Also, if our plans remain intact, he's going to join 'Team V' within a few years, so it's not like he really needs a brand-new vehicle.

Part of me wants to give him something he needs, since his mom is not exactly rolling in money. She's way better off now with the new job. Ronan no longer wonders *if* they'll have a real dinner at night as opposed to a single slice of bologna on bread. Hunter's got this thing about money. My family isn't rich, but compared to him, we basically are. These days, the kind of money my parents make barely qualifies us as middle class. Mom earns more than Dad, something that Uncle Hank really hates and has commented on more than once.

No one even told him anything. He simply assumed that a lawyer for Boeing makes more than a work-at-home programmer who spends most of his time developing software for business clients. Yeah, he writes super boring crap. Finance programs, inventory tracking... that sort of thing. Nothing cool. Dad doesn't mind that Mom makes more than him. He's doing what he loves and he never has to leave the house. He's not making bad money, though.

Hunter, on the other hand, takes after his jerk of a father in one way. It bugs him that he can't 'provide for me' so to speak. No matter how many times I've tried to tell him it doesn't make him any less of a man not to be able to shower me in expensive crap, he hates being reminded that I have more money than he does.

So, I can't buy him an expensive gift as it will upset him.

I still want to give him something useful. Maybe I could go dopey and romantic. Find a place that does like custom snow globes and get one with little figures that look like us inside. Nah. That's cute but too impractical. And very breakable. Is he old enough not to hate shirts? I could get him some clothes.

Nah. He's nineteen now. That's still young enough to roll his eyes at a gift of clothing. Oh whatever. I'll just get him a $100 gift card for Steam. He plays games on the computer more than the PlayStation. That works.

Don't need to go to the mall for that either.

I'm still here so... I meander around for a bit on my own. The place is full of Christmas stuff. There's a mall Santa with a line of kids waiting. It's cute, so I swing by a coffee place, grab a caramel latte, and spend a few minutes watching the kids tell Santa what they want. Makes me a little nostalgic for being young enough to think Santa was real.

Huh. I wonder.

I mean... leprechauns exist, as do vampires, dryads, and other things. Maybe there's something to the whole Santa thing. Obviously, the story is wrong. I mean, there is no supernatural being that runs around to every single house and leaves presents. Something like that would be really hard to hide. Kinda makes me wonder what an actual Santa Claus would really do? Run around de-grinching certain people? Showing up disguised as relatives and giving stuff to poor kids?

Hell, if I was Santa, I'd run around to hospitals and cure sick people.

This is why people with a working conscience never get super powers like that.

I glance down at the coffee cup in my right hand, steam wafting up into my face. My fingernails briefly extend into claws and go back to normal. Oh, right. I did get super powers. Sorta. That's me, the Christmas Vampire.

Oh, maybe I could 'ghost of Christmas past' some stingy bosses? Fly around the area and mind wank people into being nicer to their employees or something. Really tempting, but I have a feeling that would come back to bite me in the ass. Seems like every time I try to help people, the metaphorical teeth of fate find my butt.

On the other hand, I think I'm karmically in the black right now. Ashley and I got blown up for nothing. Meh. Whatever. I'll save that karma for when I really need it.

None of the parents or kids in the Santa line have anything on their minds that worries me. The ambiance of the mall around this time of year is so nice. Yeah, I know a lot of people hate the constant Christmas music everywhere. Not me. It's warm. Even Dad, who is about as unreligious as is possible to be, loves the season. If my father ever decided to join any faith, it would be the church of Bill & Ted. They only have one commandment: be excellent to each other.

Hmm. Since I'm here without Ashley, I might as well get her something for Christmas. Fortunately, she's easy to shop for: anything pink, plush, or unicorn themed will be a big hit. I hit a few stores and grab a couple small plush unicorns, a super floofy pink sweater that's like wearing a blanket, and finally snag a bunch of anime on Blu-ray. So what if physical media is dying out. If we have it on disc, we won't lose access to it if the streaming service shuts down or there's no internet.

If nuclear war wipes out electronic power in general, then they wouldn't do us any good.

Though, if that happens, I think we'll have bigger problems than lack of anime movies.

Loot in hand (or bag rather) I leave the mall and fly home long enough to stash the gifts in the attic. I can be super sneaky if I want to be, apparently. No one noticed me go in and out. Well, no one except maybe Max. It's pretty difficult to hide from the hellhound in the backyard. Not a big deal. He can't exactly tell anyone what I got them and ruin the surprise.

It's almost eleven now, so Hunter should be getting home from his job at the restaurant soon.

My eagerness to see him gets the better of me. As in, I arrive at their house before he does. This results in me sitting in the living room with Mrs. Lawrence and talking for a while. We get along okay, even if I do feel a bit awkward talking about any potential future with Hunter. She is not in the know, so to speak. Bad enough Ronan is. So, I have to play it straight with her and act like an ordinary girl dating her ordinary son.

Considering we're technically only nineteen, she's not really pushing too hard or even mentioning the M word or the G word. (That's grandkids by the way). Mostly, she asks me about school and whatnot. For the time being, I can still answer honestly. While I intend to stop going to SCC, I'm finishing out this semester. Not sure why. It just feels less bad to do that than simply stop going and abandon the classes.

After only about twelve minutes of talking to her, Hunter walks in. He pauses inside the door, giving me a 'whoa, you're here already' kind of glance. "Hey."

"How was work, hon?" asks Mrs. Lawrence.

He shoves the door closed and removes his coat. "Usual. Mix of decent people, loud kids, and Karens. Who the hell goes to a restaurant named *Mi Tierra* and acts shocked the menu is full of Mexican food."

"Oh boy," I mutter. "That sounds fun."

"Some people." Mrs. Lawrence rolls her eyes. "Well, I'll be going to bed fairly soon. You two go have fun and try not to make too much noise."

Hunter blushes a little. "Thanks, Ma."

Whew. Good thing it's totally out of my personality to make a raunchy joke in front of his mother. Doesn't stop me from *thinking* of one. I am not, however, going to say I could run home real quick to borrow Ashley's ball gag. Honestly, she might not even have it anymore. Some girl she dated months ago gave it to her. Really don't like thinking of that sort of thing in the context of my best friend-slash-sister, but it's hard to pretend it didn't happen.

I'm definitely not saying anything like that to Hunter's mom.

Pretty sure Hunter wouldn't appreciate the humor either. He's not into that sort of thing. Neither am I. Scott convinced me to let him tie my hands behind my back once. I was legitimately scared the whole time. That should've been a giant red flag waving in my face to get the hell away from him. I didn't. Even that oblivious jackass sensed my discomfort. Thankfully, he never asked me to do that again.

Of course, that only happened like three months before he killed me so, there's that.

Anyway...

Hunter and I go upstairs.

As soon as we're in his room, I hug him. "I'm so sorry I missed being here for your birthday."

"What happened?" He brushes a hand across my cheek, worry in his eyes.

Deep breath time. I guide him to the bed, plant his butt on the edge of the mattress, then sit next to him and explain everything.

Emotions go by on his face like the wheels of a spinning slot machine. Fear, anger, worry, relief, love… everything. He's not happy about the fact there isn't much he can do right now to protect me.

"Don't be upset. You couldn't have done anything about that." I smooth my hands down my legs over and over. "Heck, not many people could have."

Maybe Aziz could have shrugged off that bomb. The thought of him standing there charred like something out of a Bugs Bunny cartoon and just saying 'ouch' after the blast almost makes me laugh.

"I feel so useless." He sighs.

"You're absolutely not useless." I lean against him. "Right now, you are my beacon of sane normality in an otherwise ridiculous existence."

He gives a weak chuckle and strokes the back of my hand. "Your existence isn't ridiculous."

I smirk. "My sister has a teleporting kitten she made out of magical mushroom dust."

Hunter coughs. "Okay… maybe it's a little ridiculous."

"You seem distracted. Is everything okay?"

Finally, he makes eye contact. "Distracted?"

"Yeah, you weren't looking at me. Seems like you're thinking about something else."

He flashes a little smile, seemingly amused I'm not reading his mind. "I was thinking about you, honestly. Just… worrying."

I lean into him. "It's nice to have someone to worry about me. But you don't have to worry that much. I'm a little tougher than an ordinary girl."

"True, but you also get into situations that an ordinary girl wouldn't." He holds me close. "Just wondering if like you 'die' too much, will it cause permanent damage or maybe affect you mentally?"

"You think I might turn into a monster if I get my ass kicked too often?"

"Not thinking you will. Just worrying if it might be a risk."

I bite my lip. Never really thought about that too deeply. Do we stay the same forever or are all vampires set on a path to gradually become less and less like people and more like folkloric monsters? Does 'dying' hurry that process up?

Relax, luv, says Dalton's voice in the back of my mind. *If that were true, I'd be a cosmic horror by now.* He chuckles.

That's good to know. So, we don't have nine lives or something before we go full Cthulhu?

Nope. It's not even as bad as a mortal being knocked out by a concussion. Obviously, you would be better off doing your best to avoid ending up in the deep sleep. We're particularly vulnerable until we wake up.

Come to think of it, Eldon suffered a whole lot more damage than I did and he seems fine.

"I'm fine." I squeeze Hunter. "Got it on good authority it's nothing to worry about."

"Good authority?"

"Dalton's whispering to me."

He makes a face of unease. "That's one thing I'm not looking forward to... having someone watch me all the time."

"It's not like that." I shrug. "Most of the time, there's no connection at all. The rest, it's basically like having a speakerphone on next to me and everything I think is spoken out loud."

Hunter fidgets. "Still. The idea of having someone permanently plugged into my thoughts is kind of weird... unless it's you."

"Hold on there." I chuckle. "That sounds romantic now? But... I don't want to drive you off. If I'm in your head 24/7 and you can't have a spare thought without me possibly listening in on it, that might cause problems."

"But…" He looks hurt for a moment, then seems to get what I mean.

"Yeah. Exactly. Like if someone works with their spouse all day, then goes home and is with them all day, but worse. I don't want us to end up hating each other."

He nods. "So, what are we going to do about that?"

"About what?"

"About who does the… you know." He makes a biting gesture.

"We'll have to find someone we trust, and who would be willing to lose a little power for a while."

"Lose power?" He raises an eyebrow.

I nod. "Yeah. Making another vampire takes a lot out of you. Every one you make takes some power away and it regenerates super slow. I don't think Dalton's fully recovered from what he did for me yet."

Not quite. Almost there.

"Wow. That French girl must really like you." Hunter whistles.

I laugh. "Don't let Aurélie hear you call her 'that French girl.' I think she'd be insulted."

"She's what, sixteen maybe?"

"Wow. No. She was like twenty-three or so when she died. People were shorter back then."

"Oh. But I mean, she's like super powerful and old right? Nice of her to give up some power."

I tickle him. "It's not giving up. It's loaning. It comes back. Just takes a while. And, I think the more powerful they are, the less they notice. Oh… hey, I got you something."

"You didn't have to do that," says Hunter, already preparing to give me a hard time for spending money on him.

"Check your email." I wink.

He pulls out his phone, looks at it… then finds the email with the Steam gift card. "Oh, cool. Thank you."

"You're welcome. Happy birthday, even if it's late."

We kiss.

As soon as our lips meet, all my worries disappear in an explosion of relief and joy.

~

UGH. I DON'T WANT TO MOVE.

Kinda have to soon, though. It's almost five in the morning. Surprisingly, we didn't do anything more than make out a little... then spent a few hours cuddling and talking. Sex is great but... it just didn't happen tonight. What does it mean that I'm totally fine with that? Being with him was wonderful. I got to let out all the anxiety I had saved up from the Gomez situation, which mostly boiled down to me not wanting to be responsible for causing the mortal world to discover the existence of vampires.

He thinks I'm being too paranoid about it.

Obviously, some mortals in the past have become aware of vampires or there wouldn't be so many books and movies and folklore stories about them. Attempting absolute secrecy is a foolish pursuit. No one, and it doesn't matter who you are, can keep a secret perfectly. That's why Dad laughs at conspiracy theorists. He likes to say the government couldn't keep Bill Clinton getting a BJ from that woman secret. There's no way they could keep a lid on something major like the Kennedy assassination or that the moon landing was faked. If it was faked, *someone* would've revealed the truth already.

Hunter might have a point. Maybe I shouldn't be so worried about it. It's Follows Rules Girl doing it to me, though. Just like anything in life, I get told what the rules are and I go out of my way to walk on eggshells hoping not to break them. I'm such a lame-o that I never even stayed up past my bedtime reading under my blankets with a flashlight.

The thought that I'm now equipped to break into places and steal whatever I want is super ironic. Of all the possible vampire power sets to get, it's weird that fate gave me the sneaky stuff. Fate got Ashley spot on. She's always been charming and helpful. Giving her powers of supernatural adorableness is completely appropriate.

I'm not complaining though. Vampirism changes a person, even Follows Rules Girl.

The random character generator gave me rogue, so I'm going to run with it. Just because I *can* do stealthy things doesn't mean I have to embark on a crime spree. I can be a spy, not a thief. Sneaky does not require theft.

Anyway… it's almost five in the morning and the sun's coming up soon. I should go home, even if it is nice and cozy here. I've been clinging to Hunter for like two hours now since he fell asleep, like he's some sort of giant plush teddy bear.

Gently, I extricate myself from him and go out the window. Yeah, *that* window. The big one and main reason I can't simply sleep here.

Spending the night with Hunter recharged my emotion battery. I can't help but smile all the way home.

CHAPTER 10
NOT THIS AGAIN

TUESDAY NIGHT

S o much for being a slacker.

I had about three hours between getting home from my art history class and getting a call from one of Wolent's people with another job. At least this one isn't sending me out of state, just to Seattle. Specifically, to the West Industrial District, Terminal 5 area.

This is another 'quick run and grab the thing' type FedEx quest, which means I'm preparing for war.

Chloe's upstairs, hanging out with the Littles. I'm in my bedroom with Ashley staring at my wardrobe, trying to figure out what to wear for this. Everything I start to grab for, I put back because I don't want it to get shredded, lit on fire, or disintegrated at an atomic level.

"Dammit. I should storm out of the house naked, just to save the Universe the trouble of destroying my clothes again."

Ashley laughs. "You're not serious."

"I'm closer to serious than you think." I rake my hands through my hair. "Maybe if I do that, we might not end up in the morgue again. Do I just need to prove to the powers of fate it's not going to embarrass me anymore?"

"I don't think the Universe is setting out to embarrass us." Ashley side-eyes the door. "That's the upstairs bathtub."

"You think the tub is somehow feeding off embarrassment?" I purse my lips. "Like it's alive?"

She shrugs. "I dunno. Maybe when Soph used it to enchant Sierra, it absorbed some of her insecurities. Isn't her greatest fear something like being suddenly naked in front of everyone at school?"

"Not really." I sigh. "Her greatest fear is someone she loves getting killed. But, yeah… the school thing is her greatest *irrational* fear."

"She created Fuzzydoom based on her childhood nightmare." Ashley pulls her hair off her face. "I bet she accidentally cursed the bathtub. Anyway, speaking of being thrown out of the house with no clothes… you're not serious about that, are you?"

"Not really." I sigh, returning my attention to the wardrobe.

"Good. Our life is supposed to be a *silly* anime movie, not a hentai." She giggles.

I smirk. "Are you sure about that? We have giant tentacles in our closet."

"Bad." She covers her face. "Don't make me think of the void octopus that way. It's funny, not perverted."

"Yeah. True. It came from Soph's subconscious so it's innocent as can be." I trade my nice house sweats for an older black shirt, black jeans, and some beat up black Converse I haven't worn since my sophomore year. "This'll do."

Basically, I'm wearing nothing that would upset me to lose.

And yeah, Dad would say I kinda look like a kid going to a Nirvana concert. All I'm missing to complete the look is throwing a flannel shirt on over this. If I dipped my head in lime green paint, Sierra would say I'm doing a bad Billie Eilish impersonation. Whatever. I don't care about this outfit or what I look like. I am a post-fashion vampire. Not going to pile on any more grunge couture.

Gonna make do with the katana as my only accessory. Yes, I'm bringing my sword this time. I'm not ending up losing another week if I can help it.

Ashley's keeping me company again, which I am grateful for. One of the main reasons she took the vampire challenge was to 'hang with me and do stuff.' That, and she'd become ever so freaking tired of being the helpless best friend that the Forces of Evil™ kept picking on.

She doesn't really do the emo wearing all black thing. I don't either, as a matter of fact, though I do have more black clothes than she does. A pinksplosion isn't exactly good for stealth missions, so she's borrowing some of my stuff. Only real difference between our outfits is she's got a black skirt on over black yoga pants instead of black jeans.

Chloe runs into the room, emitting this long, "Eeeeeeeeeee" scream. She crashes into me, clings, then yells, "Don't let them eat me!"

Ashley raises an eyebrow. "What the heck are the Littles up to? Did Sophia summon something?'

I crouch to eye level with kiddo and try my best to be reassuring. Poor thing is shaking, crying, and looks terrified. "What happened?"

She sniffles and wipes at her tears. "There are hungry cougars nearby who want to meet me."

Ashley clamps a hand over her mouth; her face reddens.

"What?" I blink. "Where did you hear that?"

"On my tablet! A box popped up and told me." She shivers. "I don't wanna get eaten by cougars!"

Ashley loses it. She bursts out laughing.

Chloe stares at her halfway between terrified and angry. "Why is she laughing?"

"Umm... because someone is trying to trick you. There are no cougars around here." I hug her. At least not the feline kind. "Kiddo, do me a favor? Ash and I need to run and do something for Mr. W.

Can you bring your tablet to Dad and tell him about the cougars? He should be able to fix it."

"Umm. Okay." She sniffles. "Try not to get blowed up again."

"Definitely on my list." I chuckle.

The three of us head upstairs. Chloe darts left to run to the living room while Ash and I go out the sliding patio door. It's tempting to lurk and listen in on what's about to happen in the living room. Ashley is still giggling about that. Someone out in Internet land is really messing up their targeted advertisements.

Shaking my head, I leap upward.

Over the next few minutes, we fly to the dock district.

This is the part where I am once again super grateful for the whole flying thing. Trying to do these vampire jobs for Wolent would absolutely suck in a car. Once we arrive at Harbor Island, we start looking around from the air.

Our 'simple' mission sounds pretty basic. There is supposed to be a briefcase waiting for us here as a blind drop. Something, something, *vampires from California dealing with Wolent*, something. I don't know the deets, again. 'Go and get this briefcase' is the extent of it.

Given what happened in Gomez, I am more than a little concerned this briefcase might be a bomb. I'm not going to be an idiot again. Maybe I'm a little on edge, but tonight there's a more-than-bad chance that my sword is going to come out of its scabbard a little faster than might be reasonable if something gets strange.

At least this time we have more information to go on in terms of where to look.

They didn't simply say 'the pier' the same way we got a 'somewhere in this motel room.' Finding a suitcase 'somewhere on the wharf' is probably about the same level of annoying as searching a motel room for a USB stick. Thankfully, we don't have to do that. We were told the case is hidden 'by a trashcan.'

So, we start at the north part at the Jack Block Park viewpoint.

Hmm. No public trash cans here. Just concrete platforms with a view of the water. Heading south, we skip past a lot of piled up cargo containers. I scan a little parking area to my right, nothing. A little south of the giant cranes that pluck cargo containers off ships, there's a blue metal building. I spot a trash can near the wall by the door. Might as well check.

Ashley follows me down.

There aren't too many people on the dock at this hour. Only a couple security guards. One guy in a little while pickup truck that has a flashing yellow light on the roof keeps driving around the cargo containers. Poor guy. Security has got to be one of the most boring jobs imaginable. I could never do that.

We land on the blue roof and wait for a guard to go by, then slip over the side and drop down to the pavement. The garbage can smells like coffee cups, egg sandwiches, and various microwaveable lunch meals. There's no sign of any briefcase behind or under the can.

"Please tell me they didn't chuck the thing we're after into the trash," whispers Ashley.

Cringing, I peek into the can. "Hope not... That would be kinda reckless, right? What if someone changed the bag before we got here."

Ashley plucks the lid off and holds it. "Look under the bag."

"Ooh. Good idea." I gather the plastic bag away from the edges and lift it out of the container.

"Score!" whisper-shouts Ashley.

I lean forward and peek into the can. A thin metal briefcase lays flat on the bottom of the trash can. No wires connect it to anything, so I'm reasonably sure picking it up won't kill me. However, I'm not completely sure.

I set the trash bag on the ground and pull my phone out, sending a text to my brother to request Blix for a moment.

Engine noise approaches.

"I got it," says Ashley in a calm tone.

The security guy in the little while truck drives right past us without reacting to our presence. Drives is a bit of a strong word.

That truck is meandering along at not much faster than a human walking pace. Figures. We get the one security guard in Seattle who's actually doing their job and looking around for suspicious activity.

All of a sudden, the radio inside the truck blares to life at full volume, blasting some sort of screamo-metal.

I'd like to say I handled the sudden loud noise with coolness, but that would be a lie. My phone goes flying as I jump and scream. Ashley shrieks and falls over. Somehow, I manage to scrape up enough mental faculty to go into combat mode, accelerating my reflexes past human speed. Time seems to drag to a crawl as I float downward in a derpy jump-scare pratfall.

The poor security guard about shits himself. He's screaming and flailing around inside the tiny pickup truck's cab so hard the entire vehicle rocks on its wheels.

Thanks to my ability to fly, I launch myself horizontally, skimming a few inches above the surface of the tarmac, and catch my iPhone before it smashes itself to bits on the concrete. Ashley lands on her side, curled up in a ball. The only reason she's not still screaming is that her lungs are empty.

I rotate over so I'm facing down and stop flying, dropping to my hands and knees.

The guard finally manages to turn the radio off. He grabs a walkie-talkie and starts yelling at someone named Bill for messing with the radio in the truck.

Tiny laughter from above me draws my attention to Blix.

I narrow my eyes at him.

He flashes a cheesy smile at me as if to say, 'sorry, I didn't mean to scare you, just the guy in the truck.' His next overly innocent face basically says, 'sorry, I'm an imp. Can't help a little mischief sometimes.'

I sigh.

"Ooba?" asks Blix.

"Sec," I whisper.

Ashley sits up, gasping for air and staring at me with a WTF expression.

"Guard." I point.

She hastily collects herself, then nods at me. "On it. He can't see us."

"Whew." I stand there watching until the truck pulls away out of sight behind the side of the small building. Good thing that music was so damn loud. He didn't hear either of us scream. "Blix, there's a case in the bottom of this trash bin. Can you tell if it's a bomb or not?"

The imp zips over to the trash can and peeks inside for a few seconds, then nods at me.

"It's a bomb?"

He shakes his head.

"Then why did you nod?"

"Because, he *can* tell if it's a bomb or not." Ashley smirks.

Blix gives her a thumbs-up.

"Okay, just because I'm super paranoid after Nevada." I point at the trash can. "That thing isn't going to explode?"

He shakes his head so hard his leathery ears thwap back and forth.

"Cool. Thanks." I salute him.

Blix makes a weird happy noise, then disappears in a puff of black smoke.

I reach in and grab the briefcase. It's one of those slim ones, only about three inches thick. Silver edges, black faces grooved in horizontal lines. It's a little heavier than I expected. Doesn't rattle when jostled. Interesting.

Ashley replaces the trash bag in the container after I remove the case, then puts the lid back on it.

My iPhone beeps.

I look. A text from Sam says, 'no problem. Blix says it's full of little gold ingots.'

Eep. I raise both eyebrows.

Someone left a small fortune in gold in a freaking trash can on a dock all day? Maybe not. It's possible another vampire dropped it off here only an hour ago. Still. Eep. I don't want to be responsible for a box of gold any longer than I absolutely have to be.

"… chance to finally reshape vampire society," whispers a voice from behind me.

I turn. The voice seems to have come from behind a giant stack of cargo containers a few hundred feet of parking lot away from me, past a pile of scrap metal.

"Did you hear that?" whispers Ashley, using the silent technique.

"Yeah."

"Should we eavesdrop?" She grins. "Sounds important."

I glance down at the case. If I lose this, Wolent will probably be angry with me. The exchange rate of gold is something way beyond my skill set. No idea if this case is more or less than what the leprechaun gave me. Could be more. Probably is. If I have to pay Wolent back for losing this, I'm going to be back to nothing. Hey, I'm not greedy. Don't really care about gathering wealth, but having some *is* a nice cushion. I'd rather not lose it if I can help it.

She's kinda right, though. 'Reshaping vampire society' sounds pretty epic. The big guy might want to know about it.

I set my phone on record mode and fly-glide toward the cargo containers. There's nothing more silent than a floating vampire— except one of Sam's killer farts. Ashley follows me.

"That sounds like a bunch of horse shit," says a guy on the other side of the containers.

"Legit. I swear," whispers the first man.

We glide up to the top of the containers. I tilt forward into Super-girl pose, then edge forward until I can just barely peek over the side.

Two reasonably average looking guys are hanging out here, directly below me. One's leaning against the containers vaping. He's dressed kind of like a biker dude. Lots of denim, black T-shirt, boots. Unnecessary chain on his wallet, and so on. Other guy is standing to his right, not vaping. That dude's in an ordinary jacket and jeans, like any random average guy might wear around here. He looks kinda familiar, as if I've seen him somewhere, but not enough to remember his name.

"You don't just 'reshape all of vampire society'" says vape guy with more than a little sarcasm. "You're being conned."

Other dude holds his hands up. "Swear. This is on the level. Sounds crazy, but this girl Natasha's found a way to flip things over so we're in charge of mortals. We won't have to keep hiding anymore if her plan works."

Ugh. I almost bonk my head on the container beneath me. Not this bullcrap again. Didn't I make it clear to Natasha she needed to leave this the hell alone? Now I know why this dude is familiar. He was with her when I confronted them. I think his name is Seth.

I hold my phone out to get some video of these two.

Seth spends the next almost ten minutes trying to convince Vape Guy that Natasha has a Plan™ and it won't fail. Or at least if it doesn't work, no one will notice or care and everyone will be just fine.

"C'mon," Ashley silent whispers. "Press him for deets. What's the plan?"

"At least come listen to what she's got to say," asks Seth. "It's not like you've got anything to lose if you don't want to help."

Vape guy takes a long pull and exhales. "What the heck can I do? I ain't got no special skills."

The cloud rises into my face. Hmm. Grape. Never understood the whole vaping thing. If you want to enjoy a flavor, have a Tic Tac or gum. Tastes better and you don't look like a pretentious douche.

"It's not a matter of specific skills. We're trying to find something. The more eyes we have out there, the better." Seth pats the guy on the arm. "C'mon, Head, aren't you tired of hiding?"

"Don't call me that," says Vape Dude. "The name is Headbanger."

The cringe is strong with this one. What is he, some kind of biker? He dresses like it. Long, scraggly black hair, too. I swear I've seen someone like this in one of those old music videos Dad liked as a kid. Motley Crew or something like that. I'm probably spelling it wrong. Eighties metal bands did NSFW things to the English language, like sticking umlauts where they don't belong. Surprised his name isn't Hëadbänger.

"Sorry, Headbanger." Seth chuckles.

"What's this Natasha chick got that every other vamp in the city doesn't?" asks Headbanger.

"We got a scholar or something working with us now. He found some stuff in an old book. I can't really explain it because she's the brains." Seth chuckles. "She'll answer your questions."

If Natasha is 'the brains' of their group, I really shouldn't worry.

Headbanger takes a pull off his vape stick again, letting the fog flow out of his nostrils on a long, somewhat impatient sigh. "If it'll get you to shut up, I'll talk to her, but I smell bullshit."

Ashley nudges me. "Should we smack some sense into them?"

I slide backward away from the edge, shaking my head. "Nope. I'm a spy, not an enforcer. Besides..." I pat the case. "This needs to go to Wolent immediately. I'm not going to risk losing it over idiots."

"Fair." She nods. "But don't you think Wolent would want to know if there's anything to this?"

Argh. I want to scream, but don't. "Yeah... you're probably right."

Seth and Headbanger walk over to a little red hatchback and hop in, Seth driving.

I know I'm going to regret this... but... "Okay. Let's follow 'em."

CHAPTER II
ANOTHER END OF THE WORLD SCENARIO

THURSDAY

Makes total sense why the police use helicopters sometimes to track speeding cars.

Following a vehicle from the air is seriously easy, and the target has no idea they're being followed. There are no traffic lights or other obstructions up here for us to get stuck behind. Okay, so it's a lot easier for us than the cops. Learning to fly a helicopter has to be one of the more difficult things a person can do, right up there with neurosurgery and developing the skills necessary to make it through the entire run time of *There Will Be Blood* without falling asleep.

Sorry. Dad loved that movie. I couldn't stay awake.

Seth's little red hatchback leaves the docks and goes south. We follow them for a few minutes past Youngstown to a narrow strip of civilization flanked on one side by Puget Park and on the other by a massive waste of land: a golf course.

The little red car pulls over and parks on a street in said little swath of civilization.

Ashley and I dive out of the air, landing near a sign for "Bee's Plumbing."

Seth and Headbanger get out of the car and approach a one-story grey house three doors away from the plumbing place with a big For Sale sign in the front yard. I've heard rumors that Lost Ones like to squat in empty houses sometimes. Things get rather fuzzy with the 'lair' rules when a vampire is transient, though there's some-thing to it. I'm talking about rules in the sense of 'laws of physics' here, not actual political rules vampires are expected to follow. Specifically, that whole 'wake up no matter what time it is if there's danger coming' deal.

Some believe we are more powerful in our lair. I can't see how that's even possible, really. It's not like we load the place up with runes for magic or build our lairs on ley line intersections. If anything is true about that, it must be psychological. Somewhere between castle doctrine and cornered rat.

Right. Anyway...

I glance down at the case of gold bars. This is dumb. I shouldn't be risking this. Then again, officially, I don't know what's in the case. No one told me and I didn't ask. That's not going to help me much since I *do* know. Wolent will know I know what I lost if I lose it. Grr. On the other hand, I've already been given a job to stop this Natasha idiot from doing stupid things. So, technically speaking, I'm not going off on a wild side mission of my own creation. This is home-work I didn't quite finish coming back to bite me in the ass. Is the Universe punishing me for being too nice? Should I have destroyed Natasha last time?

Nah. I can't go around just destroying every vampire who might be mildly inconvenient in the future. That's really damn psychotic. It's also completely not who I am. I even feel bad about destroying vampires who've legit tried to kill me.

Except Scott.

I don't feel bad about that. Not only was he a complete jerk to me in life, he murdered me. And then he turned into a half-formed vampire abomination that honestly could not be allowed to exist. As satisfying as it was to cut his head off and burn him to final death... some of it was literally a mercy.

Great. I'm already on edge over the whole getting blown to pieces in Gomez thing. Now I had to think about him again. I'm totally going to vent my anxiety on someone tonight if I'm not careful. At least I have the advantage of actually knowing how to use a sword. Sorta. I mean... I *do* really know how to use a sword, just not a katana. Not really. There's an entirely different technique involved for them. Dalton's not a samurai. He's never even been to Japan. All the knowledge he gave me regarding swords is strictly European style.

Mind you, having real knowledge of sword combat plus knowing that katanas are slicing weapons is enough to catch almost anyone off guard. *Very* few people seeing me with a katana would expect me to be anything but a stupid kid who watched too many YouTube videos. Honestly, even among vampires, the sword thing is a dying art. Guns are so much more efficient, after all.

But they are loud.

Mom would kill me if I brought a gun home, too.

Don't even want to think about what might happen if the Littles or Chloe found it. My brain starts to say 'none of them would dare touch it' but, yeah. Everyone who's had the unthinkable happen has said the same thing. I don't feel like going through all the hassle of getting a gun safe and whatnot. The sword is just fine.

Maybe I'll find a proper longsword or saber one of these days.

Once Seth and Headbanger disappear inside the little grey house, I exhale the word, "Dammit" and start walking toward it.

"What's wrong?" Ashley glances at me.

"This feels stupid."

"Why?" She tilts her head.

I pat the case.

Ashley ponders. "You could run that to Wolent's place and I'll keep an eye on this until you're back."

Umm. Okay. Wow. That's an obvious answer I never even thought of. "Are you... of course you're going to be okay. They won't even notice you exist."

Ashley beams. "I may look cute and innocent, but I am no longer the helpless plot device that keeps getting kidnapped to mess with you."

"Heh. Good." I grin at her. "Be right back."

She nods.

I look around to make sure the coast is clear. Seeing no one looking directly at me, I feel safe enough to launch myself into the air. Go Ashley for being smart. I didn't want to lose Seth, so I followed him even though I am carrying this case. Hopefully, it won't take me too long to zoom back and forth.

Flying at a sprint is a bit like having a leaf blower pointed right at my head. Maybe a cheap one, since I can still see where I'm going. It makes me wonder... if I'm 'slow' in the air compared to some vampires, do the others need to wear motorcycle helmets when they fly at full speed? According to a navigation app on my phone, my top speed is approximately 120 MPH. That's basically all ideal conditions: wearing no baggy clothes, perfectly horizontal for minimum wind resistance, and no pigeons smashing into my face. Pretty sure I can push past that in moments of real panic, fear, or desire to be home. We made really good time returning from Gomez.

Oh hey, there's that lair thing again.

"Player has gained buff 'lair empowerment!' Plus twenty percent flight speed when traveling directly home."

Heh.

I am such a dork.

A few minutes later, I spot Wolent's manor and bee-line for the front door. Dutiful as ever, Aziz is standing at his post beside the entrance. Poor guy doesn't go out much, but I can't blame him. He's ridiculously big, almost inhuman. His biceps are bigger around than my waist. Aziz has the kind of physique only seen in Marvel Comics or secret experiments in some East German laboratory during the height of the Cold War. If he went out and about, people would stare. He'd stand out in their memory.

Yeah, that's a Beast problem. The older they get, the bigger they get... to a point. I mean, he's not going to become 'infinitely swole' or whatever they call it. Still, there's a reason Beasts back in the day used to wander off into the woods and live alone. Good chance they are the inspiration for Bigfoot legends. Then again, it wouldn't surprise me if those exist too. I mean, once leprechauns turned out to be real, I suppose any mythical creature is probably out there... with the possible exception of an altruistic politician. Some faerie tales are just too out there to potentially be real.

I swoop down and land on the stairs. "Hi, Aziz."

"Hello, Sarah." He nods in greeting.

"Here." I scurry over to him and hand him the case. "Can you please make sure Mr. W gets that?"

Aziz raises his eyebrows. "Do you not wish to go in and see him?"

"I do, but not right this second. In the middle of something." I can't help but chuckle at how tiny the briefcase looks in his hand. "There is some idiocy brewing and I'm investigating. That Natasha person is trying to stir up some morons to help her in her plan to reshape vampire society."

He blinks, then makes a face of 'you have to be kidding me.'

"Yeah, that's about how I felt." I sigh. "They're having some sort of meeting right now. I need to get back there and spy on it. Hopefully Mr. W understands. I'll be back as soon as I can."

"Understood." Aziz nods once. "Stay safe, kiddo."

"Will try..." I back down the stairs so there's no longer a roof over me. "Can't be worse than what happened in Gomez."

His eyes open wider. "What happened in Gomez?"

"I got into an argument with a bomb."

He cringes. "That's never fun."

"Nope. Can't say it hurt, though." I chuckle. "Didn't feel a thing." Aziz shakes his head.

I wave to him and zoom back into the air.

~

NOT QUITE TEN MINUTES AFTER LEAVING ASHLEY TO WATCH THE HOUSE OF
Derp, I return.

She's standing on the porch, bent slightly forward with her face
against the window.

Oh, that's real subtle.

Yeah, I know she's using her charm powers to make sure no one
sees her, but that doesn't mean the situation isn't hilarious to look
at. She's basically the cute red-haired version of a bear perched
behind a two-inch thick tree trying to hide. I don't know if her abilities will include me if she isn't aware of my presence, so I do my
best to really sneak up to the house. Halfway across the small front
lawn, I get the brilliant idea to take some pictures. Out comes my
phone. I snap images of the house, the for-sale sign, and the yard.
Not sure if this will be helpful. Better to have it and not need it,
though, right?

Ash is looking at me. She either heard my sneakers squishing in
the grass or the noise the phone makes simulating a camera. Oops. I
hope the vamps inside didn't hear me taking pictures. Well, at least
the case is out of harm's way now. I'm not going to lose Mr. W's gold.

After stuffing my phone back in my pocket, I hurry over to the
porch. "What'd I miss?"

"Not much. Mostly small talk and introductions." Ashley starts
ticking off names with each finger. "Natasha, Seth, Lorri, Robbie,
Topher, and this Headbanger guy. Oh, they've also turned the realtor
selling this place into a thrall. I'm not sure if that's related to their
plot or just a way to keep the house empty longer."

I shrug. "Could be both. Did they say anything important while I
was FedEx-ing that thing back to the manor?"

"Not really. Just that Headbanger used to be in a biker gang back
in the Nineties and Seth thinks he might be helpful. Apparently, that
Topher guy is important, too."

"Okay. Ready to engage cloaking?" I ask.

She scrunches her face up a bit. "Are you making a *Star Wars* or *Star Trek* joke?"

"Trek. They don't have cloaking in *Star Wars*."

"Damn. I don't know Klingon." Ashley winces.

"You could just do the spacey redhead nature witch thing if you want." I grin.

Struggling not to laugh, Ashley waves her hands around in a manner somewhere between fantasy cosplayer and fortune teller. "Okay. Cloaking engaged."

I take her hand, since hey maybe it helps her hide me. Also, call me immature, but I feel safer.

The front door opens as if unlocked when I try to enter. Neat. This definitely explains why some vampires have a rather loose understanding of personal space and property. It's so damn stupid but I can practically feel the 'rents standing behind me watching, ready to shower me with disapproval if I steal things.

Okay, maybe there is a downside to being turned into a vampire at eighteen. I'm permanently stuck in a mental place not having crawled out from under my parents' wing. There will always be that specter of getting in trouble hanging over me, which is going to get super weird in sixty years when Mom and Dad aren't around anymore. Meh. Who am I kidding? They're totally going to haunt me. I'd honestly prefer that to them going away permanently.

Dammit. Now's not the time to get maudlin. I have a job to do. No, Mom, I am not breaking into this house to steal anything.

We slip into the living room, which is thankfully empty. From the sounds of voices in the air, everyone's gathered in the kitchen. I sneak up to the hallway and lean against the wall by the arch, peeking around the corner. From here, I can only see shadows moving on the floor and wall. Dammit. Gotta get closer. C'mon Ash, turn up that cloaking field to eleven.

I glance at her.

She gives me an 'I got this' nod.

We move down the tiny hallway to the opening to the kitchen. As soon as I am able to see into the room, I freeze in place and do my best not to move. This feels absolutely ridiculous. We're standing like six feet away from a group of vampires... in plain view. And none of them are aware of our presence.

To cover my ass, I pull out my phone, flick it onto silent mode, and start video recording.

Of course, Natasha is sitting at the kitchen table. She's the one with the super fake maraschino-cherry red hair. The woman looks like a real-life version of a Power Puff Girls' version of La Femme Nikita. The tank top, military BDU pants, and combat boots only add to the vibe. For some silly reason, there's a bottle of Absolut on the table. No one is drinking it, though.

The other woman in here must be Lorri. Except for obviously being an adult, she's in the same club as me: brown hair, brown eyes, painfully average in every way. Okay, maybe I'm a little bit shorter and thinner than average, but whatever. We're both in the 'no one really notices us at school' club. Or whatever equates to that when you're almost thirty. She looks close to thirty, and kinda bored. Guessing if vampirism hadn't happened to her, she'd be receiving her crazy cat lady starter kit in the mail any day now.

Except for Ash and me, the youngest vampire in the room is Robbie, who still looks older than us. By appearance, I'm guessing he was probably our age when he got his Transference... but unlike us, the process didn't make him look even younger. He's like one of those guys who could buy alcohol at sixteen, as in he could pass for being twenty-four if you didn't really pay attention to him.

Now there's the other guy. Looking at him is giving me a weird disconnect. As in, he's got the face of a younger man—twenty, if that —but feels older. We're not talking Eldon old here, just... older than me. Old enough to sense, which means he's gotta have been a vampire for at least fifty years. The guys' got these big ol' round glasses on and is sitting at the table with a pile of dusty books. He's kinda got a bookish quality. Longish face with a sharp chin. He is a nerd. An athletic nerd, but still a nerd.

As opposed to me, being a geek.

Nerds are the smart people who make microchips and do rocket science.

Geeks like video games and anime and Dungeons & Dragons.

Nerds can be geeks and geeks are sometimes nerds.

I am not a nerd... at least not fully. I cruised through high school getting mostly As while barely doing the work. I'm like Sierra that way, kinda lazy. Had I been super motivated, I'd probably have been taking AP courses and doing something crazy like theoretical physics. My biggest problem with that was not being able to figure out what I wanted to do for a career. It's hard to apply oneself with laser focus when you don't even know what direction the beam should be pointing.

Sucks that society expects kids to make decisions about what our entire life is going to be when we're still kids. I mean, they don't trust us to rent cars yet; how can we be trusted with making decisions that so deeply affect our entire life?

Oh well. At least I'm out of that rat race now.

Ashley's making a face at Topher as if she recognizes him.

I nudge her and silent whisper, "You know that guy?"

She shakes her head and replies, "He totally looks like someone cosplaying Milo."

"Milo?" I tilt my head.

"From Disney's *Atlantis*." She pulls her phone out and taps at the screen. A moment later, she holds up a picture of the cartoon guy.

"Hmm. Sorta."

I can somewhat see where she's getting that from. He's not wearing an outfit you'd go doing Indiana Jones stuff in, just a plain white shirt and khaki pants. But yeah, the hair and general face shape do fit Milo.

For the moment, the man I assume to be the Topher she mentioned is completely absorbed in one of the big old books, not adding to or even seeming to care about the conversation going on around him.

Everyone in this room is a vampire. That much, I can tell. Alas, either due to my short tenure as an undead or perhaps my bloodline, I can't determine which kind of vampires they are. Some of the Old Guard can just 'read' what bloodline someone is. Me? Not so much. Outside of cases like Aziz, where it is super obvious, I'm clueless. Maybe that's the tradeoff for me having vampire stealth: meaning, other vampires looking at me often mistake me for a mortal. Innocents are *very* good at faking normality.

My trip to return the case to Wolent before I lost it seems to have taken less time than their small talk. Natasha is still droning on and on about how tired she is of having to hide herself from mortals. Listening to her talk, I want to reach out and slap whoever wrote this script. She sounds so cartoony. Okay, sure, *some* vampires really do talk like that. It always bothered me to hear them call people 'humans' as if we all didn't start out that way ourselves. Vampires are not some alien species from another planet. We are former humans given a bunch of sweet powers, and a few real pain in the ass drawbacks.

Again, I got lucky. The biggest drawback (that whole sun deal) is a whole lot less epic for me. Still, having to drink blood isn't the greatest. It's awkward and intimate. I don't think it will ever be not awkward. That's mostly from my personality, though. There are people out there who wouldn't care at all that they have to suck on some total stranger's neck a few times a month. And yes, I have heard the chatter at the soirees. Necks are not the only place that gets bitten.

Thankfully, before my brain can dwell too much on that subject, Natasha finally stops bitching about how insulted she feels having to pretend to be mortal. Damn, she'd really get along with the Oblivare. They have similar opinions on mortals. As in: mortals are farm animals to be harvested for food. Though, I think the Oblivare take it a little farther. Natasha only wants to be in power over humans. The Oblivare derive great pleasure in terrifying the peasants. They long for the old days where we were literal monsters swooping out of the air, tearing people to ribbons, and getting all covered in blood under the moonlight.

Yeah, they are nuts.

Natasha isn't that far off the deep end. She just wants power, and to be out in the open.

"All right, so what's this great plan supposed to be?" asks Headbanger, still sounding skeptical.

"Topher here"—Natasha pats the Milo-looking guy on the shoulder to no reaction from him—"has discovered the existence of an ancient elder."

"Bravo." Headbanger claps sarcastically. "Ancient elders exist. I did not know that already."

Natasha's glare is hilarious. "I didn't get to the good part yet. Yeah, no shit elders exist. But this one is seriously ancient. And... he thinks the same way we do. Once he awakens, he will send shockwaves across society and return us to our rightful place at the top."

The others, except for Headbanger and Topher, bow their heads almost reverently at the mention of this old vampire.

I fight the urge to facepalm. Natasha's people have made the transition from fringe weirdos to a proper cult. It's almost like they worship this guy.

"That sounds way too simple and easy." Headbanger folds his arms, making his leather jacket creak. "What's the catch? You're not going to tell me I have to buy a bunch of Tupperware or some shit to join this club, are you?"

Seth chuckles. Robbie and Lorri stare cluelessly at him.

"What the hell is Tupperware?" asks Lorri.

"No." Natasha leans back in her seat and heaves a sigh. "This isn't a MLM. I'm not going to ask you for money. Frick's sake, man. This is the chance of a lifetime."

"There's got to be some catch or you'd already have woke this guy up," says Headbanger.

"We gotta find him first." Robbie points at Topher. "Brainiac here is working on that part."

Lorri yawns. "And then there's some magical sort of whatever we need to do in order to wake him up."

"We've figured out that the sarcophagus was brought to the States in the early 1800s," says Natasha. "It was briefly owned by a museum, but got moved to an actual tomb at some point by unknown parties."

"Right now, we're trying to figure out where that tomb is," adds Seth. "Which is why we need more people. There's a bit of legwork involved. Going out to places and checking."

Headbanger makes a face of contemplation. "You're saying this thing could be anywhere?"

"Not entirely *anywhere*," says Topher. "I believe he is in the Northwest. However, that could be as far as Northern California or even into western Montana. Perhaps even Vancouver. You will need to forgive my vagueness here. This is verging well away from proper science into... less predictable things."

"He means magic," whispers Lorri.

A subtle sneer on Topher's face makes me suspect he's probably an Academic. It takes a certain degree of willful ignorance to blithely disregard the existence of magic when one happens to be a freaking vampire. There is no science explanation for our condition. Or how I can fly. Or how Ashley is just making them all ignore the fact that we're standing close enough to throw bits of popcorn at them.

I'm not doing that, mostly because I don't happen to have popcorn with me.

"Once we locate him, all we need to do is figure out how to break the forces keeping him trapped." Natasha holds her arms out to either side like some sort of high priestess. "He will be grateful for our releasing him, then proceed to take over the world and put vampires back in our rightful place at the top of the power structure. With us as his most favored minions."

Ashley starts bonking her head into my shoulder.

Yeah, seriously. And to think I almost got concerned here. These people are batshit.

I stop the recording. My phone can only hold so much cheese before it overloads.

We back out of the hallway to the living room, then slip outside.

Ashley closes the door super gently, as if she's handling the warhead of a nuke.

"What are you doing?" I whisper.

"I'm closing the door gingerly so no one hears us."

I raise an eyebrow at her. "Everything you do, you do *gingerly*. You can't help it."

She gives me a quizzical look. Four seconds later, she facepalms. "Ugh."

Before laughter gets the better of me, I run away from the house and down the street a bit, then burst out.

Ashley catches up to me, shaking her head. "That was bad. We should tell Dad that one."

"Are you sure? If Sierra hears it, she might stab us."

"Heh."

I glance back toward the house. "Well, so much for that. I don't think we're characters in a silly anime. We're stuck in a B movie with idiots trying to destroy the world."

She giggles. "Right? At least they seem pretty clueless."

"Yeah. That's true." I shift my jaw side to side in thought. "Except that Milo looking guy. He looks like he's taking it seriously."

"Oh, yeah." Ashley stops laughing. "You think he's up to something? Maybe manipulating those idiots?"

I shrug. "Could be. But... if he is, I really doubt he's trying to destroy the world."

Yeah, because that sounds ridiculous.

CHAPTER 12
HOMEWORK

THURSDAY, LATER

We head right back to Wolent's manor, by way of a small stopover in downtown Seattle for a bite. Hunger is a bit more intense than usual. Not worried about it. I'm confident it's a side effect of the whole bomb thing and not any sort of warning sign that I'm changing. We spot a guy trying to break into the back of a store, though leave him be. Good chance of him being a tweaker or someone addicted to something. While drugs don't directly work on vampires, drinking the blood of someone who is high can transfer the side effects.

The *last* thing I need is to get addicted to tainted blood. My parents would be so disappointed.

After making a snack of some random pedestrians close enough to an alley to lure out of sight, we proceed to visit the boss.

Aziz smiles at me as we land on the steps. "Hello again, Sarah. Miss Ashley."

She can't help herself but chuckle at that. "Hi, Aziz."

We go inside.

"Miss Ashley." Ash grins to herself. "Not sure if that makes me feel like I should go put on one of Aurélie's dresses and fake a southern accent or if I'm an English orphan protagonist in a mystery novel."

"Heh."

A long hallway leads us into the back, through an outer sitting room to another hallway and finally Mr. Wolent's office door. This house is so big, five or six of mine could fit inside it with room left over. Not jealous, just saying. In fact, I'm the opposite of jealous. The bigger the house, the more work it is to clean. He can have it.

The big man himself is seated behind his enormous carved wooden desk. It looks like it would take two of Aziz to move it.

Paolo and Stefano haunt nearby wingback chairs like a pair of gargoyles installed to scare off lesser vampires.

Wolent emits a soft chuckle, which he conceals under a cough.

Uh oh. My face warms as I really hope the other two weren't looking at my thoughts. Neither one makes faces at me so, probably not.

"I appreciate you securing the case. I trust you didn't run into any complications at the wharf?" asks Wolent.

"Not like that, no." I pull out my phone, open it, go to the photos page, and pull up the recordings of the idiot brigade. "Stumbled across something else, though."

He leans forward as I offer the phone.

Paolo gives me a look that makes me think he wants to say 'oh, you've found a phone. How quaint.' He's not so dumb as to think I'm being impressed by an iPhone. While his overt hostility has kinda toned down a bit since I've been doing decently well at this 'job,' he's never going to fully accept me until I stop living with my mortal family.

Guess he's never going to fully accept me.

At least not until time does the inevitable.

Wolent stares at the phone almost the same way Uncle Hank

looks at a television remote. Maybe I'm making assumptions based on his body language, however, it looks like he's not really sure what to do with it and is wondering why I'm showing him a picture of an orange cargo container surface.

I hurry around the desk to stand next to him and poke the screen so the video plays.

He gives me this little grandfatherly smile, even though he doesn't appear old enough to be a grandpa.

As the first recording I took of Seth talking to Headbanger at the wharf plays, Paolo and Stefano get up and walk over to watch as well. Once that video ends, I flick to the photos I took outside the grey house.

"We followed them here."

I flick to the video from inside, then poke the screen.

They watch Natasha's meeting. If the look on Stefano's face is any indication of anything, I am no longer at the top of his hate list. Well, maybe not hate. 'Contempt' would be a better word. It's too much to say that Paolo and Stefano 'like me' now. However, I think they've at least shifted to a position of resigned tolerance. They just needed to get to know Follows Rules Girl. She can adapt to the rule set changing. I'm not here to rock their boat. Since I insisted on staying at home with my mortal family, I'm sure these two expected me to just break *all* the rules and be a real pain in the ass.

"Idiots," says Stefano.

"Fools." Paolo shakes his head. "You didn't need to take our time up with this."

As opposed to your sitting around here staring at the walls? Sorry to invade that critical task.

Wolent almost smiles. "There are few things as dangerous as a committed fool. It seems unlikely this woman and her companions will manage to do anything of consequence. That being said, I'd like you to keep an eye on the situation and advise me if it escalates."

His tone is not *quite* dismissive, but I still feel like a little kid trying to play detective and being humored. "Sure thing."

Wolent hands me back the phone.

As I stuff it again in my pocket, I can't help but get this weird sensation in my gut, almost as if the Universe is telling me not to blow this off. Dammit. I'm only a few months away from being done with school and free from homework. So much for that. Seems my 'job' is going to come with plenty of homework.

At least the workload is lighter.

Hopefully.

CHAPTER 13
ADVANCED PLACEMENT

FRIDAY

I don't have class on Friday.

Last one for me each week is Chemistry on Thursdays with Dr. Markov. She's really energetic and loves practical demonstrations. Gotta say she's one of the best teachers I've ever had. Never a boring moment in her class. Had I still been mortal, she might've been responsible for me figuring out that I could get into science and chemistry. It's interesting for sure. Not much real point in me working on a career now, though.

Oh, by the way, Dad fixed Chloe's tablet. Apparently, what we thought was a brand-new tablet was really a return. It had previously belonged to a guy in his fifties who returned it after only a week. No idea why it had been returned. Apparently, the tablet still thought its user was an older guy, hence the targeted ads about cougars. We got lucky. The dude didn't leave anything on the tablet a seven-year-old shouldn't see. Dad wiped it out and reset everything, so hopefully, the tablet now understands its user is a child.

No more cougar alerts.

Anyway, despite me not having classes, I am still on my way to SCC. Why? Because Sierra.

So, weird things happened. Not 'floating kitten' weird. More ordinary weird. Perhaps unconventional is a better word than weird in this context. Sierra is really taking the art thing seriously. When she figured out that she had some talent as well as the fact that doing artwork could allow her to be part of the video game industry without having to do all that icky math stuff, it was as if a bomb went off in her head.

Best part is, the more she immerses herself in art, the less she worries about school shootings.

Her therapist is on board with her redirecting her energy in this creative direction. I happened to notice an art class going on Friday nights at SCC thanks to a posting on the wall in my art history class... so I made some arrangements for her to go.

By that, I mean a few surgical taps with the mental hammer on the instructor.

It's the same professor, Pedro Guillermo, who teaches the art history class. This is an introduction to illustration module. Mom kinda freaked out at the idea of me bringing Sierra to a college level art class. She was worried about live nude models. I'm ninety-nine percent certain that's not going to happen in this class. It's too 'beginner' level for that. Pretty sure that 'life drawing' is an entirely separate course. The only 'apples and berries' on display in this one are literal fruit. If I'm wrong and we show up one night to find some woman or dude in a towel and nothing else, I can easily whisk her out of the room before she sees anything inappropriate.

If she wants to work on human anatomy drawings before she's a little older, she can use photographs of statues. There are plenty of those out there.

My mental tinkering with the professor amounted mostly to getting him to disregard Sierra being twelve. She's also off the books, which means she's not earning any official credits here. On the upside, that also means we're not paying for this either. Win-win.

She's basically auditing the class. Professor Guillermo will give her grades and feedback but not enter anything into the school's system for her... and not really realize he's doing that. Her name is not officially anywhere.

The experience is what matters.

It's a 7:00 p.m. to 10:00 p.m. class, which I basically hang out in and watch while playing mental goalie on any of the other students in case someone has a problem with a kid being here. So far, there haven't been any issues. Sierra is a big fan of baggy sweatshirts, so it's possible everyone else here is just mistaking her for a short woman. Waited tables my junior year summer. This other girl who worked there was like twenty-four but looked more like twelve, a tiny little thing with purple-dyed hair. Always bitched about how she got carded trying to buy alcohol and no one ever believed her ID was real.

Never had that problem myself while alive, mostly because I never tried to buy alcohol, only being eighteen. Yeah, I know. I look even younger now. Sigh. At least I'm not as short as... oh what was her name. Tori? Something like that.

I sit there watching Sierra sketch with charcoals, trying to capture the form and essence of a pile of fruit in a bowl. They are learning the rudiments of volumetric shading and how to convey the direction light is coming from.

So weird to see Sierra laser focused on something that isn't a video game. She practically turns into a different person here. Less withdrawn, less creeping around trying to make as little noise as possible. While she's far from going full extrovert, she's gone up a few ticks to normal. It's obvious that she's no longer worrying about violence at school... at least not while she's lost in her art.

Whatever annoyance I might feel toward this class eating my Friday night is easily thrown aside. This is really helping her, not only in the sense of developing her skill, but helping her heal. That shooting might have only been a nightmare; however, it came from a demon. In the moment, it didn't matter it wasn't real. Worse, the demon altered her reactions, forcing her to feel scared and helpless. I'd like to think that if anything crazy ever happened for real, she would protect herself.

Here's hoping nothing ever happens.

At least we have Coralie to warn us ahead of time... and Sophia's enchantment on the school. She's too sweet and innocent to do anything like cause pain, injury, or death. Instead, she cursed the entire school, so if anyone brings a gun onto the property with intent to do bad things, they get struck with sudden explosive diarrhea. Suppose that's one way to handle it.

Anyway... bad thoughts go away.

Sierra seems happy now. That, I dunno... constant air of being mildly annoyed all the time is totally gone. Well, maybe I am a tiny bit jealous. I never figured out what I wanted to do with my life, even after I graduated high school. Sierra knows she wants to be a professional artist and she's still only in sixth grade.

I exhale and peer up at the ceiling. Hopefully, artists will still be a thing by the time she's an adult. If they ever figure out how to teach AI to get the proper number of fingers on a person, it's going to be a crap show out there. One day we've got AI stealing jobs. The next, Skynet's online and terminators are chasing us down.

You'd think people would learn to listen to warnings by now.

CHAPTER 14
MILDLY INCONVENIENT

SATURDAY

S am sat cross-legged in the tub, surrounded by suds.

The strawberry fragrance of Sophia's shampoo still hung in the air as she'd gotten dibs on the bathroom before him. Between her using the tub as a vessel for the ritual she enchanted Sierra with and the incident of flushing the essence of pure evil down the toilet, a palpable energy filled the room. It had enough of a presence to unnerve Soph's friends Priya and Megan, both of whom said they felt 'creepy' upstairs and even worse in the bathroom... as if something had been watching them.

That might not have been entirely incorrect as Coralie lurked around the house. She tended to remain in the basement or downstairs. Sam also doubted the ghost would bother keeping an eye on Sophia's friends.

He'd already finished the boring parts of the bath and now played with some of his action figures and a toy boat. His special operations team were investigating a bizarre white foamy mass that suddenly appeared without explanation upon the ocean.

Perhaps Sam added a bit too much bubble bath. He hadn't expected it to froth as much as it did, which seemed almost supernatural. Maybe the magical bathtub affected the suds.

Blix sat at the opposite end of the tub wearing a blue swimming cap despite neither having hair nor anyone in the house owning such a cap. He tried his best to stack gloopy handfuls of suds into something of a castle shape, though it kept drooping over as fast as he worked.

Sam guided the boat through the suds as his soldiers 'fought' the invading creature. Any minute now, Mom or Dad would knock on the door and tell him to get out of the tub, dry off, and go to bed. Alas, bedtime still existed on Saturdays even if the 'rents were a little more relaxed about it compared to school nights. He wondered if Sophia could do some magic to permanently eliminate bedtime... and homework, too. Whether or not she could, it would be futile to ask. She'd be too scared of getting in trouble. Not to mention, the often unpredictable nature of her magic made it risky to do anything so big. If Sophia cast a spell to eliminate 'bedtime,' it might backfire and simply destroy all beds. So, Sam figured he'd be stuck having to obey bedtime for a few more years.

While eight years didn't seem like that much in the grand scheme of things, he'd only been alive for ten... so to Sam, it may as well have been an eternity away.

If it takes me longer to grow up than normal, am I going to be stuck with bedtime?

How would his parents react to him technically being eighteen if he still looked like a kid? He debated this in his head while making 'pshoo' gunfire noises as his action figures did their futile best to fight the suds. Blix said something recently that got him wondering about the future. Somehow, Sam had made a deal with demons without even realizing it. He did favors for them, so they did one for him: longevity. The details remained somewhat elusive, but Sam had a feeling he would live for a really long time... unless something killed him. Immortality and agelessness weren't the same thing, after all.

Big question was: would he grow up gradually over an elongated time or reach adulthood normally and then stop growing older? Both had their advantages, though at least if he grew up at a normal pace, he'd be free of bedtime sooner. If he took decades to stop looking like a ten-year-old, he'd probably have to suffer bedtime... but he could get away with stuff longer. Kids could get away with things that grown-ups couldn't. For example: if a demon needed him to sneak into some place, he wouldn't get in too much trouble getting caught as a kid. As an adult? He'd probably end up being arrested—or having to resort to tricks he didn't yet have to escape.

Which only meant any sneak-into-places-he-didn't-belong type jobs in the future, he'd have to take seriously and carefully. It probably wouldn't be a bad idea to look for a way to influence people. *Star Wars* movies had a great idea with the mind trick stuff. If only he could figure out some way to do that for real, like Sarah.

"Uh oh," said Blix.

Sam looked up from his boat at the imp, whose eyes had gone huge.

The walls of the bathtub glowed bright red, glittering and sparkling as if covered with fine powdered ruby dust.

Before he could say 'oh crap,' the bottom of the bathtub disintegrated out from under him.

"Gah!" shouted Sam as he fell straight downward, surrounded by sudsy water.

He landed with a wet slap, a noise as though someone dropped a fifty-pound raw steak on a metal surface. Half a second later, his brain processed the information that said metal surface happened to be about twenty degrees Fahrenheit, quite a bit opposite to a nice warm bath.

Sam shrieked and tried to get up, flailing and slipping around in the soapy mess. After the seventh or eighth time he wiped out, he stopped struggling and lay on his side, teeth chattering, gazing out at the glimmering nighttime skyline of Seattle Downtown. The wind continued to remind him he'd landed outside, wet and soapy, in December.

It had only been seconds, but already the cold numbed his fingers and toes.

Crap! I'm gonna freeze!

Before any part of him froze to the metal surface, Sam dragged himself sideways out of the soapy water—that had already begun to turn to ice in spots. Once on a dry patch of ground, he grabbed onto a section of metal railing and pulled himself upright. The cold stabbed him everywhere like a million needles in the hands of a million angry bog faeries. Behind him, a grey column roughly double his height occupied the center of the platform, which happened to be the same shade of grey. A few big upward-pointed searchlights stood around the outside of the relatively small platform. He didn't see any doors or obvious ways down. A square hatch appeared to cover a potential means to enter the building below him; however, it would almost certainly be locked.

Crap. This is not good.

"Okay, you?" asked Blix after landing nearby.

"Mostly. Just don't tell anyone I shrieked like a girl." Sam shivered.

Blix grinned. "Cold. Anyone shriek."

"Yeah, but not like that. I sounded like a wimp."

"No wimp. Cold. Even man sound like girl when ice go down back." Blix wagged his eyebrows.

Clinging to the railing, Sam surveyed his surroundings. He'd definitely landed on the central platform atop the Space Needle. "Well, this is getting really annoying."

Blix nodded.

"Stupid tub." He kicked at an imaginary rock since he had nothing nearby to actually kick. "Oh, crap. My boat!"

"At house." Blix pantomimed falling over backward and flinging his arms. "You threw to sink."

"Cool." Sam folded his arms. "Did Soph mess up?"

Blix shook his head. "Something mess with her. All the time. Make magic misbehave."

Sam started to nod, then went completely still, staring at his friend. "Wait. What? Are you saying something is actually messing with her? She's not really bad at magic?"

Blix tilted his hand in a so-so gesture. "She learning. But also, something mess."

"Grr." Sam tapped his foot, unable to control his shivering.

"Something different mess with tub." Blix shook his head. "Not Soph blame."

Sam turned in place, looking around at the Space Needle's roof. "Why the heck did it put me here?"

"Same as Sierra. Maybe has one place go to." Blix shrugged. "Portal. It want make embarrass. Spectacle big."

"Well, it failed. I'm not embarrassed. I'm annoyed." Sam shifted his gaze to the horizon. "Which way is home? I need to get inside before things I don't want to lose start to freeze."

Blix snapped his fingers.

Jeans, socks, sneakers, a shirt, big winter coat, mittens, and probably underwear appeared on Sam in an instant.

"Neat. Thanks." Sam wrapped his arms around himself. The cold had already gotten its claws into him pretty good, but the clothes definitely helped blunt the icy fangs. "How the heck am I going to get home?"

Blix rubbed his pointy chin.

Sam eyed the hatch. "Can you open that?"

"Can open." Blix nodded. "But you maybe get caught. Security guard. Cameras."

"I could c-cover my f-face," whispered Sam. "Just get to a bathroom in the restaurant and jump in a mirror. Let them chase me."

Blix stared into the distance. "Mirror risky this far. Possible. Risky."

"Worse than frostbite?" asked Sam. "Or getting grounded?"

"You no grounded." Blix shook his head, making his ears thwap. "Mom understand tub broken."

Sam approached the hatch and kicked it lightly. It sounded heavy and solid. Maybe too heavy for him to open. "Not much other choice."

"Fly," said Blix.

The idea of taking his coat and shirt off made him shiver all over again. "It's too cold. I can't wear a shirt with the wings out."

"I fix." Blix smiled.

Going through the mirror world definitely had its dangers. Sam didn't worry *too* much there since he had an imp guide, which made navigating such a strange world safer. Still, some risk existed. Flying home might be seriously cold but he couldn't possibly end up getting paralyzed by an evil slug that way... or make a wrong turn and end up in a different dimension. Besides, he found flying to be immensely fun. He could pretend to be Superman.

"Ugh. This is seriously a pain in the butt." Sam huffed. "Okay. Fine. I'll fly."

Blix snapped his clawed fingers again. Sam's coat and shirt disappeared, leaving him bare-chested. The sudden cold air on his skin slapped a gasp out of him.

"Wings?" Blix flapped his.

It took Sam a moment to summon the willpower to force his way past the shivering to conjure the wings Olmaz gifted him a while back. They snapped out into existence with a great leathery fwoof.

"A-are y-you sure a-b-b-bout t-this?" asked Sam through chattering teeth. "I'm going to freeze solid in midair and hit the ground like a dart."

Again, the imp snapped his fingers. A ridiculously huge, red Christmas scarf appeared on top of him, immediately knocking him to the ground out of his hover under a pile of fabric. Sam laughed. He stood there shivering, arms tucked against his chest, unable to really move very much. Blix crawled out from under the scarf, then flew up and proceeded to wrap it around Sam from neck to waist, covering everything except his wings and face, his arms still wrapped around his chest in a feeble search for warmth. That done, Blix conjured up a bunch of oversized safety pins and secured the scarf in a few spots so it wouldn't unfurl.

The coat was better, but this definitely beat nothing. He looked over the cartoonishly enormous scarf, shrugged, and walked over to the edge of the grey platform. "T-thanks. T-this m-might w-work. Which way is home?"

"Follow." Blix darted into the air.

Sam slipped past the metal railing and leapt forward over the curved outer roof of the Space Needle, stretching his wings. The awesomeness of being able to fly distracted him from the cold air... mostly. Blix waited for him to catch up, then zoomed off, leading the way home.

A short flight later, teeth chattering, Sam hurried a landing on the back deck at home. He approached the sliding glass door and stared at it. Both his arms remained trapped under the scarf wrapping. He squirmed and wriggled, but may as well have been wearing a straitjacket.

"Little help here," whispered Sam. "I can't get my arms out."

"Warm." Blix nodded, smiled, then snapped his fingers.

The scarf and safety pins disappeared.

Sam gasped again at the cold air hitting his bare chest and back. As fast as he could move, he yanked the door open and leapt into the kitchen, then slammed the door shut behind him. The warm air in the kitchen washed over his temporary wings, feeling amazing.

Dad pulled away from the fridge, spinning toward the sound of the opening door. "Sam? You're not supposed to be out of bed at this hour, much less out of the house."

"I know." He turned away from the sliding door. "Wasn't my idea."

"What the heck are you doing outside without a shirt on? Do you know how cold it is out there?" Dad shut the fridge door.

Teeth chattering, Sam winced. "Yes, I am well aware of how cold it is. It was significantly colder when all I had on was soapy water."

Dad blinked. "What?"

"I got bathtubbed." Sam grumbled and dispelled his wings.

"Your lips are blue." Dad put a hand on his shoulder and ushered him toward the hallway. "Go sit on the couch and wrap yourself in the blanket. I'll make cocoa."

"Cool." Sam smiled at him and meandered into the living room.

He kicked his conjured sneakers off, flopped on the couch, and burritoed himself inside the blanket Sophia usually wrapped herself in for movie nights whenever the film happened to be scary enough to make a five-year-old cry.

A few minutes later, Dad walked in and handed him a steaming mug. "Here you go, champ. Sip it slowly. It's hot."

Sam leaned forward and took the mug in both hands. "Thanks."

"That damn tub." Dad sat on the couch near him, shaking his head. "Maybe I should get it replaced."

"Probably not a good idea." Sam sipped cocoa. "It would be risky letting anyone near that thing with tools. No idea what could happen."

Dad winced. "Oh, good point. So, what do we do?" He paused, then chuckled. "I'm asking you for advice. Ugh. Things are getting weird."

"They've already gotten weird." Sam grinned. "They're going to get even weirder."

"I am afraid," deadpanned Dad.

"Be very afraid." Sam slurped cocoa, already feeling much better as a core of chocolatey warmth gathered in his gut.

Dad sat in silence for a few minutes before looking over at him again. "I realize you're ten, but you have demon friends. Any idea what we might be able to do about the bathtub?"

Sam pondered, holding the cocoa close to his face so he could enjoy the smell—and heat. "Use the basement shower, or hope you get a good magic save."

"Hah."

"I'm only half kidding." Sam shrugged. "It hasn't thrown Sophia outside yet. She's probably got the best magic save of all of us."

"Oh boy. We better do something about that tub before it gets her." Dad leaned back into the sofa. "I don't even want to imagine what kind of magical mushroom cloud she'd set off if this happens to her."

Sam nodded. "Maybe we should all just use the basement shower."

"There is no telling the girls they aren't allowed to take long, luxurious baths. I'm not going to be the one to break that news." Dad cringed as if tasked with feeding a dangerous velociraptor. "And that includes your mother."

For an instant, the idea of Mom ending up teleported to the Space Needle seemed kinda funny. Then Sam got angry. Whatever was going on in the bathtub might do something mean to Mom. He wasn't going to stand for that. He had demonic friends to call on for help. This sounded like a serious enough problem to play that card. Whether or not he had limited favors to call in, he didn't know. Maybe he only got like three wishes. Maybe they'd keep doing favors for him as long as he repaid them somehow. Good chance they'd want a favor in return, but he'd gladly do that to protect his mother and sisters. Dad never used the upstairs bathtub. He always showered in the basement mini bathroom.

"I'm gonna see if Olmaz can help," said Sam. "Once I'm done with this cocoa."

Dad gently grasped Sam by the chin and turned his head to look at him. "Well, your lips aren't blue anymore." He let go and smiled. "You realize it's past your bedtime."

"Yeah. I know." Sam drank the last of the cocoa. "What's worse between me staying up a little later than normal or Mom getting bathtubbed?"

"Well... it *is* Saturday. No school tomorrow." Dad winked. "I won't tell her if you don't. Just try to be in bed before midnight."

Sam smiled. "I will."

CHAPTER 15

DEALS, FAVORS, AND DEMONS

A LITTLE LATER, SAME SATURDAY

Sam marched upstairs and went to his room.

After changing into his PJs, he crawled into bed and waited for Mom to pop in for the usual goodnight. Blix hovered by the PlayStation, glancing back and forth between him and the TV as if unsure if he should start playing a game yet.

Sam lay in bed for about ten minutes, then figured Mom wasn't going to suddenly double back and catch him. He pulled the covers aside and got up. First order of business: push his door almost closed so Mom walking by wouldn't see immediately that he'd gotten out of bed. That done, he approached his closet, grasped the knob, and concentrated on his desire to go visit Olmaz.

When he opened the door, the closet contained a portal to wherever Olmaz lived rather than closet stuff. A cave-like tunnel of brown stone led forward and downward into the Abyss. Without hesitation, Sam stepped inside and pulled the door closed behind him. The stone beneath his feet warmed as he descended. By the time he reached the bottom where the passage flattened out, the heat from the rock reminded him of the driveway in August. As long as he didn't stand still in one place for more than a few seconds, it didn't hurt too much. Not exactly comfortable, but he *definitely* preferred this to the top of the Space Needle in December.

He hurried forward into the cave chamber, gazing around at stalactites and stalagmites with a rainbowy sheen like gasoline on water.

"Olmaz?" called Sam. "Can I talk to you?"

"Of course," replied an inhumanly deep voice.

Sam turned to face the approaching demon, which, of course, appeared behind him amid a billowing cloud of dense, black smoke.

Olmaz, in all his crimson-skinned bare-chested glory, towered over Sam. His muscular upper body would make a WWE wrestler feel small. His neat black hair and pointy beard gave him a look reminiscent of a djinn. Sometimes Olmaz had human-like legs. Today, he had black furry goat legs with giant hooves. His massive dragon-like wings would've blotted out the sun if there happened to be one down here.

Despite his fearsome appearance, Sam sorta felt like a kid visiting a mall Santa. If said mall Santa happened to genuinely possess supernatural power.

"What is it you require, Samuel?" asked Olmaz.

"Do you know what's going on with our bathtub?" Sam peered up at the big demon. "Why does it keep teleporting us to the Space Needle when we're in the middle of a bath?"

Olmaz stroked his fingers down his long, pointed beard. "It is similar to, how is it humans say? On the fritz?"

"Busted microwaves leave the center of Hot Pockets frozen. They don't strand us on top of skyscrapers." Sam chuckled.

"Then you have never encountered a truly broken microwave." Olmaz winked.

Sam puffed at his hair. "I'm serious. The tub is getting annoying. It's going to attack Mom or Sophia soon, and I don't want that to happen."

"Ahh." Olmaz patted him on the head. "Commendable of you. There is a mischievous demon tinkering with your enchanted bathtub."

"A demon?" Sam stood taller. That was right up his alley. Stopping a bad demon was something he could do for sure. One Nerf dart could solve all their problems. "I can stop it, right?"

"Most likely." Olmaz nodded. "You could either fight it or make a deal with it. Fighting would be quicker in the near term, though I suspect it might haunt you down the road. Dealing with it seems like it would take more work right now, but ultimately be less complicated."

Sam looked down, fidgeting his weight back and forth so his feet didn't burn. The uncomfortably warm ground didn't leave him too much time to stand there thinking. "Okay. I'm going to fix that stupid tub."

"I'm sure you will, Samuel." Olmaz smiled. "Was that all you wanted to talk about?"

"Y—" He paused. "Umm. Maybe not. Since I'm already here... is there anything you can do to help Sierra be better at art?"

"Better at art?" Olmaz lifted his right eyebrow, pausing in mid beard-stroke.

Sam nodded. "Yeah. I'm not saying she stinks at it. She's pretty good, but I mean... she's not a professional yet. Stuff she draws still looks like a kid made it. Doing art makes her happy and gets her to stop thinking about bad stuff. I don't want her to get discouraged and give up. So, can you maybe like give her some free skill points? Like Dalton helped Sarah learn swords?"

"Hmm. Usually, I get asked for wealth, fame, immortality, power..." Olmaz laughed. "This is a first."

"Does that mean you can help her?" Sam continued hopping from foot to foot.

Olmaz reached down among the multiple leather pouches and satchels hanging on his ornate belt. His clawed fingers picked at them in turn, one after the next before he settled on a bright orange, thoroughly modern fanny pack. The demon opened the zipper and removed a rolled-up scroll too large to have been inside it.

Sam couldn't help but laugh at the lone fanny pack among all the properly medieval-looking pouches.

Olmaz couldn't keep a straight face and smiled back at him before offering the scroll. "Here you go. Favor for a favor. When you use this scroll, it will open a portal to another sub-realm. Look there for a demon named Tedium."

Sam took the scroll. The paper seemed ancient but felt more supple than he expected, almost as if it wasn't paper at all, but some sort of extremely thin, soft leather. "Okay..."

"I owe Tedium a favor." Olmaz nodded to Sam. "Settle my debt to him and I will repay you with a muse elixir that shall do what you ask for your sister."

Sam eyed the scroll. This sounded like an awesome adventure, even if the demon he had to see was named Tedium. Dealing with him would probably be a chore, but the idea of having a scroll to open a portal had to be the coolest thing ever.

"Oh. You will need this..." Olmaz rested his enormous hand atop Sam's head. His eyes glowed brilliant crimson for the span of five breaths.

Tingly warmth spread over Sam's entire body. Ripples of orangey-red light swirled around him, down to his toes and back up again. Nothing other than a few dancing lights appeared to happen.

Olmaz removed his hand from Sam's head, seeming pleased with himself.

Sam looked himself over and felt the top of his head for potential horns, which he unfortunately did not have. He hadn't sprouted any new body parts. Alas, Olmaz hadn't given him a demonic tail. "What was that?"

Olmaz pointed down.

Sam looked, but didn't see anything weird. "Huh?"

"Your feet," said Olmaz.

Sam wiggled his toes. Everything looked completely ordinary. "They didn't change."

"Oh, Samuel." Olmaz chuckled. "Give a boy wings once and he expects big changes every time. Look at your feet."

Sam did, still not seeing anything weird.

"You are no longer dancing back and forth."

It took another moment for it to click. The floor didn't feel hot at all anymore, no different than had he been standing in his bedroom. "Oh, wow. That's neat."

"It is another spell I have given you knowledge of." Olmaz clasped his hands. "When you use it, your body will not be affected by fire or heat for a short time. You may also enchant others with the same effect. Do be aware that the protection will fade away if they leave your presence."

"That's awesome." Sam grinned. "How long does it last?"

Olmaz scratched at his beard. "Oh, about an hour or so. Tedium's realm is not intended for mortals to visit. It is much warmer there than here."

"Understood." Sam nodded. "Thanks! You're the best."

The demon's facial expression said 'I know,' though he didn't say anything so conceited out loud. Demons, after all, gained power and or energy from being worshipped. While not exactly a cultist devotee, the unrestrained adoration of a small boy no doubt gave him a nice jolt of power. Sam, of course, knew this but couldn't help but feel the way he felt.

Olmaz was awesome.

"Thanks!" Sam bounced on his toes. "Sorry to leave so fast, but I'm going to get in trouble if Mom catches me out of bed."

"I understand, Samuel. Be careful dealing with your bathtub demon."

Sam tucked the scroll under his arm and started walking toward the cave back to his closet. "I will. Thanks!"

Olmaz collapsed once more into a massive cloud of black smoke.

Thrilled to bits, Sam ran back up the tunnel and shoved the

closet door open. His room looked the same, the door still mostly closed. That proved Mom hadn't come back to find his bed empty.

Awesome.

Sam stashed the scroll in his toy chest atop the Transformers, GI-Joes, and other things... then dove into bed, even though he knew it would take him a long time for excitement to fade enough for sleep to happen.

He had an adventure coming, and couldn't wait to start it.

CHAPTER 16

A COLLECTION OF IRRITATING INESCAPABLE ANNOYANCES

SUNDAY EVENING

I'm looking forward to another night of being a slacker.

Nights where my most critical decision is the choice between sweat pants or just a long T-shirt are wonderful. Meh. Pants are overrated. Long shirt it is. We're not going anywhere tonight. Ashley's wearing one of her nightgowns that makes her look like a giant six-year-old. She likes cute stuff. There's another advantage to being a vampire: we can wear pajamas for the normal time period in which we're active and it won't seem weird. Not like I let that stop me before. In high school, I'd worn pajama pants more than once on lazy days.

Chloe is the oddball. She doesn't go for sleepwear tonight. Nope. She adores those little doll dresses Aurélie gave her. Kiddo absolutely looks like the creepy ghost child who ought to be haunting the 500-year-old English mansion out in the middle of nowhere. Only thing missing is the accent. She can't do a British accent at all.

Hmm. Maybe we could get her watching *Peppa Pig*. I heard somewhere that kids watching that show pick up British accents. It would either be adorable or annoying. Not sure which.

Anyway, we're getting our geek on tonight. Ash and I are doing more or less the same thing we usually did whenever we hung out before our leap into the world of vampirism: watching anime and playing video games. About the only thing that really changed is we aren't talking about drama-slash-news about other kids at school. Not that we spread rumors or anything. Just... being in high school gave us stuff to talk about. It would almost be tempting to go back to high school if not for the slight problem of my being unable to wake up before, like 2:30 in the afternoon.

I'm not really serious about that, by the way. I'm glad to be done with school. Though, it is fun to think about all the crazy stuff we could've done if we happened to have vampire powers back then. Yeah, yeah. I know. We wouldn't have done anything crazy because we are tragically lame and uncool.

Chloe is somehow simultaneously watching a cartoon on her tablet, playing with dolls, *and* playing a video game on the PSP all at the same time. Wonder if I should be concerned about over-technology-ing a child. Meh. It's not like she's going to suffer developmentally anymore. She's not developing. What you see is what you get, so to speak. I'm going to spoil her. This vampire existence is basically the reward/make-up she gets for having such an awful mortal life.

Speaking of that, I feel like ice cream.

Right as I start to get up to fetch the frozen awesomeness, a knock comes from my bedroom door. Since I'm sprawled on the floor by the TV, I roll over and sit up.

The Littles all walk in, Sam leading the way with Blix perched on his shoulder like some weird version of a parrot. He and the girls walk over and stand in front of me like they're about to try talking me into doing something we'll get in trouble for. Well, maybe not too much trouble. Sophia is still participating, so it can't be too bad. Speaking of Sophia, her face is painted white with light purple swirls on her cheeks and glittery, darker purple around her eyes. She's dressed similar to Ashley, in a super girly nightgown.

Sierra's got PJ pants on with a T-shirt and purple socks. Her one nod to girlishness is that her socks have frills. My brother hasn't changed over to pajama mode yet. He's still in his Halo T-shirt, jeans, and plain white socks.

"Uh oh," I say. "Who broke what?"

"I am making a deal with Olmaz to help Sierra," says Sam.

"Say what?" I blink. "Is that wise?"

"Coralie hasn't warned us about it." Sophia shrugs.

I glance at Sierra. "What's wrong?"

"A lot of things." She chuckles. "But it's not help like that. Olmaz is going to teach me art stuff."

"Oh." I wipe a hand down my face. "You're selling your soul to the powers of darkness for talent?"

Sophia emits an, "Eep!"

"No." Sam shakes his head. "There's no selling of souls involved. Just a little favor."

I glance down at myself, the long T-shirt, the comfort, the not planning on leaving the house tonight, and sigh. "What's this going to involve?"

Sam holds up a scroll that resembles a prop from a D&D stage play. "Olmaz owes another demon a favor, so I agreed to help settle that. We have to go talk to this other demon and do something for it."

"Sam..." I stare at him. "You have no idea what this other demon is going to ask of you and you already agreed?"

He fidgets. "Technically, I only agreed to go talk to him. I'm not going to do anything bad. I don't think Olmaz would've sent me to this guy if he expected it would be a problem."

Blix nods at me, waving in a 'don't worry about it' manner.

"This is going to require pants, isn't it?" I mutter.

"Probably not. It's a portal. And it's warm there." Sam walks out of my room to the big open main basement area.

Ugh. That reminds me. There are laundry piles waiting.

"Oh, I have to see where this goes." Ashley springs upright and scurries after him.

I stare at the ceiling, knowing that somehow, I am going to regret this. Still, it seems like the Littles are going to do this with or without me. Better I'm there to make sure things don't get out of hand. There must be some insecurity in Sam or he wouldn't have asked me to help.

The girls follow him. I get up and go after them.

Sam walks to the middle of the basement, stands in a sufficiently dramatic, wizardly pose, and opens the scroll. It's covered in red writing that makes me think a four-year-old tried to learn Japanese calligraphy. Of course, the symbols are not actually Japanese. They're not normal letters, either. Whatever it is, it looks sloppy and chaotic.

My brother stares at the scroll for a few minutes.

In the middle of the silent expectation, I glance over at Sophia. "What's with the face paint?"

"I'm trying to work out the look for the sugar plum faerie." She smiles. "What do you think?"

"It's cute. Sugar plum faerie?" I ask.

Sierra grins. "She's the only one there small enough and cute enough to be the faerie."

Sophia bites her lip, seemingly unsure if she was just praised or insulted. "Dance class is doing Nutcracker. It's a big production with two other dance studios... like at a real theater."

Whoa. She is so nervous *I'm* starting to feel uneasy, but she's evidently not chickening out. Support mode time. "Nice. You're going to be amazing."

She gives me this super anxious uneasy smile totally worthy of Charlie Brown.

"Are you gonna do it?" whispers Sierra.

"Yeah." Sophia grinds her toes into the carpet.

"Not you." Sierra points at Sam. "Him. He's just staring at the scroll."

Sam doesn't respond.

"I think he *is* doing it," whispers Sophia.

"But he's not saying—" Sierra freezes as a red ball of light appears in the air.

The glowing orb is about the size of a baseball, floating at Sam's eye level a few feet in front of him. It hangs there, pulsating and glowing for a moment before expanding into a floating oval of fire with blackness inside.

Sam rolls up the scroll and sets it on the floor. He appears to do something meditative for a few seconds, then steps through the portal. Sierra moves to follow, but recoils as Sam leaps back into the basement, looking a little surprised.

"Something go wrong?" I ask.

"Not quite." Sam looks at Sierra. "You should take your socks off."

"What?" Sierra blinks. "Why?"

Sam holds up his right foot. His sock is burned off up to the ankle. "The floor is a little warm in there."

"Gah!" I blurt. "How the hell are you not covered in blisters?"

"Olmaz taught me a new spell." Sam beams.

"They're not spells." Sierra rolls her eyes. "We're not actually D&D characters."

"What would you call it, then?" Sam folds his arms. "I can do magic at you and you can't be burned for like an hour until the magic wears off."

"Sounds like a spell to me," says Ashley.

Sierra makes a face like she just realized she's probably wrong, but doesn't want to admit it.

Sam takes that as victory and doesn't bother to push her to actually say it out loud. He stoops to remove his socks, then looks around at the rest of us. I'm already barefoot. So is Chloe, but she's not joining us.

Sierra, Sophia, and Ashley remove their socks. Ashley goes the extra step of hugging her super fuzzy socks and baby talking them to reassure them that she's not going to let them get burned. Did I mention Ash can get a tad 'extra' sometimes?

One by one, Sam makes faces of concentration at us all. Then nods as if proud of himself. "Okay. We can go in now."

He steps through the portal.

Sierra follows him without hesitation. Sophia creeps up to the opening, swallows hard, then peeks inside. A moment later, she steps the rest of the way through.

Ashley looks at me, making an 'are we really doing this' face.

"Not the first time we've been to hell. Can't let them go alone." I tap my foot, wondering if this is going to require pants... or at least something else under this long shirt. Meh. I bet it's full of fire in there and the odds of me suffering another catastrophic wardrobe malfunction are above average. Whatever. I wasn't planning to leave the house today at all. Hell can suffer me in my sleep shirt.

I step through into a shockingly normal looking corridor, like something out of any corporate office building. Grey carpet, grey walls, white drop ceiling tiles. About the only odd thing is how warm it is. Feels like the heat's set to 99.

The Littles are a few steps ahead of me, looking around with a mixture of confusion and awe on their faces.

"Whoa," I whisper. "Was kind of expecting the usual hellscape cave or whatever with lava pools."

Ashley emerges from the portal behind me. "This is weird."

"Generic bland office building," I say.

"That *is* hell to some people." Ashley chuckles.

"Fits." Sam starts walking. "I forgot to tell you. The demon I need to see is named Tedium."

Sierra groans.

"Oh boy." I whistle. "This is going to be the opposite of fun, isn't it?"

One of the many doors in the hallway in front of us opens. Six demons walk out. They kind of resemble imps, being that they are bald with big heads, huge ears, spindly limbs, and no hair. Unlike

Blix, these guys are almost human sized and happen to be wearing suits and carrying laptops. Pretty sure those are Macs. Dad would say 'that figures'. They file out of a small conference room like a bunch of employees having just had a pointless meeting with their supervisor.

They all give us a 'what are you doing here' sort of look, but say nothing as they walk right past us down the hall.

Sophia shrieks.

Since she's in front of me, I don't have to spin to look what happened. Still, I'm not entirely sure. She's standing there with her shoulders hunched upward in the unmistakable pose of 'I just stepped in something awful.'

"Soph?" asks Sierra.

"It's cold and sliiiiimy and it's oozing through my toes!" wails Sophia. "What is it!?"

I shift my gaze down to her feet. She's ankle-deep in a beige glop.

Blix leaps off Sam's shoulder and glides to land beside the puddle. He sniffs it, then swipes a single claw at the substance, which he then puts in his mouth, smacking his lips a few times like a connoisseur wine taster. After a nod, he babbles.

"Cat puke," says Sam.

I nearly throw up, realizing Blix tasted it. Sierra retches once but doesn't hurl.

"Ewww!" shrieks Sophia, half in tears. She hops back on her left foot, holding the puked-on one in the air.

Sierra cringes a little, but leans closer to look at the slimed foot. "How is that cat puke cold? Why isn't it boiling off? Didn't this floor cause your socks to burst into flame?"

"It did." Sam nods.

"Get it off!" wails Sophia.

And this is the biggest problem with her magic. She could easily clean herself, but she's too upset to even think to do it, much less have the ability to focus enough to use magic at all.

Thankfully, we have a Blix.

He snaps his tiny little fingers and the cat puke slides off Sophia's foot and plops back to the floor.

After a moment of looking at each other with 'okay, that was weird' faces, Sam resumes walking.

Not four seconds later, Sierra screams. It starts as a yelp of surprised pain, and ends with an F-bomb.

Sophia gasps.

"What happened?" blurts Ashley.

Sierra glares at her, then swings her leg up in a 'here, look at this' manner. Two big Lego bricks are embedded in her bare sole.

I almost laugh, but yeah... I've stepped on Legos barefoot before. It's not fun.

We all look at the scattering of Lego bricks on the floor that are somehow not melting.

"Grr." Sierra contemptuously kicks to the side, flinging the plastic caltrops off.

"Everyone, watch where you step." Sam continues forward down the hall.

More 'business demons' occasionally emerge from side corridors or doors. They all give us curious looks but none of them stop long enough to speak.

I manage to avoid stepping in a smear of something greasy, puddles of various liquids, and more Legos. The inconvenient hazards seem to appear out of thin air mere seconds before we'd step on them... and disappear as soon as we're past. So annoying.

Feels like this corridor is endless.

Sophia screams and falls to the floor, cradling her right foot in both hands and bawling. Her nightgown begins to smoke wherever it makes contact with the floor. Blix rapidly waves his little arms, seemingly fighting the heat back.

I stare blank-faced at a phantom bedpost just standing there in the middle of the hallway, not attached to a full bed—merely one corner. Her pinky toe has turned bright red. Can't help myself but cringe in sympathetic pain. I've done that more than once in the normal world.

Not much to do here but pick her up and carry her. I can't break the face of something responsible for causing my squishiest sibling to cry. However, I can prevent her from stepping on anything else. As soon as I've got her up off the floor, the melting/smoldering spots of her nightgown shrink away and disappear, leaving the garment looking undamaged once more. Blix wipes nonexistent sweat from his brow.

"Son of a..." Sam sighs. "Blix, please..."

I cringe at the sight of the imp dispelling dog poo from my brother's left foot. I really do not want to know what it felt like to step on that.

"Eww." Sierra shivers. "Maybe this isn't worth it after all. We don't have to do it."

"It's fine. The dog poo was kinda warm." Sam examines his now-clean foot and continues walking.

"Eww," chorus Sierra, Sophia, and Ashley at the same time.

"I did not need to know that." I wince.

After what feels like an hour of walking, the corridor finally ends at a big room full of office cubicles. Hundreds of demons, varying in size from scrawny little imps to fat little critters so round it doesn't look like they can get out of their chairs to ones bigger than humans crammed into comparatively tiny seats.

Sam goes left into a passage between two rows of cubes.

Bizarrely, the demons working here have computers—naturally they are Macs. Dad would totally get a kick out of that.

"What the heck are they doing?" asks Sierra, face scrunched in a 'you gotta be kidding me' expression.

Sam peers at the demons around us. Blix babbles to him. "These ones here are managers of field teams."

"Field teams?" I ask.

"Yeah." Sam spins around, walking backward for a few steps so he can nod at me. "The ones here are out in the world tipping people's forks and spoons into their plates so they sink into sauces or soup."

"Ugh," says Ashley. "I hate that."

We reach the end of the cube row and take a ninety-degree right into more cubes.

"These guys," says Sam, translating Blix, "are managing demons that run around twisting USB plugs when you don't look at them so they're oriented wrong. That's why it takes so many tries to plug them in sometimes."

"Evil bastards," I mutter.

Two of the 'manager' demons smile at me as if to thank me for the compliment.

Sam points. "That guy's team goes to gas stations and pokes the pumps so people end up with a stray cent or two above or below."

"What's the point of that?" Sierra sighs. "That's dumb."

"It really bugs some people not to get exactly ten dollars or twenty dollars." Sam shrugs. "It must bother them when the pump stops at like $10.02 or they wouldn't be doing it."

My right foot suddenly freezes. I look down. Gooey awfulness squishes between my toes and suctions my foot to the carpet. Ugh. My turn for cat puke. The chilly, gelatinous mass is nasty enough. The faint aroma of partially digested fish only makes it worse.

"Blix," I say. "Please de-puke my foot."

He snaps his fingers. The foul substance slurps off and flops to the ground with a plop.

We keep walking among the cubes.

I spot one cube wall with a bunch of video game posters hung up and a fat little goblin like demon sitting at the workstation. His screen's split into a dozen different windows like a security camera view.

"What's this one doing?" I ask, almost afraid to know.

Sam looks at Blix, who babbles. "Umm, you know how Dad hates the *Ghosts & Goblins* effect?"

Boy do I. When my dad was a little kid, he had a Nintendo 8-bit system, the NES. One of the games for it, *Ghosts & Goblins*, was a side-scrolling platformer. It was also super bitchy. Very easy to die and some of the levels were incredibly frustrating. Dad coined the term '*Ghosts & Goblins* effect' based on his experiences with that game: specifically, levels he got stuck on.

He'd try over and over and constantly die at, say, seventy-five percent of the way through a level. Then, he'd have a great run and make it almost to the end... but die to something cheesy before he could finish the board. After that, he'd keep dying at less than twenty-percent for at least ten tries, when before he almost finished it, he'd easily make it to the halfway point or farther. It felt like the game was punishing him for almost beating the level by making him die repeatedly at a much earlier point that he used to easily cruise right by.

I imagine this game really upset him if he still talks about it this many years later.

"Yeah, Dad really hates that," I say.

"Well, this guy's managing a team of demons that do it." Sam exhales. "They poke the systems so you die over and over after making progress you never made before."

"I'm tempted to punch him... for Dad," I mutter.

"Wouldn't suggest that." Sam shakes his head. "If you ever want to play a video game ever again and not end up smashing the system to pieces."

Sigh. Not fair. Why do they get to do stuff to us but revenge only makes it worse?

Shaking my head, I force myself to leave the bastard in peace.

We make our way through the cube farm. I hope Sam knows where he's going. I'm already lost.

Demons around us manage teams that steal stray socks, send luggage to the wrong airport, make sure toilet seats are extremely cold, and the evilest one yet: causes people's coffee to get cold faster than it should.

Gah. This place is awful.

"Whoa, look at that." Sierra points into a cube.

The walls of the cubicle space are covered in smartphones. There sits a demon with the body of a huge imp and the face of a beautiful Asian girl. I can only imagine what their team is doing.

"I smell catfish," says Ashley.

Sophia sniffs. "I don't smell anything."

"Where's the puke?" Sierra turns in place, studying the floor.

I don't bother to correct anyone.

The demon in the next cube is typing furiously like that animated gif of Kermit the frog.

"Dare I ask what that one does?" I point.

Blix babbles.

"His team posts short videos to social media that start telling interesting stories, but stop before the ending," says Sam. "Like, I caught my husband doing this or that, or caught my kids doing this or that... and then it just stops without finishing the story."

"Ugh. I hate that!" Sierra scowls.

"C'mon let's get away from that darkness." Ashley pushes me forward.

I chuckle.

We head around another corner into a long row. All the demons here are wearing business casual. White button-down shirts, dark pants. They might be demons but even they seem miserable. At least a hundred workstations all look more or less the same, as if they're all devoted to the same function.

Blix mutters.

"Telemarketers," says Sam.

"Quick, run!" I blurt. "Lest their unsavoriness taint our souls."

"No!" Sierra flails her arms. "Don't run! We're all barefoot. If we run, we will step in bad crap... or smash our toes into randomly appearing bedposts."

"Okay. Okay. Walk very quickly then." I scurry forward, still carrying Sophia who does not at all mind.

It's a good thing I have supernatural strength. Soph's eleven now and not *that* much shorter than me. At least she's scrawny and light.

We rush to the end of the telemarketer row, go past a few manager demons whose field teams appear to be responsible for making drivers swerve into puddles and soaking pedestrians, then pass two teams who lurk in restaurants and wait for someone to ask for Coke or Pepsi, and then change reality so the restaurant only serves the one they don't want. Finally, we end up hitting a dead end by a pile of small papers.

"What the hell is that?" Sierra stares.

Blix says something.

"The demons here make gift cards expire a day before they get used," says Sam. "Every time someone throws their gift card in anger, it ends up here." He indicates the pile blocking our way.

We backtrack a bit and take the next possible alternate turn, going by more and more cubicles. It occurs to me that someone farted.

Sierra coughs at the smell, too.

Sophia's blushing and trying not to breathe. No, she's not embarrassed for having farted. She's embarrassed that a fart occurred at all. Pretty sure I would have heard it if she were responsible. In fact, I would've heard it if anyone here let fly. Sam would totally claim it if it had been his.

Even Blix is pinching his nose.

"I don't want to know," deadpans Sierra.

"We've found the Awkward or Inconveniently Timed Bodily Functions department," says Sam, again translating Blix. "These demons make stuff happen at inconvenient times."

"Ugh!" We all groan at roughly the same time.

Two cubes later, a manager demon steps out into the corridor from the cube they were in. This one seems to be a woman... sorta. Tall, rail thin, generally imp-like in appearance despite being five-foot-two. Honestly, she kinda resembles the evil gremlin from *Gremlins*... with boobs.

This demon hands Sierra a paper card and says something unintelligible.

"She wants your autograph," says Sam.

"Why?" Sierra flattens her eyebrows at him.

The manager demon smiles sweetly, and extends a dark crimson set of glasslike, translucent double dragonfly style wings.

Oh, shit. This must be the Red Faerie.

I hurriedly set Sophia down on her feet and wrap my arms around Sierra from behind, holding her back because I know as soon as she realizes what's going on here, she's going to try to murder this demon.

"I'm not telling her that," whispers Sam. "She'll kill me."

"What," demands Sierra.

"Think," says Sophia. "This is the Awkward or Inconveniently Timed Bodily Functions area, where demons make body stuff happen at embarrassing moments. She's got big red faerie wings... and wants your autograph like you did something famous."

Sierra shudders in rage. "I'm gonna rip her tits off!"

I hold her back.

Yes, it takes a lot of effort. She's really damn strong.

Her fury seems only to make the Red Faerie happier. I don't think this demoness wanted her autograph as much to grind her gears even more. She seems to be feeding on the rage and shame roiling inside my sister.

After a few seconds, Sierra goes still. "Let go."

"Nope. Listen." I lower my face, whispering in her ear. "She's doing it on purpose to get a rise out of you. The angrier you get, the happier she is. The more embarrassed you are, the more she feeds."

Sierra hangs there in my grip for a moment, clenching and releasing her fists. Finally, she huffs. "Okay. I'm fine. You can let go. I promise."

I give her a reassuring squeeze, then let go.

Sierra snatches the paper card from the Red Faerie and looks around. "I need a pen."

"Good luck," mutters Sam. "Every pen you find here will be out of ink."

Blix babbles and points down the row.

"He says there's an entire team dedicated to drying out those pens they leave out for public use in banks and post offices that way." Sam lightly jabs his toe repeatedly into the bland grey carpet.

The Red Faerie seems almost disappointed at the warning.

Blix conjures a pen.

"There." Sam hands it to her.

Sierra signs her name on the card and offers it defiantly to the big, skinny demon with red faerie wings.

The demoness appears a little disappointed, but takes the autographed card. She turns her attention to Sophia, offers a saccharin sweet 'see you soon' finger wave, then returns to her workstation.

Sophia reaches her arms toward me and says, "Uppies" in a baby voice.

Yes, she is totally kidding.

Still, I pick her back up.

A few cubes in front of us, a demon manager leans out to look us. He smiles and points at Sam in a 'just you wait' manner.

"What's he want?" whispers Ashley.

Blix babbles.

"Oh, come on." Sam stares at the imp. "You can tell me."

Blix shakes his head, then points at me.

"But she can't understand you."

Blix babbles.

"Fine." Sam looks up at me. "He says he's gonna tell you why that demon's looking at me and it's up to you if you tell me."

"Oh boy." I glance around at the awkwardly timed embarrassing bodily functions demons, dreading what this could possibly mean.

Blix conjures a small dry erase board and writes on it before showing it to me.

'That's the demon of random uncontrolled erections in public places.'

I burst out laughing. Blix ignites the dry erase board into a fireball, rapidly ashing it over.

"Uh oh." Sam looks up at me. "What is it? Is it going to attack me?"

I wince, but still can't stop chuckling since I remember some of the boys getting real awkward in like seventh and eighth grade sometimes. You know what's going on when they refuse to get out of their seats to write on the board. I didn't really understand it at the time, but looking back on it, it makes sense. Yeah. Apparently, there's an age where boys' little friend will randomly wake up for no reason. I'm not really equipped to have that talk with Sam.

"It's nothing to worry about. Nothing unusual. Happens to all boys," I say.

"That's not helping me decide if I should be worried or not." Sam folds his arms.

"You don't embarrass easily, so probably not a big deal." I fidget. Yeah, I'm the one that's embarrassed. No way am I talking about unprompted boners with my little brother, especially not while he's still only ten. "Look, I'll tell Dad and he can explain it."

Sam nods. "Okay."

"Can we get out of fart alley, please?" whispers Sophia.

"Good idea." Ashley marches forward.

We hurry along, passing a few demons who appear to me making kids in various schools really need to pee in the middle of class. A nameplate on one cube wall reads 'Epicus Flatulus, Lord of Elevator Farts' along with an 'employee of the month' placard with the heading '10,000 funerals achievement'.

Ugh.

Not worrying too much about stepping in slime anymore, we run out of the Awkward or Inconveniently Timed Bodily Functions Department as fast as possible into an area where demons cause lottery numbers to come up missing the win by one digit. Another hides car keys. The one next to him runs a team that changes online passwords. He shares cube space with a manager whose imps sneak up on people trying to log into computers and press the shift key so they get their password wrong even though they typed the correct thing.

One cube stands out as weird since all the stuff inside it is impossibly arranged. The monitor is like halfway embedded in the wall. The keyboard is all jumbled up. Some of the decorations on the walls stick out horizontally.

"Whoa," whispers Sierra. "Does that demon run Bethesda Studios?"

Sam and Sophia snicker.

I can't help myself but lean in and adjust one picture that's tilted a few degrees to the side back to straight. As soon as I move it, every other object in the cube slides crazily out of place. Some even flip upside down.

The demon working there grunts at me as if to say thanks.

"What the heck?" I ask.

"Word," says Sam.

"Huh?" Sierra blinks.

"This demon's team made Microsoft Word," says Sam.

"Oh. Ack. Quick. Back away before we get corrupted." I recoil from the cube and hurry off down the aisle.

In the next aisle, Blix explains the demons here cause power failures in the middle of major sporting events or at critical moments in video games. Others make traffic lights turn red faster than they should... and stay red longer. Toward the end of the row, we find the manager of a field team that whispers in the ears of network executives and makes them cancel shows everyone loves.

"Holy cow this place is awful," I mutter.

"We really are in hell," says Ashley.

"Not exactly," chirps a voice behind us that's not obviously male or female.

I spin.

A fat goblin-shaped demon in a top hat and suit stands there, beaming at us. He looks like a guy, but his voice is high pitched, likely due to his being only three feet tall. I'd say he has a double chin but it's more like a quintuple chin.

He holds his arms out wide. "Welcome to Heck. I am Nalfoz, and you don't belong here."

CHAPTER 17
STRAIGHT TO HECK

STILL SUNDAY EVENING

Sam approaches Nalfoz and shakes his hand. "Hi."

"You are still here," says Nalfoz.

"What's he, like the security or something?" asks Sierra.

Nalfoz grabs the lapels of his suit jacket and tugs. "I am the senior manager of Heck."

"Oh, the big boss?" I ask.

"No, I am the senior manager. All these field team managers you see report to me. I report to the Supervising Manager of Heck, who reports to the Director of Heck, who reports to the Senior Director of Heck, who reports to the Vice President of Heck, who reports to the big boss."

Sierra looks at me. Her expression says 'burn the corporate world to the ground.'

"None of you have ID or name badges," says Nalfoz. "I'm afraid I must ask you to leave. This is not 'take your mortal to work' day."

"Some of us aren't mortal." I raise a hand.

"It is not 'take your immortal to work' day either," replies Nalfoz without missing a beat.

Sam puts on his best 'aww please' face. "We won't stay long. I just need to speak with Tedium."

"No one simply walks in and speaks with Tedium." Nalfoz shakes his head. "You really should leave."

Sam sighs. "Olmaz owes Tedium a favor. He's asked me to come here and do something for Tedium to pay that back."

Nalfoz rubs his massive chin. It swells from the underside of his face like an overfilled water balloon. "Hmm. Well. Perhaps we can do something. But first, you must follow the rules. This way."

Nalfoz waddles off.

We follow him out of the cube farm to a small conference room with a round meeting table upon which sits a few black markers and a shoebox. We eye the little grey round table and chairs. No one sits down. Everything in here is incredibly hot, even though we don't really notice it with Sam's spell on us. Any butts that touch those chairs will soon be burned bare. The magic does not protect our clothing or any objects that are not from this place.

"Everyone, fill out a name tag." Nalfoz points at the box.

Ashley opens it. The box contains a bunch of blank 'hi, my name is' stickers.

Sierra rolls her eyes. "Seriously? This is so lame."

"It's not a big deal." Sam takes a sticker out of the box and grabs a marker. "Just do it."

I'm with Sierra on this. Feels cringey lame. Still, I write my name on a sticker and slap it onto my oversized T-shirt. Sophia writes her name with a little heart to dot the i. Once we're all wearing name stickers, Nalfoz keeps standing there expectantly. It takes us a moment to realize he's waiting for Blix.

Sam nudges the imp.

With an air of 'fine, fine... whatever', Blix writes his name on a sticker and affixes it to his bare chest. The sticker is so big on him it extends a little into his armpits.

"Wonderful. Now that we know who you all are..." Nalfoz hands me a beach ball. "Write something on this ball complimentary about the person to your left, then pass the ball to the right."

"Huh?" I blink.

"Ice breaker. So, you get to know each other." Nalfoz grins.

"Umm. Dude." I stare at him. "We're siblings, not new hires. We already know each other very well."

Nalfoz examines his fingernails. "Rules."

Sigh.

I glance left at Ashley, sigh again, and write 'Ashley is the best friend I could ever ask for, always there for me. I couldn't imagine existence without her.' Then, I pass the ball to Sophia. She blushes a little while writing on the ball, then gives it to Sam.

The ball makes the rounds.

"All right. Read them out loud," says Nalfoz.

"Nope." Sierra stands. "No way. I don't care about the art thing that much. Let's go home. Tedium can wait on his favor."

Nalfoz nibbles on his fingernails. "All right. Fine. We can bend the rules a little bit there."

"So, we can speak to Tedium now?" asks Sam.

"Not quite yet." Nalfox shifts his gaze to Sierra. "Since I am bending the rules..."

"Let me guess," I mutter. "We have to do a quest for you first."

"Exactly!" Nalfoz snaps his fingers and grins. "Three of our field operatives are late checking in. Abnormally late. Go find out what's taking them so long and tell them to get back here. Once you've sent all three back to the office, I will bring you to Tedium personally."

"No tricks?" Sierra narrows her eyes at Nalfoz.

"No tricks." The goblin-like demon offers a hand.

My sister seems suspicious, but eventually accepts the handshake.

"Now..." Nolfaz reaches into his suit jacket and removes a rock, which he offers to Sam. "This will lead you to them."

"It's a rock," says Sierra, sounding unimpressed.

Nalfoz laughs. "Of course it looks like a rock. Would you prefer I give him something big, shiny, and obviously magical that he will have to go to great pains to keep hidden and be a royal pain in the backside?" The manager demon pauses, thinking. "On second thought…"

"The rock is fine!" Sam grabs it and stuffs it in his jeans pocket. "We'll get your demons back."

"Very well." Nalfoz makes a face of annoyance, like he really didn't think the whole rock thing through well enough. He missed a chance to be seriously annoying. "Make sure you have your name stickers when you return."

And with that, Nalfoz walks out of the little conference room.

Sierra nudges the beach ball under the table so no one can read it.

"Now what?" asks Ashley.

"We gotta go back to the normal world and track down some imps." Sam starts for the door. "We better hurry. It's almost bedtime."

CHAPTER 18
AN ALARMING DEVELOPMENT

SUNDAY NIGHT

As soon as we go back through the portal to our basement, Sierra reaches up to peel the name sticker off her shirt.

"It won't go back on," says Sophia.

"So?" Sierra scowls.

"You'll get in trouble when we go back to Heck."

Sierra's face looks so much like Mom's when someone says something painfully stupid, it almost makes me burst out laughing. Miraculously, she doesn't rip the sticker off. "I look like a dork."

Before becoming a vampire, I would totally have responded to that with something like 'that's not the sticker's fault.' Obviously teasing, but, yeah. I hold it back now. Even if she would take it as a joke, I don't want to make her feel bad. Yeah, so what. I'm squishy now. Deal with it.

Sam pulls the rock out of his pocket, holds it in his palm, and stares at it as if it were a crystal ball. "We're going to need to go out."

"Dammit." I sigh. "So much for staying comfortable all night."

"You don't have to change." Ashley pokes me. "You'd only freeze for a minute or two like that."

"Yeah, but going outside in only a long shirt will attract attention." I head for my room to get dressed. "Not the best thing to do while trying to blend in."

To make things even more tedious, I'm driving.

No, I'm not driving in order to make things worse. It's not much of a choice. I could fly and carry one sibling. Ashley could fly and carry another. That leaves one of them out. Blix isn't strong enough to carry anyone while flying, at least not in any way that would be comfortable. When imps drag people through the air, it's usually only for a short time while they throw them into swimming pools or other chaos—and it usually involves six to ten imps.

Sam could, in theory, fly himself around... but not in December. His flight isn't like vampires, powered by whatever magic we use. His wings don't get along with shirts and winter coats. I am not going to be responsible for my brother getting frostbite or pneumonia.

A reasonable person might have decided to leave the girls home and only bring Sam since he's kind of required to deal with the demon stuff. Sierra insisted on going because this is all for her benefit, so she feels bad not helping. Sophia didn't want to be left out and made the argument that her magic might be helpful.

So, yeah. I'm driving, which is going to make this take a lot longer than it might have otherwise.

I'm sure Tedium would approve.

Somehow, Sam can stare at this plain little rock and get directions. He keeps telling me where to turn and generally where to go. From the sound of it, the rock is basically a pointing arrow with no indication of distance.

Eventually, we arrive at 'Redmond Place Apartments.' I pull into the complex and park in a random available spot.

"It's in here somewhere," says Sam, still staring at the rock. "The demon we're looking for is supposed to be running around in there making alarm clocks malfunction, so people are late for work."

"So, what do we do?" I ask.

"Go inside. Find it. Send it back to Heck." Sam shrugs and opens the back door.

Ugh. I cut the engine.

We all get out of the car. Sam leads the way, walking past rows of parking spots covered by metal awnings toward the buildings on the farther side of the lot from where I parked. Naturally.

"Are we going to have to search every apartment?" asks Sierra.

"Nope." Sam smiles. "This rock is going to lead me right to it."

"That's good." Sophia nods while exhaling into her hands to warm them.

"So, are we supposed to just walk into someone's apartment?" I ask.

"Basically." Sam nods. "Yeah. Can't really help that. Umm. You can do that, right?"

I stare at nothing in particular with a 'yeah that figures' face. Thanks Universe. Making me break and enter even more. At least it's for a good cause. I think. I mean, sure the goal here is collecting personal power of sorts for Sierra, but we are also saving someone from being late to work in the morning. That has to count as a benefit to the person, right? "Yeah. I can."

Sam leads us over to a building, then goes up the stairs to a second-floor entrance. "This is it. The demon's in this one."

"Ash?" I ask.

"On it." She makes pointlessly elaborate mystical gestures. "Okay. As long as everyone stays close to me, no one will see us."

"Whoa, you can turn people invisible?" Sierra gawks.

"Not invisible. Brains just don't process seeing us." Ashley winks.

Sophia frowns. "But what if there are anti-vaxxers? They'll still see us."

"Huh?" Sierra blinks.

"They don't have brains," deadpans Sophia.

I snicker.

"They do, but they're as mushy as tapioca." Ashley winks. "A lot easier to control."

Sam tries the door. "It's locked."

I grab the knob and open it. "No, it isn't."

"Cheater," he whispers through a grin.

"One of these days, I might get used to this and not feel awkward." I shake my head and proceed to barge into some total stranger's apartment.

The Littles crowd in behind me with Ashley at the rear.

Two people sit on the sofa watching the *Deadpool* movie, a man and a woman, both with dark hair. They look late twenties and reasonably normal. Neither of them reacts to us walking in. Yeah, that whole thing about having to invite vampires? Not real. Just a story vampires made up to give mortals a fake sense of security.

Sam grins at the TV screen briefly, then walks down the hall to the bedroom. The rest of us follow.

My brother glances at the rock, looks around the room, then heads over to a large black dresser. He squats and pulls open the bottommost drawer. At first, nothing seems unusual... until Sam lifts some of the clothing out of the way to reveal an imp lying there unconscious, cradling a huge plastic bag full of marijuana bigger than it is. Or at least it *was* bigger than the imp. Looks like the little bastard chewed a hole in the plastic and ate about a third of the contents.

The small demon ate half its body weight in weed.

Oof. No wonder it passed out.

"Are we supposed to help it mess with people?" whispers Sierra.

Sophia cringes. "I hope not. If we have to be mean to people, I wanna go home."

Sam shrugs. "Nolfaz didn't say anything about helping them finish their jobs. Just telling them to go back to the office."

"Cool." Sophia smiles.

Sam opens his winter coat and pulls out a bright orange Nerf pistol. Like something out of Pulp Fiction, he calmly aims at the imp and blows its head off. Gloopy black slime goes everywhere from the resulting explosion. Thankfully, all evidence the imp ever existed disintegrates within a few seconds.

"Eep!" Sophia gawks at him. "Why did you do that? We're supposed to *tell* them to go back. You didn't have to kill him."

Sam puts the Nerf gun back in his coat. "Nolfaz said send them back. That's what I did. You can't *kill* demons in our world. Destroying them only boots them back where they came from. And, I don't think we could have talked to him. He was out cold."

"True." Sierra nods.

"Okay." Sophia wipes nonexistent sweat from her brow. "Normally, I don't support violence, but darting that imp is better than messing with people."

"Are we done here?" whispers Ashley.

Sam nods, recovers his Nerf dart, then replaces the clothing so the drawer looks untampered with. "Yep. This house is clean."

We head out of the apartment, leaving the couple to their movie, unaware of our visit. At least two people in this complex aren't going to be late for work in the morning. See that? We are doing good for society.

CHAPTER 19
THE SAUCE MISER

SUNDAY NIGHT, PAST BEDTIME

Our next stop is a Wendy's in Kirkland, off 124th Street.

By the time we get there, it's well after the Littles' bedtime. Since our phones haven't exploded with texts, I'm guessing Mom hasn't realized we aren't home. It occurs to me that we left Chloe to her own devices without asking the 'rents to watch her. Oops. Umm. Hopefully, she went upstairs on her own.

"What the hell is a demon doing at a Wendy's?" asks Sierra, sounding like she's about to laugh.

"I can think of several things." Ashley frowns.

"Oh, come on. Their food isn't bad." I tap my fingers on the Sentra's steering wheel.

"Not that. I mean..." Ash gestures at the building. "There are lots of machines in there that can malfunction. Getting orders wrong. Making food cold. Tripping people, so they spill their milkshakes."

I nod. "Oh, true. Any idea what this one's up to?"

Sam looks at the rock. "Yeah. He's supposed to be stealing the sauce packets out of drive through orders so people think the workers forgot to give them sauce."

"Truly the work of darkness," deadpans Ashley.

"Hey, this is Heck after all." I wink.

"Yeah, but it's the little annoyances that really suck the most." I open the door. "C'mon. Let's hurry this along. It's getting late."

"Yes, Mom," says Sierra.

I raspberry at her.

She raspberries back at me.

We both laugh.

"So, what's that demon going to do to me?" asks Sam.

"Nice try." I pat him on the head. "It's nothing you need to worry about until at least seventh grade. And it's not dangerous. Only embarrassing."

He sighs. "Will you at least warn me when I make it to seventh grade?"

"Okay. Fine. I promise I will tell you when you are old enough if Dad doesn't already do it by then."

We go into the Wendy's. No reason to really use cloaking or weird powers. The place is still open. It's not *that* late. Merely late compared to the bedtime of ten-year-olds. A handful of people in the dining area ignore us as if we'd been hiding. A few workers mill around behind the registers. One girl gives me an 'ugh, more customers' glance. I get the feeling she can't wait for her shift to be over. Looks tired.

Sam glances at his rock, then back up. "I think the demon is in the back. We're going to have to go where people who don't work here aren't supposed to go."

"Okay." I stare at the tired worker and give her a mental poke to forget she saw us.

"Cloaking engaged," whispers Ashley.

As if we own the place, we go right into the kitchen area, careful not to physically bump into anything or anyone. Like one of the colonial marines from *Aliens* with a motion tracker, Sam holds his rock in front of him, staring at it and rotating side to side as he walks around. Did I mention *Aliens* is Dad's absolute favorite movie? We've watched it at least twenty times. He also insists the franchise stopped there. The movie after that does not exist. He won't even speak its title. I'm guessing one of the demons of Heck was responsible for that script. Though, maybe it came from lower down.

Sam stops by the door to the big walk-in refrigerator. "It's in there."

I open the cooler door.

We enter, going past shelves of frozen french fries and burger patties. There, in the back corner of the cooler case, a lone imp stands trapped behind a quarter circle of salt. Poor little guy looks equal parts scared and furious. He regards us with a dismissive huff of contempt—until he notices Blix on Sam's shoulder. At that point, he stares at Sam and erupts in a frantic babbling conversation.

I hear babbling. He's actually talking, but I don't know demonic. It's not too different from me walking by a couple of people arguing in Chinese, Russian, or Spanish at high speed.

"Wow." Ashley laughs. "Guess these Wendy's workers have some secrets."

"Special sauce," deadpans Sierra.

Heh. I chuckle.

"Someone here knows a little mysticism." Sophia looks around at the cooler. "I can sense a ward. It's pretty weak."

"What's he saying?" asks Sierra.

"Begging me to let him out of the salt line so he can get back to work." Sam shrugs, then swipes his foot across the salt barrier.

The imp lets out a cheer, salutes my brother, then disappears in a puff of smoke.

"Why did you let him go?" Sophia blinks at him. "He's going to mess with people now."

Sam turns toward her. "He's making sauce packets disappear. It's not dangerous or harmful, just annoying. In fact, it's probably healthier for people."

Ashley snickers. "Corporate probably even likes the little guy for saving them money on not using up as many sauce packets."

"Ugh. Kale has to be the work of demons." Sierra sighs.

"Hey wait a sec." Sam waves in a 'come back' manner.

The imp he freed reappears in front of him, one eyebrow up.

"Nolfaz wants to you get back to the office."

Gesturing at the room, the imp babbles at him.

"Yeah, I know you didn't finish, but Nolfaz wants you to check in. At least go back and tell him why you're late."

With an air of 'okay, fine' the imp hangs his head and disappears again.

"Our work here is done," I say in an overly serious tone.

Before we leave the place, Ashley and I help ourselves to a snack. Since we're already here and it's convenient.

Yes, Wendy's workers' blood *does* taste like hamburgers.

CHAPTER 20

THE THIRTEENTH MOST INSIDIOUS EVIL

SUNDAY, WAY PAST BEDTIME

The next stop on our crazy post-bedtime mission is the Alderwood Mall in Lynwood.

It is, of course, closed by now. That's not a problem for me, other than the whole 'contributing to the delinquency of minors' by bringing three under-eighteens with me while breaking into a place after hours.

Follows Rules Girl isn't entirely thrilled, but our motives are close enough to pure that she's not doing much more than giving me this slightly disappointed look. To avoid sticking out and raising suspicion, as well as security cameras, I park in the lot for the Home Depot across the street from the mall.

We get out, group up, and walk to the sidewalk corner, then cross the street south to the mall property. I do my best to keep us off any security cameras that might be running. Ashley's looking around for living people she needs to make not notice us, though it's fairly deserted here.

The road into the mall is split in two lanes with a few tiny trees down a grassy island in between. We head toward a 'Bittyfish Sushi' place and cut right, passing a Nordstrom's on our right, then heading for the entrance to the mall itself, not going into any particular store.

Predictably, the doors are locked, not that they are for me.

Within seconds of us entering the mall, a man's scream echoes in the distance soon followed by the clattering of wood. Sounds like mops falling over on a hard floor.

"What the heck?" whispers Sierra.

Sam peers at his rock and starts walking left—which happens to be toward the scream.

"What's happening here?" whispers Sophia.

"This demon's job is sneaking into bathroom stalls after someone goes in, and stealing the toilet paper so they're stranded with no paper," says Sam.

"That's awful." Ashley shudders. "This is why I don't use public bathrooms."

"I thought you didn't use public bathrooms because you no longer have to poop," says Sierra.

Ashley stifles a laugh.

Rapid footsteps come toward us, echoing through the mall.

We duck for cover behind a big mall directory pylon. I peek around the side at a wide-eyed security guard running as if he had a lion chasing him. The guy dashes past us, slowing to a stop a mere ten steps behind us, out of breath.

He's not overweight, just apparently out of shape. Kinda skinny and it looks like he's had a few rough years. Possibly a recovered meth addict. The guy is probably about Dad's age and shivering like a human version of a chihuahua. We aren't really hiding from him anymore, at least not by virtue of this mall directory. Nothing separates us but air, though he's not aware of our presence.

The guard looks around, listening to silence. His eyes are so wide they'd probably pop out of their sockets if someone snapped their fingers behind his head. This guy is seriously high strung. Reminds me of the hapless first victim in a cheesy horror movie. We stand there in perfect silence for a minute or two, waiting for this guy to go away.

Sam picks that moment to release a fart. It's short and a bit squeaky.

Not sure if that's the work of the awkwardly timed body function demons, or just an ordinary ten-year-old boy.

"Aaaah!" screams the guard, before running away from us toward the other side of the mall.

Sierra makes a gagging gesture, then starts pushing on me like she really wants to move.

"Sorry," whispers Sam. "That wasn't waiting."

"Rancid," gasps Sierra.

She's overreacting. It doesn't smell that bad. I've been assaulted by much worse.

"Lead on," croaks Ashley.

Sam, again looking at his rock, steps out from behind the directory pylon and makes his way deeper into the mall, swishing side to side to see how the stone reacts. Whatever he's seeing, I am not. The rock appears no different from an ordinary rock to me.

We keep going until reaching the entrance to the public bathrooms. Just as we get there, two more mall security guards emerge, walking right toward us. I sidestep slowly, giving them plenty of room to go by without bumping into any of us. The Littles and Ashley follow my lead.

The guards are barely three steps past us when my phone rings.

Both of them jump, and spin to face us... and now it's kinda obvious they are looking right at me. Ashley's charm has limits. Actively making noise is one of those limits.

Dammit. Oh well. At least they are mortals.

"Hang on a second." I wallop them both with the Derp Hammer, leaving them staring in a stunned stupor, and pull my phone out.

It's Mom.

Uh oh. There's no ignoring her. Don't care if I was in Wolent's office, if she calls, I have to pick up or the consequences would not be worth it.

I flick the screen to answer. "Hi, Mom. What's up?"

"What's up? Where the heck are you?"

"At the mall."

She's silent for a few seconds. "Isn't it closed at this hour?"

"Yeah. It is."

"Then what are you doing there?"

"Weird stuff. Nothing bad." I twirl my hair around my finger, swishing back and forth. "Should be home soon."

"Are the Littles with you?" asks Mom.

"Yeah. We're together. Everyone's fine."

"Do you realize what time it is, young lady?"

I cringe. That tone makes me feel twelve again. "I'm sorry, Mom. It's taking a little longer than I thought it would. Nothing is out of control."

"Yet," mutters Sierra.

"That's not filling me with confidence, Sarah." Mom pauses. "Get home, okay? Your siblings should be in bed."

"Swear it will only be a few more minutes. We just have to find an imp."

"Oh dear." Mom exhales. "Did Soph lose control of something?"

"No, not her fault. I'll explain when we get home. Promise like ten minutes." I stop myself. "Wait, no. I drove. Longer than that. Won't be too long though."

Mom sighs. "You better have a good explanation for this. And I am not going to bed until you five are inside the house."

Ashley grins. Mom said five.

"Understood. Oh, umm. Sorry to ask, but would you mind watching Chloe until I get back?"

"Already doing that," says Mom in an unamused tone. "As a matter of fact, she came upstairs a while ago. I didn't think anything of it until it started to seem like she was really trying to keep me distracted. Trying a little too hard to hold onto my attention."

"Oh wow."

"Yeah." Mom chuckles. "I think she was running interference for you, so your father and I didn't notice you snuck out after bedtime."

"Mom, I don't really have a bedtime, now."

"Semantics." Mom gives a frustrated chuckle. "You snuck the Littles out after their bedtime. I know I can't expect you to be in bed by midnight anymore. Honestly, I'm kind of impressed Chloe didn't mind-zap us."

Aww. "Mom, she loves having real parents who care about her... and she respects you guys. She knows mind-controlling the 'rents is a big no-no."

"Well, I appreciate that," says Mom. "Are you sure collecting demons can't wait for tomorrow?"

"Not really... it's kind of a timed quest," I say.

Mom grumbles. "You shouldn't have gotten involved in an inter-dimensional scavenger hunt on a school night."

I sigh. "I'm really sorry, Mom. I didn't even want to leave the house at all tonight. Just kinda cropped up. Can we get off the phone so I can hurry this along and get home faster?"

"All right. Just... make sure everyone is safe."

"Sure, Mom. This isn't dangerous... just..."

"Tedious," adds Sierra.

"Yeah, that. Tedious." I exhale hard.

Mom's silent for a few seconds. "All right. I trust you. Just get home as fast as you can without being reckless."

"I will. Promise."

"See you soon. I am not going to bed until you are home," says Mom in *that* tone.

"I understand. We'll be quick."

We hang up.

I turn my attention back to the guards. "You didn't see anyone. You can go back to whatever you were doing."

Sam heads into the bathrooms.

Leaving the two guards in Derpville, I follow.

Sam heads to the men's room. "He's in here."

Sophia shakes her head, not wanting to go in there. Sierra's expression says she'll go in if she has to but would prefer not to. Ashley wouldn't care. Neither do I.

I hold up a hand to Ash. "Rock paper scissors?"

"For what?" she asks.

"To see which one of us goes with Sam and who stays out with the girls."

"Easy. You go. I'm keeping the Mall Special Forces from seeing them." Ashley winks.

"Good point." I hold up one finger. "Very good point."

Sam goes into the bathroom.

I follow, pausing just long enough at the door to listen and make sure there's no one in there before going in. Kinda silly considering the mall is closed now. But hey, a security guard might be in there.

"What are you still doing here?" asks Sam, his voice echoey inside the massive empty bathroom.

Impish demonic chattering responds.

"But you have to go back to the office," says Sam. "The mall is closed. There won't be anyone else pooping in here for hours. Nolfaz says you have to go back."

An imp comes flying out of a stall, zooming right at me since I'm still in the passage to the doorway out.

I raise my hands to catch the little fiend... and my pants fly down to my ankles as hard as if one of the football jocks from high school grabbed them. Thank the Universe for vampire reflexes. The little bastard yanked everything, panties included. I am fast enough to manage to stretch the front of my shirt down, covering things before Sam realizes what happened. Of course, doing that means my hands are not available to catch the imp, which zooms right over my head.

At this point, Sam realizes what happened. He looks angry for a second, then turns his back.

I pull my clothes back where they belong. "Okay."

He spins around and runs toward me. "Let's get him."

"What happened?"

Sam runs past me toward the door. "He got distracted messing with that guard. The guy's really jumpy and easy to scare, so he's been tormenting him for hours."

I run after him. "That's how ghost videos end up on YouTube."

Sam sprints past Ashley and the girls, pulling his Nerf gun out of his coat like a tiny version of a cop from an action movie. Everyone chases after him, which isn't too difficult. He's still only able to run as fast as an ordinary ten-year-old.

Blix launches off his shoulder like a missile, veering upward and zipping around close to the ceiling.

Sam races to the other end of the mall and goes into a little hallway marked 'Employees Only.'

He slows to a sneaky walk about fifteen feet after entering the off-limits area and approaches a door, behind which a man emits continuous nervous whimpers. Ashley, Sophia, and Sierra skid to a stop at the end of the hallway, seeming hesitant to go in.

The door bursts open as the imp rockets out, raking its claws at Sam. He ducks. I snag the little leathery bag of hate in a one-handed grip as it tries to dart around my head. It immediately chomps down on my hand. Those needle-like teeth aren't very big, but they sting like fifty giant Asian hornets all at once.

Reflexively, I let go. My hand just kinda opened by itself in response to such pain.

The imp zooms down the Employees Only hallway toward the mall.

Sophia holds her hands out, glaring an 'oh no you don't' expression at it.

With a surprisingly loud *boom*, the tiny imp smashes face first into an invisible force barrier, splatting against the magical wall in the manner of a *Looney Tunes* character, arms and legs splayed out in an X, before sliding down to the floor with a 'wet squeegee being dragged across glass' sound effect.

Sam takes aim and fires. Alas, since he's using a Nerf gun and not a real one, he's grossly underestimating the range. The foam dart hits me in the face. Since I am not a demon, it bounces off me harmlessly in the manner in which Nerf darts tend to do.

"Oops," says Sam.

The imp screeches and chatters, jumping back into the air and clawing at the force barrier.

"You are not going to call my sister that!" yells Sam.

Sierra tries to punch the imp. Her fist stops on the barrier with another loud *boom*. Her eyes say 'ow, that really freaking hurt' but her expression remains hard.

Sam 'Terminator walks' toward the imp.

Realizing it's not getting out of the hallway, the imp launches itself back down the hall. Expecting it to pants me again, I clamp my legs together with all my strength and prepare to catch it... and my shirt flips up over my head, then knots.

Sigh.

My attempt to still grab the imp based on sound doesn't work too well. I reach up and grab the knot that is so damn hard to the touch I know the only way out of this is to rip my shirt off. Again, sigh.

A small finger snap comes from nearby. The knot releases. I yank the shirt down to find Blix floating in front of me.

"Thanks, Blix."

I spin a fast 180, then zoom down the hall to the doorway where Sam's standing halfway in a doorway. Right as I get there, Sam fires a dart. Thanks to my combat reflexes having activated, everything around me unfolds in slow motion.

The high-strung security guard is sitting at a desk in a tiny office, looking about ready to wet his pants. A single light above him sways back and forth because the imp is hanging on it like a tiny Tarzan. Sam's Nerf dart spirals forward and up toward the imp, who shoves himself sideways at the last second—then gives my brother the finger.

Blix crashes into the back of my head, arms, legs, and wings wrapped around my skull. He gingerly removes his teeny claws from the right side of my forehead and points at the other imp.

A spark runs down the lamp wire, jolting the other imp into a paralytic convulsion.

Sam fires again.

That dart flies true, practically going up the bad imp's nose. The little bastard explodes in a shower of grey slime that splatters all over the back wall. Some of the goo lands on the guard. He looks back at the stain running down the white wall, screams, and faints.

Sam blows over the barrel of his Nerf gun. "You can run, but you can't hide."

Seconds later, the imp goo disintegrates.

"What the hell was his problem?" I ask.

"That guy." Sam points at the guard. "He was too easy to scare. The imp didn't want to stop tormenting him."

I walk over and grab the guy by a fistful of hair, lifting his head so I can peer into his eyes, and thoughts. Oh boy. Might need a hand with this. "Ash?"

She appears in the doorway a moment later. "Yeah?"

"Help me wipe this guy's memory of the last two hours..."

Ash hops up on his desk like a big cat while I loom over it. We do brain surgery. Well, more like memory surgery. That imp had this guy hearing noises and seeing shadows ever since the mall closed and no one used the bathrooms anymore today. Dude is so high-strung there's nothing for us to do but make him entirely forget everything. He's going to lose a few hours of time, but a gap in time is better than him having a breakdown or worse, going public with what he saw. Not that anyone would take him seriously, but still.

Once we're sure the memory deletion will hold, we back out of the office. It's much easier to delete memories when the person doesn't want them.

"Okay, that's all three." I nod at Sam. "Mom's not going to bed until we are home."

"I know... but we really should turn in this quest before Nolfaz gets any more ideas of crap to make us do."

"And I want to stop wearing this stupid sticker!" yells Sierra from the far end of the corridor.

Grr. He's not wrong. He's not right either. But he's not wrong.

Sam whips out the scroll and gives me a questioning look.

"Yeah, sure. I can fly back and get the car later." I blink. "Oh crap. We ran across the mall. We're definitely on camera. I can't mess with cameras if we move too fast."

Blix babbles.

"Don't worry about the cameras," says Sam. "Blix got it."

"Cool. Thanks."

Blix gives me a thumbs up.

"They're going to have to replace the entire camera system, but we're not on the recording," says Sam.

I wince.

Blix shrugs in an 'it is what it is' sort of way.

Yeah, he's an imp. That means he thrives off chaos and mayhem. He might not have *had* to permanently fry the camera system, but it was fun. And, well, I suppose I can't fault him that little pleasure for all the help he's given us.

The girls run over to where we are, both still giggling at my shirt mishap.

Sam casts the fire protection spell on us, then opens the scroll. "Take your shoes off if you don't want them to melt."

Since none of us want our shoes to be destroyed, we take them off as well as our socks. It's diabolical, really. A realm that forces us to be barefoot and constantly conjures up piles of awfulness to step in. Ugh. What kind of evil mind came up with that?

The portal opens... and we step once more into Heck.

CHAPTER 21
TEDIUM

A FEW HOURS LATER

We make our way down the corridor.

Despite our diligent caution, we hit several land mines. Not literal mines. I'm talking cat puke puddles, dog poop, Lego bricks, and one cooking oil spill. The damn messes appear the nanosecond we have any tiny lapse in concentrating on where we put our feet.

So irritating.

I hate this place.

Sam leads the way back to the cube farm, but goes around it to the same little conference room on the outer wall of the massive chamber. Nolfaz is there waiting for us. The imp from the mall points at Sam and babbles angrily.

Nolfaz waves dismissively at the imp. Even though I can't understand demonic, I assume he's saying something along the lines of 'you should have been done and back in the office by then. It's your fault.'

"Excellent work, Sam." Nolfaz smiles. "All right, I suppose I shall hold up my end of the deal."

"Thanks." Sam nods.

"Oh. The rock?" Nolfaz holds out his hand. "Can't leave that sort of thing in circulation."

Sam gives it over.

Nolfaz drops the rock into his shirt pocket, pats it flat, then walks out of the conference room. "This way."

We start to follow.

The mall imp wanders out, points at Sophia and mutters something.

Sam whips around, grabs the imp by its tiny neck, and holds it against the wall before pressing his Nerf gun to the creature's forehead. "What do you think this will do to you here? If you touch my sister, I will track you down to the lowest levels of the pit and make sure you are ended."

No one would really think a scrawny ten-year-old with kinda long hair to be the least bit intimidating. At least, not usually. This imp seems to disagree. He about wets his pants, except for not having any, and starts making begging noises.

Sam drops the imp. "You didn't go back to the office when you were supposed to. All I did was what your boss told me to do. If you wanna be mad at someone, be mad at him. *Don't* mess with my sisters."

The imp races off.

Nolfaz clears his throat impatiently.

Sophia hugs Sam.

Sierra smiles.

I'm impressed she didn't make a comment. She's older than him and likes to think of herself as his protector, not the other way around. Aww man, I'm going to be lame and squeeze them all. My sibs are awesome.

Somehow, I fight off the urge to be that twee in public.

Nolfaz leads us out of the cube room, down another hall full of strategically placed messes, and into a big empty room with one of those common-feeder lines where red velvet ropes make a back-and-forth queue. It's entirely empty. A thousand people could fit in here and there is no one.

Sam starts walking around the velvet rope poles.

Nolfaz coughs, shakes his head, and points.

Sam sighs. "Okay. Fine."

"Tedium will be with you soon." Nolfaz looks us over, seemingly checking that we are all still wearing our 'my name is' stickers. Satisfied we are, he nods once, and leaves us here.

"Tedium's already here," whispers Sierra.

We navigate the back-and-forth line, crossing a room almost as big as a football field. Yes, that means we have stepped on almost every inch of floor in this massive chamber by the time we reach the end. A small chain hangs draped across the exit of the queue. Beyond it, a tiny brass plaque on a post reads 'please wait to be called.'

The innermost wall has about thirty teller windows like you'd see in a bank. Only one of them has a demon in it, who appears to be reading a computer screen off to one side.

We stand there.

After about ten minutes, Sam clears his throat.

The clerk demon continues staring at its screen.

"Why are we waiting?" whispers Sophia. "There's no one here."

Sierra hangs her head. "This entire realm is a manifestation of pointless annoyance. We're waiting to wait."

"We are going to be in soooo much trouble," says Sophia.

Blix babbles.

"Not any more than we already might be," says Sam. "Time works weird here. It's not the same as the normal world."

We stand there in the otherwise silent room for what feels like an hour.

"I gotta pee," whispers Sophia.

"Why did you say that out loud?" Sierra squirms. "Now I do, too."

A faint metallic *ploink* noise comes from in front of us. I glance toward where the sound originated. Another brass plaque on a post —that wasn't there a second ago—reads 'stepping out of line for any reason resets your position in the queue.'

"Uh oh." Sam fidgets. "If we go to the bathroom, we're going to have to wait all over again."

Sophia whines.

Blix snaps his fingers and a small plastic potty appears on the floor behind us.

Sophia gasps. "No way. Are you kidding? Right out here in the open? I don't have to go that bad."

With a 'suit yourself' shrug, Blix snaps again and the potty disappears.

We continue to wait.

Sam squirms. Sierra fidgets. Sophia is definitely doing the pee dance.

I can't help but think about that whole cube area dedicated to awkwardly timed bodily functions and wonder if someone from there is messing with us. Suddenly having to go to the bathroom really bad in a situation where you can't is definitely their doing. Usually, those demons ambush people on long car rides. Of course it's not *always* the work of demons. Still. All three Littles at once? That's suspicious.

Time drags on.

"Okay. Fine. Make the plastic toilet," says Sophia. "Nobody look."

Before Blix can snap his fingers again, the clerk demon finally looks out at us and waves us forward. "Next."

Sam hurries forward.

Ashley and I follow, with Sophia and Sierra close behind. The girls continuously bounce on their toes and shift their weight back and forth. Ugh. Watching them is making *me* want to pee.

"I need to speak with Tedium," says Sam. "Olmaz sent me."

The clerk looks at his computer screen for a moment. Nods once. He stamps something and hands Sam a little card, then points to the right, saying something in demonic.

"Thanks." Sam smiles at the clerk, then hurries off to the right.

We fast-walk past more empty clerk windows and continue to a doorway. Sam goes through, leading us into a short corridor that looks like we've gone up to the executive floor in a corporate office with wood paneled walls, nice carpet, and expensive looking lights overhead.

One small door on the left side of the hall about halfway to the office at the end appears to be a bathroom. We stop at it. The Littles exchange glances. Sophia smiles thankfully at the other two and opens the door.

Despite the opulent surroundings, the extremely tiny bathroom looks like something you'd find in a gas station on a highway in the middle of nowhere. Stains, both yellow and brown, cover the floor. Still-liquid puddles of pee are everywhere. The toilet seat is up, covered in dried poo and crawling bugs. Unidentifiable grey water floods the sink. If I'm not losing my mind, something tiny and alive is swimming around in that sink water.

Not even going to go into how bad it smells.

Sophia screams.

"That's just cruel," says Sierra. "I wouldn't walk into a *clean* public bathroom barefoot. That is... a horror movie."

Sam steps up to the doorway. "Wow, that's... horrible. Wonder if I can hit the toilet from here."

Sierra laughs.

Sophia blushes.

Ashley snickers.

Hang on. I know Sam. He's not kidding. He's completely serious. In four seconds, my brother really is going to try his best to hit the toilet from the doorway. I put a hand on his shoulder. "Can you hold it a bit longer?"

"Umm, not really."

Sophia shivers in disgust. "No way. I got this."

She glares at the foul bathroom and starts waving her arms around like Mickey Mouse in *The Sorcerer's Apprentice*.

All the foulness in the room flies up and into a disgusting swirl of awfulness. The torrent of ick compresses into a little poop cyclone that she forces into the toilet. Seconds later, she flips her hand over and the whole bathroom fills with roaring flames.

"Whoa." Sierra leans back. "Way to be sure."

Blix claps.

Sophia looks over the now-immaculate bathroom. "Okay. I won't take long."

"Be careful," says Sam. "Remember, everything in this place is very hot. If your nightdress touches anything, it will catch fire."

She nods, steps inside, and closes the door.

A few seconds later, she shrieks.

"Are you okay?" I rush forward and grab the knob, ready to barge in if she doesn't reply.

"Yeah." Sophia's voice wavers from inside. "Seat is cold."

Eventually, the door opens and she steps out looking much happier. Sierra goes in next. She, too, shrieks, then yells, "How the hell is this stupid seat *this* cold after Soph just used it?"

"It's how this place works," says Sam.

Once Sierra's finished, Sam takes his turn.

After all the Littles are done, we continue down the hall to the double wooden doors at the end.

Sam grabs the gold knobs and opens the doors.

The office beyond is huge.

The demon at the desk, not so much. He's average sized.

More than any other demon here, he looks generally human. Both of his hands have five fingers. His face is slightly monstrous, as in there are traces of goblin in the shape of his ears and jawline, but for the most part, he could pass as a weird-looking human... albeit one with little black horns sticking up from his temples. The guy is skinny, a bit nerdy, and is wearing a tan suit complete with a plaid bowtie. Behind him on the wall, a large frame seems to hold a giant diploma. The words 'Infernal Business School' scroll across the top in intricate calligraphy. Below that, a whole bunch of indecipherable runes and symbols say stuff I can't read. The signature at the bottom appears to be written in blood... that's still dripping.

Sam approaches the desk and stands there patiently waiting to be acknowledged.

Huh. Where did my brother get manners like that from?

Ashley, the girls, and I file in and stand behind him.

"Hello there," says Tedium in a surprisingly normal voice. "I understand you are here at Olmaz's request to return the favor he owes me?"

"Yeah. That's the plan." Sam nods.

Tedium rubs his chin. "Well, I suppose it wouldn't be smart of me to pass on an opportunity to have a mortal working for me for a short time. You can do things our normal minions don't quite have the strength to."

"Like?" asks Sam.

"Care to cause a train derailment and delay passengers for fourteen hours or so?" asks Tedium.

Sam squirms. "Umm. People can die in train derailments."

"Yes. That's true. But the ones who live are significantly inconvenienced."

Sierra puts a hand on Sam's shoulder. "This is a bad idea. I don't want you to hurt people just for my benefit."

"Yeah." Sam exhales. "Sorry. I really would rather not hurt anyone."

Tedium mulls for a moment. "Well, I suppose causing a traffic accident and an hours-long snarl is out of the question then, too."

Sam nods. "Yeah, no. Someone would get hurt."

"Topple one of the loading cranes at the pier. Shut down cargo operations for a few days," says Tedium. "You can wait for the area to be clear so no one gets hurt."

Sophia gasps.

Sierra grimaces.

"Wow, this is serious mayhem," whispers Ashley.

"Umm." Sam exhales long and slow. "I dunno. All I wanted was to help my sister be happy and do something she loves. I can't really agree to something like that. Some people wouldn't work for days and might not be able to pay their bills. What if someone gets blamed for the accident that didn't do it? What if the cops figure out it was me?"

Tedium raises an eyebrow. "You're saying you don't want to inconvenience others for personal gain?"

"Basically, yeah." Sam shrugs.

"Wow." Tedium leans back, eyes wide. "What kind of demonologist are you that you don't want to take power at the cost of another's suffering."

"Umm." Sam blinks. "Not a butthead demonologist?"

Tedium taps his fingers on the enormous desk, staring at Sam.

"I mean, I'll sit on an ice-cold toilet seat if it helps Sierra." Sam flaps his arm. "Or get stuck on top of the Space Needle with no clothes. If it's *me* that suffers, that's fine."

"Ugh, don't remind me about that." Sierra blushes.

Sam peers at her. "Didn't mean that. The tub got me yesterday."

"Wait, what?" I blurt. "You were on the Needle? *Yesterday?* It's freezing outside."

"Yeah. It's okay. I got home just fine." Sam shivers. "Was really cold though."

Tedium continues to regard Sam as if he's not sure what to make of him.

"Sorry for wasting your time." Sam turns. "We'll go."

"Hold on, boy." Tedium leans forward. "Olmaz has been blowing me off for centuries. I may as well take advantage of this opportunity in any form I can."

Sam pauses. "I'm listening, but I'm not going to do bad stuff to people."

Tedium reaches down, opening one of the lower drawers of his desk. He lifts a silver bottle into view. Looks like something a fancy executive might serve whiskey or some such liquor in. The base is wider than the top, almost conical in shape. He sets sit on the edge of the desk near my brother, making an audible *thunk*. That bottle seems quite heavy. "Would you object to not causing suffering but merely collecting it?"

"What does that mean?" asks Sam.

"Use this vessel and fill it with the purest essence of inescapably insufferable boredom, the misery of time standing still, the likes of which cause brains to melt out from a mortal's ears." Tedium smiles. "You won't need to cause that sensation, merely be near those who are already experiencing it."

Sam stares at his warped reflection in the angled surface of the bottle. "Where the heck am I supposed to find that?"

"History class?" asks Ashley.

"Oh gawd," I mutter. "That guy was soooo boring."

"Well." Tedium flicks at a bit of lint on his sleeve. "If you intend to generate it yourself, you could watch golf on television. I don't recommend that, though. Most mortals cannot survive."

Sam picks up the bottle. "How does it work?"

"Simply bring the vessel near an appropriate subject, remove the stopper, and it will siphon off them. When it is full, return to me." Tedium nods.

"What is an 'appropriate subject?'" asks Sierra.

Tedium waves his hand in a deliberating manner. "Well, you could try security guards. They are my favorite creation."

I blink. "*You* created security guards?"

The executive demon smiles. "No, I created the concept of night security. Specifically, that part where the guards are not allowed to do anything like read, use their computer, or do anything but sit there, erm... guarding."

"Ack." I cringe. That sounds awful.

"Eww," says Ashley.

The double doors behind us swing open. A pear-shaped demon waddles in, his tiny ears flapping like itty bitty wings. He stops a few steps past the door and bows at the desk. "Sir, Insurance needs more staffing to keep up. They're requesting another two dozen managers."

"Insurance?" I blink at them.

"Ahh, yes." Tedium leans back, smiling to himself. "My finest creation. The greatest evil humanity has inflicted upon itself—with my help, of course."

"Greatest evil we did to ourselves? Wouldn't that be organized religion?" I ask. Sorry Dad. I'm stealing your line.

Tedium winces, then snaps his fingers. "Oh, you do have something of a point. Very well. I created the *second* greatest evil humanity has inflicted upon itself."

"Companies that deny health claims are horrible," grumbles Ashley.

"Eek!" chirps the pear-shaped demon, acting like Ash just dropped an F-bomb in fourth grade.

Tedium waves at her in an 'oh no, wait a minute' gesture. "I don't do medical insurance. That's way too evil for me. I'm in vehicles and flood insurance. If you want to gripe about medical coverage, you'll need to go down to nine."

"Nine?" asks Ashley.

"The ninth layer," says Tedium.

"Where the darkest evil dwells." Sam shivers.

Tedium nods to him. "I believe medical insurance is Asmodeus' domain. You'd have to talk to him, but I wouldn't recommend it. You all are so innocent and young. He's nowhere near as cordial as I am."

"Yeah, let's not do that." Sam hefts the silver bottle, needing to use both hands. "Okay. One bottle of coalesced boredom coming up."

CHAPTER 22
UNSPORTING

SUNDAY NIGHT

It's almost midnight when we exit the portal directly into the basement at home.

The girls are quite done and head up the stairs, eager to go to bed.

Sam looks at me. "Can we fill this real quick?"

"Mom is going to stake me if I keep you awake any longer." I sigh at the ceiling. "Go to bed. We can collect the pure essence of boredom tomorrow night."

"Aww come on." He fidgets. "I kinda feel like we have a time limit here before Tedium changes his mind and wants me to do something worse."

"Okay. Look. I'll see what Mom says. If she's okay with it, we can start."

Sam makes a face like I just said no way. He sighs. "All right."

We go upstairs to the living room.

Mom's waiting for me on the sofa. Since it's not quite midnight, she isn't up past the time she usually goes to bed. "That wasn't exactly fast."

Chloe's cuddled up to Mom, her attention glued to her tablet.

"I know. Sorry. We got stuck in Heck."

"Heck?" Mom raises an eyebrow.

"You know, like Hell but not quite as bad." I chuckle.

Mom stares for a moment. "Are you messing with me?"

"Nope." I sit on the sofa nearby and explain everything that happened, including Sam refusing to do horrible things like cause a train derailment.

It's apparently so far past my mother's limit of weird that she simply blows it off with an, "All right, but please don't drag the kids to hell on a school night again."

"Sure thing Mom. I should've realized it was Sunday and waited for the weekend." I shift my weight. "Oh, umm. One more thing."

"Hmm?" She looks over at me.

"Sam *really* wants to get this finished. We have to collect the physical manifestation of boredom for Tedium. He thinks there might be a time limit. Can you give him like fifteen minutes?"

"What are you going to do?" asks Mom.

"Figured since it's just him, we could fly over to the pier and follow some security guards. Supposedly they are the best source of this energy."

Mom winces. "I really would rather you not take him flying right now. It's freezing out there."

I cringe.

Sam looks down. "Yes, Mom."

"If you simply must do that tonight, take a mirror to Boeing. There are plenty of security guards there. You can stay inside where it's warm."

Sam and I look up at the same time in shock. Did Mom just really say that? We spend another half a breath's time gawking at her, look at each other for a second, then scramble to our feet before she can change her mind.

"Sweet!" chirps Sam.

"Thanks, Mom." I jog toward the kitchen. "I'll have him home in fifteen minutes or so."

Mom responds with a sort of 'mm-hmm' noise that sounds a bit like she's overwhelmed, or maybe she's merely tired. I do feel a bit guilty pushing the boundaries of time on a school night. Still, I think the entire family is nervous when it comes to Sam dealing with demons. Yanno, come to think of it. Mom is a lawyer. Maybe she could teach Sam how to make deals and avoid being taken advantage of. I mean, seriously. How much difference really is there between making bargains with demons compared to government lawyers?

"Ash, need you," I say while going into the little basement hallway toward the mini bathroom.

"Argh. What's up?" calls Ashley from my room.

"Quick stealth mission." I stop at the bathroom door and let Sam go past me.

Blix leaps from his shoulder onto the sink, eyeing the mirror.

Ashley pokes her head out of my room. "Seriously? We just got home."

"Yeah. Gonna take Sam to Mom's office real quick to see if he can fill the jar off some security guards."

"Wow." Ashley blinks. "Mom's gonna kill both of you."

"She said it was okay," calls Sam. "We don't have much time. Fifteen minutes."

I whistle. "Yeah, I was going to go to the pier, but Mom suggested using her office, so Sam stays warm."

The look on Ash's face is the Wikipedia entry for 'holy shit.'

She emerges the rest of the way from our room in a long, pink T-shirt and her big fuzzy unicorn slippers. "Already got comfy, but who cares. No one will see us."

"To Mom's work," says Sam.

Blix scratches his little claws down the mirror surface. In seconds, the reflection shifts, basically reversing itself. It's no longer a reflection but a window into the shadow world, or mirrorverse. I pick my little brother up under the armpits and stuff him into the mirror. Then leap/fly through. Ashley glides in behind me.

It's neither cold nor warm on the other side. This is basically still our bathroom... only its shadow version.

Blix opens the door and we step out onto a street that's simultaneously foreign and familiar. It's kinda-sorta based on the neighborhood we live in, but different. Sam tried to explain it to me a while ago. Something about how this is an amalgamation of hundreds of years of how the place looked. That's why we sometimes see really old cars or buildings that aren't around anymore. It's like a memory echo of the past, forever preserved in the ether of this parallel dimension.

We follow the imp down the street and into a small forest. All manner of weird noises come from everywhere around us. A black bear the size of a garbage truck sits up and peers at us. He's wearing one of those transparent plastic green visor headbands and sipping a mojito. The absurdity only deepens when the bear waves at us in a 'oh, hey, what's up' sort of manner.

"Yo," says Sam, as if he knows the bear.

We keep going.

A moment later, four growling Jack-o'-lanterns come bouncing out of the woods toward us. They aren't any larger than one might expect them to be, though they are on the bigger end of pumpkin possibility. Two of them drool seeds and mash while snarling menacingly at us.

"Go away," says Sam. "I don't have candy."

"What the fudge?" blurts Ashley.

Something jumps on me from behind, clinging to me. I scream, momentarily thinking a goblin's eyes are bigger than its brain and some three-foot-tall critter has convinced itself it's going to take me down. I'm half a second away from grabbing the little arms encircling my chest and power-bombing the thing into the ground when it, too screams.

In fear.

I know the voice.

It's Chloe.

Kiddo screaming makes Sam and Ashley yelp and flail.

A glop of orange goo and pumpkin seeds rises up next to the biggest Jack-o'-lantern almost like a hand. It points at itself, then at Sam, then back at itself in an 'I'm watching you' manner.

Chloe whines and clings to me. "I don't wanna get eaten by a pumpkin!"

Once the jump scare of Sudden Appearing Child™ has worn off, Sam laughs at her.

Ashley gasps. "Chlo, what are you doing here?"

"Hey, that's my line," I deadpan. "Chloe?"

"I wanted to go with you," she says. "I'm good stealth too."

Ashley opens her mouth to say something, hesitates, then shrugs. "Kid ain't wrong. I had no idea she was with us until just now."

The three Jack-o'-lanterns somehow convey a sense of turning and wandering back into the trees like a bunch of mobsters.

"What the hell was that, Sam?" I ask.

He holds his hands up innocently. "They think I owe them candy. I have no idea why. Swear I did nothing to them. I think they just go around here at Halloween and shake kids down for spare Milk Duds."

I'm not sure whether to laugh or be concerned.

"Oh." Sam biffs himself in the forehead. "I think I know what happened."

"Do tell." I raise an eyebrow.

"One of the houses gave out candy corns this year." He sticks out his tongue. "I might've tossed them into the trees. I think they're mad at me for giving them candy corn."

"That would do it." Ashley chuckles. "Maybe you should give them something to make up for such an insult."

My brother makes a 'they're pumpkins. What are they possibly going to do to me' face, then shrugs.

We keep walking.

Blix leads us through the woods for what feels like about five minutes before the trees part to reveal the airplane parking lot near the Boeing HQ. Some of the planes parked here look like they belong in a World War II movie. Legit bombers or something. Others are more modern. The instant I look at this airplane graveyard, the distinct impression that something exceptionally dangerous lurks here comes over me.

"Hurry up. There's something bad here," I whisper.

Blix nods emphatically, babbling.

"He says don't stand under anything heavy. There's a gremlin king here and it will try to kill us if we give it the chance."

"A gremlin king?" Ashley blinks. "Like Mogwai?"

Blix cackles, then rambles in demonic.

"No. Not at all cute," says Sam, translating again. "Nothing like the movie. Real gremlins are sorta like imps but half the size. They infest technology and make it malfunction. If we walk under a wing, it's probably going to fall off and crush us."

"Eek." I cringe. "I'd be grounded for four centuries if you got killed."

Blix puffs up his little chest in a 'that's not going to happen' manner.

We take a careful path through the field of airplanes until Blix decides to go up a portable staircase that's parked against something that looks like a 737. The laws of this place are intensely weird, so I don't question why he seems intent on entering a plane.

At the top of the stairs, Blix snaps his fingers and the airplane door pops open. My brain struggles to process the sight waiting for me inside. It's not the interior of an aircraft, but a corporate bathroom. The shimmer of a mirror boundary hovers in the plane's doorway.

This is why having an imp to navigate this realm is so important. None of it makes sense. Trying to do the logical thing by walking to the actual shadow copy of the Boeing building wouldn't have taken us to the interior of the building, since that's apparently hidden inside this plane.

We all climb through, back into the normal world. It's a little chilly in here but hardly as cold as it would've been had we flown here. It's also a men's bathroom given the presence of wall urinals. Huh. Weird. I figured it would smell horrible in here. Guess they pay their cleaning staff well.

Ashley does her thing.

I do mine, keeping us off cameras. "Remember, we can't run or move too fast or we'll show up on security cameras. No one can see us unless you make noise or touch someone. Stay calm."

"I know, know." Sam rolls his eyes.

We creep out into the hallway and start looking for a security guard.

Thinking the best bet would be the ground floor lobby, I do my best to remember how to get there. We make our way downstairs, not using the elevator. Sure enough, three guys and a woman in security uniforms are hanging out talking. Looks like two of them are supposed to be there at the desk, the other two guys are standing to chat.

We sneak closer. There's no perfect angle here. The two men standing are facing the desk while the other two in the chairs are facing the doors to the outside world. Our best approach is on the side where neither pair of guards would be looking directly at us... but it's still not perfect. Not sure why I'm concerned. If they *do* manage to see us, they're only mortal.

Once we get within spitting distance of the guards, Sam holds up the silver bottle and pulls out the stopper.

All four security guards are soon surrounded by a faint hazy mist that seems to sweat out from their entire being. The mist gathers into a thin tendril from each guard, which flows over the course of several seconds into the bottle. Before too long, no trace of it remains visible.

Sam, likely assuming the vessel has taken all it can, puts the stopper back. He peers down at the bottle and frowns. "Wow. That barely moved the needle."

"The needle?" I ask.

My brother holds the bottle up so I can see the bottom. It's got an empty-full meter kinda like the strip on batteries that shows the charge level. This thing is barely at two percent.

"Four guards, two percent. Oof." I cringe. "That's going to take forever."

Chloe tugs on my shirt.

I peer down at her.

"I found more guards." She points at a hallway, then starts walking for it.

With a shrug, I follow.

Ash and Sam stay close.

Two guards sit on backless cushioned benches in the hall, seeming asleep. Another five lay slumped about randomly, like someone's been playing *Assassin's Creed* and using this hallway to store bodies.

"Whoa. What the heck is going on here?" I whisper.

Chloe beams. "I collected them."

Oh, that's only a *little* creepy.

It finally occurs to me that one of the guards seated on the bench has his shirt collar opened. I'm guessing she was hungry.

"Most of them." Chloe points at the guy she fed from. "He was already sleeping."

Sam shrugs, seeming unfazed at this. He unstoppers the bottle and siphons more mist from the guards. It takes about a minute before the vaporous tendrils stop. Then, he looks at the bottle. "We're up to six percent."

"That's not really a one percent per two guard reliable ratio," I say. "This is..."

"Tedious," adds Sam.

Ashley shrugs, flapping her arms. "Maybe these guards are happy working here? We could try looking for a place where the security guards are incredibly bored and hating life. Otherwise, it's going to take a really long time to collect this much anguished boredom."

Sam peers down at the silver decanter. "Yeah. This seems cruel and unfair. Night security is bad enough without doing whatever we're doing to them."

"I dunno." I scratch my head, glancing back at the main lobby. "The guards didn't seem to notice you did anything to them. In fact, I think they seemed a little happier after you drained them."

"Do you want to play with me?" echoes Chloe's voice from the far end of the hallway, sounding weird and ghostly.

A woman's voice screams in terror. Another security guard comes sprinting around a corner into view, pale as a ghost. She sees the five guards sprawled around the floor here and screams again.

Oh, shit. Chloe....

Fast as I can, I zoom over to this terrified guard and wallop her with the Derp Hammer, then dive into her thoughts. She didn't see kiddo, just heard a ghostly child voice. The bigger problem is her seeing Security Guard Jonestown in the hallway. She doesn't need to remember that.

While I'm deleting that scene from her mind, Sam siphons her.

That done, I point at the other guards. "Ash, help me move them around so they're not all in the same place like a massacre just happened here."

"Okay."

We spend a few minutes relocating unconscious security guards to different rooms and chairs, positioning them so it looks like they just sat down for a break and passed out. To be clear, none of them are dead, nor even injured. Merely sleeping. I think Chloe just hit them with a 'sleep' command. That's kinda unsportsmanlike. If we're talking D&D creature terms here, the Night Security Guard has a vulnerability to sleep spells and charms. Their save is penalized against those kinds of effects.

Anyway...

I set the last guy in a chair behind a desk and hurry back to the others in the hallway. Only the one guy who Chloe initially found sleeping there remains. Ashley's already rebuttoned his shirt for him.

"Damn." Sam sighs. "We're almost out of time and this thing isn't even ten percent full yet. This isn't going to happen tonight."

"Oh. I have an idea." I snap my fingers. "Anguished boredom. Let's come back to this tomorrow."

Sam yawns. "Okay."

We hurry to the nearest bathroom and hop a mirror home. On the way back, the Jack-o' lanterns pop out to stare at Sam. One of them's holding a wiffle bat. Yeah, holding. A pumpkin. A thing that has no arms or hands is holding a bat. It's a glop of seeds and pumpkin guts in the shape of a floating hand.

Ugh, this is so strange.

CHAPTER 23

NIGHTMARES OF NIGHTMARES

LATER, SUNDAY NIGHT

We get Sam home and in bed.

A little after one in the morning, a faint nagging chewing on my brain finally gets the better of me. I'm worrying about the whole Natasha waking up an ancient vampire thing. The worst part is that I don't know how much of her scheme is wild nonsense and how much could be a potential threat.

I start talking about this with Ashley, who is equally clueless. Our conversation leads me to suggesting we ask Aurélie about her opinion. So much for staying home, right? Alas, this *is* going to require pants. Grr. Once Follows Rules Girl realized I was actually taking my job (with Wolent) seriously enough to think about job stuff instead of just being lazy, she's not going to let it go.

Ashley and I change. T-shirt, long sleeved purple sweatshirt, jeans, and Uggs for me. Ash goes for a fuzzy pink sweater and a denim skirt over yoga pants, giant purple socks that are likely the illegitimate offspring of leg warmers and normal socks, and also Uggs.

Chloe insists on going with us. She doesn't change as she's still wearing her frilly doll dress. Kiddo also decides to stay barefoot because whatever.

Does it make me a bad mother-slash-big-sister that I'm not throwing a fit or making her put on a heavy coat and shoes? It's not like any of us care about the cold. Other than the initial shock of changing temperature zones, it doesn't matter. We don't get sick. We don't get frostbite. I could walk six miles barefoot in the snow and my toes would be fine.

Guess the rules change a bit when we're talking about parenting a little vampire.

I'll save the arguments for things that matter. We're not exactly planning to go out in public among normal people, so no one should see her and call CPS.

We head upstairs and go out the patio door.

Chloe gasps and starts shivering.

In fairness, so do we. Maybe not so much since these Uggs are super warm and fuzzy.

A few minutes later, the bite of the cold loses its grip on us and 1:19 a.m. on a December morning feels like room temperature. We leap into the air and climb high out of sight from the ground before veering toward Seattle.

Before long, we arrive at Aurélie's high-rise apartment... as much as owning an entire floor counts as an 'apartment'. Sometimes, it's hard for me to process the truth of her existence. She does not appear like what anyone would expect a really old vampire to look like. Aurélie is almost too pretty to seem real. She looks like an anime character brought to life. Depending on how the light strikes her, she seems anywhere from sixteen to early twenties. Sigh. Unlike me, she has a choice in whether or not she appears childish. Some of that is due to makeup, most is due to her charm aura. Out in public, she always goes for the drop-dead gorgeousness where no one would ever possibly mistake her for a teen. Since she favors the 'French Nobility' look, which I guess nowadays has kinda turned into what they call 'sparkle goth,' she gets away with having skin as white as copier paper. It looks like she's wearing cosmetics to turn herself into a porcelain doll, even though she isn't.

It works, and it keeps the mortals from freaking out.

Even at home, when she's not trying to be pretty, she can't help it. Her powers are largely charm focused. Beauty is her thing. Also, unlike me, any innocence in her appearance is a complete disguise. I am tragically lame, naïve, and generally a goody-two-shoes. Aurélie only looks like one. She's not evil. That's not at all what I'm saying, but she does *not* have a Follows Rules Girl living in her head. She's got a Makes The Rules girl... or however you'd say that in French.

One thing that is true about her: she is *thrilled* to see Chloe.

You'd think I'd brought the little one to see her grandmother who hasn't seen in her in months. Can't really do the grandma jokes since Aurélie barely looks twenty.

Visiting her is a most bizarre combination of hanging out with a friend, going to your boss's house, having a super famous celebrity friend, and some sort of old-fashioned socialite gathering. She's from a time way before the existence of social media, television, movies, electronics or that sort of thing. When she was mortal, girls generally tended to amuse themselves by hanging out and talking, or telling stories. Rich girls anyway, the ones who weren't stuck working all the time.

So, yeah. It does feel a bit old school as we're sitting here talking and no one is using a phone or a tablet or anything. She *did,* however, get an enormous television and a PlayStation. I think we opened her mind to the idea of finally trying it out. She initially got the electronics for Sierra's benefit, I think as a bribe to get her to pose in a fancy dress for a painting. I suspect Aurélie has tried to play video games when no one is watching. How funny would it be if she likes

Assassin's Creed. I think one of them is set in historical France, right? Not sure. Haven't played them myself.

Aurélie loves dolls, especially haunted ones. She has tons of them. A few of the less delicate ones have made an appearance in the living room for Chloe to play with. Good chance that a part of the reason she so loves Chloe is that kiddo basically *is* a haunted doll. Other than being much larger than the dolls, she totally looks the part in that dress. The one thing about coming here and watching Chloe play with Aurélie's dolls is it's impossible to tell if she's playing pretend or if the dolls really are talking to her.

No, that's not going to give me nightmares. Not at all.

Ashley doesn't mind the old school socializing thing to a point. She finds it neat and interesting for a while; however, there's definitely a point when she's had enough of it and wants to return to being more modern. That means electronics. For her, it's like we're cosplaying for a bit and she gets into character.

Eventually, an opening presents itself in the conversation for me to finally get to the main reason we're here. Obviously, Aurélie knows we're here because I have questions for her. It would be just as foolish for me to think she doesn't as it would for me to try rushing past the niceties of the social call. Not only can she read our thoughts, Ash is a vampire because of Aurélie. They've got the same mental connection like I have with Dalton. And in doing that, Aurélie gave me the best gift anyone could possibly have: the ability to be with my best friend forever. For that, I will always be grateful. It's the kind of gift that I'll never be able to repay.

By 'opening in the conversation' I mean Aurélie asks me how things are going with Wolent lately. That's basically her saying it's okay to ask the question I wanted to ask now. No, I'm not in a rush and I do not begrudge the time spent hanging out and being social. Still, this isn't home. It's not the same as watching anime or playing video games in my PJs.

"Good as far as I can tell," I say. "Stefano and Paolo still think I'm an insult to vampirism but whatever. They're warming up to me... might take a few decades, but it's a work in progress."

She chuckles. "I believe they were most concerned you would influence a new trend of staying with one's mortals."

"They probably don't have to worry about that." I fidget. "Pretty sure there aren't too many people out there as lame as me who'd run straight home to the parents in a panic after waking up a vampire."

Ashley laughs. "You aren't lame. You're just lucky to have a good family."

"Well if Dalton had done his proper duty, things would certainly be different." Aurélie glances down at her fingernails.

Ugh. I don't want to think about a reality in which I was whisked away from my family and told to 'play dead' and never have contact with anyone who knew me in life. My nightmares have already beaten that particular horse to death.

Aurélie raises her gaze to make eye contact with me, and smiles. "I'm glad he's disorganized."

Have I said I really love Aurélie?

"There is something else you wanted to ask about?" She tilts her head at me.

"Yeah." I explain the whole Natasha situation. "Wondering if you ever heard anything about this ancient vampire sarcophagus and if there might be anything to worry about here?"

She regards me with a blank stare. "You have not really told me much of anything. Do you know this supposed ancient one's name? Where they came from?"

I bite my lip. "Nope. They just kept calling him 'the ancient one.'"

"Well..." She sighs. "Without more information, I can't say much. I am not aware of any such stories as a very old vampire who would wake up and upend all of mortal civilization. It is foolish. A waste of energy."

"Tell that to Natasha." Ashley rolls her eyes.

"Oh, I already have, couple weeks ago. Probably going to try again soon." I laugh. "Whether or not she believes me is another question."

Aurélie tsks. "You should explain to her that it is much easier to control the mortals by allowing them to think they are in charge. People do not like to be oppressed. No matter how powerful the oppressor is, eventually the tormented will rise up and strike out. If there is a vampire of great age involved, he would certainly understand this."

Considering she saw the French Revolution in person, she knows what she's talking about. If I remember right, she got her Transference in 1640 something, so she would have been a vampire by the time of the French Revolution and have been able to easily keep herself safe.

"Assuming he's not insane." Ashley cringes. "The way these idiots were talking about him, it's like they're already a cult worshipping this dude."

"What about Milo?" I ask.

Ashley giggles.

Aurélie raises an eyebrow at me. "Milo?"

I pull my phone out and open the video I took of their meeting. "His name's not actually Milo. He just looks like a cartoon character named that. I think his name is really Topher. He had a lot of books and seems to be the reason Natasha knows about this old sarcophagus."

Aurélie watches the video. She makes the same faces Dad makes whenever he's on YouTube watching fail videos where people try out for the Darwin Awards. Like that one where the idiot sits on a tire and they detonate an airbag mechanism under him and he goes flying.

"I do not know him." Aurélie frowns. "The way he carries himself, I suspect he may be an academic. There could be some meat to his theory."

"That sounds bad." Ashley winces.

Aurélie sighs. "Unfortunately, I cannot think of any truly old vampires who might be their promised destroyer."

"Darn." I exhale. "Oh well."

"I do know of someone who might be able to give you more information." Aurélie flashes a coy smile. "Alas, Remi is still in Paris."

Not a master of Frenchness here, but I think Remi is a boy's name. That look on her face is kinda obvious. She might still have a thing for this Remi guy. Wonder if he's cute.

"Oh, sure." Ashley nods. "We'll just pop over to Paris and ask him."

"If you do, please tell him I think of him." Aurélie smiles at her.

Yanno. This is the kind of thing that people invented telephones for. Or email. Or even snail mail. We shouldn't have to physically travel to Paris in order to ask one dude a question. There are probably flights scheduled late enough for Ashley and I to do this. Not like I can't afford plane tickets.

Still, for a day that started with me not wanting to leave the house, going to freaking France is way off the deep end, especially considering that Natasha and her people are almost certainly idiots who have no idea what they are doing. It's probably not important enough to go to the trouble of hauling my ass all the way across the ocean.

Besides, Euro vamps are weird. They're all into this ancient political crap us Americans have no time or patience for. Like, I'd have to figure out how to properly request permission to enter their city as a guest before I go there or they'll get pissy with me.

Bleh. Probably not worth it.

"It probably isn't." Aurélie winks at me. "We vampires are rife with stories about long-gone ancient ones who sleep in mysterious places and may or may not wake up one day to do something drastic."

"Like vampire bogey men?" Ashley blinks.

"Something of that nature, yes." Aurélie grins.

She doesn't seem particularly scared of this theoretical sarcopha-gus-dwelling elder, so I'm not going to worry.

Much.

Ashley bursts out laughing.

"What?" I ask.

It takes her a bit to stop laughing enough to talk. "Just finding it funny that even vampires have nightmare creatures they're scared of."

Aurélie makes a 'not this vampire' face while examining her fingernails.

"Makes sense. I mean, we're still not too different from mortals, at least mentally." I nod toward Chloe. "I mean, she screamed at Jack-o'-Lanterns."

Ashley laughs more.

"I did not." Chloe narrows her eyes at me. "Those were not Jack-o'-Lanterns. They were monsters. Jack-o'-Lanterns do not move."

Aurélie raises both eyebrows. "Oh, you simply must tell me what happened."

"Okay. One quick question first?" I ask.

She nods.

"Why would a really old vampire go into a sarcophagus and sleep for years?" I fidget. "Is that something that happens to everyone at a certain age?"

"*Non.*" She shakes her head. "There are two reasons an elder can sleep for a long time. Most commonly, it is because they are bored with existing. They sleep a century away and hope the world has become more interesting."

"Oh." I shrug and kinda nod along with her. Makes sense. I mean, all of these super old vampires would've been awake in a time before the Internet, so yeah. I can see how they'd get bored.

"The other is severe injury. When we reach great ages, it takes much more to harm us significantly... but also much longer to recover. We—" Aurelie stops as Chloe jumps up into her lap.

"Not pumpkins. They were moving and growling and scary," says Chloe, seeming a bit frightened even thinking about them again.

Uh oh. Is she going to have nightmares about them?

"What happened?" asks Aurélie.

Well, that's about as much as we're going to learn about some theoretical vampire bogey man in a box tonight. I relax in the super soft sofa and share the story of our recent trip through the mirrorverse.

CHAPTER 24
THE MOTHERLODE

MONDAY AFTERNOON

Some is better than none, so they say.

We got home from Aurélie's place a few minutes past four in the morning. That left us a few hours to enjoy being slackers. Sunrise hit at about 7:55 a.m. Mom has her alarm set for six and she's out the door on her way to work by seven. Ugh I could never tolerate a job that expected me to be in the office by 8:00 a.m. Even if she has the advantage of getting to go home at four in the afternoon, it's not worth it.

I am not a morning person... even more so now.

Ash, Chloe, and I get in bed right as the sounds of activity come from upstairs, the Littles waking up and getting ready for school. I think this might be their final week of classes before Christmas break. That was amazing. I remember being a kid and thinking about how the holiday break was so long and epic and wonderful. Really, it's only like two weeks. But to a grade-school kid, that's a really long time.

Shame that adult jobs don't give everyone two weeks off

between Christmas and New Year's the way schools do. They should consider that. I suppose it might totally shut down society for two weeks, but who cares? People could really use the break.

I lie there staring at the ceiling, waiting for the sun to knock me out and thinking about my plans for the day. With any luck, my 'brilliant idea' is going to help Sam deal with his Tedium problem. I guess we shall see if I'm being smart or just too cynical.

NEXT THING I KNOW, I'M AWAKE AGAIN.

The clock on the nightstand reads 2:29 p.m.

Vampire fact: in the absence of major injuries, we are not groggy when we wake up like mortals are. (Or at least like I used to be.) Getting up in the morning had been one of the great chores of my childhood. I can't even claim Christmas morning as an exception because the 'rents let us open our gifts on Christmas Eve. It's a lot easier for kids to fall asleep when the excitement and anticipation over what presents we got is already past.

Yeah, quite out of character for me, I jump out of bed right away. After a quick trip to the mini bathroom for a shower, I head back to my room and finish drying off, then throw on some clothes, including a winter coat. I might not need it, but the more I cover up, the easier it is to fight off the sun. Also, people will look at me weird if I'm running around in December without a coat. Ash and Chloe are still sleeping. No point disturbing them, so I slip out, brace myself, and go upstairs into the day.

The sky is overcast and gloomy—shocking, I know. If ever an ideal place for an Innocent vampire existed to live, the Seattle area is it. Days like this make it feel almost easy to handle sunlight.

I head up to Sam's room and grab the silver bottle, which he hid in his toy chest. Damn this sucker's heavy. Prize in hand, I head downstairs and outside to the Sentra... then wait. May as well start the car and let it warm up inside.

Eventually, the bus rolls by and drops the Littles off.

When they walk past my car, I open the window and look at Sam. "Get in, loser. We're going soul harvesting."

All three of them laugh.

"Wait, seriously?" Sophia blinks at me, fidgeting.

"No, not really. Just umm... boredom harvesting. Souls are remaining intact." I wink.

"If you want to harvest boredom, you should go to Mrs. MacDonald's class," deadpans Sierra.

There is stupid, and then there is taking up a career in teaching with the name MacDonald. Yes, it's not exactly McDonald, but ask a bunch of sixth-graders to care about the difference. The jokes are relentless. It's worse because Mrs. MacDonald is not a great teacher. She's nice enough, but she's suuuuuper boring and very unmotivated. She's the kind of teacher who brings out the video cart three times a week and lets the DVDs do the teaching for her. Worse, kids get excited when they see the cart, but then the video is so dry and boring it could put a chihuahua with ADHD to sleep. I'm not sure if there's some sort of universal law that states history (sorry, 'social studies') teachers need to be boring as crap but holy cow.

I remember having her class years ago. To this day, I still do not know how I never got in trouble for falling asleep.

"I can't do that," says Sam. "I'm only in fourth grade. She'd kick me out."

Sierra waves dismissively. "She wouldn't even notice."

"Maybe not, but Miss Moore would notice I was missing." Sam grins, then darts around to the other side of the car and climbs in. "Where are we going?"

"To feast upon the anguished boredom of the masses." I drop the car in reverse. "Put your seatbelt on."

Sierra and Sophia head inside, evidently not interested in prime boredom.

I plop my iPhone in the dash holder and pull up the navigation app.

Sam is content to let me surprise him, not pushing me to answer his question.

"So, you got bathtubbed?" I ask.

"Yeah." He shakes his head. "That was really annoying. My butt practically froze to the roof."

I squirm. "Wonder if Soph will ever be able to fix it."

"My butt doesn't need fixing." He chuckles.

"You know what I meant." I smirk. "The tub."

Sam blinks at me. "Didn't I tell you already?"

"Umm. Maybe? I think I forgot."

"It's not her fault. There's a demon messing with the tub. I'm working on it."

"Crap."

"Relax. It's one of the annoying ones." He huffs, then swipes hair out of his eyes.

Heh. His hair is getting kinda long now. It's turning into a big fluffy brown orb. Sam looks like the adorable little boy from an anime cartoon. Uncle Hank would totally lose his mind if he saw a boy with hair like that. He'll probably ask for a trim sooner or later. Sam doesn't want *long* hair to the point he resembles a miniature version of Eighties glam rocker—like Ronan. He likes looking like an anime character.

"How is that going?"

"Ehh, tricky." He grumbles. "The demon has a connection to the tub somehow. I've been trying to figure out how to manipulate that energy and drag it out so I can deal with it. Haven't found him yet. Need to work on it more if I can get in there for long enough. Sophia keeps chasing me out."

I chuckle.

"Maybe it's not a great idea for her to use the tub until this problem is fixed." I cringe. "She would not handle getting flung out of the house with no clothes well at all."

Sam shrugs. "It won't get her. She's too protected."

"That's good." I slow to stop at a red light.

A sudden glint of sunlight reflecting off the chrome of a truck in front of us stabs me in the left eye like a red-hot needle. It's sudden and unexpected enough that I blurt an F-bomb and grab my head as if I've been shot.

"Whoa... Sare?" asks Sam. "You okay?"

"Aww... hell." I cringe, rocking side to side. Head down, I open my eyes. Dammit. Left one isn't working right now. "Yeah, fine just... sun in the eyes. That hurt."

"Want me to drive? Can you see?" asks Sam.

"One eye is still working." I grumble. "And no, you're not driving. I'm offline right now. If we got pulled over, we'd be in deep poop."

A tiny finger snap comes from the space between the front seats.

Sunglasses appear on my head.

"Nice. Thanks, Blix."

"*Neem noba*," says a tiny voice.

Pretty sure that's demon for 'no problem' or 'you're welcome,' or something. He says that a lot. Either I'm hearing that phrase no matter what he says or it's like 'smurf,' a word that means anything depending on context.

When the light changes, I resume driving. In a few minutes, I experience one of the worst sensations. No, not stepping in a cold puddle with sock feet. Not sensing an imminent fart while I'm standing in front of a class doing a presentation. No, this is worse than both of those (but not by much).

My left eyeball itches so bad it feels like it's been replaced by a wad of angry fleas.

I white-knuckle the steering wheel and try my best not to scream.

The itching is still going on when I pull into the parking lot of the DMV office. I'm almost tempted to wait in the car, but it would attract too much attention for a boy Sam's age to walk alone into a DMV. He's a bit young to apply for a learner's permit.

Sam picks up the silver bottle and hops out. I cut the engine and exit the car with my left hand pressed into my left eye. Getting stabbed in the head by a sun dagger is not fun. My fault for forgetting sunglasses.

We cross the parking lot and go into the DMV. It's only going to be open for another hour or so. I think they close at four. Only an idiot goes to the DMV an hour before closing. As expected, the waiting area is packed. Doesn't even look like there are any open seats. Nice. Good thing for me I don't actually need to do anything here. Such a huge crowd is exactly what I was hoping to find.

There's gotta be over a hundred people there. The place has sixteen counter windows, but only three of them appear to be open. Another eight windows have clerks seated there, but they aren't dealing with people. One is obviously eating something. The others stare at their computers. Swear one lady is painting her nails and trying to be subtle about it. Not subtle enough. Maybe she's doing it on purpose, so people realize she's doing it and making them wait for no reason.

"Oh, wow…" Sam leans toward me, whispering, "Half the people working behind the counter are demons."

"Why am I not surprised?" I chuckle.

"That woman painting her nails has horns," whispers Sam. "But she's hiding them."

"Yeah, that tracks." I press my hand into my super-itchy eye. "Argh. Stop already."

"I'm not doing anything."

"Not you. My eye is healing. Itches like mad." I shudder from the horrible sensation of not being able to scratch this. They don't make anti-itch eyedrops strong enough for vampires. "Go on, do the thing."

"Huh? Here?" Sam looks around. "But we're not even hiding."

"No one will notice. Just walk around with the bottle. Act like a bored kid wandering randomly." I head over to one of the tables near the entrance and pretend to be searching for the form I need.

The cop, or perhaps armed security guard, standing there doesn't pay me too much attention. Nor does he seem to care that 'my kid' decides to go wandering around the waiting area. At least with this coat on, hood up, and sunglasses on, it's not obvious that most people think I'm too young to drive. I should hide my face more often.

It's so tempting to pluck my eyeball out. I'm sure that would only make it worse—not to mention freak the hell out of everyone in here. So, I tolerate it as best I can while fumbling at the papers.

After a few minutes, the mad itching fades. Sight returns to my left eye, albeit with a whole bunch of bright sparkly swirls. Since the itching is done, I peek toward the waiting area. Sam's slow-walking behind the chairs holding the silver bottle. Dozens of thin vapor strands connect the people waiting to the narrow top end. These strands seem much thicker and denser than the ones we got from the security guards. In an odd sort of paradoxical way, the people seem a little happier once the siphoning is done.

Huh. I guess my brother really is *taking* their boredom.

The strands stop all of a sudden.

Sam peers down at the bottle, then hastily puts the stopper back before fast-walking toward me.

I go back to rummaging for forms.

"Sare," whispers Sam, wide-eyed in awestruck horror. "It's full already and I didn't get half of the people. Holy crap. What is this place?"

"DMV at peak hour," I say, then add, "Crap. I forgot the stupid paper," while patting my pockets down. "Grr. Going to have to come back."

"What paper?" whispers Sam.

I take his hand and head for the door, acting annoyed at myself for being scatterbrained.

Sam follows, giving me the raised eyebrow all the way to the car. Finally, as he grabs the door to open it, he gets this 'ohhh, right' expression.

We get in and close the doors at nearly the exact same time.

"Well, that's done." I smile at him.

"Your eye is all red and puffy." Sam cringes. "That looks painful."

"It feels fine."

He nods. "Good. Umm. Are you gonna go with me to Heck again?"

"Yeah, sure. Let's go home first. Don't want to leave my car here."

Sam exhales in relief. "Cool."

CHAPTER 25
POWER OF THE SACRED BEAN

MONDAY AFTERNOON

Upon returning home, we go to the basement by way of Dad's office.

I lean in just long enough to let him know we're alive and everything is under control. He laughs his head off when I explain about going to the DMV to fill a magical jar up with the purest essence of anguished boredom. He can't help but suggest monthly financial meetings at his job as another potential source. Still haven't told him all the demons in Heck seem to be using Mac computers. He'd never stop laughing or randomly blurting 'Hah! I knew it.'

Hopefully, Sam won't need to do this again.

We head downstairs. I ditch the winter coat, Uggs, and my socks.

Sophia and Sierra come running downstairs and race into my room.

"Are you going to Heck now?" asks Sierra.

"Yeah." Sam nods.

Sierra wiggles her bare toes. "Okay. I'm ready."

Sophia squirms uneasily. She plucks off her fuzzy pink socks and tosses them on my desk. "I don't like it there."

"No one likes it there." Sam chuckles. "But if you're a demon, it's way better to have a job in Heck than farther down."

"I'm surprised you guys didn't run into an HOA there," says Dad from the outer basement.

"What's an HOA?" asks Sam.

"The Devil's work." Dad grumbles.

"Oh. Well... then that would be lower than Heck." Sam nods. "Probably on two. Maybe three."

Look at kiddo talking about the levels of Hell so casually.

Dad pokes his head into my room. "I feel I would be somewhat remiss in my parental duties if I failed to inquire as to why my children are literally going to Heck. Should I fire up the Nerf machine gun?"

"Nah." Sam grins. "This isn't a combat mission. I'm just helping Olmaz settle a favor."

"I see." Dad rubs his chin. "You're doing this for some reason other than just being nice?"

"Yeah." Sam nods toward Sierra. "Olmaz is going to help Sierra learn art stuff so she can do it and make money enough to live... and be happy... and umm, be happy."

My brother doesn't want to say 'stop thinking about school violence' out loud in front of Sierra.

He doesn't have to. Sierra knows exactly what he almost said. For two tenths of a second, she looks pissed. Then gets this resigned expression before showing a reluctant sort of gratitude at her little bro for trying to help. She's not upset at him for what he said or what he's doing. She hates having her vulnerabilities made public. That part, she's getting better at dealing with. Sierra has opened up to me about it. She's in the process of admitting to the 'rents exactly how scared she's been.

If Dad picked up on the unspoken second reason, he's not

showing it. He keeps smiling at us. "Okay then. I'll be upstairs if you need backup." He makes a 'racking a machinegun' gesture. "Still got the mega nerf cannon ready."

"Thanks, Dad." Sam grins. "But we're just turning in a FedEx quest."

"This wasn't a FedEx," I say. "It was a collection quest, one of the ones where we just click on the creatures instead of having to kill them for a drop."

"Oh, true." He laughs.

Sam pats himself down. "Poop. I left the scroll upstairs."

Blix pulls the scroll out of seemingly nowhere and hands it to him.

"Cool." Sam flops on the rug and takes his socks off.

He does the fire protection thing on all of us, then stands and opens the scroll. After a few minutes of concentration, the red ball of light appears and expands into an oval portal.

"Oh wow. That looks exactly like the portal spells from *Diablo*," says Dad.

I shrug. "Maybe there are actual demons working for Blizzard."

Dad laughs. "Wouldn't surprise me."

Sam steps through, then leans back to give us a 'c'mon' wave.

We step once more into Heck, arriving in the near infinite boring business corridor.

Sophia tries to climb me, so I pick her up.

Careful to watch my step, I make my way down the plain grey-and-white passage.

Sierra is the first to get caught off guard by a land mine. More cat puke. Lovely.

Surprisingly, she doesn't shriek, scream, or freak out. She simply holds her foot up so Blix can de-slime her.

Minutes later, it's my turn. Despite my diligence, I'm suddenly standing in stickiness. The floor doesn't *look* different, but it feels like I'm walking across a puddle of semidry pancake syrup. Never really thought about how awful it is to walk barefoot in sticky. Oh, sure there are far more horrible things, but this is the perfect level of uncomfortable annoying to be near intolerable. Wait, no. That smell. The sweet foulness mixing butter and coke, the perfect balance point between sticky and slippery. This isn't syrup. I'm standing barefoot on 'movie theater floor.' Spilled soda and popcorn butter are the tamest things likely to be in this miasma. Eww. I hurry away from the awfulness, then fly-hover so Blix can deslime both of my feet at the same time.

We head down the hall to the big cube area, then turn left to follow the open space outside the cube farm around the perimeter of the giant chamber. It takes us almost fifteen minutes to walk to the other side of the room where all the clerk windows are. As before, we end up standing and waiting in the common feeder line for a while.

Finally, the single clerk demon waves us forward and points.

We go down that same corridor with the tiny, filthy bathroom and the ornate double doors at the end. This time, however, the double doors don't lead directly to Tedium's office, but a small waiting area full of cushioned benches. An imp seated at a desk looks up as we walk in.

Despite its tiny size, about the same as Blix, it speaks with the tone and depth of a normal human man. "Tedium will be just a moment. Have a seat and wait."

Sierra hops on one of the benches.

"Nooo!" yells Sam.

Sierra makes a 'huh what?' face. Then her jeans start smoking. It takes her a second to realize she's sitting in a cloud of smoke before she jumps up, fanning at her backside. Two egg-sized holes have burned completely through the seat of her pants, exposing her unburned butt and the charred edges of her underpants.

"Everything in here is seriously hot," says Sam.

Sierra's face is so red she could pass for a demon. Not sure if it's rage or embarrassment. Probably rage. More of her backside shows when she's wearing a bathing suit than the burn exposed. I think she's just feeling furious she was so naïve and did a derp.

Blix snaps his fingers and repairs the fabric damage.

Sierra glares at me, Sophia, Sam, then looks down and sighs. "Okay. Fine. Laugh. That was dumb of me."

The imp at the desk seems mildly amused, but also disappointed that only one of us fell for it.

Sophia has too much sympathetic embarrassment to laugh. Sam restrains his reaction to a smile. Ashley giggles.

We stand there for a while, waiting.

I think all of us realize this is Tedium's domain, so some level of torture is going to be expected. The trick is not to dwell on it, not to get bored, not to be upset at having to wait. Just take it in stride and deal with it.

Finally, after almost an hour of waiting, another set of double doors at the opposite end of the little waiting room area opens. Four pear-shaped demons waddle out of Tedium's office, grumbling and talking to each other in demonic. They're all wearing white button-down shirts, neckties, dark pants, and shiny black shoes that resemble sneakers trying to pretend to be dress shoes. It seems they'd been in a meeting. They're on the short side. The tops of their heads barely come up to my chin—and I'm not the tallest critter in the world.

"What are those?" whispers Sierra.

"Middle managers," says Sam.

"You can go in now," says the desk imp.

"Thanks." Sam nods at him.

We enter Tedium's office, which looks the same as it did before, only now it smells like stress and charcuterie burps.

"Ahh, Sam." Tedium smiles. "That was surprisingly fast."

"Sorry." My brother sets the silver bottle up on the desk. "I filled it."

Tedium picks up the bottle and examines it. "So you did." He unstoppers it and sniffs. "Oh, my. This is wonderful. Exquisite." He spins his chair around to face away from us and sets the silver bottle on a cabinet beside some tumbler glasses.

Oh wow. That thing really is a liquor decanter. Does he *drink* the essence of anguished boredom? Did this demon just basically send us on a liquor store run?

"Now then." Tedium spins to face us, his bowtie practically twitching with excitement. "I suppose it would only be fair of me to consider the favor Olmaz owes me repaid."

Here we go. It would be fair but...

Tedium opens a drawer and pulls out a length of fancy scroll paper, which he unfurls on the desk. "Would you mind doing me one more small, tiny favor?"

Sam squeezes his hands into fists. He's fighting the urge to say 'we had a deal.'

"It is very small." Tedium picks up a giant quill and dips it in blood red ink from a bottle nearby. "And not required for me to send this document to Olmaz. It's a side request."

"Oh." Sam relaxes. "What is it?"

Tedium continues writing for a moment, then sets his quill in a holder before puffing at the scroll. Smoke peels off the writing as if his breath ignites it. "A simple delivery." He rolls the scroll up, sets a small cube of red wax on the seam, then picks up a baseball-sized silver imp statuette. As soon as he presses it down on the wax, a tiny scream of agony fills the air. I can't tell if it's coming from the wax cube or the imp statute... but it's really unsettling.

Ashley raises both eyebrows. Soph and Sierra lean back.

"There you go." Tedium sets the statuette back on its base and hands the scroll to Sam. "Give that to Olmaz."

"That's the delivery?" Sam tilts his head.

"No, that is your favor complete." Tedium opens another drawer and pulls out a small envelope that looks a bit like a gothic holiday card all black and purple, also wax sealed. To our surprise, he leans forward and offers it to Sierra. "This is the delivery. My dear, would you be so kind as to give this to Mrs. MacDonald?"

Somewhat stunned, Sierra reaches up and takes the card with a 'say what' expression. "Umm. Okay. It's not gonna hurt her, is it?"

"Not at all. In fact, she will be quite happy." Tedium smiles. "She's earned a holiday bonus this year for excellent performance."

"Wait," I say. "MacDonald is a demon?"

Tedium glances at me. "Isn't it obvious? No mortal is capable of making an entire room of eleven-year-olds fall asleep in under five minutes simply by talking."

Heh. Yeah, that tracks.

Sierra laughs. "Umm, sure I'll give it to her. She's going to freak the hell out that I know."

He waves dismissively. "It will be fine."

Another pear-shaped demon barges in. "Sir, Insurance is falling behind. The Obscure Justifications and Minutiae Technicalities teams need support, pronto."

Tedium sighs, then looks at us. "My apologies. There was a flood in Florida last night. My people are struggling to come up with creative ways to disqualify insurance claims." He looks at the middle manager in the doorway. "All right. Reallocate teams 1140 through 1155 for the rest of the week. That should be enough."

"Thank you, sir." The pear-shaped demon bows graciously before scurrying off.

"I think we're done here." Sam also bows at Tedium. "Thanks."

The boss demon nods once at us.

We waste no time leaving before some other complication comes out of nowhere and bites us in the butt. Naturally, we cannot simply make the portal right where we are, and have to walk all the way across the building to the place we arrived. Six puddles of cat vomit, two hairballs, nine Lego brick ambushes, three 'employee in a hurry crashing into us, spilling coffee all over us' and two pinky toe-to-the-bedpost collisions later, we reach the portal.

Like battle-hardened veterans of some distant desert warfare, we stagger over to it and step through to our basement. The wonderful cat-puke-free carpet is amazing. A small demon pokes its head out behind us, cackles madly, and snaps its fingers right before the portal closes.

Out of nowhere, I have to pee as bad as I've ever had to pee.

Ashley's doing the dance, too. If the expression on the Littles' faces is any indication, all five of us are seconds away from wetting ourselves.

"What the hell?" I blurt. "That's not supposed to happen to me anymore."

Sam grunts. "Five of us. Three bathrooms."

"Ugh!" blurts Sierra. "I can't hold it anymore."

"I wanted to go right to Olmaz..." Sam grabs himself and squirms. "They love being annoying and inconvenient."

Sierra takes one step before deciding that sprinting would be a grave mistake. She shuffles down the hall to the mini bathroom.

Sophia has to go so bad she's crying. Whoa.

"Uhh. I'll take her upstairs," I say. "Ash, can you wait for Sierra to be done down here? Sam, use the toilet downstairs."

With a battle plan in mind, we break up.

I rush all the way up to the second floor, carrying Sophia to the bathroom with the cursed bathtub. I set her on her feet by the door and wait, dreading what's going to happen when my turn comes. How the hell do I have to go? I didn't drink anything. What, exactly, is going to come out of me?

A few minutes later, I knock. "Soph, you okay in there?"

"It's *still going*."

"What the hell?"

The echo of her voice grumbling around the bathroom comes through the door. "It's trying to be as annoying as possible, making us wait."

I squirm and try my best to hold it. Good grief I'm tearing up it's so bad. What the actual frick is going on?

Swear I'm literally half a second away from saying to hell with it and just going outside to the backyard. I have to pee so bad it's getting to the point I no longer care if anyone catches me watering the lawn.

Finally, Sophia shoves the door open and staggers out into the hall looking exhausted. "I hate demons. That was not nice."

"Yeah…" I gently pick her up, rotate ninety degrees, and set her down out of my way, then rush into the bathroom.

Five minutes later, I am baffled.

I haven't had to go like that since the Family Summer Road Trip when I was ten and I forgot to go before leaving the house. Yeah, I was literally crying it hurt so bad by the time Dad finally pulled into a rest station on the highway. There's a point where after holding it so long and having to go so badly, it's actually difficult to get things started. I thought my plumbing broke. I was freaking out. Like, how can I have to go *so damn bad* but nothing's happening.

Fortunately, that did not happen to me now.

What *did* happen was… cartoonishly weird. Let's just say there is no way *that* much should have come out of me. Freaking demons. If I ever end up in Heck again, I'm going to punch one of them for that. Then again, maybe not. If they can make a vampire go to the bathroom, who knows what they could do to me if they were genuinely angry. That was a parting prank, not an attack.

Eventually, we all reconvene in Sam's bedroom.

"No one shall ever talk of this event again," says Sierra.

"Why did they do that to us?" whines Sophia.

"Because it's annoying… and they probably thought it hilarious." Sam shrugs. "Okay, everyone good?"

We all nod.

Sam opens his closet, revealing a cave tunnel going downward.

By now, his fire spell has worn off us, but it's not a huge problem. This cave isn't as hot as Heck. It's warm, for sure, but it's no worse than summer beach sand. We file down the cave to the giant chamber at the bottom.

Olmaz is waiting for us. Guy's bigger than I remember. The massive wings are a nice touch. He kinda looks like a big scary thing from a Frazetta painting, though far more handsome in the face— like if someone made a cross between a stereotypical demon lord and... like... Robin Williams' genie from *Aladdin*. Though Olmaz isn't anywhere near as funny. He does seem to be nice, though. Obviously, he's got a soft spot for Sam.

"Here." Sam offers the scroll. "This is from Tedium."

Olmaz breaks the wax seal on the scroll—which wails in pain again—and opens it. He glances over the writing, then nods, seeming pleased. "Thank you, Samuel." The demon collapses the scroll, tucks it in one of his belt pouches, and faces Sierra. "So, you wish to be the best artist in the world?"

Sierra blinks, glances at Sam with a 'huh' face, then blinks again at Olmaz. "Umm, no. I never said that. I just don't want to suck. I'd like to be good enough to like, umm, do art for a living. I'd love to be able to design the art stuff for video games. I'm not trying to be famous or 'the best in the world' or anything cheesy like that."

Olmaz rubs his beard in thought, then nods. He checks through several of the large pouches hanging on his belt before finding what he's looking for and opening one. He pulls out a large potion bottle. From another pouch, he takes a seemingly ordinary, plain white mug.

We stand there quietly watching as Olmaz bites the stopper off the potion bottle and pours the contents into the mug, which he then hands to Sierra.

"Drink that, child."

Sierra sniffs at the mug. "This smells like coffee."

Olmaz raises an eyebrow. "Where do you think creatives get their power from?"

Ashley mutters, "LSD?"

Olmaz coughs. "Fair point, but not where I was going."

"She's only twelve!" I swat at Ashley, making her laugh. "We are not giving her LSD." I look at her. "You are not taking LSD."

Sierra blinks at me. "What the hell is LSD?"

"Good." I nod at her.

"What?" She stares.

"Keep it that way."

"What way?" Sierra pokes me.

"You not knowing what it is." I point at the mug. "Go on, drink your coffee."

"Muse elixir," whispers Olmaz.

"Behold the power of the sacred bean," says Sam.

I laugh. "You sound like Dad."

Sierra narrows her eyes at me.

Oh damn. That's a 'you won't tell me but the internet will' face if I've ever seen one. Sigh.

She sips from the mug, then evidently realizing it's not too hot, chugs the rest. She stands there looking bewildered for a second or two, then releases a small burp. "I don't feel any different."

"Give it a few minutes," says Olmaz with a wink.

Sierra's eyes cross briefly, and she gazes into space.

Dammit. I thought that was coffee, not LSD. Well, she doesn't look high, merely... distracted like she's having the mother of all daydreams—or like Neo in *The Matrix* while they're uploading kung fu into his brain. Here's hoping it worked.

"Thanks for your help." I nod to Olmaz and take Sierra by the arm.

"Happy to be of assistance." The demon half-bows at us.

"C'mon. You look like you should lie down for a bit."

Sierra doesn't reply, continuing to stare into space. I lead her back up the cave to the normal world.

CHAPTER 26

OLMAZ THE SOMEWHAT WISE

MONDAY AFTERNOON

Sam started to follow the others, then stopped, turning back to look up at Olmaz.

"Hmm?" asked the demon.

"Was that just normal coffee?"

Olmaz grinned. "Mostly. Not entirely."

"You just gave her coffee." Sam scratched his head. "We could've done that by going to the kitchen."

"I said mostly, Samuel." Olmaz patted him on the head. "It was, in fact, a muse elixir. Your sister has what it takes already to be an artist—an overly vivid imagination. She merely needs practice."

"So, that coffee didn't do much?"

"She thinks it's giving her a boost, so it is giving her a boost."

"Did you trick us?" Sam folded his arms.

Olmaz chuckled. "No, Samuel. Not entirely. There is some power in the elixir beyond that of ordinary coffee, though you should not brush off the potency of normal coffee."

"You really sound like Dad now." Sam laughed.

"The elixir will give her a little help beyond what you might expect from the average cup of Starbucks." Olmaz plucked at his beard. "Mostly knowledge. Consider it a few years of art school in a cup."

Sam nodded. "Cool. Thanks."

"Seriously, kiddo, she only needed a little push." Olmaz glanced off in the direction the others had gone. "Some mortals do have gifts. Some don't. If you asked me to turn Daryl into an artist, that would have been a serious task. Might have had to call in a genie for that."

"Oof." Sam cringes. "Daryl's not that dumb."

"It has nothing to do with dumb. Merely aptitude and imagination."

"Oh. Okay." Sam exhaled in relief. "Umm. So, you know how you told me there's a demon messing with the tub?"

"Yes..."

"I can't seem to get it to show itself. What am I doing wrong? Where is it?"

"Where do you think it is?" asked Olmaz.

Sam frowns. "In Heck?"

"Hah." The demon laughed. "Good guess."

"So... I have to go back there?"

Olmaz made a so-so hand tilt gesture. "That would be one way to do it. There is an easier way."

"There is?"

"Yes. Use his link to the tub to summon him." Olmaz poked Sam gently in the stomach. "Whether or not you realize it, you do have some magical powers when it comes to interacting with demons."

Sam idly scratched the spot. "Yeah, I kinda figured that out by now. So... I can drag it out of the tub?"

"More or less." Olmaz moved beside Sam, took a knee, and put an arm around him like a coach showing a little leaguer proper batting form. "Concentrate on the bathtub and you should feel the demon's presence, and then the connection back to where it is hiding. Think of it like mentally grabbing the cord and pulling on it. You will be able to drag him into manifestation."

Sam found it easy to picture and feel what Olmaz described. Honestly, it seemed so basic he felt a little dumb for not having found it by himself already. Then again, he'd been a bit preoccupied doing the thing for Tedium. "Cool. Okay. Gonna try that."

"Excellent." Olmaz stood and gave him a back pat. "Remember to be careful about what you agree to if you make a deal."

"I will." Sam waved and ran off toward his bedroom.

CHAPTER 27
SCRY BABY

TUESDAY, LATE AFTERNOON

I sacrificed Monday night on the altar of futility.

That means I spent most of it doing homework. For at least the next few months, I'm still a college girl. Professor Black's writing class Monday evening hit me with an annoying assignment. I have to write a 'persuasive essay' on a randomly chosen topic. The one I got was arguing *against* the widespread adoption of electricity as a power source as would be written by someone alive during the War of the Currents. That's when Thomas Edison and Nikola Tesla got into a fight over DC vs. AC current.

Ugh. That sounds stupid but whatever. I cheated. Since Dalton was around back then, I poked him for help. He still remembered some of the stupid things the anti-electricity people used to say. It's pretty much the same thing people always do. New technology comes out and it's super scary and evil and will destroy society... right up until it doesn't. I feel like an idiot making these dumb arguments I don't believe in. I suppose that's the point of this class, right? To train students to be able to write persuasively about anything.

Oh well. At least we only have to turn them in and not present them to the class.

I hope. If Professor Black decides to surprise ambush us with an 'and now, everyone, read your crap to the class' thing... she's going to learn what vampire mind control is capable of. Nothing bad. Just going to delete that presentation idea right out of her thought process. She can read the essays and grade them silently without any public speaking involved. I'm sure the poor guy who got the assignment to argue *against* the abolishment of slavery is really going to appreciate not having to say that crap out loud—at least, I really hope it would bother him. The girl who got the argument *for* abolishing slavery probably wouldn't mind speaking about it.

So anyway, Monday was a mess. However, I'm all caught up with homework for the week. At least, homework I got from SCC. The homework from Wolent, not so much.

I'm sitting there in my room Tuesday afternoon messing around in *Skyrim* again. No matter how many times I get curious and try to play a magic user again, it ends up being frustrating and underwhelming. Why am I doing this to myself? I run out of mana after killing one creature... and my archer character can just kill tons of stuff from perfect safety without ever stopping. They totally underpowered the magic in this game.

I'm not really that focused on the game. It's merely something to do while worrying about the Natasha problem. Maybe after class tonight, I can grab Ashley and we can go back to that grey house and see what the idiot brigade is up to.

Hmm. Speaking of magic. I wonder.

No sooner do I think that thought than the house shakes with the vibrations of a fart played over a loudspeaker.

Sam, Daryl, Jordan, and Ronan all laugh.

Ugh. Boys.

A moment later, another too loud to be real fart happens.

I hear Dad mutter, "that sounded painful" from his office.

All I can picture are the boys holding a microphone to their backsides and farting into it, then laughing. Weird, but I guess that's better than trying to light them on fire.

A foamy creature walks into the room and stares at me.

It takes me a moment to realize what I'm looking at.

Chloe, covered head to toes in shaving cream.

I blink at her. "What are you doing?"

She grins, then darts out into the basement laughing.

Kiddo might be a vampire, but she's still seven. What is it about little kids and shaving cream? Why the heck is she playing in the bathtub at this hour anyway? It's not even four in the afternoon yet.

This is the suburban version of trying to catch a greased-up pig, isn't it? She was totally baiting me into chasing her. Do I take said bait?

The house shakes again with a noise that reminds me of a giant semi-truck doing that thing with their brakes. Was that a fart? Did that come out of someone's butt? If it did, someone needs to call an ambulance right away.

"What the hell was that?" yells Dad.

"Daryl farted," shouts Sam.

"Should I call an ambulance for him?" replies Dad. "Or an exorcist?"

I laugh. Yeah, I am my father's daughter. We think alike.

I spend a few minutes chasing Chloe around the basement. Yes, it is really difficult to get a grip on a soaped-up vampire child who can fly. Eventually, she makes the mistake of going back to the mini bathroom and I trap her in the dead-end hallway. She's laughing her head off as I help her clean up, dry off, and get dressed.

"Why are you taking a bath in the middle of the day?" I ask.

"Sophia told me to," replies Chloe, all innocence.

"What happened?"

"Magic went boom." Chloe holds her arms out to both sides while making a pshoo sound. "I got dirty."

Hmm. It couldn't have been too bad since I didn't hear the blast. Oh well. Remind me to replace the entire can of shave cream she wasted before Dad notices. I situate kiddo back in the room with her tablet, then go upstairs. And before anyone gives me a hard time for letting a seven-year-old bathe alone, there are several mitigating factors here. One: she wasn't in the bathtub, she used the shower downstairs. Two: she cannot drown. Three: I didn't even know she was in there.

Speaking of magic, indeed. Maybe Sophia can help me cheat on my homework, too.

I go up the basement stairs to the kitchen, cross the house, and grab the banister to swing myself around before jogging up to the second story. Our entire upstairs floor smells like a backed-up toilet. I damn near vomit immediately upon taking a breath at the top of the stairs. This cannot be ignored. I hold my breath and storm over to Sam's room, flinging the door open.

The boys are sitting on the floor, gathered around the PlayStation. Blix is there, too... though only Sam and Ronan can see him. Sam, Ronan, Jordan, Blix, and half of my brother's bedroom are covered in dark char as if they'd been at ground zero of a Wile E. Coyote bomb exploding. Daryl is attempting to cover a blast hole in the seat of his jeans. He's the only one not blackened. Dark smoke peels upward from his butt like a howitzer that's just been fired.

Naturally, the boys are *still* laughing.

I facepalm and give Blix a 'knock it off before the Persons In Black show up' stare.

Blix cringes.

The charring disappears. Daryl's pants go back to normal. The smoke stops... all illusions. Even the smell ceases, apparently illusory as well.

Whew.

Fingers crossed if the boys mention the epic fart to anyone it will be dismissed as kids being kids and not an imp with illusion powers and zero impulse control.

At this point I realize it has been a little while since my last visit to Sam's bedroom. He's got a huge plastic habitat on a new little table right next to his frog terrarium. Four or five little furry critters scamper about among the sawdust. The interior is decorated with little plastic houses and a whole bunch of tiny windmills.

I wander over and look more closely at the enclosure. Sure enough, my little brother must have talked the 'rents into allowing him to get pet hamsters. There is little doubt in my mind that Sophia getting to keep Klepto played a small role in this. Rodents in a cage are quite a bit less disruptive to a household than a cat or dog would be, so I'm guessing a compromise occurred.

"What's this?" I ask.

"Oh, I got hamsters." Sam grins. "Early Christmas present."

"Neat." I smile. "Umm… what's up with the windmills? That's kinda weird."

My kid brother wags his eyebrows at me, pauses just long enough, then says, "It's Hamsterdam."

I cringe. "Let me guess, you said that and Dad was immediately on board with letting you get hamsters."

"Exactly." Sam beams, proud of himself.

Considering none of the four hamsters are dead, I'm going to assume Blix spared them experiencing the illusionary farts.

Satisfied there are no major issues here, I cross the hall to Sophia's room.

My kid sister is sitting cross-legged on the floor by a ritual circle of crayons, dolls, and plushies with her back to the doorway… crying into her hands.

Uh oh.

I knock lightly and step in. "Soph? You okay?"

She lifts her head and looks back at me—in a gas mask.

I'm not ready for that sight and jump. "Gah."

"Where did you get a gas mask?" I blink.

"Conjured it. Sam and his dumb friends won't stop farting." She exhales hard, sounding like a tiny Darth Vader.

"The smell is gone." I take a deep breath in my nose. "Was just an illusion."

She grabs the mask in both hands and pushes it upward off her face. One test sniff later, she seems satisfied and takes it off the rest of the way before throwing it aside.

"Why are you crying?" I walk over and sit next to her.

"I stink at this." Sophia grumps.

"No, you don't. You're scarily powerful." I reach over and rub her back.

"I set off a mud explosion." Sophia sniffles. "All I was trying to do was practice a basic levitation and I filled my whole bedroom with mud."

"Is that why Chloe took a shower?" I ask.

"No, she took a shower because I ruined the bathtub. And I told her not to use the tub." Sophia sniffles.

"You did not ruin the bathtub. There's a demon messing with it." I keep rubbing her back. "Why did Chloe need to clean up? Your room looks clean. You got rid of the mud."

"Oh, that happened before the mud. She wanted me to give her an illusion of faerie wings."

"Aww. That sounds cute."

"Except I covered her in..." Sophia flails her arms. "Molasses or something. Magic resistant molasses. I couldn't get rid of it."

I cringe. "Well, whatever it was, she managed to wash it off."

Sophia rests her chin in her hands, elbows on her knees. "I am such a failmage."

"You are not a failmage. Something is messing with you." I pat her shoulder. "Olmaz said so."

"Huh?"

"There's an outside force interfering whenever you try to do magic. It's not that you're bad at it or can't control it."

Sophia sighs. "Thanks."

She doesn't sound too convinced.

"I'm serious, Soph. There's something out there trying to make you think you're doing magic wrong. You aren't." I pull her into a one-armed squish hug. "We'll figure out what's doing it and punch it in the face."

"Think it's another demon?" She glances over at me.

"Maybe. Demon, some sort of critter, probably." I exhale. "Hey, since you're amazing at this, I was wondering if you could help me do something."

Sophia's glumness evaporates. "What's up?"

Behold the power of adored big sister. I hold her emotional well-being in the palm of my hand. I shall not abuse this power... at least not anymore. That whole almost dying and getting back up as a vampire thing has rearranged my priorities. The most important thing to me now is protecting my family, especially the Littles.

But... having a magical sibling is definitely a bonus I shouldn't ignore.

"So, there's a problem I'm dealing with and I'm kinda drawing a blank." I shift to face her, both of us sitting cross-legged on the floor. On a basic level, I explain the Natasha situation. "... so I was wondering if you could maybe attempt to do that scrying thing and figure out what this supposed ancient vampire's name is?"

She bites her lower lip. "Umm. Maybe. I don't suppose you have any pieces of him."

"Nope. I'm not even totally convinced he's real."

"So, you have nothing at all?" She sighs. "That's going to make it difficult."

"Umm. Just a video of them talking about it." I pull my phone out and show her the meeting.

"Wow. They sound like the bad guys from *Scooby Doo*." Sophia rolls her eyes.

I laugh. "Kinda."

She watches the video again, pausing it when there's a good view of the table with the books. A moment later, Klepto the kitten appears in a flash of pink-violet light in front of us with one of those books.

"Holy cow." I laugh. "Did you just yoink one of Topher's books?"

"Yeah. Only borrowing it." Sophia pulls the cover up and peeks inside.

"Better put it back fast. He's an Academic."

"So?" She peers over at me.

"He will absolutely know one of his books is missing and freak out."

Sophia grimaces at the indecipherable writing and closes the book. "Good thing he's dead tired right now."

"Hah." She's got a point. "True. He can't notice his book is missing if he's not awake."

Sophia runs to the bathroom to fill one of her plastic bowls with water, then hurries back. She spends a moment making some adjustments to the ritual circle. To me, it looks like a kid playing with toys, yet, she seems to be double checking the exact positions of every doll, crayon, strip of yarn, strange rune symbol made of construction paper, or small plushie.

Maybe someday I'll get her a real crystal ball. I mean, I got Sierra a dedicated art computer. Might as well do a similar thing for my other sister's talent interest, right? Granted, giving Sierra a computer won't possibly result in anything blowing up or being flooded with pudding.

My sister places one hand on the stolen book, then stares intently into the water bowl.

We sit there in total silence for a few minutes, listening to the sounds of video games and boys laughing from across the hall.

"Eep!" Sophia jumps back, wide-eyed. She looks more startled than scared.

"Everything okay?"

She exhales hard. "Yeah. I think so. Just saw a scary face. I broke the connection before the eyes opened."

"Probably a good idea."

"Rabanus," says Sophia.

"Say what? What the heck is a Rah-bannus?"

She looks at me. "Rabanus. That's the name. Rabanus Vesperus."

"Crap." I grab the phone, open a note app and type that in taking a wild guess at the spelling. "Does that mean there really *is* a dangerous vampire elder out there?"

Sophia shrugs one shoulder. "It means there's definitely an elder out there that this book and the vampire who owns it is looking for." She shrugs both shoulders. "Dunno if they're dangerous, though."

"Did it feel dangerous?"

"Umm. He looked scary. I didn't stay long enough to feel anything."

"Looked scary..."

"Yeah, kinda like a mummy, all brown and corpsey."

Considering this is Sophia, we're probably talking *Scooby Doo* levels of scary, not something from an R rated movie with an actual special effects budget. Most non-Innocent vampires sleeping would freak her out. They look much more corpselike than I do. I just get paler and my lips turn grey. If anyone happened to lift my shirt up, they'd probably see an open knife wound in my chest. Fortunately, it doesn't bleed. This explains why I've ended up in a morgue twice when found by mortals. Though, I think I had a few more marks on me than Scott's knife wound in Gomez. Stupid bombs.

"Dammit."

"What?" asks Sophia.

"This guy is real. Now I have to go to France."

She grimaces. "Why?"

"Aurélie knows someone there who might be able to tell me about this Rabanus guy. I need to figure out if he's really an apocalyptic threat or not."

"Daryl's butt is an apocalyptic threat," mutters Sophia.

I laugh. Yeah, this is the kid who has stopped up our toilet almost every time he's come over. I Don't know what his parents feed him but they need to change his diet.

"Umm." Sophia bites her lip and gives me this nervous look. "I could try opening a portal if you want."

Ashley pokes her head in. "Who's getting slapped by the void tentacle this time?"

Sophia huffs. "No one." A second later, she whispers, "I hope."

Again, the floor shakes under the oppressive weight of a wet blast of flatulence boosted by concert arena speakers.

Sophia reaches for her gas mask.

"Sam?" yells Dad from downstairs. "Will you *please* stop casting Power Word: Fart?! I can smell it down here."

The boys laugh their fool heads off.

"Eww," deadpans Sierra from her room. "Soph? Can you conjure a cork?"

CHAPTER 28
POKING THE VOID OCTOPUS

TUESDAY

I ponder the situation—with Rabanus—for a moment before rubbing my forehead.

"Wait, hang on... everyone calm down." I exhale. "There's a lot we need to figure out before just going to Paris."

"Like what?" Ashley tilts her head.

"Well, like time difference for one." I rake my hands through my hair. "It's like 4:30 now. Is it even dark over there?"

Ashley looks at her phone, her thumbnails clicking at the screen for a few seconds. "Um, it's like ten at night there. Should be fine."

"Okay, Ms. Google. What about that Remi guy?" I gesture at her. "There's gotta be thousands of men named Remi in Paris."

"How many are vampires?" asks Sophia.

"Okay, there's gotta be at least a few dozen." I smirk.

Ashley gets a distracted look for a few seconds. "Remi Durand. We should be able to find him pretty easily, according to Aurélie. Just find a vampire and ask them."

"Wow." Sierra blinks. "You found that on Google?"

"Nope." Ashley laughs. "Aurélie told me."

"Umm. Okay. Yeah, I suppose that makes sense. If he's her friend, he's probably pretty old. Every vamp around here knows who Aurélie is."

Sam runs in, with Ronan right behind him. "Ooh. I wanna go with you to Paris."

"No way." I shake my head. "Mom would kill me."

"Only if she finds out," says Sierra, strolling in as well.

I fold my arms. "As if she won't. This is Mom we're talking about."

Sam, Ronan, and Sierra all give Sophia the look. Mom is definitely going to find out because Sophia will not be able to resist telling her we did something questionable. Guilt will eat at her and eat at her until she confesses.

"Whatever." Sierra shrugs. "It's easier to ask for forgiveness than permission."

"Nope. No way." I shake my head. "I'm going to talk to vampires. I am not bringing four children with me."

Sierra examines her fingernails. "But, we're not ordinary kids. We're... special." She glances at Ronan. "Well, three of us are."

"Still." I hold a hand up at her. "Mom nearly had a heart attack the last time I brought you on a vampy job."

"Aww, Sare..." Sierra stomps. Logic is failing her, so she's slipping back to childish begging.

Okay, that's not like her. She must really want to go. I don't want to be the bad guy here. Aha! I will do what Dad does.

"Look. Fine. If you want to come with me, go ask Mom if it's okay. If she says yes, then fine."

Sierra looks at me like I just said 'no way in hell.'

Sam shrugs. "She let me go harvest suffering from the guards at her work way after bedtime. She might say yes."

Before anyone can say anything else, Sam runs out.

"This is not going to end well." Sierra sighs. "You should've just taken us with you."

"I don't want you to get hurt. We have no way to tell how Euro vamps are going to react to us. Especially you guys. Stefano and Paolo still think I'm the worst vampire ever for hanging out with my mortal family."

"Stefano and Paolo are buttheads." Sierra frowns.

Sam walks back in with Mom in tow. She's still got her coat on, which means she hasn't been in the house for two full minutes yet after getting home from work.

"What's this about Paris?" asks Mom.

"Sec." I give Mom a 'one moment' finger and look at Sam. "Where are Daryl and Jordan? We're talking about this stuff and they're right across the hall."

"It's fine," says Sam. "Blix froze them."

I blink. "He froze them?"

"Yeah. Put them in a limited time loop. They're fine." Sam waves in a 'no big deal' way. "Paused them like a PlayStation game, not frozen like ice."

Not sure what to say to that, so I ignore it for the moment and look at Mom. I explain the Natasha situation and how we need to go talk to Aurélie's friend to see if they know anything about this old vampire and how much of a threat they are.

"So, you're going to Paris to talk to vampires?" asks Mom.

"Basically yeah. Just asking a few questions. It shouldn't take that long." I shrug.

Mom shifts her weight from leg to leg. "I really would rather the Littles stay here. This sounds dangerous."

"See?" I gesture at Sierra.

"Not fair. Sophia gets to go to Paris." Sierra grumbles. "Why can't we all go?"

"Oh, no. Sophia is not going anywhere either." Mom folds her arms.

I wince. "Uhh, Mom? Soph kinda has to."

The Glare of Doom™ falls upon me.

"What?" barks Mom.

I am an immortal vampire with powers beyond mortal comprehension, yet the way Mom is glaring at me makes me feel like I just messed up bad. "Uhh... because she has to open the portal there. If she doesn't go with me, I'm going to be stuck there and have to figure out a way to get back here."

Mom relaxes. Whew. No longer feels like I'm going to get grounded for forty years. "Can't you just take a mirror?"

"No way." I shiver. "Too far. *Way* too far. Even with Blix leading me there, we'd never make it. The mirrorverse is dangerous. The longer the trip, the more risk. Going to Paris from here is basically suicide... or maybe just ending up trapped permanently in the mirrorverse unable to escape. Something horrible would happen to us."

"You could get trapped forever on the Dr. Phil show," says Ashley.

"Gah. I'd rather hug the sun." I fake cower.

Mom frowns. "And bringing Sophia near old vampires isn't dangerous? That's like waving a cupcake at a room full of fourth grade boys."

"Eep!" squeaks Sophia. "I am not a cupcake!"

"Mom, Remi is Aurélie's friend. Possibly ex umm, *friend,* if you know what I mean. They're not going to bite Sophia if she's with me."

"So, you say." Mom paces. "All right. I really don't like this, but if it means you are there and back again in a few minutes, I guess there's no choice."

Sierra grumbles.

Mom seems intent on staying right here to make sure the other kids don't follow me.

That's fine. I appreciate the backup and not having to be the bad guy here.

Sophia approaches her closet door, widens her stance, and holds her arms out toward it.

It occurs to me that she's not dressed to go outside, wearing a plain dress and barefoot. Come to think of it, I'm still in my night shirt. Not great to meet with elder vampires. I zoom downstairs to my room as fast as I can go without damaging the house, and hurriedly change. Ugh. Might as well make a reasonable impression, so I do the nasty and put on a skirt suit with a nice blouse, like I'm going to a job interview at Mom's company. Bleh. I feel awkward. I haven't worn stockings and kitten heels in a while.

By the time I finish getting dressed, I realize Ashley's in here with me also having changed. She went for the adorable dress. Great. I'm ready for a job interview and she's ready for an 1890s social gathering. Whatever. That portal's going to be open any second now. No time to argue.

We rush back upstairs.

Everyone is still where we left them.

A small black cloud of annoyance hangs over Sierra's head. (Not literally, this is a metaphor). Sam seems bored but also faintly smiling like he's up to something. Oh no.

Magical light flashes out from the seams around the door.

I rush around and gather up Sophia's winter boots, a warm pair of leggings she can pull on under her dress, and a winter coat.

Sophia opens the closet door revealing a long dark passageway that ends in the distance at another closet, more likely a storage room considering the brooms leaning against the side.

"We good?" I ask.

Sophia nods. "Yes. I'm completely sure this goes to Paris."

I step in first. The passage isn't cold, which is a good sign. We are, after all, going to another building there.

Ashley follows, with Sophia right behind us.

We're about ten steps in from the closet when a startlingly loud wet *slap* comes from behind. I twist around to look back right as a giant black void tentacle extending out of the nothingness above us yanks Mom into the darkness after having wrapped around her head.

Sierra's clinging to Mom's legs, and Sam's wrapped around Sierra's legs.

Mom crashes into Sophia, shoving her into Ashley, and all of them slam into me.

The rest of the black passageway zips by in an instant. I go face-first into the wooden door at the other end, burst through it, and do a double lutz faceplant on a stone floor. Judging by the pain in my back, most of my family is on top of me.

"Ouch," I mutter.

"*Quesquecette merde?!*" exclaims a woman nearby, along with the sound of something heavy being dropped.

"That means 'what the F,'" whispers Ashley.

"Yeah," I groan. "Kinda assumed."

CHAPTER 29
MERELY THE KING OF FRANCE

TUESDAY

Sierra groans and rolls off the top of the pile, tumbling down to land on the floor beside me, both hands clamped over her nose.

"You okay?" I ask.

"Yeah. Just mashed my nose into Mom's back."

"Sorry." Ashley shifts her weight to the side and climbs off me.

I push myself up off the floor. We're in a basement of some kind. Mom's sitting on the stone floor, her whole head covered in black slime. She looks unhurt but disoriented as hell.

A grandmotherly woman stares aghast at us from about fifteen feet away at the bottom of a stairway near the box she'd been carrying—and dropped when we exploded out of her closet. It appears to contain a few dozen fist-sized globs of dough wrapped in some sort of cloth.

Ashley's already on damage control, having derped the poor old lady.

Sam runs out of the closet into the basement, looking around with an expression of 'wow, this is cool.'

"So that was the plan, huh?" I fold my arms at Sam. "Set off a void tentacle to grab Mom and then follow her?"

Sam shakes his head. "No. Honest. We didn't do that."

"Then why were you smirking before Sophia opened the portal?" I raise an eyebrow at him.

"Because I kinda figured *something* would happen." He shrugs. "Just kinda felt it coming. My smile was an 'oh, this is going to be good' smile. Not a 'we're going to get away with something we were told not to do' smile."

"I legit tried to stop Mom from being pulled through." Sierra sighs, sounding genuinely annoyed. "Being strong doesn't help me much since I still only weigh forty pounds. That stupid tentacle yoinked us both like we weighed nothing."

She is, of course, understating things. She's not forty pounds. Of course, she is skinny, as are we all. Thanks, Dad. If not for Mom's influence on my genetics, I'd probably still look like a stick. Didn't get hips until I was like fifteen. Anyway... we made it to France.

"Mom's going to be mad," says Sam.

"Mom?" Sierra pats her on the cheek. "Mom?"

"I'm here." Mom looks around. "What the heck happened?"

"Void tentacle," we all say at the same time.

Mom looks at Sierra. "We're in Paris?"

"I think so." Sophia gazes around. "Smells like bread in here."

"Definitely France." Ashley gestures at the older woman. "I can't understand anything she's thinking. Sounds like French."

Sierra flashes an apologetic grimace-smile at Mom. "I tried to stop it from grabbing you, but it just pulled me in too."

"Sorry, I suck at magic." Sophia looks down.

Well, there goes my developing theory that Sophia did it on purpose to avoid the argument. If she yanked everyone through the portal, then no one would need to fight over us not bringing Sierra and Sam along. Though, Sam would've accepted Mom's decision without being grumpy about it. Sierra probably would have been surly for the rest of the day.

I hand Sophia her winter stuff. "Here."

"Thanks." She sniffles.

"You don't suck at portals. Something is messing with you, remember." I pat her on the head.

Mom looks at me, her expression like she can't figure out how angry to be.

"Relax." I grimace. "Going to Paris and talking to old-ass vampires are two completely different things."

My mother raises an eyebrow.

"We're here, yeah, but that doesn't mean I need to take the Littles with me to find Remi." I gesture at her. "Since you're here, you can stay with them and check Paris out until we're done."

Sierra grins. "Sare's got a point. I just wanted to see Paris, not the vamps. Seeing them would've been cool, but I can accept it's probably too dangerous for kids. But... umm... if you get into a fight, you might need backup."

I laugh. "I am not getting into any fights here. This is just a go and talk thing. Really not thinking they'd be terribly open to the idea of letting mortals in there, especially little ones."

"It would be like waving a plate of cupcakes at them." Sam laughs. "We're like candy."

"Ugh." Sierra looks down. "Okay. You're probably right."

"Why is that old lady staring into space?" asks Ronan.

"Because she's not going to remember seeing us." Ashley grins at us. "We've got about five minutes to get out of here before she snaps out of it."

I head for the stairs. "Come on. You guys can explore Paris while Ash and I do the thing."

"Sierra, you are not going outside like that," says Mom. "Where is your coat?"

"At home," says Sierra in a more than slightly sarcastic tone.

"Where else would it be? If I was really planning to sneak through, wouldn't I have it with me?"

Mom sighs, clearly annoyed at the tone. "True. That does present a bit of a problem."

Blix snaps his fingers, and a heavy winter coat appears on Sierra. It's not *her* coat, but it will do.

"That is cool." Sierra looks down at herself.

Blix babbles.

"It's a temporary conjuration." Sam waves at the imp in a 'my turn, hit me' manner. "They'll last for about an hour."

Blix conjures a coat for Sam as well... then Ronan, who also needs temporary boots since he's in socks.

"We should be back before that." I exhale. "Unless unforeseen complications happen."

"Young lady, so help me," says Mom, "If you get blown up again, I don't know what I'm going to do. I forbid you from setting off another explosive device."

That's overload. I hug her. "Okay, Mom. I promise I won't do that."

Blix conjures a small towel for Mom to wipe the void tentacle slime off her face. He then makes a 'duh' face before throwing it aside and de-sliming her the same way he got rid of the cat puke in Heck.

We make our way upstairs into what seems to be a bakery shop on a street corner. Ashley radiates her charm enough that the older guy and two young men working there don't notice us until we're outside on the street.

"All right," says Mom. "How long do you think this will take you?"

I shrug. "No idea. Never did this before. It depends on how long it takes us to find this guy. Once we find him, probably not much more than ten minutes unless we have to go through some super annoying 'we're sorry for entering your city without asking first' bullshit task."

"That's a thing?" Sierra scrunches her nose.

"Yeah. Euro vamps are weird like that." I shrug.

Mom blinks at me. "Sarah?"

"Yes?" I look at her.

"I just realized what you're wearing. You look great. You should dress up more often."

"Thanks." I fidget.

"She looks like a kid dressed up as her professional mother for Halloween," deadpans Sierra.

I stick my tongue out at her. "I am a mature adult!"

"Uh huh." Sierra laughs.

She shares my opinion of dressing up. I'd much rather live in sweatshirts and jeans, or just pajamas. Not a huge fan of stockings. Skirts are meh. Heels are awful, which is why these kittens are as high as I go. Even they are kinda annoying. I hate clicking when I walk.

"Okay then. Meet back here in forty-five?" asks Mom.

"That works." I look at my phone. It's 4:54 p.m. Of course, that's Washington time. A few finger taps bring up an app with Paris local time. "Uhh, problem."

"What?" asks Mom.

"It's 1:54 a.m. here. Probably shouldn't run around with kids." I show her the phone.

Sophia waves her hand in a circle above her head. In seconds, she, Sierra, Sam, and Ronan all rapidly age into their early twenties. Or at least look like they do. The sounds of their breathing still comes from the same height it was before. Sophia looks pretty much the same, but taller. Sierra's still thin but almost has this Linda Hamilton from *Terminator* badassery around her. Sam sorta looks like Dad, but younger. Ronan totally resembles one of those long-haired pretty boy dudes from an Eighties glam rock band.

This is clearly Sophia's guessing how they'd look like as adults and not what will happen naturally.

"Gah!" blurts Ronan, his voice still that of a nine-year-old. "What the hell?"

"Illusion," says Sophia. "No one will mess with us. Just, uhh, don't talk 'cause we still sound like kids."

Oh, this isn't possibly going to go wildly wrong in any of a thousand ways.

Might as well get it over with fast. "Okay. Meet back here by 5:50 p.m. our time."

Mom nods. She looks around, seeming no longer upset at this change of events. There's kind of an 'I always wanted to visit Paris' gleam in her eye. Uh oh. It might fall on the Littles to make sure Mom is back here on time.

Heh.

I nod to Ashley. We dart off to the nearest alley away from the handful of pedestrians still out and about at this hour. Once we have the cover of shadow, we fly. As per protocol, at least as best as I can remember, since we arrived without prior notice, we are expected to make ourselves known right away to the power structure. It's tempting to find this Remi guy, talk to him, and disappear, but Follows Rules Girl is there staring at me with 'you remember what happened last time.'

Yeah. Better to deal with the formalities and then go look for Remi, so I don't get stuck spending a week doing an apology quest to make up for the insult of ignoring the political power here.

The two of us cruise around in an expanding circle, checking out anyone we see on the ground. It takes us about six minutes and close to a hundred people spotted before we finally encounter a vampire. He's an older guy, probably in his thirties, hanging out near the mouth of an alley, leaning on the wall and waiting for a victim.

Or so he looks to be.

Maybe he's just bored and enjoying the night.

I fly down to land deeper in the alley, far enough away not to seem threatening but close enough that he spots me right away. Ashley floats down to land beside me.

The French vampire blinks at us.

Not sure if he's never seen flying vamps before or if it's merely the contradiction in our outfits. I look modern and all business while Ashley stepped out of the screen of a historical anime. She is cute, though. That dress is totes adorbs.

I open Google translate on my iPhone and type in, "Hi. We just got to Paris and need to announce ourselves. Also, we're trying to find someone named Remi Durand, if you know where we can find him, that would be amazing."

I hit the speaker button on the French side of the translator and let the AI voice speak.

The man looks at us, at the phone, and back to us.

"You are American?" he asks in heavily accented—but passable —English.

"Yes." I nod.

"'Ow long you stay?" he asks.

"Just a few minutes. We only need to ask a question or two and we're going right back home."

The guy makes a face that could only mean 'Americans are so strange' before shrugging, then waving at us to follow him.

He walks briskly out of the alley onto the street. With nothing else to do, I follow, holding Ashley's hand like we usually do when slightly nervous in unfamiliar surroundings. Like something straight out of *Grand Theft Auto*, this vampire jumps in front of the first car to roll by, forcing it to stop. The driver leans out and starts shouting at him angrily. Vamp dude reaches in the window and yanks the guy out one-handed, glares into his eyes, then tosses the derpified man to the sidewalk before getting in the car behind the wheel.

"'Op in."

Ashley blinks at me.

Follows Rules Girl is having a complete meltdown. Ash eventually grabs me and sorta pushes me into the car while I'm not really able to make myself do it. We get in the back like this is an Uber or taxi. The French vamp doesn't seem to mind that neither of us sit up front with him.

I stare into space, trying to process the fact that we legit just carjacked someone. Only the knowledge that the owner of the car didn't get hurt keeps me from having a total meltdown. Instead, I sit there in numb silence, begging Karma not to bite me in the ass for this.

We careen through the narrow streets of inner Paris at a speed far too high for comfort. At least the driver has superhuman reflexes, probably the only reason we don't end up in a twisted mass of burning metal. Some of these streets seem too narrow to be real. Like... are they even meant for driving on or just bicycles?

Guilt over stealing a car puts me in enough of a mental fog. I'm not really aware of time going by until the car stops. We're parked on the street in what appears to be a nice residential area surrounded by big, expensive looking houses.

Our guide gets out of the car and starts walking toward one of the houses where a large open area in front of it holds a fountain and circular courtyard where a smattering of cars are parked. This place isn't quite a mansion or manor. It's still big, and three stories tall. Looks old but in a good way. Not run down at all. Just... old and probably expensive.

I scramble to get out of the stolen car and hurry after the guy, who isn't waiting for us.

The click of my dress shoes on the pavement feels as loud as gunfire. After like ten steps, I float the rest of the way to make the noise stop.

By the time I make it to the front door—the place doesn't have a porch or stairs—the vampire who led us here is already talking to a butler-looking guy who answered his knock. He gestures at us while chattering rapidly in French.

The butler type guy says something about Americans, then gives us an almost impressed look before nodding at the carjacker vamp.

I have no idea what he really said, but I'm going to guess he's shocked that American vampires are doing the custom thing and going straight to the head vampire in the area to announce ourselves.

"Good evening, ladies," says the butler. His English is much better than the other guy's. Still has an accent, but it's nowhere near as thick.

The one who drove us here waves to me before heading back to the car and driving off. I assume he's going to ditch it somewhere. Ugh. I hope he doesn't destroy it and the poor man gets his car back.

I look away from the distancing car to the butler. "Hi. Umm. Good evening."

"Hello," says Ashley.

"Come in, please. It's frigid out there." The man backs away from the door, opening it more so we can get in.

I step through into an ornate antechamber that connects to a wide corridor going straight into the building. This is all so lavish and opulent looking but, I'm just used to normal size houses. Nothing here looks overly expensive or a conspicuous showing of wealth. It's merely a massive house full of stuff that has likely collected over many, many years. There's even a suit of medieval plate armor on a stand in the hallway. Neat.

"You have been commanded to present yourselves here? Snacks?" asks the butler.

"Uhh, no. We're not mortals."

He tilts his head at me in mild confusion.

Ashley and I exchange a glance, then both extend our fangs at the same time.

This gets him to raise both eyebrows. "How curious. You both must be very new."

"I'm sorry if this is inappropriate," I say. "I'm not exactly very experienced at visiting places. I do remember it's tradition to announce ourselves to the person in charge when arriving."

Butler guy smiles. "Indeed. It's not too often visitors from the States honor the old ways. It is good to see some of you know to show respect."

Yeah, that's me. Follows Rules Girl.

"Might I inquire as to who your sires are?" asks the butler.

This is either going to be no big deal or get me in a heap of trouble.

Hey, says Dalton in my head. *I'm not that famous. Or nefarious, as the case may be.*

I fight back the urge to chuckle. "Dalton Ames."

The man shows no reaction to the name beyond a simple nod of acknowledgement. Whew.

Ha. Ha.

Ashley can't resist the coy smile. She looks like the young intern who's about to tell the manager that's been giving her a hard time that her dad owns the company. "Aurélie Merlier."

The butler blinks, then stares at her. "You jest?"

"No. I'm not making that up. She gave me the Transference." Ashley smiles innocently.

"Well, I should warn you... it will be difficult to pretend in there." He smiles.

I nod. "Yes, we know. Older vampires can read our minds just like we read mortals. We're being honest."

"Very well. Come this way."

The butler leads us down the big hallway to the end, then left at a T. At the end of another long hallway, we go through a set of double doors into what's probably a ballroom. There's no ball going on at the moment, merely about a dozen people in period dress hanging out and being social. Feels like we stepped through a time gate into the Victorian age.

Everyone in here is a vampire. Except for two guys who look well into their forties, the others all seem to have been turned somewhere in their early to mid-twenties. Being here, I can't help but start hearing Marilyn Manson's *The Beautiful People* playing in my head.

As the butler guy leads us into the room, the vamps take notice of our arrival.

Much to my surprise, we don't get stared down at. I do not consider myself to be movie-star pretty no matter what Hunter says. Ashley's always been girl-next-door cute more so than hot. With the whole Innocent thing, the cuteness has increased for both of us. So, we're getting looked at like someone brought their super adorable kids to work for the day.

Butler guy heads right over to one of the two men who looks fortysomething. He speaks briefly in French before nodding and walking off, leaving us there.

The vampire—who at this distance is radiating vibes of oldness and power, even more so than Wolent—approaches us. He smiles politely at us, then gives Ashley a head-to-toe look over. If anyone in this room is the head vampire of Paris, it's this dude. No one else here feels as powerful.

"My name is Sarah Wright. I'm from Washington State in America. We've just arrived and I'd like to officially make myself known and ask for your permission to visit Paris."

The assembled vampires exchange glances.

Wow, I feel like the biggest dork. I've never done this before. What was I supposed to say? Did I just make a total fool of myself.

The man nods at me, then turns his attention back to Ashley. "My, my. What has finally convinced Aurélie to take on the mantle of sire?"

"I asked her really nicely," says Ashley.

The man chuckles. "There must be more to it than that."

"Umm. Well, Sarah is my absolute best friend in the whole world," says Ashley. "We're basically sisters. She accidentally got turned, and I thought she died, and I couldn't handle the idea of not being with her anymore, and then I found out what happened to her. I didn't want her to have to deal with me getting old and dying someday, so..."

"How did Aurélie come into this?" asks the man.

I explain my somewhat awkward entrance to vampire society and how Aurélie took me under her wing, eventually leading Ashley to meet her since I still kept mortal associations and one thing led to another.

"Ahh, that sounds like her." He gazes into the distance. "I do wish she would visit sometimes."

"Wait." I blink. "Are *you* Remi Durand?"

He smiles, then laughs. "You did not even know this? Of course I am."

"You're the head vampire of Paris?" Ashley raises her eyebrows. "Am I supposed to curtsey?"

He waves dismissively. "No need to bother with that level of formality. Though it is France... not merely Paris."

Oh wow. Aurélie's ex-boyfriend is the vampire king of France. Or maybe ex-boyfriend. He does seem kind of fond of her, and she did seem a little wistful talking about him. Maybe they're not so much ex as merely separated by distance. Then again, Aurélie is kinda umm... polyamorous. So, who knows what the heck the story really is. I don't need to pry.

"Sorry if I'm doing this wrong," I say. "I'm not really a political critter."

He laughs. "Don't worry about it. I was wondering why you were being so formal."

Cheesy smile is all my brain can summon in response.

Remi puts an arm around Ashley. "Come. Let us sit and talk."

He's escorting her in a rather familial sort of way. Dude's not creeping on her at all. It's more like she's the daughter of his sister or perhaps even stepdaughter. Ashley doesn't seem to mind.

We go to a small private table and sit... and proceed to make small talk. A mortal guy stops by long enough to set three goblets of blood on the table like a waiter bringing wine. Takes a second for my still normal brain to get past the ick factor of blood in a cup. Once I get a whiff of it (smells like cherry Coke) I cast aside any hesitations and help myself. It would be rude not to.

A slightly longer than brief period passes where every vampire in the room makes the social duty of stopping by to greet/welcome Aurélie's progeny. Not that I'm yesterday's cat food that's been left out overnight, but... Aurélie is apparently a big deal here. They are pleasant to me and say hello, but it's very obvious they're curious about the girl she agreed to give the Transference to.

Finally, the parade of vampires—picture me saying that with an overdone French accent—ends and we resume having a more or less private conversation with Remi.

He is mostly asking us simple questions about how we're handling the adjustment to vampire life, plus a lot about Aurélie. Yeah, this guy is quite fond of her. As much as I am growing more and more anxious to get back to the bakery at the agreed-upon time to meet Mom, there is no way I'm cutting this guy off or interrupting him. Ashley seems completely fine chattering away with him right up until her entire body posture shifts and she starts speaking fluent French with him.

Oh boy. That's not Ashley anymore. I think Aurélie has borrowed her body.

Really hope they don't do anything icky. If Ashley technically counts as Aurélie's vampire daughter, that would be super messed up. Remi gives off no weird vibes, like he's thinking of her as some sort of manifestation of Aurélie here. She's basically a paranormal version of a cell phone. This goes on for about fifteen minutes or so before Ashley returns, fighting the urge to laugh. I'm sure it felt rather strange to lean back and let someone else take over her body.

Remi shifts his attention to me.

"I can tell you are pressed for time and in something of a hurry," says Remi. "Your... mortal family is waiting?"

"Yeah." I grimace smile. "Aurélie thought you might know something about this problem I'm dealing with." I explain the situation with Natasha. "Have you ever heard of a vampire named Rabanus Vesperus?"

At that, Remi blinks. "That is a matter of concern."

"Uh oh." A sinking feeling weighs in the pit of my stomach. "How bad? These idiots think he's in a sarcophagus and they're hoping to wake him up."

"According to legend," says Remi, "to unseal that sarcophagus would destroy the vampire doing it."

"Ouch," says Ashley.

Remi nods. "It could not be done by accident. They would need to understand what they are doing and willingly surrender their existence. Rabanus would then awaken, mad with the hunger of a millennia of slumber. He would certainly consume upwards of twenty lesser vampires before he regains his sensibilities. Please tell me you are not contemplating releasing him."

"No. No way." I shake my head. "Exact opposite. My job is to stop some idiots from doing that. Honestly, I had no idea if the elder they were looking for was even real or if they're chasing ghost stories."

"Unfortunately, Rabanus Vesperus is quite real," says Remi in a hushed tone. "At one time, long before I even existed, he was the ruler of our kind over most of Europe. He last walked the Earth in the waning days of the Roman Empire."

"Wow. That's old." Ashley blinks.

"Assuming he is still intact, he would be more than two-thousand years old." Remi adjusts his glass, rotating it absentmindedly. "His waking up would not be good for any of us. Vampires, in his time, operated under an entirely different set of rules."

"Yeah, I bet." I cringe. "Right, so this guy waking up is bad. Got it."

"Umm, so just destroying vampires near his crypt won't open it?" asks Ashley.

Remi shakes his head. "As far as I understand the stories, they must be willing to be destroyed specifically to break the seals upon the sarcophagus."

"Wow." I click my fingernails nervously on my glass. "He must have been really bad to end up sealed in a box with rituals."

"The stories talk of an international war among vampires. The new and the old. His side lost. Our current age began." Remi sips from his cup, seeming nervous but contained. "If these people you mention do manage to find this sarcophagus, they must be stopped.

We thought it lost long ago, never to be recovered. Perhaps dumped overboard at sea."

I give an uneasy chuckle. "Well, maybe that is true. I mean, they haven't been able to find it as far as I know. Maybe they won't find it." I swish the remaining blood around in my glass. "Dumb question. If this guy is so dangerous, why did they imprison him in a box rather than destroy him?"

"Because that's the rules," says Ashley in a somewhat derpy voice. "Ancient evils like this must be locked away so they can be a threat in the sequel. Killing them for good is too simple."

I roll my eyes. "Stefano or Paolo would say that vampire kind wanted to keep this guy around as a secret weapon in case mortals ever discovered us and started a war to wipe us out."

Remi chuckles. "That is a possibility, though I dare say the consequences of releasing Rabanus upon the world would be worse than not, even in those circumstances."

"Great. He's a nuclear weapon." Ashley whistles. "Even if the war is going badly for you, it's still an awful idea to use one."

"Exactly." Remi toasts us. "To our continued existence without the start of vampire Armageddon."

We clink glasses.

Wow. Did I really step in it this time? This Rabanus situation feels like it's way, way, way above my pay grade. Fortunately, Natasha and her morons are not. They might be older than me, but I doubt any of them know how to use a sword. If I do things right, it won't come down to violence. I really hate the idea of vampires needing to be destroyed permanently... but if it's either that or the world ends, she's not going to give me much choice.

For a little while more, we keep talking on much nicer topics.

Eventually, Remi seems aware that our timer is running out. He also has stuff to do, you know, being the freaking Vampire King of France. Oy. Eventually, we are able to take our leave in a socially acceptable manner.

The same butler meets us at the exit of the ballroom and escorts us to the front door.

"Good evening, girls. Mr. Durand hopes you will call again sometime."

"Sure. Yeah. I can do that, hopefully once we're no longer worried about a bunch of morons setting off the vampire equivalent of a nuke." I exhale hard.

"That certainly sounds unpleasant," says the Butler. "I wish you luck with that."

"Thanks." I smile at him and start walking across the little courtyard, heels clicking.

Ugh. I hate loud shoes.

"Well, that was nice," says Ashley. "Remi seems really nice."

"Of course he'd be nice to you." I nudge her. "You're basically like his stepdaughter."

"He was nice to you, too." Ashley grins. "I think he's genuinely a nice man."

"Yeah, I guess. We didn't even get sent on a fetch quest in exchange for his information." I wince at the time on my phone. We're ten minutes late. "That took longer than I thought it would."

She laughs. "True. C'mon. Let's get back to the bakery before Mom freaks out."

CHAPTER 30
FOR ONCE, IT WORKED

TUESDAY

Ash and I fly back to the little corner bakery shop.

That sounds simple, doesn't it? Wasn't quite that easy. I was too busy being all sorts of upset about the carjacking that I didn't pay too much attention to where we went. At least we only spent about six or seven minutes in the car, so we could not have gone *too* far. It might've been ten minutes. Honestly, I wasn't terribly composed.

Don't really need Google satellite view when I'm here and can fly. It's basically the same thing without the internet load times. Getting from Remi's house to the bakery involved flying in a search spiral while studying the layout of the city below us for familiar buildings.

Sophia managed to choose a fairly recognizable place: a corner bakery with large windows.

Threw us off that the lights were out by the time we spotted it. Made it harder to pick out from the sky. Yeah, the people who work there have gone home for the night—or at least upstairs. I think they might live in the same building. Don't blame them. It's getting on toward three in the morning here.

We land in the closest shadowed alley that offers enough cover not to be seen coming out of the sky, then walk half a block to the corner. No sign of Mom or the kids. We stand there for a few minutes, waiting before I start to worry.

Out comes my phone.

I send a text to Mom. 'Sorry we're late. At the shop now.'

She replies, 'we're already downstairs.'

"Oh wow." I put the phone back in my pocket. "They went inside already."

Ashley blinks. "Really? Which one of the kids can pick locks?"

"None of them, as far as I know. Had to be Blix." I grab the door and open it as though locks weren't a thing.

Once Ashley's inside the bakery, I close the door and think about it being locked again. Not going to be responsible for this place getting robbed. Careful not to disturb anything, I make my way across the bakery to the back room and down the stairs to the basement.

Mom and the Littles plus Ronan are all there, looking bored and impatient.

"Sorry." I offer an apologetic smile.

"Unexpected complications?" asks Sierra, with an eyebrow raised.

"Not in the usual way." I pantomime wiping sweat off my forehead. "No extra quests or tasks. So, this Remi guy?"

Ashley flaps her arms. "He's just the vampire king of France."

"Oh, is that all," deadpans Mom.

"Yeah... so uhh, it wasn't exactly easy to rush through talking to him. Had to let him set the pace." I look at Sophia. "Ready to open the closet?"

"Did you learn anything useful?" Sam tilts his head at me.

"Yeah." I nod. "This trip was informative."

"Good or bad?" Sierra bites her lip.

"Oh...." I rock heel to toe, letting my arms sway back and forth. "The morons back in Seattle are only trying to set off the vampire equivalent of a giant nuclear bomb."

Mom lets out a long, slow breath. "I sincerely hope you are not being literal."

"She's not." Ashley leans on me. "They're trying to wake up an old vampire who's going to be insane with hunger and go on a rampage that is likely to destroy modern society and send us back to the dark ages where feral humans scramble to survive in a world dominated by vampires and are either prey or slaves."

"Fuck that," blurts Sierra.

Mom looks at her, then sighs. "It seems rather silly to be upset over language in this situation."

Sierra fidgets, blushing slightly upon realizing she just dropped an F-bomb in front of Mom.

I'm sure her complete lack of defiance is why she's not getting in trouble. The apology—subtle as it is in her body language—is enough for Mom to pick up on.

"Chloe swears all the time and no one complains." Sophia taps one of her winter boots on the floor.

"It's cute when she does it." Ashley laughs.

"And she's from New Jersey." I shrug.

"Am I not cute?" Sierra holds her arms out to either side, totally doing a *Gladiator*—are you not entertained—thing.

Mom palms the back of Sierra's head and pulls her into a hug. "You are adorable. The difference is that Chloe doesn't really know what she's saying. She's repeating stuff she's heard. You know full well what you are saying."

"Oops," says Sierra in a flat tone.

"All right. Everyone's here. Let's get home. It's almost time for dinner." Mom rakes a hand through her hair. "It's going to be a little late."

"That's okay." Sam shrugs. "This was worth it."

Sophia faces the closet, kneading her hands.

I walk up behind her and rest a hand on her shoulder. "You are not a failmage. You can do this. Something out there is messing with you. We'll figure it out."

"You think so?" Sophia looks down.

"Yeah. I do."

Two breaths later, Sophia lifts her gaze off the floor and directs it at the closet. She thrusts her right hand out toward it, setting off an immediate glow of light from behind the door. Both her eyebrows go up and she lets her arm flop to her side.

"Umm. It's open."

"That was fast," I say.

She gives me this 'I know, right?' stare. "Yeah. Umm. It felt a lot different this time."

"Maybe it's the smell of fresh bread." Sam grins.

Mom gingerly opens the closet door, revealing Sophia's bedroom. No black tunnel, no distance, no weird portal effects. It's simply as though this door leads directly to her room. Most important of all, we don't have a void octopus waiting to slap someone.

We all hurry through before the Universe changes its mind about her magic working.

Once everyone's back home, Sophia closes the closet door, concentrates for a second or two, then re-opens it to reveal her closet being all normal and totally not a gateway across the world.

Everyone stands there in a moment of stunned, impressed silence.

"Nice." Sam smiles, then hurries out into the hall. "Blix, please unfreeze the guys."

"*Eem oorba*," chatters the imp.

"Wow. See?" I nudge Sophia. "You did it perfectly. Nothing went weird."

Sophia rubs her chin. "Hmm."

Mom looks at the closet, at us, back at the closet, then sets her hands on her hips. "You did say there is some manner of outside influence harassing her. Do you think it simply lost track of her since we traveled so far in such a short time?"

"Ooh!" Sophia looks up. "Yeah, probably."

"Interesting thought." I tap my foot. "That would imply that whatever is doing this has to know where she is to interfere, which means it or they are doing it actively and it's not like a curse on her."

"Grr." Sophia stomps.

Yes, a tween in purple moon boots stomping in anger is cute. Well, at least in Sophia's case, it is adorable.

Soph paces around. "I wanna stop this thing from messing with me. Maybe I can scry for it."

"If you find out who or what is messing with you, let me know and I will go slap some sense into them." I pat her on the head.

She beams adoringly at me.

"Don't scry over spilled milk?" offers Sierra.

We all groan.

"Daaaaad!" shouts Sophia. "Sierra is punning without a license!"

This, of course, is a joke in reference to one of the small gifts I got him for his last birthday. It was a 007 joke. 'Licensed to pun' instead of kill, on a little gold plaque the size of a business card on a wood backing. He's proudly hung it in his office.

"Uh oh." Mom wags her eyebrows. "You're in trouble now."

"You guys are back?" calls Dad from downstairs.

"Yeah." I shout.

"C'mon down," says Dad. "Dinner's almost ready."

Mom makes one of those nauseatingly gooey faces. Yeah, Dad took care of the cooking while she was busy with us. Ugh. Oh no. They're going to... do stuff tonight I bet once the Littles are asleep.

I just realized I have class tonight.

And, crap. I *had* class this afternoon. Wait, it's not quite over yet. Still have twenty minutes before six. If I get there before everyone leaves, I can make Professor Guillermo think I was there the whole time.

"Blix! Need a mirror please!" I run across the hall to Sam's room.

Does it mean anything that Follows Rules Girl barely looks up from her video game to be annoyed at me for that idea?

CHAPTER 31
THE LESSER EVIL IS STILL EVIL

TUESDAY NIGHT

Blargh.

So, I did it.

Thanks to a mirror and a helpful imp, I made it to SCC before my art history class dismissed. Fortunately, I didn't have to do any mind poking on the teacher. I'm still stuck in high school brain mode. College doesn't take attendance. Guess they figure people are paying for it so if they don't go there, it's on us. It's all about passing the tests and doing the projects.

I did read his mind a little to get an overview of the lecture. Nothing I can't make up for by reading a few chapters in the textbook later. An hour after that class ended, my life science class started. Dr. Calvin Reed is a nice guy with an engaging voice... but he's also a fan of dumping homework on us. Normally, I'd be horrified at the idea of just giving a teacher a mental program to believe I did an assignment. However, I've got a vampire nuclear war to stop. That's a tiny bit more important than his research project.

Not like I'm pursuing a career in science.

Didn't mind poke him yet, but I'm not sweating the deadline. If I manage to fix this Natasha problem fast, then I'll do his homework. If I never find the time for it, well. Sorry Dr. Reed. Making him think I did the project and got a B on it is not going to hurt anyone but me. And it would only hurt me if I actually needed to learn from that project. Again, my future isn't dependent on education anymore so, whatever. And yeah, a B. I'd feel less guilty that way than cheesing an A out of him.

I'm having trouble concentrating on the class anyway since I'm worrying about, you know, the end of the world as we know it. And yeah, I realize that girls my age call everything the 'end of the world as I know it,' but this is honestly literal. My brain constantly teases me with imagined future scenarios ranging from terrifying horror vampire apocalypse scenarios where mortals take one wrong step and are instantly torn to shreds by inhuman savage vampire-like beasts to low-budget cheese-fests. There's even a moment where I caught myself daydreaming about a version of vampire apocalypse in the tone of *Shaun of the Dead*.

Send help.

Ashley is waiting for me outside SCC when I finally escape. Yeah, I could've said screw it and left early... but, Follows Rules Girl knows all my pressure points. It's absolutely silly that I'm so vulnerable to her. I'm in school, so leaving early isn't a thing that good girls do. Ugh. This isn't high school. I'm not going to get detention for cutting class. What the hell is wrong with me?

"You look stressed," says Ashley as I walk up to her.

"Something like that."

"Bad day at class?" She tilts her head.

"Nope. It's the impending ancient doom threatening to devour the world."

"Oh." She nods. "How did you know Dylan blew up the bathroom again?"

I facepalm. Obviously, she knows exactly what I am talking about. "Ugh. Again?"

"Yeah. Stopped it right up... and then went home without telling anyone."

"Typical Dylan. Poop and leave." I frown in no particular direction and start walking down the street like I'm going to the parking garage.

"Sophia's probably still screaming." Ashley falls in step beside me.

"What now?"

"Oh, she just found the turd."

I cringe. "Dad plunged it already, I assume?"

"Nope." Ashley winks. "Sophia fixed it."

"Uh oh. There's no way Sophia used a plunger. Dare I ask?"

"Assuming nothing went wrong with her magic, she sent the turd to Dylan's house." Ashley scrunches in on herself like she's close to throwing up. "She said she put it in their toilet, but you know how her magic likes to do strange things. She might've filled their entire house with crap."

I shudder. "Please, Universe. No."

Ashley laughs. "I'm sure that didn't happen, or she'd be calling one of us to rush over there and make everyone forget."

"Dylan's lucky she only moved the stopped-up toilet to his house and didn't drop the mess on his head." I shiver. "He's abused our toilet long enough. Surprised Mom hasn't banned him from using the bathroom by now."

"Hah." Ashley stops beside me at the corner by the parking garage. "What are we doing?"

Since there are people around us, I say, "Getting the car and going home," before walking into the garage.

Somewhat confused, Ashley follows me up to the third story roof parking area. Nice. No one here. Now, I leap into the air.

She follows, giving me a quizzical look. "Where's the car?"

"Are you for real or messing with me?"

"You said car." She flails her arms.

"People listening. Just trying to sound normal." I veer around in a circle and head toward Wolent's manor.

"Oh duh." She grins. "So, what's the plan?"

"Gonna go tell the boss what we learned in Paris."

Ashley looks down at herself briefly, then smiles. "Okay."

I think that was a pajama check or something, making sure she had on an outfit appropriate to meet the higher-ups. She's good. Pink sweater, black leggings, and Uggs. I, on the other hand, rushed out of the house so fast I'm still wearing my skirt suit outfit. Gah. No wonder people at SCC were staring at me. I'm overdressed for community college. Oh well, this outfit is perfect for meeting Mr. W.

AFTER SPENDING A FEW MINUTES TALKING WITH AZIZ, WE HEAD INSIDE.

I like to talk to the guy. Just saying hi and walking past him feels wrong. He's not a servant or a bit of scenery. Bad enough the poor guy is basically stuck at the manor since he looks the way he does. Someone his size walking around in public would end up on YouTube every damn week. There is a reason some vampires back in the day became hermits. If you're going to be *that* big and out in public, you'd better be an ordinary mortal so no one finds proof of supernatural wonkiness.

Anyway...

One of the mortal workers leads us into the back, to a slightly different room than the one where Mr. Wolent usually hangs out. We're let into a conference room with a huge table. Wolent, Stefano, Paolo, and seven other people—two women and five men—sit all clustered up at one end of the table. Makes sense. This table is big enough for fifty.

Three of the guys and one of the women appear to be metaphorically crapping bricks. They're mortals, for sure. Possibly thralls, but definitely mortals. Wolent doesn't seem happy. Granted, he's also not angry. A wall projector's throwing some sort of line graph up and it doesn't look good. The line isn't plunging, but it's also kinda not going anywhere.

Oh, this probably some sort of boring as hell financial meeting.

Must not be super important since I was allowed to just walk right in. I'm not that big a deal.

The air is thick with tension, making me think everyone was waiting for the big guy to say something in response to whatever went on in here before I arrived. All eyes shift to me as I break the uncomfortable silence by entering.

All the mortals give me some variation of 'uh oh' looks, like I'm some new district manager that's going to be a pain in their collective asses. Ugh. This is another reason I hate wearing outfits like this. People see 'professional attire' and make all sorts of assumptions about the person wearing it.

Two of the guys give off more of a 'wtf' vibe than an 'oh, this must be the consultant who's about to ruin our day' vibe. I glance at them while making my way around the empty end of the table toward the big guy. Yeah, figured. They think I'm a kid and are confused as to why I'm wearing this suit. Well, I mean... to some people, eighteen is still a kid. But I mean, they think I'm closer to fourteen.

Sigh.

This is one of those things I'm going to have to learn to accept or it will drive me insane. Weird how being able to come off childish is just fine when I'm using it to my advantage, but it annoys me otherwise. Kinda hypocritical of me. Not like I'm going to change, so... all I can do is embrace it. I think about how some women hate getting older and wish they could be in their twenties again. I should be happy that will never be me, even if some people treat me like a kid.

Hey, if they think I'm a kid, that means they will let me get away with stuff.

I ignore the two guys giving me 'what are you doing here' stares and approach the end of the table where Wolent, Paolo, and Stefano are sitting.

"Sorry to interrupt," I say. "Got some information I thought you'd want to hear right away about the Natasha problem."

"Ahh." Mr. Wolent looks at his watch. "I suppose this would be a good time for a break." He looks at the seven mortals. "Why don't you all stretch your legs, grab a snack, or something. Come back in fifteen?" He glances at me.

Should be plenty of time. I nod.

"Fifteen minutes." Wolent leans back.

The mortals get up and hurry out wordlessly.

I watch them go until the door closes behind them. "Bad news?"

"Nah." Wolent waves dismissively, chuckling. "Merely average news. Problem with mortal employees is they tend to get nervous in our presence."

"That happens to mortal bosses, too... if they're high enough up on the food chain." I clasp my hands in front of myself. It happens to immortal employees as well. The whole 'one wrong word can get you killed' thing is real. Not that I am afraid he'll order me destroyed. It's super unlikely I would ever say or do anything to make him angry. Not only is that totally against my nature, I genuinely like him.

"Right, so..." He looks me over, half smiling at my thoughts.

I fill him in on what we learned from Remi about Rabanus Vesperus, including the part where the destruction of several vampires is a necessary process to breaking the seals holding him in whatever enchanted sarcophagus he's trapped in.

"You know," whispers Ashley to no one in particular, "this really sounds like a video game."

Without thinking about it, I laugh at her comment. Two seconds later, I realize I'm standing in front of Wolent, Paolo, and Stefano and slam on the metaphorical brakes, trying to keep a straight face.

Then Wolent laughs.

Both Paolo and Stefano barely contain their 'why is he humoring the grandchildren' slash 'how is that supposed to be funny' energy.

Wolent looks toward them. "Do any of your people have any idea where this sarcophagus might be located?"

"It isn't exactly the sort of story we would ordinarily take seriously," says Stefano.

Paolo points his gaze at me. "Are you saying Remi Durand believes this?"

I try to keep as straight a face as possible and not give away how nervous I am at getting in trouble. "He really seemed to. I mean, I suppose he could have been teasing me... but it didn't seem like he was. Not like I can read his thoughts."

"You can't read his thoughts, but I could feel his mood." Ashley fidgets. "Remi was worried."

Paolo and Stefano exchange a glance.

"And you guys right now are feeling like the traditionalist background characters who were just shown proof that magic is real and are struggling to find any plausible normal explanation so you can continue not having to acknowledge the weird stuff." Ashley shrugs. "This isn't *that* weird. It's just a really old vampire who's likely to lose his mind when he wakes up."

"The weird part," I whisper, "Is the magic keeping him asleep and stuck in the sarcophagus."

"Oh." Ashley offers a cheesy smile. "That's right. Yeah, that is kinda strange and hard to accept. You know what I say whenever things get that weird... teleporting kitten."

All three elders look at us like we're annoying kids babbling nonsense.

I am pretty sure Wolent knows about Sophia and her kitten, since my mind is an open book to him. Still, it sounds so strange to hear spoken out loud.

"Well, uhh." Wolent exhales. "See what our people can find out about it. Also, I want eyes on this Natasha. If they get close to finding this thing, they forfeit their right to exist."

Eek.

Wow.

Umm.

Why do I feel like the tattletale who got someone expelled from school? I mean, sure if Natasha's plan actually works, she's going to cause a whole heap of suffering and misery on everyone, mortal and immortal alike. Still, being present for a destruction order is super awkward and uncomfortable. Or a delayed destruction order. He hasn't ordered her ashed immediately, only if they get close to finding the sarcophagus containing Rabanus.

So, what do I do now? Wolent's sending other people after Natasha to watch her, vampires more threatening than I could hope to be. Should I surrender to my squishy side and try to save Natasha's unlife by messing with her so they never find this old vampire? Do I just go home and enjoy being a permanent teenager with no responsibilities?

Wolent shifts his attention back to me. "Good job with the information. A spontaneous trip to Paris was going above and beyond what I expected from you."

"Thank you, sir."

"I'm not expecting the two of you to get involved with the unsavory parts, if it goes that far." Mr. Wolent nods at us, then his expression softens. "Let us hope it does not need to go that far. However, like everyone else in our little family, if you see Natasha or those she has convinced to join her cause, you should do whatever you can to make sure they don't wake this guy up."

The more I can slow her down or throw her off track, the less likely it is she ends up filling an urn. I can do that.

"Of course, sir."

Wolent gives me this look like I'm the Don's daughter and he's mildly uncomfortable at me calling him sir. "All right then, Sarah. Enjoy the rest of your night."

I smile. "Will try to. Thanks."

There, I managed to answer without calling him sir.

Paolo and Stefano are still on their phones talking to underlings when I turn to leave. Neither of them pay me any mind, so I don't interrupt them with any sort of formal goodbyes. Ashley follows me out of the conference room.

Once in the hallway, she nudges me with an elbow. "So... are we going Natasha hunting?"

"Yeah. But first, I'm going to go home and change out of this damn suit."

CHAPTER 32

A BARGAIN OF EPIC ANNOYANCE

TUESDAY, TWO HOURS EARLIER THAN THE LAST CHAPTER.

S am's entire face hurt.

He lay on the floor of his bedroom, out of breath from laughing so hard. The sound of Daryl's father on the phone yelling 'why is my house full of shit?' would forever remain one of the funniest things ever.

Sophia was a little annoyed at him stopping up the toilet for the sixtieth time. She overcorrected. Or perhaps whatever force out there constantly messed with her magic caused her to 'miss.' She only intended to teleport the backup from their toilet to Daryl's toilet where it belonged. Somehow, she'd set off a massive poo bomb instead.

At least she didn't screw up the localized time rewind magic.

Weird how she could do something so powerful without any problems, but a simple thing like trans-poop-location proved hard to control. Sam tapped his foot on air, wondering to himself if her emotional state helped. She only ever used the time rewind when she panicked over getting in trouble. Perhaps sufficient fear made her magic so strong the outside force couldn't affect it.

Crisis averted, at least.

She managed to undo the poo-splosion and reattempt the tele-poop. On the retry, her magic did exactly what she wanted. The second time Daryl's father called him, the yelling was far less epic, but still funny. Daryl got in trouble for 'dropping a bomb' in the bathroom and not flushing it before he left the house.

Naturally, this confused Daryl who insisted it wasn't his since he'd been at Sam's place all afternoon. Sam could only imagine the hilarious argument going on now over at his friend's house.

The guys had all gone home for the night. School nights were annoying in that regard. Everyone had to go home early.

"Done laugh?" asked Blix, holding up a PlayStation controller.

"Yeah." Sam sat up. "Hang on. I wanna try something before we game."

"What?"

Sam crawled over to his toy chest, opened it, and grabbed his big Nerf rifle.

"Uh oh." Blix set the game controller down. "Who make you mad?"

"Bathtub demon." Sam checked the rifle over to ensure he had a dart loaded, then got to his feet. "If he's not going to deal, I'm going to deal with him."

Blix started to nod, then got a look of inspiration in his eyes. He zipped over to the window, peered out, then waved. "Sam. Look."

"Huh?" He meandered over to the window.

Blix pointed at a neighbor outside at the end of the cul-de-sac, opposite Mr. Niedermayer's house. Sam didn't really know the guy's name, only that he lived there with his wife. They were thirtysome-thing and didn't have kids. The guy was out fussing with Christmas lights on the front of their house.

"I prove." Blix snapped his fingers.

"Prove wha—?"

The rain gutter on the neighbor's house bent, setting loose a waterfall of icy slush that poured all over the poor man—who promptly released a rather high-pitched shriek.

"See?" Blix folded his spindly little arms. "Even man shriek when cold."

Sam felt a little guilty about laughing, but did anyway. The neighbor didn't suffer anything worse than what had already happened to him. Well, maybe. Being stuck in freezing wet clothes did sound worse than simply being teleported outside with no clothes. At least the man was right next to his house, so he didn't have to *stay* stuck in wet things.

The neighbor ran inside, still screaming.

Blix snapped his fingers again and the rain gutter bent back to its normal shape.

"Okay. Okay." Sam bowed to Blix. "You're right. I didn't sound like a wimp because I screamed at the cold."

Blix gave him a thumbs-up.

"Okay, tub demon." Sam racked the Nerf rifle. "Let's chat."

He marched out into the hall and went to the bathroom. Sierra had gotten into the habit of using the basement shower, which opened up more time that the upstairs bathroom wasn't in use. Everything there seemed normal and unassuming.

"Okay, out." Sam stared at the bathtub.

After a few seconds, he felt the presence of something demonic slithering through the material of the bathtub like feelers or a spider web. It seemed to be a fragmentary scrap of consciousness, as though a single strand of infernal awareness monitored the tub to be alerted when someone dared to use it. He mentally seized upon the strand and gave a yank.

In a flash of reddish light, a goblin-like demon about the same height as Sam appeared standing in the tub. He wore a little green dress coat that kind of made him look like a hideously warped leprechaun. The creature resembled Nalfoz, only not as fat. His long, floppy ears had bands of dark green tiger striping all along their twelve-inch length. Numerous rings of various precious metals ran up the lower edge of both ears. In one breath, he smelled like the stuff they threw on vomit at school to clean it up. The next, he gave off an odor like a tissue that's been sitting in Grandma's purse for six years waiting for the perfect moment to be needed.

For a few seconds, the demon wobbled in place, waving his arms as if off balance. Then, seemingly realizing he got yoinked, set his fists against his hips and glowered at Sam. His beady yellow eyes glowed with indignant hatred.

Sam pointed the Nerf rifle at him.

The demon laughed. "Did you enjoy the Space Needle?"

"No. But you didn't embarrass me." Sam frowned. "It was annoying. Not embarrassing."

"That's the point." The demon examined his gnarly, wavy claws. "Next time, I'll drop you at school."

"Still wouldn't embarrass me." Sam shook his head. "I take baths right before bedtime. No one would be there then. Still just annoying."

"Annoying is the point." The demon let his hand drop and sighed. "You aren't getting it, are you?"

Sam flicked the safety off. "I understand. Look, I don't want to blast you back to Heck, but I need you to leave this tub alone. Sophia is already insecure about her abilities, and she thinks all of this is her fault."

"Excellent." The demon wagged his furry eyebrows. "Bonus points."

"You're not helping." Sam tapped his foot. "I'd prefer not to fight you. What will it take to make you leave this bathtub alone?"

The demon grasped the lapels of his little green coat. "It is a deal you seek?"

"Depends on your terms."

"Hmm." The demon paced back and forth in the tub, toe claws clicking on the porcelain. "I would have been done with this place and gone already if not for one little snag."

"What snag?" Sam tilted his head, but kept watching the demon over his Nerf gunsights.

"I have been trying to drop Sophia out of the tub into a public place." He grumbled. "It's just not working."

Sam narrowed his eyes, finger tightening on the trigger. "Why would you do that?"

"Because." The demon faced him, eyes wide and greedy. "The emotional explosion would be epic. We're talking well past ordinary embarrassment and into worst fear come to life territory."

"And so would the lifelong trauma and therapy bills." Sam grumbled. "You will not do that to my sister."

The demon clasped his hands together. "Do you want me out of this tub or not? Your sister's magical defenses are too strong. There is a particular root, the tea from which would be enough to weaken her defen—"

"No," said Sam. "I'm not going to help you do that to Soph. I'd rather go to war with you for 300 years. Something else or I'm going to move on to Nerf negotiations."

At last, the demon seemed genuinely worried. His fear lasted only a few seconds before the nervous pacing resumed. He seemed to think back and forth several times before finally stopping and turning to face Sam.

"Pull an epic prank that extremely inconveniences a lot of people, and I will release this tub."

Sam sighed. "I'd rather not mess with people. You know I could just shoot you in the face."

"You could..." The demon rocked heel to toe, nodding. "But, do you really want to go to war with me for the next four centuries?"

"I said three centuries."

"Terms may change without warning or notice." The demon held up one finger.

Ugh. "No. Not really. I don't want to be at war that long." Sam let out a long sigh. He didn't worry so much about getting in trouble for pranking people as he felt genuinely bad at the thought of being such a giant pain in the butt to other people. "Umm, couldn't I do something embarrassing instead of pranking other people? What if I streaked the mall?"

The demon shook his head. "No. You wouldn't be embarrassed enough. And your willingness to sacrifice your dignity is too noble. Disgusting, honestly. You must inconvenience a lot of people. Solve my monthly quota in one shot. Do that, and I will forever leave this tub."

Sam squeezed and relaxed his grip on the Nerf gun, causing the plastic to creak. Stupid demons and their stupid knack for just knowing things, especially about mortals. True, Sam wouldn't really be embarrassed if he streaked the mall. Such a thing would be incredibly embarrassing to most people, but wouldn't really bother him. Probably why he suggested it. Odds were good his parents would be twenty times more mortified when the police called them to pick him up. Getting grounded would be worse than doing it. At least Sam's willingness to redirect badness onto himself instead of others made the demon feel sick to its three stomachs.

"Well?" asked the demon. "I've got places to be, wardrobe malfunctions to cause, accidental emails to send."

"Huh?"

"I'm with Public Embarrassment," said the demon, offering a clawed handshake. "Neifos the Ever Cackling, at your service. You can call me Niffy if you prefer. We do things like make pants rip at work, remove deodorant off people in the office so they think they forgot to put it on, or nudge people into sending mortifying emails to the person they're talking about instead of their friends, cause employees to spill coffee on the big boss, that sort of thing."

"Do I have to make the prank embarrassing?" Sam frowned.

"Ideally yes, but..." Niffy waved in a 'whatever' manner. "If you inconvenience enough people all at once badly enough, I can overlook the embarrassment part."

"Inconvenience, not hurt." Sam shook his head. "Not going to hurt anyone."

"Agreed." Niffy kept holding his hand out. "Just be really annoying. I'm sure you can do that. You're a ten-year-old boy."

Somewhat reluctantly, Sam lowered the Nerf rifle. Being annoying to a whole bunch of people for one solitary prank was definitely mean. However, he wouldn't be doing it simply to find amusement in the misfortune of others. This would free his home of a severe—and potentially even dangerous—annoyance and allow his mother and sisters to use the bathtub without fear of ending up stranded somewhere super embarrassing or even harmful. Neither Mom nor Sierra could get themselves off the Space Needle without help. Either one of them could end up suffering severe frostbite or even die if they got bathtubbed during winter.

"All right." Sam braced himself for regret, then accepted the handshake. "One question, though."

"Non conditional. You've already agreed."

"I know. I just have a question."

Niffy grasped his lapels again. "All right. Ask."

"Why the Space Needle?" Sam scrunched his nose.

"Ehh, I got the idea from your big sister. She seems to like the place." Niffy shrugged. "Figured it would be a huge public spectacle. Kid stranded on the top of the Space Needle. Cops, news reporters, everything."

Sam tapped his toes into the floor, not sure if he liked the answer. "Kinda dangerous. I could've frozen to death."

"Nah, I knew you'd be okay." Niffy chuckled. "Contrary to what you might think, we're not in the business of killing people. Can't embarrass the dead."

And with that, Neifos the Ever Cackling cackled, and disappeared in a puff of black smoke.

"Did I screw up?" asked Sam.

"Nah." Blix grinned while doing weasel hands. "Nothing wrong with good prank."

CHAPTER 33
BIG RED MONSTER

THURSDAY, NOT QUITE DINNERTIME

Not sure if I'm going about things the right way, but the past two days have been almost fun.

Late Tuesday, Ashley and I snuck back into the grey house to spy on Natasha. Unfortunately, they weren't there. Still had the feeling they used the house and hadn't left it for good, so we had some fun. By that, I mean we messed with Topher's notes. Ashley did her best to forge his handwriting and made small changes here and there to hopefully keep them going in circles or changing his conclusions.

Even if he doesn't fall for it, as an Academic, he'll probably spend the next three months freaking out that someone tampered with his work so badly he won't be able to make progress. While she did that, I got my gremlin on. Every laptop in the house, I hacked. Changed passwords, renamed files, deleted stuff that looked like it related to the hunt for the sarcophagus, and so on. I also sent an email from Robbie's computer to Lorri's email making it sound like he was having second thoughts and wondered if Natasha was simply crazy.

That should make for an interesting conversation.

We went back Wednesday night. Stuff had been moved around. The laptops were gone. Topher's books were also gone. None of Team Moron was there, though. We spent like an hour searching the area. Of course we didn't find them. I think tonight I might go ask Glim for some help. Maybe he or the Shadows have heard something.

Then again, if he did, and this is as serious a problem as Remi thinks it is, he'd probably have come to me to warn me... or not. Glim is kinda protective of me. Why would he bother telling me about it rather than just go slap some sense into Natasha directly? Now that I think about it, if a truly apocalyptic event was on the horizon, the Shadows would totally hear about it and do something.

Maybe I really don't need to be worried. I am, after all, just a baby vampire. It's not like I'm the Chosen One™ or anything. The fate of the world and the universe rests solely in the hands of the naïve, newbie teenage girl who knows nothing about anything but just so happens to be the main character.

Hah.

Yeah, that's not me.

This problem is more likely to get solved by vampires with a higher pay grade than me.

I'm starting to understand a lot of what Mom has said over the years. Being responsible for Chloe is an adventure. Kids are crazy and unpredictable. One minute, she's playing with her tablet. The next, she suddenly says 'I miss farting' for no reason whatsoever and gets upset that she can't fart anymore, being a vampire.

This probably has something to do with Blix's illusionary butt bombs from the other day.

The boys found them hilarious. All boys find farts funny. Even Dad can't hold back laughter if a fart happens. That's something I'm never going to understand about the universe. One day humanity will unlock the secrets of cold fusion and cure cancer and make colonies on Mars... but we will never understand why boys laugh at farts.

It may or may not have been a mistake, but in an effort to make kiddo stop crying and feel better, I explained that we, as Innocents, can still eat food. If we eat the right things, we might actually still manage to fart.

Of course, Ashley had to ruin things with logic. Since our bodies don't process anything we eat—it just goes right through us—there is no gas produced. This got her crying again. And yeah, kids cry over weird things. I remember Sophia being like two and screaming her head off because the receipt Mom got at the store was too long.

Yeah, no idea either. Really small kids cry at the strangest things.

My second very likely mistake of the night was buying Chloe a fart machine. It's on order, so not here yet. But she's at least stopped crying. This may or may not prove to be a disaster. Time shall tell.

For now, she's calmed down and we are watching *Teen Titans* on streaming. Yeah, so it's not really anime but it's still a cartoon. I really should be doing homework. Meh. Can't find the urge to bother. Spending time with kiddo is more important... even though she's as immortal as I am. It's the Littles and 'rents who have a time limit.

Sophia lets out a blood-curdling shriek of terror from upstairs.

This could be anything from finding cat poop on her pillow to hostile vampires crawling in her window. What counts as a shocking horror worthy of a scream like that to her is a long list. Still, I have to check. Much, much better for me to zoom upstairs in a panic and find out it's nothing at all than for me to assume she's being a drama queen and something truly bad happens.

If I were a cartoon character, I'd have zoomed straight out of my pajamas at this speed.

Fortunately, I am not a cartoon character.

I fly-sprint across the basement, up the stairs, through the downstairs floor, and up to the second floor. The screams come from Sophia's bedroom along with a disgusting glorpy-gloopy noise as though someone tried to process a live giant octopus in a butter churn.

Mildly horrified, I burst into her room and stop short with my hand still on the doorknob and my mouth open in shock.

Sophia's floating up near the ceiling, thoroughly wrapped up in thin, bright red tentacles. The mass of tentacles sprouts from the back of an enormous, fat, goblin-like creature embedded to its waist in the middle of the room, right in her crayon-doll-construction paper-plushie ritual circle. It's like the demonic fat kid from sixth grade tried to squeeze through the cat door and got stuck. He claws at the rug, though I can't tell if he's trying to pull himself the rest of the way into her bedroom or push himself back down to wherever he came from.

The tentacles have coiled around my sister, pinning her arms to her sides and trapping her legs together. At the moment, it doesn't seem to be doing anything worse than holding her in the air and struggling to either free or dislodge itself.

Sierra runs out of her room, darting over to stand beside me. She seems ready to attack... at least the instant I go first.

"Whoa," I whisper to no one in particular.

"What is all that noise?" yells Mom from the living room.

The toilet flushes. Sam comes running out of the bathroom and joins us in staring at this thing in bafflement.

I lean back into the hallway and shout toward the stairs, "A giant red monster is attacking Sophia."

"Heeeeeeelp!" shouts Sophia while squirming and trying futilely to kick at the creature. "Get it off me!"

The 'rents race up the stairs and hurry over to me. Mom and Dad peer into the room.

"Okay, maybe my red monster attack wasn't really that bad." Sierra blushes slightly.

"This is *not my period!*" shrieks Sophia. "It's not that kind of red monster! I dunno what the heck this thing is!"

"Demon?" I ask.

Sam shakes his head. "Nope. Kinda looks like one, but it isn't a demon."

Mom folds her arms, seeming a little casual about this situation. "Sophia, I thought we agreed you would not summon any eldritch abominations into the house."

"Probably against the HOA." Dad rubs his chin. "Oh, there's a thought. I wonder if Sophia's magic might be able to get rid of them."

"I'm not sure, Jonathan." Mom glances at him. "Do you really want to ask our eleven-year-old daughter to take on such a powerful, ancient evil?"

I gesture at the creature. "Not sure that counts as a powerful ancient evil."

Mom smirks. "I was referring to the HOA."

The creature swings Sophia around, making her scream. Despite its efforts, it is neither pulling itself up any farther nor sinking back down. Halfway deep in the floor, the thing is only a little shorter than me. If it got to its feet, it would tower over me.

"Get off her!" I lunge forward and punch the goblin in the face as hard as I can.

My entire fist disappears into its head, like I'm slugging a massive Jell-O mold. Feels rubbery and soft. The creature flies away from my fist, careening over backward and smacking into the floor, flat on its back. If this thing has a spine, it's totally broken. Nothing with a skeleton can bend ninety degrees backward at the waist and not at least need to make an appointment with a chiropractor.

Sophia, in the mass of tentacles, flies into the wall and bounces off with a loud 'Oof.'

The creature springs back up off the rug and stares at me with a hilarious WTF expression.

"Be right back," says Sierra. "Sword time."

"Put her down or I'm going to hit you again," I say.

It heaves a huffy snort, as if to say 'what's a scrawny little thing like you going to do?'

I slug it as promised, hammering it into the floor like one of those inflatable punch dolls that keep bouncing back up to get hit again.

Sophia bumps the wall. "Stop it! Ow."

The creature rises upright again and glares at me. Doesn't seem injured at all. In fact, I'm pretty sure he's only angry because my punches actually move him and he can't laugh at me.

Sophia shrieks as the tentacles swing her downward at me like some sort of blonde ball and chain weapon.

I duck. Sophia flies over me, stops, then comes zooming right back.

This guy's not terribly fast. An ordinary mortal with a little bit of training would be able to dodge the Sophia flail. For me, it's beyond trivial. After the fourth time he fails to club me over the head with her, he growls.

"I'm gonna puke," yells Sophia.

Mom and Dad run at the creature together. I'm too busy ducking Sophia again to do anything about them. The monster ends up grabbing both my parents by a hand around their throats and throwing them aside. They land on their backs and slide a few feet away in opposite directions. Mom bumps into the bed; Dad hits the wall.

"We need a better plan," says Dad. "*Get him* didn't work."

Sierra comes charging in the door with her sword up over her head like Red Sonja. The creature tries to do the same thing to her it did to Dad (reaching to grab her by the neck) and is totally not prepared for her being almost as fast as a vampire. Her chopping blade passes between two of its fingers, slicing its right hand in half completely and stopping about three-quarters of the way down the length of his forearm.

Everyone freezes, cringing in sympathetic agony.

"Ooh, that looks painful," says Dad, cradling his right hand to his chest.

It's not exactly horrific since this creature is not bleeding at all.

The look on his face is somewhere between shock at the injury and complete surprise she's so fast.

I take advantage of its bewilderment, sprout claws, and leap into a big swiping rake. My weaponized fingernails slice the narrow tentacles as easily as spaghetti noodles... if spaghetti noodles were two inches thick.

Sophia drops straight down on top of the thing's head, bounces off, and slides to the floor. She wriggles out of the limp rubbery cords and speed-crawls over to Mom.

The big red monster lets out an agonized scream. Either those tentacles are a sensitive spot or this is the vampire claw effect. My claws might be small, but they seriously hurt.

Sierra yanks her blade out of its arm into a backspin, then leaps up and brings her sword up and over her head in a massively telegraphed barbarian chop straight into the middle of the creature's face.

Somehow, her blade goes all the way to the floor, stopping with a *thud* on impact.

The big red monster splits in half down the middle, screams, then promptly explodes into a brilliant scattering of energy. Sophia's carpet in the ritual circle area ripples in the manner of a liquid for a few seconds before going still and solid again. A cloud of pinkish-peach hued light from the exploded creature hangs in the room for a few seconds before coalescing into three head-sized orbs. Said orbs zip about randomly for a brief instant, then rocket out the window despite it being closed.

"Nice." Dad sits up. "You Voltronned it."

"What?" asks the Littles all at once.

Dad looks sad. "Damn. I am remiss in my duties as a father. You shall all soon understand what Voltron is."

"It's an old cartoon," I say. "Big robot ended almost every episode by chopping some big monster in half straight down the middle."

"Oh," says Sierra, sounding unimpressed.

"Neat." Sam shrugs. "I'd watch it."

Giant robots and farts. Don't need much more than that to keep a boy amused and entertained.

"Oh, Sierra..." Mom gestures at the slash in the carpet. "The rug..."

The average person would be confused as to how my mother could witness a giant creature throwing one of her kids around in a mass of tentacles and be more upset at a sword slash in the carpeting. Bear in mind this is the woman who forbids the wearing of shoes in the house to protect the rugs. It's almost an OCD thing with her. Might legit be OCD. I'm not totally sure. If she does have it, it's a super mild case.

"Sophia can fix that slice." Sierra gestures at the big red goo puddle in the middle of the ritual circle where the creature had been. "She can also get rid of that *enormous stain*."

Mom looks ready to faint.

Okay, now I think she's overacting. Is this her coping mechanism? It's not every day fat, ten-foot-tall magical beasts end up half-embedded in your floor.

Sophia's already crying because she thinks she's going to get grounded.

Dad walks over and puts an arm around her. "It's okay, Soph. You're not in trouble."

Mom looks up with this 'she's not?' expression.

The next words out of Sophia's mouth are critical in determining how long she gets grounded for.

"What were you trying to do?" asks Dad.

"Umm." Sophia's voice quivers. "You know how there's a force messing with my magic? Or Sam thinks so?"

"There is." Sam nods. "Olmaz said so. I'm sure he's right."

Sophia sniffles and wipes at her tears. "I was trying to scry to figure out where the interference is coming from... and that *thing* burst out of the floor."

Mom furrows her brow. "So, you're telling us you weren't trying to summon something on purpose?"

"No," wails Sophia. "I promise! I was just trying to figure out why my magic keeps messing up."

"That's for sure." Mom rubs her temples. "Your magic certainly does run away from you too much."

Blix babbles.

"Mom," says Sam. "The Forces of Evil™ want her to get discouraged from doing magic. Please don't say stuff like that. It really isn't her fault."

"Well... I mean..." Mom sighs. "I'm not trying to be critical. Just... how could it be anyone else's fault?"

Blix babbles.

Sam eyes the imp. "I'm not sure I want to say that to Mom."

The imp waves in a 'go on, it's fine' manner.

"What did he say?" Mom raises an eyebrow.

Sam fights the urge to laugh. "Umm, if someone was about to take a swing at golf..."

"Okay...?" Mom looks at him.

"And someone shot him in the nuts with a BB gun right as he swings, so he totally misses the ball, would you say that guy is bad at playing golf?"

Dad bursts out laughing.

"All right. That does make sense in a bizarre sort of way." Mom stands and neatens her shirt. "Sophia, can you fix this carpet?"

The look on Sophia's face is tragic. Her eyes say 'I dunno. I could try but it would probably destroy the house.'

I scoop her into a hug. "Yes, Mom. Sophia can totally fix this carpet."

CHAPTER 34
MAGICAL MESSES NEED MAGICAL SOLUTIONS

THURSDAY, CLOSER TO DINNERTIME

S ophia emits a faint sigh, still shivering.

I keep holding her. "It's okay, Soph. I'd be rattled, too, if a giant red monster came out of the floor and attacked me."

"You got this, Soph." Dad pats her on the shoulder. "You opened a portal to Paris. Fixing a carpet is no big deal."

"Yeah. Kick ass," says Sierra. "Err, butt. Kick butt."

Mom squeezes Sophia's hand. "Sorry. I know you're doing your best. I only said that because things have gone awry most times you've done magic. It's not your fault."

"All right." Sophia sniffles. She looks down at the rug.

"Remember how it felt when we were in Paris and you opened the closet back here." I squeeze her. "It's all about confidence. You *know* you can do this. Don't worry about it. You definitely know how to do it."

Sophia breathes for a while, then finally raises her hands and points them at the damaged rug. Her 'I'm going to burst into tears again at any minute' expression hardens to a glare of annoyance.

The goo leaps upward off the rug, gathers into a baseball-sized orb, then rockets out of the room. Seconds later, a wet *ker-ploink* comes from the bathroom. Then, the small sword cut disappears.

"See?" I grin.

"Is whatever that was safe to flush?" asks Mom.

Sierra grinds her toes into the rug. "Umm. I dunno."

Blix babbles.

"He says it's basically liquid magic." Sam pauses to listen to the imp for a moment, then says, "If you flush it, it might end up empowering something random. Better keep it in a jar."

"Eww. It's already in the toilet." Sophia cringes.

"I got it. Gimme a jar," says Sam.

"Be right back." Dad walks out.

Mom shakes her head, sighs, then heads after him. "Please don't send any unknown magical substances down the toilet."

"Sorry, Mom," says Sophia. "It just feels like the best way to get rid of nasty stuff."

Mom goes back downstairs.

Dad returns soon with an empty peanut butter jar he grabbed from the recycle bin and washed.

Sam takes it and goes into the bathroom.

Sierra and Sophia share a cringe at the idea he's going to reach into the toilet. Neither of them are thinking. How is my brother going to grab a blob of goo with his hand? He's not. Blix is going to levitate it.

Sam returns with the jar, now half-full of quasi-glowing red slime, which he hands to Sophia. "Here."

She eyes the jar like she doesn't want to touch it.

"The jar didn't touch toilet water. Blix floated the goo out." Sam offers her the jar again.

Sophia takes it gingerly. "What am I going to do with it?"

"I dunno." Sam shrugs. "Keep it until you need it. It's basically like magical battery power."

"Oh." She shrugs and puts it on her shelf.

We all stand there for a moment in awkward silence until Sophia stomps her foot and grabs her empty plastic bowl. She storms out to the bathroom, runs the sink, then returns carrying the bowl of water, which she sets at the middle of her ritual circle.

Sierra gives me an 'uh oh' look. I wave her off. The last thing we need to do now is damage Sophia's confidence.

She kneels in front of the bowl and snaps her fingers. Several of the crayons she's arranged around the circle ignite like candles.

Sophia stares into the water.

The rest of us stare in silence.

After about five minutes, the crayons go out. Sophia takes a deep breath and sits back, looking frustrated.

"Bad news?" I ask.

Sierra makes a 'well at least nothing exploded or turned into a huge pile of slime' face.

"Ugh." Sophia huffs. She sulks for a moment, chin in her hands, staring down. Eventually, she gives off an overwhelming sense of annoyance. "I couldn't see where the interference was coming from. There definitely is something out there messing with me. Why would something mess with me? What did I do?"

"Demon?" asks Sierra. "They seem to like to cause chaos and disorder just because. You wouldn't have had to do anything wrong."

"Maybe," says Sophia in more of a sigh than voice. "Oh, I messed up again, by the way."

"How?" I ask.

She gestures at the window. "That monster? Sierra didn't kill it. It split into three energy balls and ran away. I probably need to figure out where they went and catch them before they do something bad."

"Okay." I nod. "One: you didn't do something bad. Outside force messed with you. Two: let's go. Where are they?"

"Umm." Sophia fidgets her hands together. "I dunno. It's gonna take a bit of work to find them. More scrying. I'm also going to need to make something to catch them in first. Wouldn't be any point to finding it if I couldn't trap it."

Dad pokes his head in. "Everything okay in here?"

"Yeah." I say. "Just figuring out where to go from here."

Sophia looks at him. "Am I in trouble?"

Dad rubs his chin.

"Technically, she didn't do this." I wave around randomly. "Someone or something else out there did it to her."

"Yeah." Dad smiles. "I get that. For now, no. Not in trouble. You are intending to clean it up. I heard what you said about the three parts running off."

Sophia bites her lip. "Yeah. I'll clean it up. Just... need to make something to put it in first."

Dad wags his eyebrows. "I have an idea for that."

Oh no... I'm afraid to ask.

CHAPTER 35

MISSION POSSIBLE: COVERT EXTRACTION

FRIDAY NIGHT

When taking care of a vampire child, there are narrow windows in which open feeding may occur. This, of course, depends entirely on the social customs of where a vampire lives. It gets easier in winter since the sun goes down long before it's unacceptable for a seven-year-old to be awake.

During the summer, we have a much smaller window in which to take Chloe somewhere for feeding purposes before we risk Karens getting in our face about why our kid sister is still awake at this hour and we deal with the whole 'where are your parents' thing. The alternatives are kinda creepy and off-putting. Ashley and I could always go out into the world, derp hammer someone, and bring them home so Chloe could bite them.

That's risky since it involves bringing strange people to the house. I don't think the 'rents would approve of that. It also feels too much like kidnapping for Follows Rules Girl to go along with. Our only other option would be using Aurélie's trick and draining someone's blood into a bottle, adding a drop or three of ours as a preservative and bringing that home for Chloe to drink. Bleeding someone into a bottle also sounds a bit weird. Less weird than kidnapping, though.

Still, we have big darkness at this time of year. It's not a problem to take Chloe to downtown Seattle during times when no one would really care about a kid being awake. We roam about the downtown, enjoying the spectacle of Christmas decorations and so forth... and feeding when the opportunity presents itself.

I thought I had it good being a permanent teenager. Chloe gets to experience Christmas from the mindset of a seven-year-old over and over again forever. She'll never become jaded about it. This will always be a magical time of year for her. She'll also never get sent by some vampire boss to do strange quasi-illegal things. Talk about an absolutely carefree existence.

Okay, sure, she's still got to worry about a sudden shift in vampire politics making her a 'liability that should be destroyed.' I don't want to think about that. If I keep my head down, do what I'm told, and Chloe behaves herself, we should be fine. Even if Wolent falls out of power, the local vampires are all fairly sweet on her. Whoever might someday replace Wolent—if that ever happens—will likely be okay with her as long as we keep her from being a problem. And if we get some idiot instead? Well, I guess that's the day I finally leave home.

Fingers crossed if something like that ever happens, it's many, many years from now.

Anyway... tonight, we're having fun and being innocent.

I'm allowing myself not to worry too much about the Natasha problem. More important vampires than me are on the job. Besides, if the world is going to end, I'm totally sure the Shadows would have intervened by now. Nothing quite changes a vampire's mind like having a seven-foot-tall ghoul come out of nowhere, slam you into the wall by a hand around your throat and tell you 'change your attitude or I'm going to rip your entrails out.'

My phone rings.

I don't recognize the number, so I assume it's a telemarketer and silence it.

The phone rings again right away.

Okay, not a computer calling every number in a block. This must be a real person.

I answer. "Hello?"

"Sarah?" asks Mom, whispering more than speaking.

"Yeah. I'm here." I blink. "Didn't recognize the number."

"I need you. Quick. This is an emergency."

"Why are you whispering? What number is this?"

"Listen," says Mom. "I was enjoying a bath and—"

Oh no. I facepalm.

"—the next thing I know, I'm in Cristian Fowler's office."

That's her boss. Oh boy.

"Could be worse," I say. "The tub usually leaves us on top of the Space Needle. At least you're inside."

"Sarah!" snaps Mom in whisper-shout. "I am soapy, wet, and naked in my boss's office! Do you have any idea what will happen if I get caught here like this?"

I cringe. "Nothing good. Don't you have a change of clothes in your office?"

She sighs. "I do, but I can't go out into the hallway or the cameras will get me. Please drop whatever you're doing and help me get out of here."

This is the very first time in my entire life my mother has sounded legitimately scared. Not only is she mortified, she's watching her entire career go up in smoke. Naked in her boss's office. Her *male* boss? Yeah, that is going to start a shit show if anyone catches her.

"This is career-ending, Sarah... please," whispers Mom.

"Umm. What should I do? We can't really call Dad and have him bring you clothes."

"No. Cameras. Besides, I *have* clothes here... but they are in my office all the way down the hall." Mom exhales hard. "No way am I going to make it there without being picked up on cameras sneaking around in my birthday suit. How am I going to explain being in Cristian's office with no clothes? And even if I *could* get out of here unseen and make it to my office, security will notice me leaving the building again after I already left, without any record of me arriving. How would I explain that?"

I think. Yeah, this is definitely not something Dad can handle. It's only a matter of time before a patrolling guard catches her in that office. "Okay. I'm on it. I think I have an idea if you can put up with a little weird."

"I fell through the damn bathtub and landed in the office. This is already weird. I'm going to die if anyone sees me here like this. We are already fully into weird."

"Right..." I exhale.

"Also, when the hell is Sophia going to fix that damned tub?" snaps Mom.

"She can't." I frown. "Sam said something the other day about a demon being involved. I'll explain later, since you are in a hurry now. Just don't be mad at her for this, okay?"

"Fine. Please hurry," says Mom. "Maybe we should just get a new tub."

"And inflict that thing on someone else?" I ask.

"No, it would be sent to a landfill and probably destroyed."

I wince. "Hopefully, it won't explode."

Mom gasps. "You think it might?"

"Who knows? It's a powerful magical artifact now. Speaking of Sam, let me call him and get my plan moving."

"Okay. Hurry, before the guards find me," whispers Mom.

"On it."

I hang up and call my brother's cell phone.

"Yo," says Sam. "Demon Pizza. Always on fire. What can I get you?"

I chuckle. "Sam. We have a problem. Mom got bathtubbed. She's trapped in her boss's office at work."

"What?" He pauses. "Stupid Neifos. I made a deal with him so he'd stop messing with our tub."

"What the hell is a Neifos?"

Chloe continues staring in awe at the Christmas display in the store we're standing beside.

"That's the demon in our bathtub. He wants me to call him Niffy."

"I'm going to call him a lot of other things." I scowl.

Ashley snickers.

"He's not supposed to do that anymore, 'cause I'm working on it." Sam grumbles.

Blix mutters something in the background.

Sam lets out an '*auuuuugh*' scream worthy of Charlie Brown.

"What happened?" I ask.

A sharp *snap* comes over the line. I think my brother just slapped himself in the forehead. "I forgot to make it a condition of the deal that he stop messing with us while I'm working on it."

I wince. "Yeah, uhh... making deals with demons is tricky. You should really ask Mom to give you some tips on how to lawyer better."

"Good idea." Sam grumbles.

"Do I want to know what this demon asked you to do?"

"Just a prank. I have to inconvenience a lot of people for a nontrivial amount of time, and be annoying."

That's a stretch. No, seriously. Sam is probably the most un-annoying kid I've ever seen. He's also not much of a prankster. "Let me know if you want help with it."

"Cool. Still trying to think of something that's not too bad, but just bad enough to make Niffy happy."

"So, uhh, right. Mom got stranded at work. Can you ask Blix to mirror her home before she gets caught by security?"

"Blix?" asks Sam in the background. "Mom's stuck at work."

An 'affirmative Blix noise' comes over the line, then babble.

"Umm, is there a mirror where she is?" asks Sam. "One big enough for her to fit through?"

I shrug. "Hang on."

A little swiping later, and I three-way call back to the number Mom called me from. Alas, I go into an after-hours IVR that tells me they are closed. Grr. Why won't this stupid phone thing just put me through to her directly.

"Hello?" whispers Mom.

Say what? Did I just *anger* my way through the IVR. Hmm. These powers I have seem to be more interesting by the day.

"It's me. Sec." I three-way connect us. "Sam?"

"Yeah, I'm still here."

"Mom, Sam wants to know if you can get to a mirror."

"No," whispers Mom. "Not in here. I'd have to go to the executive bathroom and that's going to put me on security cameras, so... not happening."

Argh. This is not going to be the sort of problem I can solve by remote. I'm going to need to go there like some sort of Special Forces commando to extract my mother from hostile territory.

"Okay. Hide. We're on the way. Should be no more than ten minutes."

"All right. Be careful," says Mom.

"I'll get ready." Sam hangs up.

"You want to stay here with her?" I ask.

"Nah." Ashley smiles. "You're going to need me to hide from the guards."

"True."

"Can I come?" asks Chloe in a sweet voice. "Sounds fun."

"If you promise not to touch anything."

She nods.

"Okay."

We leap into the air and sprint home as fast as I can make myself fly.

Like a trio of some sort of weird suburban witches, we glide down out of the air and formation-land on our back deck, then rush inside. Dad's in the living room on the sofa tinkering with a bunch of metal parts to some unknown object. Looks like he's working on some sort of model kit.

"Dad," I say while fast-walking by. "Mom got bathtubbed into the office. We're going to get her out stealthily now. Get ready for emotional support when she's back."

"Understood." Dad nods.

I hurry upstairs and stick my head into Sophia's room.

She's reclining on her bed, reading an e-book. She looks over the top of it at me.

"911. Need you to send Klepto to bring Mom some clothes. She got bathtubbed. Sweats and sneakers are perfect. If anyone does see her, no one would believe it's her in that outfit."

Sophia lets out an *eep!* and tosses her e-reader aside onto the bed. "Okay. On it."

I continue down the hall to the bathroom. Sam and Blix are already there waiting for us. He gives Chloe a look, then shrugs.

Blix scratches at the mirror. As before, I lift Sam through. The rest of us fly.

We walk out of our negative bathroom into the streets of Cottage Lake. For a little while, we hurry down a paved road flanked by completely black trees. A sasquatch walks by wearing a golf sweater, those silly pants, even sillier socks, and a cap.

"Excuse me," says the bigfoot in a posh tone. "Have you seen my golf ball by chance?"

"Sorry, no." I shrug.

"Blast." The bigfoot shakes his head and walks off.

As we go around a curve in the road, the forest abruptly changes to a somewhat generic looking city street full of small storefronts. Grey-skinned people with hollow eye sockets and vacant, drooling expressions mill around.

"Oh, no! Zombies." Chloe grabs onto me.

"Those aren't zombies," says Sam in a calm tone.

"What are they then?" I glance at him.

Ashley deadpans, "People who think *Joey* is funny."

"Who's Joey?" asks Sam.

"The show." Ashley frowns. "The *Friends* spinoff."

He looks at us like we said something totally girly and uninteresting. It doesn't involve robots, aliens, or orcs, so he's not interested.

"Whatever they are, are they dangerous?" I ask.

"They're the drained remains of people who believe everything they see on the internet," mutters Sam.

"Are they dangerous, though?" I pull Chloe away from one guy staggering kinda close.

"Only if you disagree with them," says Sam. "Try to avoid getting into a conversation."

We hurry through the small bit of city, following Blix's lead over to a little grey door in the side of a tiny movie theater. The sign is total gibberish, like this entire reality was made by an AI. Ugh.

Blix opens the door to reveal a bathroom. Specifically, a giant fancy bathroom at Boeing corporate.

We hop through.

"Okay," I whisper. "Only been on this floor like twice, and both times it was take your kid to work day and I was like nine. Don't really know my way around here."

Blix pounds a fist into his chest in an 'I got you' manner.

"Nice. Okay." I concentrate on hiding us from security cameras. "Move slow and careful and we should stay off video."

"Take us to Mom." Sam nods to the imp.

"Cloaking field engaged," whispers Ashley.

Chloe tugs on my shirt. "If you need a decoy, I can go be creepy down the hall."

I chuckle. "I'll keep that in mind."

She grins.

We leave the bathroom and sneak down the hallway.

A pair of security guards come around the corner on the left, walking toward us and seeming a little bored.

Everyone flattens themselves against the wall and holds totally still until the two guys are well past us.

Blix resumes floating along.

We follow him to the last office on the left side before a right-ward bend. He points at the door.

I open it and peek inside. It's a huge office. Nice, but not ridiculously opulent. Looks empty. Uh oh. Did they find her? The room smells like soapy bathwater and lavender bath bomb.

"Mom?" I whisper. "Are you in here?"

The bottom drawer of a big file storage cabinet slides open. Mom appears to have stuffed herself into it. Her hair is still mostly wet, soaked into the baggy blue sweatshirt the kitten express provided. Mom flails at the drawer, trying to get herself out. I hurry over and help her.

"Got lucky. Bottom drawer was empty," rasps Mom. "Not as flexible as I was at your age, but at least my ass isn't too big. The sweat suit was a nice touch."

I grin. "Ready to get out of here?"

"You know it." Mom shivers. "This was totally not my fault, but I felt like I was in huge trouble."

"Yeah. Been there." I shake my head. "C'mon. Follow us and don't walk too fast."

"You're going out into the hallway?" Mom blinks.

"We are."

"What about the cameras?" She fidgets.

I take her hand and guide her along. "Don't worry about the cameras. We're not going to show up on video. Stay close to me."

"Is this Sophia's magic?" whispers Mom.

"No. It's, uhh, Dalton's magic, I guess." I shrug. "He's kind of a rogue. I've inherited some minor stealth powers. Ashley's got the guards. If we see anyone walking by, don't panic. Just stay quiet and don't move. Don't let them touch you. They won't process that we exist as long as we don't do anything to attract their attention."

"You two are getting kind of scary." Mom half chuckles. "But I'm not going to complain."

We sneak back to the executive bathroom.

Chloe can't resist. Once we're all inside, she leans out into the hallway and giggles.

"What was that?" asks a distant man. "Sounded like a little kid laughing."

"Stop saying shit like that," snaps a woman. "You're trying to freak me out."

"Chloe!" I wave at her. "Stop it."

She grins and scampers over to me.

Blix scratches the mirror.

Time to go home.

CHAPTER 36
How to Reason with Fanatics

LATER, FRIDAY NIGHT

We got Mom home through the mirrorworld without *too* much of an issue.

She made the mistake of saying the show *Joey* was a bad idea and they should've just left it at *Friends* when we told her what those zombie-like things were. Apparently, those creatures can hear very well. Yeah, they got mad. Chased us a bit. And yes, that appears to be exactly what they were. Ashley was right. Dumb as that sounds, the mirrorverse shapes itself based part on reality and part on our consciousness. As soon as she decided to joke about the wandering zombie-like creatures were 'people who thought *Joey* was funny, they became exactly that.

And they're passionate fans.

Dad was in full emotional support mode when we got home. Let's just say they got cute.

Yeah, time to get out of the house for a bit. I don't need to listen in on that.

So, I do something impulsive and maybe a little foolish. Oh, hey shocking. I'm a teenager.

No, I'm not getting involved in a land war in Asia. Nor am I trying sushi from a gas station. We went out to cruise around and brought Chloe along with us. Yeah, it's not the smartest idea in the world to go out into the world with her at this hour. We're way past any reasonable bedtime for a seven-year-old. Couldn't leave her home by herself. Didn't want to stick the 'rents with her, since they've gone to bed and... yeah. Stuff I do not want to listen in on is happening.

Oh, I have no idea if they're trying to give me another sibling. Maybe they'll end up doing that. They're just being all cute and lovey-dovey with each other tonight. Mom's in an unusually vulnerable state right now after being convinced her entire career was going to be destroyed by events totally out of her control she could in no way explain without being thought of as insane.

One thing working in our favor for this not being terminally stupid is kiddo having some stealth capability. It's clear to me now that vampires inherit certain abilities from the one who made them a vampire. While not a set-in-stone sort of rule the way all Shadows get those neato shadow powers, it seems like Lost Ones tend toward roguish-slash-stealthy abilities.

We know little about the random vampire passing by her old house who just happened to hear her screaming that night. She and I have that in common. We were both mercy vampires after someone murdered us.

Whoever he was, he must have been a Lost One. I don't *think* he was a Shadow or Chloe would totally have said something like 'a monster' saved me. She described him as a man. So, regardless of her sire's nature, kiddo is mega sneaky. She's figuring this out and itching to have fun with it. That's why she messed with the security guards. Even without Ashley's help, she could walk right up to a mortal and they'd never see her unless she wanted them to. I'm not really sure how many people she can affect at once. It might be one or two... or maybe she could walk through a crowded room unnoticed. Who knows? Not going to test it. At least not tonight.

She *does* know that she can't be seen out in public after it gets too late, or problems will happen.

Fortunately, Ashley and I don't really look like adults. So, if anyone *does* see us, it's unlikely witnesses will assume we are kidnapping her and go straight to calling the cops. They'd probably assume all three of us are in trouble somehow and approach us to ask if we need help. See? Sometimes it *is* good to look harmless and young.

I guess that's a normal thing. When you're little, you hate being called a kid and want to get older faster. When you get older, you hate getting older and long for youth. I'm stuck in the middle space where it's no big deal either way. Or at least it wasn't until the Transference shaved a few years off my face and everyone started assuming I was somewhere between fourteen and sixteen. It's like finally getting promoted to Eighteen and almost adulthood and then being demoted back to kid-dom. Like, I *just* got my real driver's license and now it's not terribly useful.

Okay, Sare. Get used to it. This is my reality. Enjoy the advantages whenever possible.

Not like I care about drinking alcohol. I will *never* be able to buy liquor without using mind control powers. Even my legitimate, real, government-issued ID is going to get dismissed as a fake if I claim to be twenty-one in two more years when I am really twenty-one. No big deal. I could drink all the booze in the entire store in an hour and all it would do is flow straight through me. Absolutely zero point to bothering, as like ninety percent of booze tastes horrible.

Other problem is it kinda burns on the way out. So, yeah. No thanks.

We fly around a bit messing with Chloe's powers because it's fun.

Ashley and I are ready to charm and mind-scrub the hell out of anyone if something goes wrong. We determine that kiddo can go so far as to brush up against someone while walking by and they don't acknowledge her presence. They *will* hear any noise she makes including footsteps, speaking, coughing, bumping into things... so it's only a visual stealth. At times she looks kinda blurry to me, so I think she might truly be turning invisible rather than doing the Ashley thing and just making people's brains refuse to process what they see.

Neat.

Of course, we can't help ourselves and mess with some rich people in a downtown Seattle high-rise apartment. As the old saying goes: 'there's nothing as beautiful as the laughter of a child... unless it's two in the morning and you don't' have kids.'

We do that for a little while, then leave. Chloe gets the bright idea to go flying around looking for Santa Claus. Ashley's quick enough to say it's not Christmas yet and he won't be flying tonight. Kiddo is disappointed but understands.

Figure it's probably long enough that the 'rents have gone to sleep by now. I suggest heading home and getting comfy. Ash and Chloe like the idea, so we jump off the roof of the high-rise and start flying home.

That is, until I spot a familiar little red hatchback zooming along the road below.

A feeling twists in my gut the instant I realize that's Seth's car. I'd been more or less ignoring the Natasha situation since I rationalized greater powers than me would totally step in and handle things if it got out of control. This feels like the Universe giving me a nudge and calling me a slacker. Kinda been slacking a lot lately, but being lazy with homework isn't going to end the world.

Okay fine.

"Detour... sec." I swing around in an almost 180 turn to follow the car.

Ashley zooms around to catch me, pulling alongside my left. "What's up?"

Chloe trails after us, looking like some sort of Victorian ghost child. Her frilly doll dress catches the moonlight, making it almost glow. The way all the frills waver and wobble in the wind as she flies only adds to the etherealness of her form.

Huh. Maybe the reason kid vampires are generally considered a taboo has nothing to do with vampires feeling sad/guilty over taking the life of a kid. Might not even be due to the awkwardness of having to hide a permanent child from society finding out they're not getting older. It's probably just how darn *creepy* they can look.

There's a reason so many horror movies use scary little kids as plot devices.

Eep. If I wasn't a vampire and I didn't know Chloe, seeing her flying at me like that would've scared the absolute hell out of me as a mortal. The cuteness only makes it worse. Like, if a Shadow came after me, that's easy. Monster. Scream, run, no big deal. But Chloe? She's simultaneously adorable and terrifying (while flying). It sets up a contradictory emotional storm in the brain. You want to run over and hug her as much as you crap your pants.

The scariness is almost entirely due to her flying—and that dress. At home, on the ground, there's nothing scary about her.

I point at the car, then look over at Ash. "Natasha's idiot."

"Oh. Umm. So, what are we doing?" She makes goofy eyes at me.

"Not sure yet. Just got the strangest feeling I should follow him."

Ashley shrugs in a 'sure why not' manner.

We have eternity to pursue comfy nights at home watching movies and such. Sacrificing one of an infinite number of such nights is a small price to pay for potentially avoiding the destruction of civilization, right?

Guess it depends on which anime we'd have put on.

Seth drives to the industrial district, eventually pulling through the gate of a fence surrounding a somewhat rundown building. It's what I'd call 'unsmall.' It's neither huge nor small. On the smaller end of huge, so to speak.

They drive up to the entrance of the building and park close to the door, near some giant concrete flowerpots that probably once held mini-trees. Now, they're collection buckets for rainwater.

He and Robbie get out of the car and go around to the hatchback, which Seth opens.

I glide down and land on the roof above the two guys. The metal is wet, so my sneaker makes a small squeak as I touch down. Neither of the two vampires react. Whew.

Ashley swoops in next to me, doing a superhero pose kinda thing. She's more Squirrel Girl than Supergirl, but it works for her.

Chloe decides to land *on* me, draping herself over my shoulders like a backpack made of child. Don't blame her. The roof is cold and wet, and she's not wearing shoes. Kiddo seems to hate shoes. At least, she never puts them on unless we specifically tell her to.

"This is ridiculous." Robbie grabs two shopping bags. "What the hell does he need 200 blank notebooks for?"

Seth also grabs two shopping bags. "He's transcribing all of his notes into a backup copy or some shit. He thinks one of us pranked him and changed a bunch of crap in his books."

"You're serious." Robbie stares at him. "He's going to rewrite all those books by hand?"

"Yep." Seth lifts his leg up, hooks his heel on the hatchback lid, and closes it. "Every single one of them. Gonna take him months."

Ashley and I clamp our hands over our mouths to hold in the laughter. Hah! It worked. Topher is totally as OCD as I assumed an Academic would be about his area of fixation. He's probably spent every waking hour since that night going letter by letter over his books, trying to figure out what we changed.

Yeah, it's a little mean, but if keeping him occupied going in circles to fix his books prevents him from locating and releasing the end of the world, it doesn't make me feel guilty. I think it was even better than just stealing his books. It's taking him longer to fine-toothed-comb every page of every book to look for alterations than it would've been for him to replace or find new source materials.

Even books we didn't touch, he's certainly giving the same treatment too out of paranoia.

"Can't 'Tasha tell him to find the thing first?" asks Robbie while they head for the door.

"You don't think she's tried?" Seth grumbles. "If that guy wasn't so important, I think she'd have told him to get lost by now."

Seth and Robbie carry the shopping bags of notebooks (I assume) into the abandoned industrial property.

I say abandoned because it looks a bit rundown and there are no security guards here, no lights on inside, and I don't feel the presence of security systems operating. Yeah, I can feel that crap now. It's really subtle and easy to not even notice if there is any other noise or activity going on. An active security system gives off a super faint sound kinda like standing in the room with a really old TV set that's turned on but tuned to a blank channel. The only reason I know that is because Dad took us to this silly little museum somewhere in the Midwest on one of our road trips when I was like twelve or so. They had a massive CRT television set from like 1979 or 1980 or something ancient like that. Of course, I had to turn it on. It filled the area with... a 'presence' of sorts. Like you could hear it being on without really hearing anything. Hard to describe.

Anyway... this building is dead electronically speaking.

The two guys head inside.

I fold my arms in thought.

Chloe rests her chin on my shoulder. "Why are they mad?"

"Because they're trying to do something really dumb and we messed with them." I chuckle.

Kiddo nods. "Are we gonna mess with them again?"

Ashley gives me this eager 'ooh, yes, let's' look.

"Maybe." I ponder the situation for a minute or so. "Now that I've got more information about what's really going on here, I'm half tempted to try and talk some sense into her."

"Seriously?" Ashley puffs her hair out of her eyes, which falls right back down. "How do you talk sense into zealots?"

"Zealots?" I lean my head side to side in a 'yeah, okay maybe' sort of way. "You think they're that far off the deep end?"

"They're talking about this Rabanus dude like he's the second coming of Freddie Mercury." Ashley gestures at the wall.

I blurt out a laugh. "Okay, possible. But... I'm going to try."

"What if they decide to attack us?" Ashley bites her lip.

I glance down at myself. This shirt and jeans are not on my 'don't care' list. The jeans are newish and this *Battle Angel* anime shirt is one of my favorites. I'd be pissed if anything happened to it. "Damn. I'm going to miss this shirt."

She cackles. "I don't think any of them have claws. Besides, Sophia could fix it if you bring her enough shreds."

I smirk. "We could also just run away instead of fight. None of them can fly."

Ashley snaps her fingers. "I like that more."

"I'll distract them if you gotta run," says Chloe.

"No way, kiddo. I don't want you getting involved." I pat her arms, which are currently wrapped around my neck.

She sighs. "I'm not gonna fight. Gonna hide and scare them with a noise if they wanna fight. When they look, you run."

Does it mean I fail at being her 'mom' because that doesn't sound like a completely bad idea? To be fair, she's a lot sturdier than a normal child.

"Okay, kiddo. The most important thing for you is not to be seen."

"Promise," whispers Chloe.

I look over at Ashley. "Just going in there to try talking some sense into them. Maybe you could try some of that charm stuff on them."

She makes a 'hmm' face at me. "Haven't really tried it on vampires before, but I suppose it's worth a shot."

"That means you've tried it on mortals." I glance at her.

"Just experimentally." She waves dismissively. "Right now, it only kinda makes people inclined to like and trust me. I can't derp slap a whole room like Aurélie can... and it's for sure not going to make anyone do something they aren't already at least somewhat inclined to do."

Right. Not mind control, just charm.

"Better than nothing." I stand. "If any of them have doubts, you can exploit that."

"Assuming it even works on vamps."

"Pretty sure it does." I jump off the roof and glide to the pavement below.

Ash hops down beside me.

I head for the door and walk right in to an empty reception area. It's small with one desk and like four chairs around a little coffee table. This is not the kind of place that seems to have expected frequent customer visits.

The sound of voices leads me to a corridor past a handful of small offices, a conference room smaller than my bedroom, and some closets. An 'authorized personnel only beyond this point' door blocks our path at the end of the hallway.

"I hereby deem myself authorized," I whisper, then push the door open, revealing kind of a locker room type area.

All sorts of signs on the walls warn that PPE is required. Some poor little cartoon man gets mangled in various different ways on the signs to show why it's important to wear hard hats, goggles, gloves, and good boots. The cartoon warnings seem absurd, but the more I see of the world, the more I'm starting to believe that some people really *are* this stupid.

The voices emanate from the hallway leading deeper into the building, so I go that way.

Chloe picks this moment to stop being my backpack. She hops down and lets us go ahead of her before dropping into an over-acted video game 'I'm sneaking' posture. She is adorable.

Natasha and her people are hanging out among the vast array of machinery in this building's largest room. No damn idea what went on here other than that it involved conveyor belts and big machines.

Hoses, too. Maybe they bottled drinks in here. I creep toward the voices, ducking under a steel roller belt and huddling up behind a giant, boxy machine. It's not a bad hiding place. Close enough to peek around the corner and observe them.

Ugh. My brain wants me to think Natasha is considering using this place to process mortals into like 'blood soda' or some nonsense. If vampires ever went mainstream, there'd be a market for commercially sold stuff like that.

Sounds ridiculous, doesn't it?

Then again, if Mom could just grab some blood at Kroger's, it would kinda make life simpler for me. I would totally *not* miss having to bite people. Dammit, Sarah. Bad thoughts. I'm supposed to be trying to talk her out of this idiocy, not convincing myself she might have a point.

Besides, I don't know for sure if she's thinking about refurb-ing this building. It might've merely been a convenient abandoned location to set up shop. Guess they got spooked out of the grey house. Or, this is just a temporary thing.

Topher's looking over several large stacks of spiral-bound note-books arranged on like a foreman's desk in the middle of the factory floor. He's stacking and restacking them as if it matters what order he uses them in. Behind him is a steamer trunk with two enormous padlocks. Oh, wow. Why do I have a feeling he's put all of his old books in there. Paranoid much? Heh. Padlocks even. I should totally sneak over there and put a Post-It note inside the locked trunk with 'find what I changed in your books' written on it—while not actually messing with any of the books.

The others are sitting around on the various bits of machinery, either relaxing or poking at laptops. It seems like everyone is kind of in a holding pattern, waiting for Topher to finish doing his side project and get back to helping them look for Rabanus.

Right, here goes nothing.

I step out from behind the machine and approach them. "Hey, guys. What's up?"

Lorri screams like something out of a scare prank video on YouTube.

Her sudden loud outburst more than my appearance makes the others all jump, yelp, and flail around—except for Topher. He continues examining the notebooks like nothing happened. Dude didn't even flinch.

Natasha starts to reach for a gun on her hip, but pauses as her brain processes me. "You again."

"Hi." I wave. "Yeah, me again."

Ashley emerges from behind the machine and walks up beside me.

Natasha kind of gives her a mildly contemptuous, disdainful look. It's the same face the pretty girls back in high school always used whenever Bree Swanson showed up. Yeah, jealousy. Ash is by no means a Bree Swanson. She is not smoking hot cheerleader material. She's the cute girl.

The way Robbie stares at her makes me expect he's seconds away from an explosion of blood flying out of his nose right before he passes out.

That's an anime thing, by the way. He's lovestruck—or looks it.

Lorrie, Headbanger, and Seth give off more of an, 'aww are you lost, sweetie' vibe toward her. In a way, it kinda makes sense. They're all adults. Robbie is our age—or looks it. Who knows how long he's been a vampire.

None of them feel old. Topher only barely has a sense of age to him, which I guess means he's been a vamp for about fifty years or so. I have a feeling he is probably the oldest (as a vampire) of anyone in the room. He does not feel *old* old. Just 'established.' I'm still not sure what the actual requirement in years is before a vampire starts giving off power vibes, but it's well past a hundred. Topher is not there yet.

"So, what do you want, good girl." Natasha swipes her artificially bright red hair out of her face. She's wearing it in this bob style like some sort of cyberpunk anime character. "Don't suppose you've finally pulled your head out of your ass and realized I'm right, huh?"

I stuff my hands in my jean pockets and wander closer, trying to seem as nonthreatening as possible. Hey, I do non-threatening really well. It's kind of my thing. "You know, I can actually understand some of the appeal of no longer having to keep secrets."

Natasha raises both eyebrows. "Whoa. Really?"

"Yeah, I mean it's a pain in the ass sometimes." I shrug. "It would be kinda nice to just be able to go out and about and not care about keeping the whole vampire thing hidden."

She slides off the big machine she's sitting on, dropping to the ground with a loud *clomp* of heavy combat boots. Various decorative chains and such on her skirt and bracelets jingle. "Your tone is kinda sarcastic."

"Not intentionally. I'm not trying to be sarcastic. There are genuine good points. However... is it really worth not having to hide anymore if civilization is destroyed?"

She narrows her eyes.

"Wait... what?" Robbie snaps out of his 'she's so pretty' haze and moves his attention to me. "Destroyed?"

Natasha scoots to the side to put herself between me and him. "Don't listen to her, Robbie. She's the Trads little pet."

"You're not wrong there." I roll my eyes. "Yeah, I'm working for the traditionalists. Path of least resistance. That doesn't mean I want the world to get destroyed."

"Or you guys to end up dead," adds Ashley. "She's trying to help you."

Natasha leans at me. "Is that a threat?"

"No. No. Frick no." I flail my arms. "Good grief! I'm not here to pick a fight with you. I decided to talk to you because I *don't* want you guys to get hurt."

Headbanger sits up off a conveyor belt with a grunt. "What's this about the world being destroyed?"

"She's so full of shit." Natasha scoffs. "She's just trying to scare us because the Trads don't want to lose their power over us."

"Umm." I raise an eyebrow at her. "Do you think that their power comes from mortal society not knowing we're real?" I chuckle. "The elders are still going to have power over us whether or not we're out in the open. It has nothing to do with it."

Ashley swishes side to side, throwing off 'cute and innocent' so thick I expect a film crew from Hallmark to show up any second.

Alas, I've lost track of where Chloe is. That worries me. However, it kind of is what I told her to do: not be seen.

"Does kinda make sense." Robbie shrugs. "If they didn't have to stay hidden, they'd probably have even *more* power over us. They could do anything and not have to worry about cleaning up the mess after."

Lorri wraps her arms around herself, seeming worried.

Topher continues studying his new notebooks as if our conversation isn't even happening.

Sensing her people developing some doubt, Natasha turns to face them and yells, "She's talking out her ass. Don't you understand this is part of the plan to keep us oppressed?"

"Umm, Natasha?" I ask.

She spins on me, almost growling. "What?"

"How is having to keep ourselves hidden from mortal society 'being oppressed by the traditionalists'?" I scratch my head. "I always thought it was a 'let's not get ten billion mortals angry and coming after us with torches and pitchforks' kind of thing."

"It's oppressive because we can't enjoy our full potential." She points at me. "We're hiding in the shadows like rats. Not ruling over the mortals."

I let my arm flop to my side. "While you aren't wrong, that's still a mortal thing, not a Trads thing. It's the mortals who will rise up and try to exterminate us if they figure out we exist."

Everyone's quiet for a moment.

"You didn't explain what you meant about the world being

destroyed." Headbanger saunters closer, hands on his belt. He's got two guns, one on each hip. Who needs a concealed carry permit when you have mind powers?

"It's bullshit," mutters Natasha.

"Don't you want to at least hear the bullshit?" Headbanger gives a wheezy, dry chuckle. "Might be worth a laugh."

"Okay fine. What do you mean by destroy the world?" Natasha folds her arms and throws all her weight onto one leg. It makes her butt stick out to the side.

I take a breath, trying to collect my thoughts enough for this not to sound like I'm a nervous nerd freaking out over nothing. "You know that Mr. Wolent is aware of your idea to break secrecy."

"Right..." She nods.

"He gave me the job of trying to figure out how dangerous you guys were and if you were any sort of threat." I idly scratch at my shoulder. "That means he didn't really think you guys were too much of an issue."

"How's that?" asks Seth.

"She's a baby." Natasha rolls her eyes. "We're the intern's project."

Heh. I gesture at her. "She's not wrong."

"He's going to regret underestimating us." Natasha clenches her fists.

I hold up a 'wait a sec' hand. "That's changed. You guys aren't really my job anymore. He's put his real people on this." I pause, thinking. "Well, technically, no one said we weren't supposed to tell you this, so here goes: he issued a standing order to destroy all of you if you get close to finding that sarcophagus. If *any* of Wolent's people —some of whom are assigned to keep you under constant surveillance—think you're getting close to it, it's game over."

Lorri fades to corpse white.

Robbie coughs.

Headbanger's demeanor doesn't change too much except for his eyes. I think that's a 'screw this, I'm out' expression.

Natasha simply looks pissed off, like the twenty-six-year-old daughter of a rich guy who's finally been told 'no' for the first time in her life.

Topher looks up. "A destruction order? Surely, you can't be serious."

Ashley bursts out laughing.

I facepalm, then start chuckling.

Laughter seems to short-circuit Natasha. She sputters, as if trying to say something but not quite able to find the proper words.

Ash and I laughing apparently terrifies Lorri even more.

"The fuck's so funny?" blurts Headbanger.

"I am serious," says Ashley in an attempt to mimic a man's voice. "And don't call me Shirley."

Headbanger starts laughing.

"I'm gonna shoot her." Natasha pulls her Beretta.

Headbanger grabs her arm and pushes the gun down. "He walked right into that one." He glances back at Topher. "Who the hell talks like that?"

I think about the seriousness of the world ending to get my laughter under control. "The problem is that this sarcophagus you're looking for contains an ancient vampire."

"We know that already." Natasha stuffs her gun back in her belt. "Dumbass."

"There's more." I frown at her. "He's kind of like the vampire bogey man. There are specific legends about him."

Topher stares at me. "I highly doubt that you have more information about this elder than I do, considering you are still essentially an infant."

"Books aren't the only place to find information." I shrug.

"It's not going to be on the internet." Topher scoffs.

"I didn't Google this." I walk over to his desk and put my hands on my hips. "What about Remi Durand?"

Topher narrows his eyes as if the name is somewhat familiar to him, but he can't quite place it. Everyone else seems clueless.

"Who the shit is Remi Durand?" asks Robbie after a moment of no one talking.

"Just the vampire king of France." Ashley examines her fingernails. "No one that important."

A few seconds pass. Topher's expression shifts to 'oh, yes, that's right.' He then smirks at me. "And we're supposed to believe he somehow spoke with... you."

"He did." I nod. "Guy's actually kinda nice for a super old head vampire. Anyway, the point is what he told us. This sarcophagus you're looking for contains a vampire who was turned back in the days of Ancient Rome. He's over 2,000 years old... and he's such bad news that someone way back then stuffed him in a box and enchanted it closed."

"And when we release him, he is going to reshape the world the way it should be." Natasha folds her arms. "With vampires at the top of the power structure. Don't listen to her, guys. She's just trying to scare us. The Trads like being the only ones with power and they don't want any vampire to be able to feel powerful, on top of society."

I sigh. There's stupidly stubborn, and then there's this girl.

"I dunno, 'Tash," says Seth. "You think Wolent would order us destroyed just to keep holding on to feelings of power?"

She glares at him in a 'well duh' manner.

"Guys, I know what you think, but trust me. Wolent didn't issue that order because he's afraid someone else might feel powerful. After I explained to him what Remi told us, he does not want that sarcophagus opened. You are going to destroy the world."

Topher rolls his eyes. "Nonsense."

I wipe a hand down my face, frustration mounting. "You guys aren't understanding me. That old vampire is not going to do what you think he's going to do. If he wakes up, he'll be out of his mind with hunger and rage. Whoever opens his box, they're going to be the first ones he consumes... before he sets off on a vampire apocalypse. You won't be around to 'enjoy' whatever's left when he's done."

"That myth about very ancient vampires no longer being able to obtain sustenance from mortals and having to resort to feeding from other vampires is just that, a myth." Topher shakes his head. "The *only* creatures capable of feeding from vampires are *sefil*. It does not matter how old our kind get, the blood of other vampires is unpalatable, even dangerous."

"How do you know that?" asks Ashley. "Those books?"

He sighs. "Not specifically *these* books. I am a scholar of history, including vampire history. Regardless of a vampire's age, we simply cannot safely consume vampire blood. All that hogwash about elders turning into monsters and feasting upon lesser vampires is effectively the same as fables made to scare children."

"Anyone could write anything in a book." Ashley waves around indicating the room. "Writing something down doesn't make it true. What if all those books were written by ancient vampires and full of lies because they wanted to trick us?"

Topher attempts to keep a straight face but can't hide his nervousness. She hit him where it hurt: doubting his research. I imagine he's going to spend the next twenty years going back over everything he thought he knew to verify the sources thrice.

Ashely glances at me. "Look, I really don't want to be a secondary character in a B-grade end-of-the-world movie. You guys are on the way to doing something extremely stupid."

"I'm also really trying to stop you guys from getting ashed." I try my best to sound as sincere as I really am. As dumb and arrogant as Natasha is, the thought of her getting destroyed permanently makes me feel guilty. "Yes, I am trying to stop you guys from carrying out your plan. It's not because I want to preserve the Traditionalists' order. It's because I'm trying to save your unlives. Wolent's people *will* end you if they think you're about to open the bad box."

Natasha fidgets. She glances at Topher, seeming rattled by his visible worry.

Ashley leans forward practically glowing with 'trust me' charm. "The elder in that sarcophagus is dangerous. Europe is full of stories about him waking up and destroying thousands of vampires. Feel free to go ask Remi if you want. We're not making this up."

"I dunno, guys." Headbanger taps his boot on the concrete floor. "Maybe we should think about things a bit more before continuing."

"Continuing?" Natasha sighs. "We haven't been doing anything but waiting for Topher to sort out his books. And now he doesn't even seem confident in what he thought he found."

"Well, erm..." Topher drums his fingers on the desk. "I suppose it is theoretically possible that the texts I had been using as a confirmed source might have been fabricated by those with ulterior motives. It will take me some time to conduct a more thorough vetting of sources."

Hah! I knew it.

"Umm. I don't want to get destroyed," whispers Lorri. "Maybe we should kinda set this project aside until we know for sure."

Robbie nods at Lorri.

Natasha looks like she's about to cry—or shoot me in the face.

"Hey." I reach to put an arm around her but back off at the glare she fires my way. "Just because we have to stay off mortals' radar doesn't mean we can't enjoy ourselves. There's a lot that's awesome about being a vampire. Don't get older. Never get sick. Never get fat. We could get almost anything we want with mental influence. Lamborghini? Penthouse? Women's clothing that has actual real pockets even."

"Hey don't get crazy there," says Ashley. "That's like asking for a real unicorn."

"Some of your ideas are good." I nod to Natasha. "The way you're going about them is... not. This sarcophagus is basically the vampire equivalent of a nuclear bomb. If you open it, you are going to be devoured."

"And it's probably going to hurt." Ashley cringes. "A lot."

"Wouldn't be much point to us having the ability to go public if 'public' is a vast ruined landscape." I shrug.

"Yeah, yeah. Okay." Natasha folds her arms. "Not making any promises, but it's worth thinking about." She turns to look at Topher. "Can you figure out if she's telling the truth?"

"Probably... though it might take a while." He resumes checking the blank notebooks.

Oof. What the heck is he doing? Checking for anything pre-written in them or something? Making sure none of them are a sixteenth of an inch too big? Maybe it's like an ASMR thing and he just adores the smell and feel of virgin, untouched notebooks. And wow, that sounded creepier than I intended it to.

"Cool." Ashley grins.

It sure seems like Natasha's crew, if not her personally, have lost a lot of enthusiasm for this plot. Nothing quite says 'hold on a minute' like a destruction order.

"So, uhh..." Lorri fidgets. "If we don't keep chasing this old vampire, does that mean the Trads are not gonna destroy us?"

"Yeah." I nod. "Wolent ordered them to ash you guys *if* you got close to opening the box. If you stay away from it, you'll be fine."

"Are they gonna know we're not going to do that anymore?" asks Robbie.

I smile, then start making my way to the exit. "Yep. They've got people watching you."

At that moment, a childish giggle echoes from the back of the factory.

"What the hell was that?" Lorri jumps. "Did you guys hear that?"

Robbie stares toward the back of the factory, his expression saying, 'no effin way.' "Sounded like a little kid."

Wow. Vampires scared of ghosts. What will they think of next.

"Time to go home," I say—mostly for Chloe's benefit. "I'll leave you guys to think. Please believe I'm not trying to bullshit you."

Natasha and her people keep quiet as Ash and I leave. Once we're outside, Chloe draws our attention to the roof with a clicking noise.

Kiddo looks quite proud of herself. She not only stayed out of sight the whole time, she managed to prank scare two vampires.

And I think I might have gotten through to Natasha.

That was honestly much easier than I was expecting... which can only mean it's not going to work.

Sigh.

Not much else for me to do right this minute other than make the unprompted leap directly to violence. Nah. I like this shirt too much. Besides... Natasha probably won't see reason, but if her people chicken out on her, she won't be able to do much. Lorri and that Headbanger guy seemed the most hesitant.

I can hope, right?

CHAPTER 37
A LITTLE MAYHEM

S
am sat at his desk in second period, listening to the math teacher talk about fractions.

Evidently, Blix hadn't been convinced that Sam believed sufficient amounts of cold in the right places could make even the most manly of guys shriek. While being teleported instantly from a hot bathtub to the unforgiving roof of the Space Needle in thirty-degree December was an extremely unlikely thing to ever happen to normal people, the school property had plenty of other sources of cold.

That morning, several older boys as well as two teachers happened to get close enough to puddles or walk too near to clogged rain gutters. Blix ensured that all of them had an unexpected meetings with almost-frozen water. One of the eighth-grade boys happened to be the only one who didn't shriek like Sophia finding a dead rat in her bedroom. He simply gasped and appeared momentarily paralyzed. Everyone else, including the two teachers, made noises pretty much the same as Sam did when his backside hit the roof.

Sam truly believed the imp, though he already did after the neighbor got doused. No, this was Blix getting his imp on, so to speak. Despite being a cool best friend, he remained an imp. The urge to cause mayhem and chaos was in his bones. Thankfully, being not quite the ordinary sort of imp, he had little trouble shifting the nature of his pranks to generally harmless, funny things rather than the dangerous, semi-deadly sort of bedlam favored by the majority of his kind.

That ability to 'go dark' remained locked away. Sam knew Blix could summon it if need be. It would stay locked away unless or until someone tried to hurt his family. For now, though, funny pranks were perfect.

The problem with pranks, at least as far as Sam thought, was how so many of them felt as if they were rooted in cruelty. Someone always got victimized by the prank and either humiliated, hurt, or made to feel bad. He needed to come up with some sort of prank that didn't do any of that, one that inconvenienced people for a decent enough time without making anyone feel targeted or shamed.

He tapped his pencil on his notebook, thinking. How could he possibly pull off a big enough prank that simultaneously inconvenienced a large number of people without hurting anyone?

Maybe I could ask Blix to kill all the cameras at the next Seahawks game? He thought a moment. *Nah. Someone might get hurt. That'll start fights.*

Likewise, shutting down all the computers and stuff at SEA-TAC was a definite no-go. While it would *massively* inconvenience a huge number of people, he couldn't run the risk of dead air traffic control equipment causing a plane crash. Way, way too evil.

The idea of asking Blix to call up a bunch of imp buddies to run around Seattle downtown and turn all the traffic lights red for two hours got some traction. Seemed like a super annoying thing to do. He almost considered it a good idea until thinking about ambulances getting stuck in the massive traffic snarl it would cause. Someone could die.

Nope. That's out.

He glanced around at the rest of his class. Neifos the Ever Cackling seemed to like embarrassing people. Could Blix summon a bunch of other imps and snap their fingers so everyone in the entire school suddenly had no clothes? Nah. Not only did that include two of his sisters, it would be far too obviously supernatural. That sort of thing didn't happen. Besides, it was really mean to do. While he wouldn't be too bothered by it, something like that could cause mental damage to others.

So no, that was right out, too.

Something that won't get the Persons In Black knocking on our door... something that won't hurt anyone. Something that will be annoying and inconvenient to a lot of people.

Blix whispered from his bookbag on the floor next to the desk, "We could make *Barney the Dinosaur* go back on TV."

Sam blinked. He had no idea what that meant or why the imp thought it so funny. Once he got home today, he'd ask Dad to explain.

Back and forth, ideas came and went. Sam dismissed them for being dangerous, mean, too small in scope, or too obviously supernatural. He had to find a balance between something that might have been done by normal people while being big enough to satisfy Niffy.

Obviously, he planned to ask Blix for help. For one thing, an imp could do things much faster than he could. For another, it offered the perfect alibi. No rational person would ever connect mayhem back to Sam, especially if said mayhem occurred while he sat there innocently in class under the eye of a teacher.

Something in the school.

Something big.

Something that would not hurt anyone.

Something funny.

Something really inconvenient.

An idea hit Sam, somewhat inspired by an old movie Dad let him watch that he probably shouldn't have at his age. Some sort of Eighties college comedy film. Most of the jokes went over his head, but the sight gags were funny.

Sam tore a small bit of notebook paper off the corner and wrote: can you get some friends (more imps), then run around school: swap all the padlocks on all the lockers randomly. Coat halls with mega slippery slime. Chaos the library and supply closets. Set off fire alarm. When FD turns off alarm and calls safe, set it off again. Eat this paper after reading.

That done, he leaned over sideways and slipped the paper into his bookbag.

Seconds later, impish cackling came out of the bag. Blix stuck one spindly arm out and gave him a thumbs up.

Sam exhaled as the sense of his imp companion being right next to him stopped. An imminent sense of approaching chaos fell on him. Using his powers over demons to attack his own school felt wrong, but also kind of hilarious. He did not suffer the same sort of crushing, constant guilt that Sophia did. He would be able to keep quiet and not confess to his parents or anyone else that he was the cause of this.

After all, no one would believe him anyway if he did.

Except the 'rents. They'd believe he *could* do it. Perhaps not so much that he actually did. It was for a good cause, though. Since Mom got bathtubbed, she might go easy on him if he got caught. If this worked, Niffy would leave them alone.

The next five minutes of math class felt like they took an hour.

Then, the fire alarm went off.

"Oh dear," said Mrs. McMurphy, the teacher. "We weren't supposed to have a fire drill today. Oh well. You know the routine. Everyone up. Hurry and grab your coats, then form a line..."

Sam tried to act as normal as possible while getting up and queuing up at the door with the rest of his class.

An adult woman screamed out in the hallway, the kind of scream someone usually makes while wiping out on a patch of ice. A few kids shrieked. Mrs. McMurphy opened the door, took a step out into the hall, and promptly ended up flat on her back sliding away.

Sensing that this was not a fire drill but could be a real fire, the kids in Sam's class surged forward out the door. As soon as they tried to step into the hall, their feet shot out from under them like something straight out of a cartoon. Kids farther back in line kept surging forward, unaware or unconcerned the ones in front of them were wiping out.

Sam clenched his jaw, bracing for it and followed his classmates, not that he had much choice being caught in the midst of the mass of bodies.

The instant his sneaker touched the slime-coated floor, it felt as if something grabbed his foot and yanked it forward. Whatever the imps used—which looked more or less like clear petroleum jelly— had to be partially magical. No natural substance could be *this* slippery.

Sam wiped out and landed on a pile of kids. He didn't really even try to get back up, knowing it would be futile.

All around him, kids screamed, teachers yelled, people struggled to stand up again and only fell right back over. A few kids grabbed onto the lockers and tried to pull themselves upright, though that didn't work either. Once the slime coated their hands, they couldn't get a grip on anything.

One kid tried to swim and ended up just paddling his arms on the floor without moving anywhere.

Some of the screaming from the kids changed tone to hilarity. Maybe a quarter of the students found this mess to be fun. The others, still thinking there might be a fire somewhere, kept trying to escape the building by dragging themselves along the floor.

Stuff crashed and slammed in the distance, likely teachers or bigger kids losing their balance and dragging furniture to the floor with them as they went down.

Absolute chaos reigned in the halls.

Sam remained calm and didn't really try to do much more than avoid being sat on. Due to the extreme slipperiness of the slime, the students turned into a flowing river of flailing children all moving toward the exit at the same excruciatingly slow pace. By the time Sam's section of the near-liquid flow of kids reached the door, some of the teachers who had made it out of the building stood on either side, plucking kids away from the ooze and setting them standing on the sidewalk.

After a great deal of slipping, sliding, and struggling, Sam carefully made his way across the school parking lot to the area where his class gathered. The coating of goo all over him made it challenging to walk even out here on the pavement. Lots of kids kept slipping and falling over.

No one seemed to be getting hurt from the falls. Sam caught sight of a few imps scurrying about begrudgingly throwing themselves under students to cushion their falls on pavement. He grinned to himself. Blix totally understood the assignment: no injuries.

He scraped his sneakers on the ground until enough slime wore off them that he didn't constantly slip and slide around, then watched the chaos. Almost everyone, teachers and students alike, looked like they'd been downwind of the Stay Puft Marshmallow Man blowing his nose. The slime resembled snot enough to the point where a few people threw up. Of course, it wasn't snot. It had to be some generic slimy substance the imps conjured into existence.

Hopefully, it would evaporate like everything else they conjured after enough time... specifically before any labs could test it to see what the heck it was.

Sam and his classmates stood there for a few minutes before the fire department showed up.

The first few firemen to try going in discovered exactly how slippery the slime was. Their commander got the bright idea to use a hose to clear the hall and learned that water made it even slipperier.

Once it became quite clear that it would take the fire department an exceedingly long time to clear the building, the teachers had the students move over to the recess area and sit. Being outside in December was not the best. Not every teacher had their kids grab coats before getting out of the building so... problems arose.

Those without coats got hurried into the gymnasium for the time being. The fire department cleared the gym, which had not been slimed. Soon, they brought the rest of the kids in there for warmth.

Two hours after the alarm went off, the fire department still hadn't been able to make it completely through the school to declare it a false alarm. The slipperiness of the goo proved a massive obstacle.

Sam tried his best to avoid laughing at the situation. Mostly, he thought about the poor janitors who would have to clean this up. Perhaps not so much the slime, since it would disintegrate soon. But, part of his idea involved the imps throwing all the books off the shelves in the library, tossing all the school supply closets, and basically making as much of a mess of anything as possible—kinda like when the imps went crazy at Sarah's friend Michelle's job and messed up all the lawyer files.

The gym had become quite loud from kids talking. Some ignored the chaos and talked with their friends about whatever. A few girls complained loud and long about their clothes and/or hair being ruined by the slime.

Like a nest of hornets someone walloped with a baseball bat, the teachers gathered near the middle of the gym, plotting their revenge on whatever students were responsible for this. One of the teacher's voices seemed baffled as this was the 'sort of thing' high school seniors would do. He didn't think it plausible that middle schoolers could've pulled this off. That got the other teachers wondering if their school had been 'attacked' by kids who didn't even belong here.

Eventually, the school staff brought food in and handed out burgers, fries, and drinks to everyone in the gym. The hallways were still mostly impassable, so getting all the kids to the cafeteria wouldn't be a great idea.

This prank inconvenienced the students. No one liked being covered in slime. Though some of them did have fun playing in the slippery hallway. It inconvenienced the teachers because they'd have to make adjustments for the entire day being wasted to cover stuff in class. It definitely inconvenienced the janitorial staff. It would probably inconvenience some cops who got called in to investigate who did this.

"Crap," whispered Sam. "Security cams."

"Covered," replied Blix from his perch on Sam's shoulder. "Today security cam all Jerry Springer show."

He held back laughter. Certainly, the angry teachers would be looking for any student laughing a bit too much, even if they didn't believe middle schoolers would be capable of a prank at this scale. He did at least have a perfect alibi. Mrs. McMurphy saw him in class this morning and he never left the room until the alarm went off.

Finally, the fire alarm stopped ringing... at 1:38 p.m.

Sam grabbed Blix as the imp began to dart off. "Nah. That was fine. Don't gotta do it again."

Blix shrugged. "Okay."

Sam looked out over the chaos he caused, his emotions a swirl of wanting to laugh, feeling guilty, and being generally annoyed at the whole situation.

This better be enough for Niffy.

CHAPTER 38
QUALIFIED IMMUNITY

MONDAY EVENING

So, yeah. I'm expecting Natasha to still be a pain in the ass.

There is only so much I can do, though. I tried. She and her people are fully aware that they risk destruction if they keep chasing this sarcophagus. They don't even have to genuinely find it. If Wolent's people even *think* that they are close to it, it'll be game over.

Something happened today. When the Littles got home from school, they were mostly laughing. Sophia complained about the day being wasted. This, of course, got Sierra to call her a nerd because what sort of kid complains about school being canceled, or delayed, or whatever happened. From what they're saying, I think the fire alarm went off and some sort of enormous mess ensued.

Sounds like the kids got a day off school. Mostly... They still had to wake up early and go there, even if not much schoolwork went on. Fortunately, from what I'm overhearing, no actual fire occurred.

Mundanity took over my afternoon-into-evening. I got to feeling a bit too much like a freeloader, so I went into cleaning mode. Spent all day (at least all day after 2:30 when I woke up) cleaning. No big deal. It's not like I hate doing it or have better things to do. Ashley ended up joining in like twenty minutes later, since it still takes her a bit longer to wake up than me for some reason. Then again, she was like that as a mortal, too. Mrs. Carter had to physically drag her out of bed some mornings or she'd have been late for school. I struggled to get out of bed in the morning, but at no point was I ever that bad. Mom never had to literally haul me out of bed.

While cleaning the upstairs bathroom, I took care not to step fully into the bathtub. Didn't feel like being stranded atop the Space Needle until sunset. Kinda makes me wonder if my family ignored the bathtub, would that demon eventually give up and leave us alone? They always say not to give a tormentor what they want and they'll go away. Pretty sure the 'they' who said that never actually suffered from a tormentor. That tactic seldom works on bullies, so I doubt it would do much good on a demon. Creatures that can wait centuries to repay a grudge tend to be modestly more patient than humans.

I also don't think Mom or Sophia would make it too long without caving in and trying to take a long, relaxing bath. At least it seems like Sophia can somehow resist that thing's mischief.

So, yeah. Lots of cleaning today in between moments of wondering how much time I bought for the Natasha problem before idiocy takes over again. Even if it ends up failing, I had to try to talk her down. I'm not the 'just kick the door down and start swinging' type of person. That's more Sierra's style. Though, in fairness, that's her style when playing tabletop RPGs. She likes warrior type characters. Whether or not she'd feel the same way in real life when actual living (or unliving as the case may be) people would end up dead, I don't know. Probably not.

It's neither of our problems. Wolent has people for that. I am not now nor will I ever be one of his 'legbreakers' or whatever the term is for it. My job's either being a harmless courier... or a mad bomber.

Yep. Two extremes. I either hurt no one or blow up an entire nest of vampires all at once.

Go me.

Unlife goals... or something.

Can't a girl just hang out with her friend and enjoy unlife? Argh. Why all the complications?

Today, at least, seems to be on track to be quiet. I'd say the worst thing about the day is that it's Monday, except that doesn't matter to me much anymore. I used to dislike Mondays for the same reasons most of the country does: alarm clocks. They're the end of the weekend, the first day where we can't just sleep until we're done sleeping. To get technical, 'Mondays' don't necessarily have to be a literal Monday. Some people work weekends and have other days off. The first day they need to obey the alarm clock is their Monday.

Me? I never have to wake up early... mostly because I can't. Not really.

Sure, if someone breaks into my bedroom with the intention of harming me, I'll wake up before my usual time... in a manner of speaking. The intruder won't get 'normal Sarah' though. They'll get something else. Something much darker that probably won't remember anything about whatever happened.

So, yeah. On that charming thought, I scrub the toilet. Gotta do something cheerful. One of the worst parts about being a vampire is having a boosted sense of smell. I think my eyes are watering. If nothing else, that means I will get this damn thing 'hospital clean.' When *my* nose can no longer detect the horrors that went on here, it will be spotless.

"Sare?" asks Sierra, poking her head in the door.

"Yeah?" I continue working the brush around the bowl.

"Mom wants everyone in the living room, family meeting." Sierra backs out and starts off down the hallway.

"Uh oh. Who did what?" I sigh at the toilet. Still getting a hint of awfulness. Though, it's nothing a mortal nose would pick up. Gonna call that good enough for now.

"No clue," says Sierra right before running down the stairs.

I put the toilet brush back in its holder and make my way down to the living room.

Dad's in his recliner. The Littles and Ashley are on the sofa. Chloe's sprawled on the floor near the sofa. Mom is standing in front of the TV facing everyone. She doesn't seem upset, nor does she give off vibes of happiness. If anything, the read I get on her expression and body language is like she's been given an annoying but not terribly demanding task she needs to do.

Uh oh. I hope she didn't lose her job or something.

Wait, no. She'd be far more upset. And I don't think she'd call a family meeting for that.

I jump over the banister about midway down the stairs and float myself to the sofa.

"Show off." Ashley grins.

"All right. Now that everyone is here..." Mom exhales.

"Is this about the bathtub problem?" asks Sophia in a timid tone. "I'm working on it."

"Might have fixed that." Sam fidgets.

Mom looks back and forth between them. "No, this meeting wasn't about the bathtub. But what's going on there?"

Sophia stares at Sam, seeming hopeful. "You fixed it?"

"Maybe." Sam swipes at his hair, which is getting long enough to hang over his eyes. "I can't explain unless Mom gives me immunity from being grounded."

"What did you do, Sam?" Mom raises an eyebrow.

"Do I have immunity?" He bites his lower lip.

Mom taps her foot, thinking.

"If he did fix it," I say, "you won't end up stranded in Fowler's office again."

Redness takes over Mom's face. "All right. Fine, Sam. You have immunity from being grounded on this one thing *if* said thing was directly related to the bathtub problem being fixed."

"Okay." Sam takes a deep breath. "There's a demon messing with us through the bathtub. I made a deal with him to stop and leave us alone but he wanted me to do something that inconvenienced and annoyed a lot of people so he could feed off that instead of embarrassing and annoying us."

Sophia and Sierra gawk at him, then burst out laughing.

"Dude..." Sierra gasps. "That was you?"

"If you're talking about what happened at school today, yeah." Sam fidgets.

"What happened at school today?" asks Mom.

Dad leans forward in his chair, making an 'oh this sounds good' face.

"Slimed the hallways, set off the fire alarm, knocked all the books in the library off their shelves, messed up a bunch of office papers, general chaos." Sam scratches idly at his chest. "The hallways were so slippery the fire department couldn't properly inspect the school to declare it safe for hours."

Sophia looks vicariously guilty. Now that she knows who did it, she's terrified someone's going to ask her and she might need to lie about it.

"At least that slime disappeared." Sierra frowns. "Do you have any idea how *funky* that felt being soaked in it?"

"Yeah." Sam nods. "I was covered in it, too."

"That had to be a mess." Dad chuckles.

Sophia cringes, making a face like she just sat in a bowl of warm snot. "It was horrible. So slippery no one could even stand back up once they fell over."

Dad whistles. "I almost wish I could've seen that."

Blix leaps off the couch above Sam to land on Dad's knee. He reaches into nothingness beside him like he's got a pocket, and pulls out an iPhone, which he flicks his little hand at a few times before holding it up to show the screen.

From the screaming, it sounds like Dad is watching a video of the chaos in the hallway. My father's expression is part horrified, part trying not to laugh himself silly.

"No one got hurt." Sam shakes his head. "That was a firm condition. Looks bad, but there wasn't even a sprain or stubbed toe."

Dad bursts out laughing. "Oh my. That looks like the kind of craziness that the idiots at my high school might have tried to pull off... if they could've gotten the funding for 500 gallons of Vaseline."

Mom facepalms. "Don't the fire alarm things have dye packs in them to deter pranks?"

"I dunno." Sam shrugs. "Blix made it go off. He probably didn't even pull any levers."

The imp shakes his head, grinning, then babbles a short two-word phrase.

"He said 'no evidence'," Sam gives Blix a high-five.

"And this somehow fixed our bathtub?" Mom continues facepalming.

"Umm. Not sure." Sam jumps off the couch. "Let me go ask."

He runs upstairs.

Again, I have no idea how such a skinny ten-year-old boy can make so much damn noise on the stairs.

The rest of us sit around in awkward silence. Except Chloe. She's absorbed in a cute little kid-friendly game on her tablet. What the heck did parents do before kids had tablets? Oh, right. According to Dad, parents just set the kids loose outside and hoped they came home when it got dark.

A few minutes later, Sam thunders down the stairs. Unlike me, he does *not* jump off halfway down and runs the entire length of the stairs like a normal person. He flings himself back onto the sofa where he'd been before, then nods.

"Yep. We're good. Niffy agreed to leave our tub alone and go back to Heck." Sam smiles. "The tub should be safe to use again."

"That's good news." Mom lets out a sigh of relief.

Sophia and Sierra cheer.

"On to the reason I called the family meeting." Mom clasps her hands in front of herself. "Got some bad news today. Evidently, Uncle Hank has passed away."

Sierra's face says, 'that's *bad* news?'

Sophia looks ready to cry.

Sam makes a 'that stinks' face.

"Aww, poor guy." Ashley sighs. "Was he alone in that home?"

"He did it to himself," mutters Dad. "I mean, how much of a jackass does someone have to be for your mother to want them at arm's length?"

Mom shifts her stare to Dad. "What's that supposed to mean?"

"I mean, your mother is one of the sweetest people I've ever met. She *was* letting Hank live with them for a while, right?" Dad raises an eyebrow. "Why did they decide to relocate him to the care facility?"

"Because his medical needs exceeded their ability to keep up with." Mom fidgets. "At least... that's the official reason."

Dad gives her a 'there, see what I mean?' smile.

Yeah, Grandma Sheridan is awesome. If someone mugged her and ran off with her purse, then tripped, hitting his head on a rock, she'd be worried about them getting hurt. Even *she* couldn't take Hank anymore... and he was her family. Grandma's father's brother, I think. Uncle Hank was like 91 or so. Grandma's in her early sixties.

Well damn. Part of me is like 'well, he won't ruin another holiday dinner.' Another part of me is trying to be sad. I mean, someone related to me has died. It's inappropriate to be anything other than sad even if I barely knew the guy. My only real memories of him are bad: holiday dinners when he showed up and was a jerk to just about everyone except for Grandma Sheridan.

"The Grinch died before Christmas," mutters Sierra.

Mom cringes.

Dad winces. "Too soon."

Sophia covers her mouth, staring at Sierra in an 'I can't believe you said that' manner.

"While I'm sure we all understand the sentiment." Dad reaches over and pats Sierra on the knee. "It would be better for everyone involved if we didn't say certain quiet parts out loud."

"I know." Sierra looks down. "Wasn't going to say anything to Grandma... or anyone not here right now."

"As you all probably expect, there's going to be a wake and funeral." Mom laces her fingers together and sighs. "We are expected to be there."

"Can I wear jeans?" asks Sierra.

Dad chuckles. "Hmm. Sure."

Mom blinks at Dad.

"Under your dress," says Dad.

"Ugh." Sierra glares at the ceiling.

Sam and Sophia almost laugh.

"I guess you're not going to let me wear a dress to the funeral." Sam tilts his head.

"No." Mom shakes her head. "Let's just be respectful for the last time we'll ever have to deal with Uncle Hank? That's not too much to ask. Just because he was a raging asshole to everyone, doesn't mean we sink to that level."

We all stare at Mom in total shock. It's so very rare that she swears.

Murmurs of agreement come from the Littles. I nod as well. Yeah, true. As much of a jerk as he was, no reason we should sink to the same level. His last hurrah messing with my siblings is that Sierra will need to suffer wearing a dress for the funeral. Hopefully, the guy won't haunt us out of paranoia Sierra or Sam might be gay.

Pretty sure neither of them are; however, according to him, girls wearing jeans is a sure sign of the absolute collapse of western society.

Or something.

CHAPTER 39
THE HUNT: PART ONE

MONDAY EVENING

Our night proceeds forward from the family meeting.

Not much changes, really. Uncle Hank, while family, was not a frequent presence in our lives. I do have some faint memories of him being at Grandma Sheridan's house when I visited as a little kid. It's kinda hard to remember exactly when he stopped living there. Part of me wants to say I'd been around ten years old the first time we went to visit and he wasn't there anymore.

I do remember the room... a small bedroom with oxygen tanks or some other stuff that smelled weird. That 'sick elderly person' smell saturated the whole room. Honestly, I have no idea what sort of issue he had other than being old. Something with his lungs, I think? Hard to say. My parents didn't really talk about it much. Uncle Hank has, for most of my life, simply been an annoying but mandatory presence at holiday dinners.

Had he been a nice guy, I'm sure he'd have continued living with Grandma... and probably been welcomed at more than just holiday dinners.

Alas. Not every old person is nice. But, like Dad said... the guy did it to himself. He just couldn't stop himself from being a jerk to anyone who existed outside his opinion of how the world should be. He gave Mom a hard time for working a job, because women should stay at home. I got a little flak for talking about college. What's a girl need an education for anyway? I'd be more upset at that if I hadn't been murdered. A *living* version of me totally would've needed an education. Now? Not so much.

Ashley and I head downstairs to our room after dinner. Yeah, our room. It's officially mine, but functionally ours. Not really sure why Sophia bothered going to the trouble to magically copy her existing bedroom. Ash barely uses it.

We hang out having an oh-so-upbeat conversation about how much it sucks to spend one's last years of life alone in a care facility. As miserable a person as my Uncle Hank was, I do still feel a little bad for the guy ending up like that. There's no way I'm going to let anything like that happen to either of my parents, or any of the grands.

In the middle of our conversation, we end up talking about being grateful to the Universe for sparing us that fate and decide to kinda 'adopt' Mr. Niedermayer. No, we're not going to have him move in with us or anything. He lives at the end of our cul-de-sac. Won't be too big a deal to check on him now and then and visit him.

Yes, Niedermayer has been a jackass to us—and all the kids in the area—but he's not the same as Uncle Hank, who was just a miserable, hateful person to the bone. Niedermayer's lonely and, I'm pretty sure his hostility to kids is coming from his not liking any reminders of whatever family he has not being around anymore.

So, we decide to visit him and offer to be there if he ever needs anything.

We've got a lot of time on our hands. May as well do some good with it.

Sophia pokes her head in. "Sare?"

I'm reclining in my computer desk chair, feet up on the desk.

Ashley's flopped on the bed. My computer is on, but I'm not paying attention to it. Ash has a tablet, but she hasn't been doing much with it while we've talked.

Chloe's still absorbed in her tablet. Should I be concerned about how much screen time a vampire child is getting each week?

"'Sup?" I ask.

Sophia walks in. She's in one of her pink dresses, has her school backpack on, and is carrying her pink-and-white sneakers. If I didn't know better, I'd say she was expecting to go outside... a little after nine on a school night.

"I located an energy fragment from that red tentacle monster." Sophia grinds her sock-covered toes into the rug, throwing off waves of guilt and nervousness. "It's not going to stay in the same place for long, so we kinda need to hurry. Can you help me?"

"Mom's going to flip." I exhale.

"Already asked her." Sophia grimace-smiles. "She said it's okay as long as we're not out *too* late and we don't cause any mayhem bad enough to end up on the news."

Wow. Okay. I'm not going to question this because there is no way in hell Sophia would lie about getting permission from Mom. "What's the plan?"

"Sneak up on it and catch it in the trap." Sophia holds up a black and yellow box with silver hatch doors. Damn thing looks really familiar.

"What the heck is that?" I blink.

Ashley bursts out laughing. "Are you serious?"

"No, I'm Sophia." She grins. "Dad made it."

As soon as she says that, it clicks in my brain why that thing looks familiar. It's a ghost trap from the movie *Ghostbusters*. Or at least it's a reasonable attempt to make something that looks like one. Wow. Never realized my father has a crafty side.

Sophia looks at the 'ghost trap' dangling on a wire from her hand. "It doesn't really work like the ones in the movies. There's no foot pedal and stuff. But it doesn't have to. I just needed a container. Was going to borrow one of the Tupperwares..."

I cringe. "Oof. I think Mom would've objected to using her food storage boxes for trapping a fragmented eldritch horror."

"Probably." Sophia shrugs. "Oh, guess what movie we're going to be watching Friday."

Ashley and I laugh.

"Also..." Sophia offers a weak smile. "It's not an eldritch horror, so we don't have to worry about our sanity getting torn to pieces."

"What is it?" I slide my heels of the desk and stand up.

"Umm." She fidgets. "I don't know what to call it. It's kinda goblin-like but also sorta orcish. Neither goblins nor orcs are supposed to have tentacles. It doesn't matter what we call it because it's not a real creature. Just a conjuration."

"Right. So, there are no crazy cultists."

She blinks. "Why would there be crazy cultists?"

"Eldritch horrors... that whole Cthulhu thing." I chuckle.

"Fish people... monsters... something." Ashley flails her arms, overacting being in a panic.

"Nope. Not that." Sophia shakes her head.

So much for making it through an entire day without having to get dressed. By 'dressed' I mean changing into something I can go outside wearing and not get laughed or stared at. Long sleeping T-shirts are great for lounging around in. Chasing magical chaos beasts, not so much.

After changing into a reasonably clean tee and jeans, I gesture at Sophia in a 'lead the way' manner.

"Hang on." Ashley scrambles off the bed. "I'm coming, too."

"Can I go?" asks Chloe.

I look at her, at Sophia, then back to Chloe. "Umm, Soph? How dangerous is this?"

"Umm." She rocks heel to toe a few times, flicking her gaze around at random. "It's either going to be no big deal or a huge mess."

"A huge mess as in dangerous or just a mess?" I tilt my head at her.

"Just a mess." She nods.

"All right, kiddo. You can go with us if you want."

"Yay!" Chloe shuts her tablet off and leaps to her feet.

Probably a good idea she takes a break from screen time anyway.

WE FLY INTO THE NIGHT SKY.

Sophia clings to me like a human backpack. She's not quite as thrilled with flying as Sam is. That she isn't screaming constantly speaks volumes as to how much she trusts me. Heights is on her long list of 'scary stuff,' though it's way below other things like spiders.

"Follow the kitten," says Sophia.

Before I can ask what she's talking about, Klepto appears in front of me amid a brief flash of purple light. The little grey kitten with glowing teal eyes stares at me, emits an adorable 'mew,' then rotates 180 degrees before rocketing off.

No, the kitten is not leaving a rainbow trail of light.

I'm not even going to make that joke or Sophia will add special effects to her kitten.

"Why are we following the kitten?" asks Ashley.

"Because my hands are busy." Sophia squeezes me tighter.

Somehow, that makes sense to her. Ashely looks baffled, but decides not to press her for more information.

Klepto races off into the distance ahead of us, turning to look back every so often, as if to ask what's taking me so long.

She is kinda hard to see, being small and fuzzy. At least her eyes are glowing, which makes it simple to follow her.

Within a few minutes, it becomes obvious to me that the kitten is heading for the school the Littles go to.

We cruise down toward the building. I slow to a midair crawl and start doing my best to keep us hidden from security cameras.

"It's at your school?" Ashley glides down and lands by the doors that go right to the cafeteria.

I follow. "Well, it is connected to her. Maybe it got attracted to places she's familiar with."

Sophia lets go of me and drops to her feet. "I don't know why it's here. Only that it's here. These fragments don't stay in the same place for very long. We've got less than an hour before it disappears and goes somewhere else."

"Are you sure we even need to catch these?" Ashley raises and lowers her toes.

"You forgot your shoes," I say.

"No, I didn't. 'Forget' implies accident." She does a little pirouette. "What's the point of being immune to cold if I still have to wear shoes all the time?"

Chloe giggles.

"Yes, we have to catch them." Sophia grabs the door handle and gives it a yank, grunting from the effort. It doesn't budge. "They're locked."

I step up. "Let me give it a try."

She half rolls her eyes at me, knowing what's about to happen.

Predictably, the lock likes me. The door opens easily when I try it. "All in the technique."

"Nice." Sophia grins. "If we don't catch them in time, they're going to gather strength and do something bad."

"Bad is bad." Ashley nods.

"Thank you, Confucius." I roll my eyes.

"What kind of bad?" Ashley enters the school. "Are we talking screaming and bleeding kind of bad or like forcing every television in the world to show Teletubbies 24/7 bad?"

"Eek." Sophia shudders. "I really hope my magic isn't capable of doing something *that* evil."

Heh.

Sophia pulls her backpack off, unzips it, and pulls out a chunk of glass. It's either glass or clear plastic and about the size and shape of a hockey puck. Dad got it from the office. Apparently, it used to be part of a copier machine that broke and they took apart. He thought it looked cool, so he kept it.

Chloe looks around. "Your school smells like farts and throw-up."

I hadn't really noticed until she mentioned it, but yeah. It kinda does... at least to a vampire's nose.

"It does not," whispered Sophia.

"Does, too," chimes Chloe.

"Does not!" Sophia stops walking to look at her.

"Really?" I rest a hand on both of their heads. "We're not doing this all night. Let's find this magical essence beastie and go home. You guys can do the 'does not, does too' thing all you want once we get home."

Chloe grins.

Sophia pouts at me. "No, we can't. Mom will tell us to stop."

"It honestly does smell like that," I whisper. "To a vampire."

"Oh." Sophia exhales. "Okay. That's fair. There are a lot of boys here. Boys are basically farts and puke held together by bubble gum and the desire to play video games."

Ashley and I laugh. Boys desire a bit more than video games... but maybe not the ones here. They have to get a little older before that starts—and I am not making that joke in front of my little sister... or Chloe.

The copier lens, which no doubt has been somehow enchanted, leads Sophia across the cafeteria to the hallway. I think she got the idea from that rock Sam used to track down the imps. We make our way down the hall, creeping along in more or less silence to allow my influence over the school's security cameras to keep us from showing up. She holds it out in front of her, almost like she's looking through it.

As far as I know, this school has no overnight security guards, only a camera system.

Chloe wanders side to side, peeking into rooms if the doors are open, and flying up to look through the windows if they are closed. Since she appears simply curious, I don't mind.

Sophia turns left at the first intersection. We go past a wall covered in fifth grade art projects. Lots of attempts to draw super-heroes, cats, dogs, and other less-identifiable things. Not every kid is an artist, apparently.

"In there." Sophia points at a door marked 6A at the end of the art installation. "Uh oh."

"What does uh-oh mean?" Ashley leans closer to peek through the window.

"This is my classroom." Sophia fidgets. "It might be attracted to places I spend time."

"Why?" asks Chloe.

"Umm. I think it's draining whatever emotional energy I might have left here." Sophia shrugs. "Or something. Whatever it is that's messing with me when I try to do magic might have sent this thing after me on purpose, so the part of the magic that's making it 'track me down' might be causing it to collect in places where I spend time."

"Sounds reasonable." I eye the doorknob. "What do we do?"

"Not much." Sophia takes a deep breath. "Unless you can do magic. Umm. Maybe one of you could try to get the trap close to it. Then, just try to keep it from messing with me."

I take the trap from Sophia and hand it to Chloe. "You're small, fast, and good at being sneaky. If you see something strange in there, try to get close to it without it noticing you."

She beams and nods eagerly, tossing her hair around wildly.

"On three," I whisper, grabbing the knob.

Everyone tenses.

"One... two... three!" I yank the door open.

Chloe zooms into the classroom.

Sophia rushes in after her.

Ashley and I go at the exact same time, crashing into each other —but since we're not that big, we fit through the doorway.

An orb of pinkish-purple light about the size of a volleyball hovers over one of the desks near the front row. I'm going to assume that's the desk Sophia sits at. Chloe dives forward into Supergirl pose, flying a mere few inches above the floor. Like some sort of slow-motion missile made of child, she drifts among the desk legs until she's directly below the orb—which so far has not reacted at all to us barging in the door.

We were not exactly subtle about it.

"Hit the button," whispers Sophia.

"What button?" I glance at her.

"On the trap. The red one." Sophia points.

Chloe peers down at the trap. She fiddles with it and the two metal doors pop open with a faint squeak.

Sophia hands me the lens. "Hold that."

I take it.

She raises her arms, palms out, fingers spread, and stares at the orb.

And that's when the proverbial shit hits the fan. A *whoosh-thunk-squish* noise comes from my right that kinda sounds like a town guard taking an arrow to the head in *Skyrim*. I barely have time to notice Ashley standing there making a derpy face with a small US flag impaled through her skull before six desks ram into me from all sides.

"Ow! Son of a...!"

The desks really smashed into me hard. My legs are tangled up in them and probably would've broken if I was mortal.

Something whooshes past me.

Sophia's scream of alarm gets cut off like someone grabbed her from behind and put a hand over her mouth. A high pitched *fweee* noise nearly drowns her out. I've never heard anything like that in my life. She keeps trying to scream through whatever's over her mouth. Chloe goes flying sideways, spinning horizontally like a human Frisbee before slamming into a scattering of kids' coats hanging at the back of the room. Several of them come to life and mummify her.

The glowing orb takes off like a cannonball, racing all the way around the classroom. Papers fly off shelves. Books in its wake leap into the air. Pens, folders, anything not glued in place gets tossed into the air like King Kong's leaf-blower hit this room on full power. After making a complete circuit around the classroom, the orb rockets straight at me. I try to dodge, but the desks crushing into my legs keep me pinned in place. I cringe, bracing for impact.

The orb hits me square in the face with no real solidity at all, and presumably goes right through me and out the door.

A sensation as though I'd plunged my head into an ice-cold river gives me the worst case of brain freeze I've ever had. The headache is supermassive... but only lasts for about three seconds. I'm seeing spots it hurt so much.

"Ow," says Ashley sounding way too calm. "The unicorns don't like peach schnapps."

My attempt to say 'what the hell are you talking about' comes out as the kind of noise Quasimodo might've made if he got kicked in the balls while simultaneously stubbing his toe. Yeah, my brain is frozen.

Sophia keeps trying to scream, and her tone is starting to sound full of legitimate panic. I'm sure no one actually grabbed her from behind since she's not being dragged away. Her voice is still coming from the same place.

I power through the brain freeze and look toward her.

She's lying on the floor, entirely mummified in duct tape, wriggling as much as she can with her arms and legs thoroughly taped together. She's panicking because the tape covers her entire face so she can't breathe. I shove at the desks, but they don't move... some invisible force continues to push them all into me.

"Ash! Help Soph! She can't breathe!" I yell.

"I'm Ashley," says Ashley. "I think. That is my name. Isn't it? You look really familiar."

"Not the time for Space Cadet mode!" I yell.

She turns to look at me. There's a small classroom flag impaled through her head. Dammit! She's not playing space cadet. She's got brain damage.

"Mmmm!" yells Sophia.

The reality that my kid sister is suffocating sets off a level of fury inside me I've never known myself capable of. I grab the desk right in front of me and shove as hard as I can, full of desperation. The desk moves barely half an inch, as though its legs mired in thick epoxy cement that hasn't quite dried. Sophia keeps freaking out.

"Grr!" I snarl, releasing a deep inhuman monstrous vampire growl that sounds more like it's coming from an 800-pound bear.

The desk moves half an inch more... then breaks free. All the force I've built up shoving on it releases at the same time, launching the desk across the room so hard it smashes through a bunch of other desks, splintering the tops and bending metal legs. Whatever magical energy animated the desks is broken; none of them are pressing into me anymore.

I pounce on Sophia.

Klepto sits on her chest, already having shredded the tape away from her mouth and nose so she can breathe.

By some absolute miracle, Sophia lays still, not moving, and appears quite calm.

Chloe shreds her way out of the coats wrapping her up. She looks angry, and unhurt.

I tug at the duct tape wrapping around Sophia's side. Her arms are thoroughly pinned to her body with the sort of tight precision only possible with magic.

"Don't rip it off," rasps Sophia. "Just cut my arms loose."

A wooden 'ploink,' 'ploink,' 'ploink' sound comes from behind me. It's so weird that I have to look now that Sophia's not in danger.

Ashley picks her fingernail at the gold-painted pointy cone at the end of the flagpole sticking out of her face. I'm calling it a flagpole but it's a stick. The whole shaft is roughly the size of an arrow. The flag hit her high in the back of the head and came out her left cheek. It's a bloody mess, but the actual damage path is pretty small.

"This feels sooo weird," says Ashley. "Like, I think it should hurt, but it doesn't."

That sounds more like Ashley. Guess her brain is recovering from the shock of being pierced.

"Piece of shit light ball!" yells Chloe at the doorway. "If you had an ass, I would *so* kick it!"

Ashley starts to laugh, then stops with an, 'Ow.'

I claw-slice the duct tape to free Sophia's arms from her sides.

She sits up and waves her hands around. Like noodles floating in water, the duct tape unsticks from her and floats up into a tangled mass. The 'fweee' noise I heard before must have been the sound of an entire roll of duct tape being de-spooled in half a second. The tape compresses into a giant wad, then falls to the ground.

Soph flicks her right hand at Ashley in an 'away with you' gesture.

The little flagpole yanks itself out of her head and floats up behind her. The flag cloth is saturated in blood, though not as much as it would've been if Ash had been mortal. Sophia snaps her fingers at it. In an instant, the flag is clean. I'd say it was nice of her to spare someone the hassle of washing it, but she's worried about evidence.

Ashley's eyes cross hard. She grabs her head and moans. "Ooh... I hate this... hate this... hate this... I can feel air blowing through the hole."

I cringe.

"Grr." Sophia stands, then looks at me. "Are you hurt, gummed up, or suffering anything I need to fix?"

"Don't think so." I look down at myself. My legs are sore as hell, but nothing broke. "The orb flew right through me. Got a massive brain freeze for a second there. It's over."

"Iiiiitching now." Ashley clenches her jaw. "This sucks."

"Lens please," says Sophia.

"I dropped it..."

"Mew!" says Klepto, appearing in a purple light flash beside Sophia, clutching the copier lens.

"Thank you!" Sophia grabs the lens and runs out into the hall. "Come on!"

I look at Chloe. She's fine. Furious, but unhurt. The coats, on the other hand, are in tatters. White fluff is everywhere back there. Yeah, kiddo has claws. They're tiny and cute, but still dangerous.

Ugh. This entire classroom got tossed like the Mafia came looking for something, didn't find it, then did more damage out of spite.

That's going to be fun to explain. Soph's already running down the hall, so I'm guessing she forgot to fix things here—or doesn't plan on it.

Chloe retrieves the trap.

"You okay?" I glance at Ashley.

"Yeah... I think." She angles her face toward me. "Is the hole still there?"

"It's a little red dot now." I gently swipe a finger at the mark. "Should be gone in another few minutes."

"Cool." Ashley frowns. "What the hell did I do? Why did it stab me?"

I hurry after Soph. "Like I have any idea..."

A massive *boom* shakes the school and sets off a car alarm or two outside. Uh oh. That was loud. Like *really* loud. The 'rents probably heard that from home.

"Was that a good boom or a bad boom?" I yell.

Sophia just growls.

Oh, screw it. There's no way I'm concentrating on the security camera thing at this speed anyway. "We're going to need to call in a specialist."

"What?" Ashley flies up to glide alongside me.

"Please shoot Sam a text and ask him to Blix the cameras here." I chuckle. "Again."

"On it." She pulls her phone out.

I round another corner at the end of the hall and stop short at the sight of two giant steel doors on the floor. They're warped as if having withstood an explosion from inside the gym, torn clear off the hinges and come to rest like thirty feet away from the doorway.

Sophia floats in the middle of the gym, surrounded by crackles of lavender lightning. Her pink dress and hair flutter around like a doll held out the window of a car on the freeway. She's got her arms thrust forward, grunting, growling, and twisting as if wrestling with a giant glob of invisible pizza dough.

I skid to a stop at the smashed doorway. "What's with the Sailor Sophia routine?"

Yes, the lightning and stuff is kinda... obvious. We've probably got only a few minutes before the police show up. Someone outside *has* to notice this crap going on.

"Traaaap!" calls Sophia.

That's when I notice the orb. It's stuck in place high in the air near one of the basketball nets, vibrating back and forth as if it's *really* trying to break free from whatever force she's using to hold it down.

Chloe skids to a stop at my side, gawking at electro-floaty-Sophia. "Whoa. Holy shit."

"Trap, now!" I say, then grab Chloe and hurl her into the gym.

I would not normally throw children like this, but kiddo can fly.

She smoothly transitions from projectile to flying, bee-lining for the floor below the orb. As soon as she lands, she opens the 'ghost trap' and holds it up over her head.

Sophia gives off an adorable snarl.

Yeah, she's pissed, but she still doesn't do intimidating well at all.

My sister thrusts her arms up, then swings them downward like she's power-bombing something foul into the trash—with contempt.

The orb zooms down through the basketball net into the ghost trap, hitting it with enough force that Chloe grunts from the effort it took her not to fall over. Kiddo reaches up and closes the doors. For a second or two, the 'ghost trap' Dad made emits smoke and fumes while rumbling and shaking about... then it goes still. I'm not sure if Dad added special effects somehow... if that's a normal side effect of whatever just happened here, or if Sophia did that on purpose so it looked like a proper ghost trap.

All the crazy lightning and wind around Sophia stops. She falls out of the air, but aces the landing without looking clumsy at all. Guess those dance lessons are useful for something after all.

"Nice." Ashley fist pumps. "Did you get it?"

"Yep. This one's caught." Sophia grins. "Sorry it got weird."

"No worries. We should get out of here." I wave Chloe over. "That was... not subtle."

Fortunately, there is a door that goes directly from the gym to the outside. I start heading toward it.

"But the classroom is a mess!" Sophia flails her arms. "I have to fix it."

"Cops are going to be here any second." I keep heading for the door.

"I can handle the cops." Ashley smiles. "They won't see us."

"Come on, Sare. Pleeease!?" Sophia pulls on my arm. "I'll feel so guilty if I leave it a mess. You know they're going to grill us tomorrow about it, and I'm not going to be able to lie."

I sigh. "You're right. We gotta do this fast."

We run down the hall, back to Sophia's sixth-grade classroom.

No sooner do we get to the room than the flashing red and blue lights of approaching police cars light up the trees visible out the windows.

Sophia waves her arms and spins about in a manner part Gandalf, part Disney Princess. Thankfully, she's not singing. Stuff flies into the air, zooming around and sorting back to where it belongs. All the stuffing bits and ripped fabric chunks jump into the air and collapse together like an explosion in reverse. The smashed desks reassemble themselves, unbend, and slide into place. The papers, books, pens, and all the crap from the teacher's desk leap off the floor and restack themselves as they were before.

... and then we spend the next twenty minutes standing completely motionless and silent while five cops wander around the school looking for whoever broke in. Ashley screws up and makes a noise when one of them finally arrives at room 6A and shines his flashlight right in her face. She can't help herself and whimpers a bit at the sudden intense glare.

We get lucky. Bright light hurt, but not enough that it ruined her concentration. He didn't see us, but he definitely heard her.

"Who's in there?!" yells the cop. "Cottage Lake PD. Show yourself."

He shines the light into the space behind the teacher's desk— where we are not. Sensing it coming back, I close my eyes in time before the stupidly bright flashlight pans over us again. Now he's looking at the rear end of the room.

Sophia's shaking. She's damn close to bursting into tears from anxiety. The kid who's never even gotten grounded once has to be freaking out at doing something we'd legitimately get in real trouble for.

Oh, what am I doing? I'm going to command this guy to go away.

"Hello," half-whispers Chloe in a creepy ghostly girl voice. "Wanna play?"

Uh oh. I stare at his chest. Time for his body camera to stop working.

The cop jumps, spinning to aim his flashlight toward her. He's shining it on the desk next to her. She grins at me, then pushes the desk so it slides a few inches to the side.

"Gaaaah!" the cop screams, then hauls ass out of the room.

I make a face at Chloe. Ooh. If she wasn't so damn cute, she'd be in so much trouble. We really should stop teasing mortals with obvious displays of supernatural stuff.

With the distraction of the terrified cop drawing the other offi-cers' attention in his direction, we slip out of the classroom and hurry to the gym. Sophia pauses long enough to magic the blasted doors back to normal, and we slip out the back to the parking lot outside. I scoop Sophia up and leap into the sky, Ash and Chloe flying right behind me. Kiddo is still carrying the 'ghost trap,' which once again looks completely non-paranormal.

Once we're high enough up not to be heard, we all burst out laughing.

Soon, we land at home and make our way into the kitchen.

Mom's waiting for us. "Did you catch the thing?"

"Yes." Sophia smiles. "We got it and didn't make too much of a mess."

"Oh no." Mom facepalms. "How bad is it?"

I wince. "Pretty bad. Entire classroom trashed. Two steel doors ripped off their hinges and bent. Lots of lightning and stuff flashing around. Someone called the cops."

Mom stares at me.

"Don't worry." I pat Sophia on the head, ruffling her hair. "She fixed it all. No permanent damage, and Chloe gave one of the cops a ghost scare. I can't imagine the stories that are going to go around for this."

Mom continues staring at us like she's not sure how to react.

Ashley grins. "There's no evidence of anything in the school. Everything looks the same. There shouldn't be anything on the video either. A lot of noise and light with no explanation. Obviously, ghosts."

"All right. Well, I suppose..." Mom sighs. "If it stops whatever magical oddity you summoned from wreaking havoc, I'll have to tolerate it."

"I didn't summon this thing." Sophia pouts. "Someone sent it to mess with me."

Mom raises an eyebrow. "Oh. Umm. Well. In that case, tell me when you found whomever or whatever it is. I'd like to make sure they know better than to mess with my daughter ever again."

The amount of relief wafting off Sophia probably registered on seismic detectors in Hawaii. She leaps into a hug and gives Mom a squeeze.

Mom pats her on the back. "It's all right, hon. Now, go on to bed. It's a little past your bedtime."

"Aren't there two more pieces to find?" Ashley folds her arms.

"Yeah." Sophia sighs. "But I have to find them. I'm working on it. It's a real pain in the butt... like something is trying to block me from seeing them."

I grumble. "Because something probably *is* trying to block you. Maybe we should teleport to France again? That might buy you a few minutes before the 'outside interference' is able to figure out where you went."

"Ooh. Wait. I have an idea." Sophia narrows her eyes... the cutest scheming weasel in the world.

"What are you thinking?" Mom raises an eyebrow.

"I'm going to make a trap." Sophia clenches her hands into fists at her sides. "I think I can do it, but I'm going to need some help from the book."

"Which book?" asks Mom.

"I'm guessing not *Fahrenheit 451*," mutters Ashley.

I groan.

Mom blinks at us. "What's wrong with that book?"

"You remember... we had to read that thing every stupid summer in high school..." I flail my arms. "Like do any of the English teachers talk to each other?"

Ashley laughs.

"No, not that book." Sophia holds up a finger. "The Tome of F Knowledge."

Mom gives me a 'should I be worried?' look. "What does the F stand for?"

"Umm. Forgotten, I think." Sophia shrugs. "Maybe forbidden."

"Or fantastic." I smile.

"Well, it's definitely not that other F word," whispers Ashley behind her hand to Mom.

Sophia blushes. "No. No, it is not. It's magic stuff. I just have to borrow it from the mystics."

"Oh, I'm sure they won't mind." I start heading for the basement stairs. "Can't object if they don't notice."

"What?" Mom gawks at Sophia. "Are you stealing books?"

"No. I'm just borrowing them." Sophia smiles cheesily. "It's only stealing if I keep it. Don't worry. The book likes me. If it didn't want me to borrow it, I wouldn't be able to."

Mom opens her mouth as if to say something, then decides against it and shoos us all to bed.

I can't help but laugh. She's either joking or is so overwhelmed she still thinks I have a bedtime.

Then again, I kinda do have a bedtime.

The stupid sunrise is far less forgiving than Mom about when I need to be asleep.

But that's still a few hours away. It's not even ten yet.

CHAPTER 40
MYSTIC RIVALRY

TUESDAY EVENING

Tuesday again.

Ugh. Lately, Tuesdays bug me more than Mondays, but not more than Thursdays. Why? It's school. I've got early classes on both days starting with T. Today's art history from three to six, and then life science from seven to ten. What was I thinking stacking two 'once a week' classes on the same day?

Oh, I remember... something along the lines of 'get it over with.' Having a piled-on Tuesday gives me Friday off. Yay. But it also makes me dread Tuesdays. Honestly, I think if the whole vampire thing never happened, this would bother me less. Going to college wouldn't feel like a waste of time. I'd have the motivational fire lit under my backside of not wanting to end up waiting tables for the rest of my life. Not that there's anything wrong with working in food service—other than the customers, the long hours, the grueling work, kitchen burns, smelling like grease, destroying your feet, and being mostly dependent on the generosity of total strangers to not starve.

A few of the kids I went to high school with were all about trade schools. This one guy, Trent, was almost as bad as a vegan for talking about that sort of thing. Apparently, a guy can make more money as a welder in much less time than someone going for a master's degree in almost anything. Good for him. Hope he makes it work. Me? I'm not really cut out for being a welder. That sounds too much like actual work.

By the way, did you know that Trent's sister was named Reznor?

Yeah, that's her first name. Their parents are big NIN fans. And their kids are probably going to disown them.

So, anyway. I'm finally home after classes on Tuesday with a giant pile of homework. Bunch of reading plus a 'compare and contrast the styles of two ancient people that 98% of the population of Earth wouldn't know the name of' for art history. Life science is all reading and studying for a test next week.

Kill me now.

Oh, wait. Scott already did that. Damn. Even death isn't sparing me from finals.

Mind control might, though.

Follows Rules Girl narrows her eyes at me.

Yeah, yeah. I'm just frustrated and venting. I said I would finish out this semester and I will.

Doesn't mean I really need to care what grades I get.

I'm sitting at my desk staring at the books and failing to summon the urge to do anything academic. Ashley's stretched out on the bed, watching a movie or something on her tablet with headphones, since she thinks I'm trying to do schoolwork.

Chloe's playing with her dolls behind me, in very much a normal way any ordinary seven-year-old might. Maybe she's abnormal, since she hasn't ripped many of their heads off yet. She's happy, which makes me happy.

Momentarily anyway. As soon as I think about the pile of books in front of me, I get all grumbly again. My gaze shifts back and forth from the books to the computer. It would be so easy to fire up a game and relax. Is it wiser to immediately start on the reading assignment for a class I *just* had, or would it be better to wait a couple days so reading the stuff feels like a reminder of the things the professor talked about? Delaying it appeals more whether or not it's the smarter choice.

It occurs to me at that moment that my computer monitor is warping, stretching upward toward the ceiling, and tilting a little. And not just the monitor. Everything in my room gradually elongates upward and skews to one side or twists—except me.

"What the fuck?" whispers Chloe.

I look over at kiddo. She's sitting on the floor near the corner playing at her dollhouse, which is now about twice it's usual height. The dolls float upward off the rug and stretch. Fortunately, Chloe is not warping... though her dress is. My clothes squeeze tight around me as they try to get taller and thinner, plus levitating. In seconds, my underpants become one of the most epic wedgies I've ever suffered. So grateful I rarely wear a bra.

The contents of my closet and wardrobes rattle around, suggesting everything in there is also trying to float toward the ceiling and stretch out. My entire bedroom looks kinda like a cartoon drawn on soft plastic film that's being slowly stretched. Everything... except for the three of us anyway. It seems whatever magical chaos is going on still considers us 'living' beings for purposes of the crazy effect.

Ashley's headphones pop off her head and glide upward, stretching and elongating as they go. Her oversized T-shirt fluffs up, though doesn't make it too far since she's sitting on it. Her expression is a mix of awestruck and clueless, then she scrunches her nose at me as if to ask 'why are you making faces like that?'

Flying upward out of my chair doesn't do much to alleviate the discomfort going on down below. If not for my jeans and shirt also trying to pull me upward, the wedgie would've already been making me scream.

My bed is now twice it's usual thickness and starting to twist around in a corkscrew. Walls of bedding rise around Ashley, framing her like she's a doll in a diorama. Judging from the look on Chloe's face, she's experiencing a similar malfunction with her underpants. While she's trying her best to look furious, she's still only seven and inches from bursting into tears.

"Chlo?" asks Ashley. "You okay?"

"No!" replies kiddo in a wavering voice, trying *really* hard not to cry.

"Wedgie from hell," I rasp. "Underwear rebellion."

"Oh." Ashley appears unbothered, not suffering the same discomfort. "Umm. Need help?"

I'm half a second from reaching down there and shredding my panties off before things can advance from 'really uncomfortable' to actually painful when everything snaps back to normal.

Chloe sits there for a moment, scraping her composure up off the floor. She manages not to cry at all, though her eyes are a little red. Once anger has fully taken over her expression, she turns her head to look at me. "Did you just see some messed up shit?"

"Yeah." I look around at my room, checking that everything is once again normal.

"That was... trippy." Ashley whistles.

Kiddo scowls and indelicately fixes her underpants by grabbing them through her dress. "Whose ass am I kicking?"

I look up at the ceiling. "I don't think that was an attack... Sophia must be trying to do something."

Chloe jump-flies to her feet, then storms out of the room.

Uh oh.

That look in her eye... she's totally about to lift Sophia off the ground with an atomic wedgie. Eye for an eye, underpants for underpants apparently. I chase kiddo upstairs and manage to grab her right as she gets to Sophia's room. She digs her claws into the doorjamb like a cat trying to resist being carried out of the house.

Sophia's kneeling on the floor at the center of her room beside her ritual circle of dolls, crayons, construction paper, and a few plastic toys from her kitchen set that kinda look like medieval potion flasks. Beside her on the right lays a massive book with gild-edged pages. It's so huge it seems impossible for Sophia to even lift it. She's wearing one of her older dresses, a less fancy one that's probably a few months away from being too small for her. Uh oh. She picked an outfit she wouldn't care about losing.

Sierra's standing beside her holding her sword. Yes, the real one Dad gave her for Christmas last year. Except for her being barefoot in a plain T-shirt and jeans, she looks ready for war.

"Let go!" yells Chloe, trying to pull herself out of my arms. "Revenge is justified!"

"Eek!" blurts Sophia. "Revenge? What happened?"

I brace my hip against the wall to keep holding Chloe back. "Whatever you just did caused all non-living material to stretch and float."

"Umm. Oops," says Sophia. "Why is she upset? Did you guys stretch and float, too?"

"No, it didn't affect our bodies... but underpants are non-living matter." I adjust my grip on the kiddo, wrapping both arms around her and plucking her off the doorjamb. Confident I've got her, I step into the room. "You wedgied the hell out of both of us."

Ashley appears from the stairway at the end of the hall, having added sweat pants to her long-T shirt outfit. Upon seeing me holding Chloe, she fake wipes sweat from her brow. "Whew. You caught her before she could attack."

"Ack!" Sophia winces. "Sorry. I didn't mean to do that. If stuff happened outside my room, it's that stupid thing messing with me."

Chloe lets out a soft growl. "Dammit."

"What?" I peer down at her.

"Not Sophia's fault, so I can't be mad at her." Chloe folds her arms and sulks.

Sophia smiles at us. "Since you guys are here, wanna help us?"

"What were you trying to do?" I set Chloe down, confident she's no longer on a mission of revenge... at least not one directed at Soph. "Expecting trouble?"

"Not sure what to expect." Sierra pats her sword, which is at least in its scabbard. "Wanted to be prepared."

"Sophia!?" calls Mom from downstairs. "Please warn us before warping linear dimensionality again. I would really prefer not to be inside a Salvador Dali painting ever again."

"Sorry, Mom!" shouts Sophia. "Accident! Or... uhh, tampering." Her expression shifts to annoyed disappointment.

I walk over to stand beside her. "Why do you look so let down?"

"Because," she whispers, glancing at the book. "I thought I set a magic trap for the tamperer. If they're still tampering with me, that means I really do stink at this."

Sierra nudges her. "Hey. You just set the trap up. It wasn't active, so they could've tampered with the setting up of the trap. Now that it's set up, they can't tamper. Right?"

"Umm." Sophia ponders, tapping a finger to her chin. "Well, assuming it actually worked. Yeah. Or not. I mean... they could still tamper with me, but it's going to set the trap off. I made a trap, not a shield."

I fake being nervous and look around. "Should I get my sword, too?"

"I'm going to try to find the next fragment of that red monster." Sophia folds her arms. "A sword isn't really going to help."

"What about the tamperer?" Ashley pads over beside me. "Will a sword work on whatever that is?"

"Ugh. I dunno." Sophia wipes both hands down her face. "I still have no clue if whatever is messing with me is a creature, a faerie, a demon, or something else."

Sierra grins. "Let's find out."

"Okay." Sophia takes a deep breath and directs her attention onto the pink plastic Barbie bowl in the middle of her circle. "I'm trying to find the next essence fragment. If something tries to mess with me, things might get a little weird."

Oh drat. She's using a bowl of water to scry with. I was going to get her a crystal ball for Christmas. I better deal with that soon. It's almost the 25th.

Sophia glances at the Tome of F Knowledge, skimming over a few pages before nodding at it and saying, "Thanks."

No sound happens, though oddly enough, the book radiates an emotion of 'no problem.'

"Mew!" Klepto appears in a violet flash, then flops down, draping herself over Sophia's head like a kitten hat.

Our little mad sorceress waves her hands around over the scrying bowl.

A sensation of my guts leaping into my throat comes out of nowhere. It's the same feeling as being on a roller coaster going into its initial big drop... or jumping off a high place. The vertigo crash lasts only a second. The bedroom around us shifts scenery in an instant, changing into a huge chamber six times the size and made of large stone blocks.

We've gone from Sophia's room to a vacant castle dining hall... or something.

There is no furniture or any decorations. Merely a plain medieval-looking room with ten huge pointy-arch windows running along one wall. Seems to be dark outside, wherever we are.

Sophia's still kneeling on the floor. The rest of us remain arranged around her in the same manner as we'd been in the bedroom. We haven't moved, reality around us did.

A confused intake of breath to my right draws my attention to a woman at the other end of the room. She looks younger than Mom but oldish to me, which probably puts her around thirty. Hey, give me a break. I'm eighteen. Everyone past twenty-five or so looks old. Okay, fine. 'Old' isn't the best word here. She looks *fully adult*. How's that?

The woman's got long, straight black hair and seems reasonably ordinary. White fluffy sweater, jeans, fuzzy socks, no shoes. Due to her lack of shoes and coat, I'm guessing she must have been inside somewhere before this happened. She also looks incredibly baffled and disoriented. Pretty much the exact expression and body language reaction any ordinary person might have to suddenly being teleported somewhere without warning.

Sophia jumps to her feet and points at the woman. "That's who's been messing with me!"

Sierra looks around at the massive chamber. "Uhh, what the heck just happened?"

"I set a trap." Sophia rests her hands on her hips, seeming triumphant. "When *she*"—again she stabs a finger in the unfamiliar woman's direction—"tried to mess with my scrying, it grabbed her by the magic and pulled us all into neutral space."

"Neat," says Ashley.

Sophia grins at me. "It's true! I'm not really a failure at magic. She's making me mess up."

"Nice." I nod at her.

Then, the most rare thing in the Universe happens: Sophia flies into a rage. She balls her hands into fists, leans toward the woman, and screams, "Leave me alone or I'm gonna send Fuzzydoom after you!"

The woman raises an eyebrow, then gives off this haughty 'you have to be kidding me' laugh.

"Vengeance is mine!" shouts Chloe.

A blur flies upward from behind the woman along with a loud *riiiip* of fabric.

The woman's eyes cross. She grabs herself and collapses to her knees, face frozen in an expression of shocked pain.

Chloe's hovering fifteen feet in the air—this place has a really high ceiling—holding the torn remains of silk underpants. I think she attempted to administer an atomic wedgie while underestimating how strong she can get while furious.

Realizing what she just did, I cringe in sympathetic discomfort.

"Ooh." Sierra winces. "So wrong."

"She kinda deserved that," whispers Ashley.

"Maybe." I tap my foot, eyeing Sophia. "Don't you think sending Fuzzydoom after her is going a little far?"

Sophia stops fuming and recoils into an apologetic full body cringe. "Oops. Yeah. Sorry. I was mad. She's mean! She's been messing with me for so long, making me think I was a failure at magic."

The woman gasps, still stunned from Chloe's revenge. She appears to be trying to do something magical, waving her right arm about, though nothing is happening.

Chloe discards the ripped fabric and zooms back over to me. Unlike most seven-year-olds who just did something mean to an adult, she is not hiding behind me for protection. She's boldly standing there, as if daring the woman to do something to her.

Again, the woman attempts to invoke magic, but nothing happens. She glares at Sophia. "Dispel this pocket dimension immediately!"

Sophia folds her arms. "You're not my mother. I don't have to listen to you."

"Insolent little brat," mutters the woman.

Klepto hisses.

"Who the hell is this bitch anyway?" asks Sierra.

The weird thing about the human brain is how it tends to produce the answers to questions it hears, even if the owner of said brain has no intention of speaking the answer out loud. As soon as Sierra asks it, the woman's thoughts give me the answer.

"Her name is Eveline Marchand," I say.

Eveline almost bats her eyelashes at me, shocked I 'know' her and mistakenly thinks she's famous or something.

"Never heard of her." Sierra frowns.

"She's obviously a mystic of sorts." Ashley shrugs. "They don't exactly run around trying to turn themselves into celebrities."

Eveline stands back up and limps toward us. After about five steps, she resumes walking more or less normally. Guess Chloe didn't do real damage. The fabric gave out before it could. "Dispel this dimension right away."

"Not until you promise to leave me alone." Sophia stares defiantly at her.

"Insolent little..." Eveline draws her arm back as if to slap my sister.

I zip in between them, moving so fast time around me seems to drag into slow motion. Eveline catches herself before she swings at me, then blinks in shock at my sudden appearance. To her, it must've looked as though I'd teleported six feet in an instant.

"I wouldn't do that." I narrow my eyes at her. "If you touch my sister, I am going to rip your arm off and shove it down your throat."

"Not up her ass?" asks Ashley.

"Eww," mutters Sierra.

Chloe giggles.

I shake my head. "No, too rude."

"I'm not serious." Ashley laughs. "That's just what they say in all those movies."

Eveline looks down her nose at me, giving off this 'who the hell do you think you are' vibe.

Sierra pulls her sword out a few inches. "Get away from Sophia. If you hit her, you're losing a hand."

"Tell that brat to dispel this pocket dimension immediately!" barks Eveline.

"No." I fold my arms.

Sophia whispers to Chloe, "Say the thing I can't say."

"Why don't you eat a bag of dicks?" chirps Chloe. "She'll dispel it when she's ready to."

Sierra's attempt to look serious and scary falters.

I almost laugh, too. What is it about little kids using foul language that's just so damn hilarious? At least she didn't drop an F-bomb.

A little blush reddens Sophia's cheeks. "You are going to stop causing me to mess up magic. All you have to do is swear to leave me alone and I will dispel this temporary dimension."

"Listen here, brat," snaps Eveline. "You don't give orders to adults."

"You're not in any position to make demands here." I lean at her because I don't loom very well. It's also rather hard to loom at someone taller than me, even if it is only one inch. "After all, that 'little kid' dragged your ass here and you don't seem terribly capable of doing anything about it other than pissing and moaning."

Eveline slaps me. "Disrespectful child."

Her smack turns my head a little to the right. I purse my lips. "Okay... my turn."

I slap the bitch so hard she spirals into a pratfall. Pretty sure I controlled myself enough not to break her jaw, though I wouldn't necessarily be heartbroken if I overdid it a little.

Sierra and Sophia grimace in the same way. Yeah, they are totally siblings even if they're two extreme ends of the girly spectrum. The difference happens about six seconds later as their grimaces fade: Sophia looks kinda concerned about Eveline while Sierra's giving me a 'that was an epic slap' grin.

"Ouch." Ashley whistles. "That was loud. Did you kill her?"

"No, she's still moving," deadpans Chloe. "Are we going to kill her?"

I shake my head. "Not planning—"

Eveline growls and points in our direction.

A hair-thin lightning bolt appears in an instant, connecting the tip of her finger to my chest. The forked bolt's second half nails Sophia. I have, unfortunately, experienced the sensation of having a stake rammed into my chest before. This feels pretty close, only without the blunt force trauma—from zero straight to a hot pain lance through my core. My body clenches up involuntarily for a second or two.

Sophia falls over sideways like a mannequin without a base.

Luckily for Eveline, Sophia stops looking dead before I regain control of my muscles. She bursts into tears, wailing and sobbing.

Ashley gives me hard side eye. "Now what?"

"Now, I'm going to have an overprotective big sister moment."

I pounce on Eveline, grab her, and throw her across the room. Her body flies at least thirty feet before hitting the stone wall and crashing to the floor. I'm on her again before she can even start trying to scramble back to her feet. Sure, it took me less than a second to run after her, but that gave me enough time to regain control of my anger and hold myself back from simply killing her.

I grab her by two fistfuls of her fuzzy white sweater, haul her off the ground, and slam her back against the wall. Yeah, she's taller than me, but I can fly. We're at eye level.

As soon as the disorientation of being thrown wears off and I'm sure she's fully aware and looking at me, I let my anger flow out of my eyes—meaning my glare is glowing, painting her face bright red.

My voice tinged with inhuman growl, I lean closer until our foreheads almost touch. "If you ever try to harm Sophia again, there won't be enough left of you for an electron microscope to identify."

Eveline trembles, seemingly too frightened to speak.

"What's that bitch's deal, anyway?" yells Sierra. She's flopped to the floor and is doing her best to hug/comfort/reassure Soph. Pretty sure that's the only reason she's not running over here to get stabby with Eveline.

The answer peeks out from behind the 'what the hell is this girl' dominating Eveline's thoughts. She somehow found out about Sophia's existence—most likely from mystics talking amongst themselves. Darren perhaps bragged about his prodigy level new student. Apparently, this is all just petty jealousy. Years ago, Eveline was the child prodigy doing magic faster than most people. She's afraid Sophia will become more powerful than her and get all the attention and fame. Fame, of course, being limited to the mystic community. Initially, she only wanted to make Sophia screw up a few times in hopes she'd get discouraged and give up on magic... and when my sister didn't give up, things escalated.

"Oh, for eff's sake," I mutter. "She's just jealous Sophia might become more powerful than her."

Ashley looks around at the big stone room that Eveline couldn't get herself out of. "I think we're there already."

"I'll leave her alone," says Eveline in a frightened voice.

Sounds good, but I can read her mind. "You're lying. Already, you're trying to come up with something else. Interfering with her won't make her give up, so you're starting to think about banishing her somewhere or even killing her."

Eveline's mouth opens.

"That... is a very... bad... idea." I snarl.

I'd be lying if I said the urge to snap her neck and be done with it didn't cross my mind. Follows Rules Girl is pulling really hard on that rope, trying to drag me back from the cliff. No question in my mind if she had really just stopped Sophia's heart, I'd have already turned her into tomato paste. It would be too much to rip this woman apart for simply making Sophia cry. I think the cracked shoulder and busted rib from getting thrown into the wall is probably adequate payback for that.

"Is she going to make us kill her?" Sierra's voice is neither eager nor hesitant.

There is a note of 'you're gonna do it if we have to, right?' to it. Sierra doesn't want to murder anyone, at least not yet.

"Nah." I let the red glow in my eyes fade. "We're not monsters."

"I said kill her, not force her to marathon-watch every episode of *Barney the Dinosaur*."

Ashley gasps in mock horror.

"I'm okay," rasps Sophia between sniffles. "Ow, that hurt so much."

"Ash?" I glance over my shoulder at her. "Give me a hand here?"

My best-friend-slash-third-sister pads across the stone floor toward us. Did I mention she's wearing a knee-length pink T-shirt with a rainbow-maned unicorn appliqué and sweat pants? There is nothing about the cute 'redhead next door' that everyone finds adorable that is in any way intimidating.

Yet, somehow, the 'ooh, what are we doing' gleam in her wide blue eyes scares the absolute hell out of Eveline, causing her to start flailing and struggling to get out of my grip. This causes her to also realize we're floating off the ground. I need to use the Derp Hammer to stop the panic attack.

"What's up?" Ashley walks up beside me, then floats to meet us at eye-level.

"Need to build a mental block in there." I nod toward Eveline. "I don't want her to be able to process Sophia's existence. Won't be able to see her. Won't acknowledge it if anyone talks about her. Won't remember this, us, or that Soph ever existed."

"Hmm." Ashley rubs her chin. "I'm not *that* good at mind stuff yet, but I can try."

"Your charm is better than mine." I shrug one shoulder. "Basically, if this bitch gets insecure again and starts trying to scry around to see if anyone's more powerful than her, her brain just won't process seeing anything about Sophia."

Ashley's body language shifts. Cute and innocent sidesteps out of the way of confident poise.

Oh, hi Aurélie.

Smiling in a creepy doll sort of way, Ashley reaches one hand out and lightly cups Eveline's chin, directing her head over so she can stare into the woman's eyes.

"This one should consider herself fortunate she continues to remember there is such a thing as magique," whispers not-quite-Ashley in a French accent she does not normally have.

A little drool dribbles from the corner of Eveline's mouth.

Soon, Ashley lets her arm drop to her side. She blinks, smiles, then chirps, "Thanks!"

Okay, I obviously love Ashley like a sister, and Aurélie is like a second mother to me. But I still kinda get the heebies watching her take over Ashley's body like that. Here's hoping it's some special unique power she has and not every sire can do that to any vampire they created.

Never tried, to be honest, says Dalton's voice in the back of my mind. *Honestly, it would feel a bit... improper.*

I can easily feel the 'ack, no' emotion coming from him. It's just like mine. Granted, he feels awkward at the idea of possessing a girl's body. I'm just freaked out by the whole losing control over myself thing, not so much if it's a guy or woman doing it. Though, yeah, having a guy at the controls of my body would be worse.

Pretty sure that's her special thing. Dalton hums. *Can't say I've heard of that happening before. This link is more or less a phone connection.*

I chuckle. Guess Aurélie sprang for the upgraded data plan.

Ashley doesn't seem to mind at all. And hey, it spared us the need to commit murder tonight, so that's a win.

Eveline is on the last train to Derpville... in first class.

"This should be dealt with." I set her down.

Of course she starts to fall over when I let go. I'm not *that* much of a bitch, so I catch her enough that she doesn't smack her head open on the stone floor.

Sophia runs over and hugs us. "Thank you!"

"So, how do we put her back where she came from?" I ask.

"As soon as I dispel this temporary realm, she'll be right back where she was before my trap got her." Sophia rubs her chest.

"You okay?"

"Still sore."

"Let me see?" I raise an eyebrow.

Sophia pulls the neckline of her dress down. A small burn on her sternum area kinda looks like she got tased. I gingerly brush a fingertip over it. She winces a little. No bleeding. Doesn't appear to have broken skin. Basically, just a bruise that ought to go away on its own. We won't need to come up with an explanation for this to a doctor. Or maybe we should.

"Ugh. It's probably nothing but I'd feel much better if you got looked at."

"You're looking at me." Sophia laughs.

"I mean by a real doctor." I wag my eyebrows.

"What would we possibly tell them?" Sophia waves her arm around as if to indicate the entire room. "Hey, doc. My sister got zapped by a crazy jealous mystic who threw a lightning bolt out of her hand."

I laugh. "When you put it that way..."

Ashley chuckles.

"The doc's gonna believe whatever we want them to." Chloe grins.

"True." Ashley nudges me. "We have mental powers. There won't need to be CPS reports. Do you really think she should get looked at?"

I sigh. "I'd rather overreact than underreact and have her get sick."

Of course, I say 'get sick' but electricity is weird. If her heart randomly stopped later tonight, I'd never forgive myself.

"Yeah." I hold my fist out to Ashley, who touches knuckles with me. "Wonder Derp Powers, Activate."

Ash laughs.

I take Sophia's hand. "C'mon. Quick trip to the ER just to be safe."

Sophia sighs. She closes her eyes and seems to concentrate for a moment. All of a sudden, we're back in her bedroom. I walk with her downstairs, where the 'rents are watching TV.

"Gonna run Soph to the ER real quick," I say.

Mom and Dad both stare at us.

"What happened?" Mom gets up and runs over.

Dad somehow gets to us before her even though he started moving after her. He fusses over Sophia but doesn't see anything obviously wrong. "Is she sick?"

Sophia pulls her dress down so they can see the burn.

I explain what just happened.

Mom continues fussing over her. "Get dressed. I'll drive."

"Was gonna fly..." I shrug. "But we can all go."

Dad picks Sophia up and cradles her. "What's the official story?"

"Umm. Something like a random person came out of nowhere and tasered her?" I offer a cheesy smile. "Wasn't really planning on lying our way through this one. Just full mind wank."

Mom and Dad exchange a glance, then shrug at the same time.

"That's fine, dear." Mom runs to grab her coat. "As long as Sophia is okay and we don't end up having to explain things to the police."

Nice. I grin to myself. Mom gave me permission to mind control at will.

Just call me double-oh-nine or something.

License to Derp.

CHAPTER 41
HOLIDAY SPIRIT

Well, we didn't manage to go hunting another essence fragment last night.

However, a doctor who is likely very confused today checked Sophia out and was sure she's fine. She got a little cream for the burn and some gauze to put over it in case having fabric rub the area hurt.

Mom was surprisingly casual about me being half a breath away from murdering someone last night. Come to think of it, so am I. Attacking my family is one of my lines that shall not be crossed, especially when the attack is totally unprovoked and against the most innocent of my siblings.

I mean, if Sierra randomly decided to pick a fight with someone and they hit her back, I'd still run over and help her... but I wouldn't be as angry with the person since my sister started it. This Eveline bitch came out of nowhere just because of jealousy. Everyone says I still look like a kid, but that bitch still acted like one. Oh noes. She's not the precious little prodigy everyone adores anymore.

Ugh. People.

And really, how powerful could she have been if Sophia—someone who's only been aware magic even existed for a little over a year—could trap her in a place she couldn't escape? Then again, if my life really is turning into a crazy anime movie, Sophia would be that crazy powerful innocent looking little kid who could crack planets in half with her mind, then want ice cream.

Speaking of Soph... it's Wednesday and I'm not going to school. Holiday break. Yay.

I'm with Sophia at the mall. Her Girl Scout troop is doing a donation drive for charity. They've got a bunch of tables set up in the middle of the atrium where the two concourses in this mall intersect, right near the fountain. They're accepting donations of clothing, toys, or money that will be given out to the needy over the holidays.

Sierra is here as well, to hang out with us, though she is not in the Girl Scouts anymore. She is not wearing the uniform—which she considers to be dorky and lame—or any more elaborate holiday costumes. However, she did relent and put on a Santa hat like the girls in the troop. Sophia, like many of her fellow Girl Scouts, is wearing a nice red velvet Christmas dress. Ashley and I are basically standing around with the other chaperones and troop leaders. We're here to protect the mall from a small army of tween girls as much as we're protecting the girls.

I'm not dressed up. T-shirt and jeans for me, though I did accept the Santa hat. Ashley showed up at the mall in a similar outfit as mine, but she caved in and went shopping. *Now* she is wearing a cute red dress with furry white trim at the collar, sleeves, and hem plus candy cane striped leggings. She looks like one of Santa's elves. Swear if any place in this mall sold prosthetic elf ears, she'd have totally done that, too.

"Thank you," chirps Sophia at a woman who dropped off a few sweaters.

The woman smiles back at her. "You girls are adorable. Nice of you to do this for the community."

After the woman walks away, Sierra shakes her head at Soph. "That dress is more embarrassing than the uniform."

"I think it's cute." Sophia brushes her hand down her chest. "And it's soft."

"You need to get these kids out of here," says a woman at the other end of our tables.

I shift my gaze off my sisters across the way to the source of the voice. A late-thirties woman with short blondish hair has decided to get in the face of Becky Stout, one of the scout leaders and also mother of Nevada Stout, a ten-year-old in the troop. Poor kid. Her parents wanted to give her an 'unusual' name. Hopefully, she doesn't get teased too much. Fortunately, she's slim. Not quite as skinny as my family—thanks Dad for the genes. She is what the average person would consider to be 'slim.' Note to any future parents out there. If you name your kid after a US state, and they happen to be overweight, the other kids at school *will* make fun of them.

Don't do it.

Anyway...

"Uh oh. Karen alert," says Sierra.

The woman continues giving Becky crap for the 'constant begging.' She rants for a good five solid minutes about how annoyed she is that she can't go anywhere this time of year without *someone* shoving crap in her face trying to guilt her into giving money away. Her problem isn't so much with the Girl Scouts, merely that they happened to be the final straw that broke her brittle back.

Ugh. I get distracted by feeling weird for calling Becky 'Becky'. The woman's thirty-five or so. Yes, she's younger than my mom and too young to be my mother. I mean, if she got preggo at fifteen maybe, but still. That's too young to *feel* like my mother. Somehow, it still feels a little inappropriate of me to call her by her first name. But also, calling her Mrs. Stout makes me feel weird. It's the same weird like 'hey, I'm not a little kid anymore.'

Argh. This is a Heck I will forever be stuck in. How does a permanent teenager refer to people a bit older than me but not old enough for it to feel normal for me to call them Mr. or Mrs.?

"... everywhere I go, there's just begging, begging, begging. Why do you people have to always be in our way trying to sling guilt around?" barks the Karen.

Sophia covers her mouth and nose in both hands. Her eyes are reddening up. Uh oh. Tearstorm imminent.

"Ma'am, it's totally fine if you're not in a position to give to charity," says Becky. "We're not demanding anyone do anything. If you can't or don't want to give, just pretend we're not even here."

"How am I supposed to do that with your huge obnoxious sign and..." Karen looks at the scouts. "You should be ashamed of yourself for making those innocent kids dress up like that to help you grift money from hard-working people. You're exploiting them."

Karen keeps ranting about how angry she is that she can't take five steps without someone else asking her to donate to this, that, or the other thing. Sophia's full-on sniffling. Some of the younger girl scouts hide behind their parents or other chaperones. The older ones vary between glaring at Karen or trying not to make eye contact with anyone, quietly wishing she'd just shut up and go away.

Predictably, the spectacle of her shouting at us has caused a complete stop in anyone else approaching us to make donations.

Sierra folds her arms and looks at me. "The overwhelming presence of charity drives is a red flag about the health of a society and is probably a harbinger of imminent collapse."

The furious woman stops barking at Becky and turns her glare onto Sierra. It looks like she's about to start barking at her. Probably would be yelling already if it didn't take her a few minutes to unpack what Sierra said and try to make sense of it.

I step around the table and put myself between Karen and Sophia. "Look, lady... you've almost made one of my little sisters cry. I'm not going to let you scream at the other one. You are being unreasonable. Unless you want to find out what it looks like if I decide to become unreasonable, I suggest you leave."

"She *did* make Soph cry," deadpans Sierra. "Soph is actively crying right now."

Karen scoffs at me. "What the hell are you going to do? Are you threatening me?"

Good. I've got her attention off Sierra.

"Sare?" asks Sierra in a sarcastically sweet voice. "Try not to get any blood on Soph's dress."

Sophia attempts to chuckle while crying. That's an odd sound.

Obviously, she is not serious. However, there's enough 'things could actually go that way if you push hard enough' in her voice that Karen starts reaching for her cell phone to record me. She probably thinks I have a knife on me or something ordinary.

I clench my jaw and dial back my sun resistance enough to free up power for a mind poke. Somewhere in the back of my mind, Captain Kirk is yelling about diverting power from shields to weapons. Thankfully, it's hella overcast today and the giant skylight above us is quite grey—not to mention covered in a light dusting of snow. This means I don't emit visible smoke, though it's far from comfortable. Basically, it feels like I walked into a 200-degree room for a few seconds.

Go home and contemplate your life choices.

After hammering that command into her subconscious, I stop fighting my own subconscious and let the sun resistance surge back to full power. While Karen stands there in Derpville, I reach into her purse and grab her wallet, which I open in search of her driver's license. Aha. Susan Daley. Apologies to anyone else out there named that. I hope you aren't as Karen-y as this one. I take note of her address.

"What are you doing?" whispers Sierra.

I close the wallet—without taking anything—and put it back where I found it. "Oh, just going to ask a little friend of ours to send some of his little friends to give this Grinch an 'imps of Christmas past' night she'll never forget." I pull my iPhone out of my pocket and type her address into a note file before I forget it, then take her picture so Blix knows the target of his mission. It'll cost me a new PlayStation game, but that's worth it. She made Sophia cry.

It seems no one else around us noticed me pickpocket Susan. Neat. That wasn't 'pickpocketing' as much as plainly reaching into her purse. That no one noticed me do it is totally supernatural. Oh, boy. Good thing for me Follows Rules Girl is not the sort of person who would abuse powers like that for personal gain.

A moment later, Susan snaps out of the mind fog. She looks at me with an expression that says 'why am I standing here', then walks away into the mall.

"You have a way with people." Becky chuckles.

"She is the Karen whisperer," mutters Sierra.

Becky, Sophia, and some of the other chaperones laugh.

Sophia wipes her eyes and tries to look all cheerful and happy again.

Fortunately, we only have another like two hours of this.

WEDNESDAY NIGHT

I'm seated in a row of theater seats with Ashley on my left and Sierra on my right. Sam's in the next seat past her, then the 'rents. The theater is fairly impressive. Bigger than I expected, though not exactly massive. Haven't been here before, but it seems like this place hosts everything from stand-up comedians to small theater companies.

Tonight, *The Nutcracker* is being put on by Sophia's dance class in association with two other dance studios and some manner of production company. All the performers are kids, the oldest being like sixteen. Sophia got the part of the Sugar Plum Faerie. It seemed a natural fit. She's the only kid in the group skinny enough to pass for an actual elf. Okay, that's not totally fair. This *is* a dance class, after all. Some of the other girls are also on the small side. Guess she either loves faeries so much fate let her do this or it's the extreme cuteness. Sure, I'm biased, but Sophia is freaking adorable. She could totally have gotten picked up by an agency and ended up making TV commercials or movies.

Except for her extreme stage fright and shyness.

While she might be more than photogenic enough for such a career, she would *hate* the spotlight and being famous. Also, Dad was kinda overprotective. Lots of horror stories about bad things happening to former child stars. He kinda discouraged that idea, which Sophia appreciated since it didn't make her feel like an idiot for not pursuing it.

Tonight is about the limit of her tolerance for being in the spotlight. She's got a small solo number. Yeah, the make-up department went nuts. The glittery purple face paint, the sparkle wings. She absolutely looks like a faerie—except for not being seven inches tall.

The show finally gets to the point where Sophia's big solo number (big for her) happens. She flits out onto the stage as the music picks up. Everything is going great for about twenty seconds until she makes the mistake of looking out at the audience. Her pace slows. For an instant, I think she's going to falter—maybe even panic and run off stage.

Then, it happens.

My clothes disappear.

Not all of them, just the outer layer. I'm now wearing a pair of *Strawberry Shortcake* cartoon print panties and a training bra... same outfit Sierra is also in... and Ashley. Sam's outfit changed to cartoon briefs. In fact, everyone in this entire theater is in underwear. I can't say *their* underwear because I'm almost certain adults do not wear GI-JOE boxers or He-Man briefs. Adult women most certainly do not wear *My Little Pony* granny panties.

At least not too many of them.

Sophia's stopped dancing completely and stares out at the audience with the most epic 'oh shit' face of all 'oh shit' faces.

She flings her arms out to the sides and sets off a blast of pink purple light. Everyone in the theater, except me, freezes as time stops. She then paces around muttering, 'oh no' to herself repeatedly.

Sigh.

I fly up out of my chair and zip over to the stage for my debut in the first-ever production of *Peter Panties*.

"Soph?" I raise an eyebrow. "Why?"

"I'm sorry!" she wails. "I just... panicked."

My sister is starting to hyperventilate. I put an arm around her as best I can without ruining her costume. "Breathe. Slow down. Take deep breaths."

She buries her face in her hands. "Everyone is looking at me."

"No one's looking at you right now, they're all frozen in time." I chuckle.

She sniffles.

"What did you do?"

"I didn't mean to." She reaches up to wipe her eyes, but stops herself. "No.... is my makeup smearing?"

I lean back and look her over. "Not yet. You should probably stop crying if you don't want it to smear."

Sophia shivers. "I'm sorry. I didn't mean to actually *do* it. Ms. Ramirez told me if I get nervous that I should imagine the whole audience in their underpants so they won't be scary."

"Yeah... operative word there being *imagine*." I flick the elastic waistband of my *Strawberry Shortcake* granny panties. "The cartoon briefs were a nice touch."

She blinks in a 'what do you mean?' way.

Ugh. Of course. She put everyone in what she thinks underwear looks like. She doesn't know anything else.

"Hey, look at me." I lightly pat her cheek. "You got this. Eveline is no longer messing with you. Your magic should do what you want it to now, right? None of those screw ups were your fault. You are really, really good at magic for being a kid who's only done it for a year."

"Almost two," mutters Sophia.

"Yeah. Exactly. Only two years and you're doing stuff like *stopping freaking time*." I gesture at the room.

"It's only inside this theater. Not all time." She exhales, the shivers slowly starting to leave her body. "And it's not going to last much longer. Like five seconds or so."

"That's plenty of time. Just rewind us back to before you did that... and dance the routine you've been looking forward to and practicing for months. You got this."

She looks down.

I put a finger under her chin and look her in the eye. "*You got this.*"

Okay, maybe I cheated a little. The Universe won't be mad at me for using a tiny bit of mental power to give my kid sister a scrap of confidence, right?

She nods. "Okay. I got it."

"Cool." I wink at her then fly back to my seat.

A disorienting—and mildly nauseating—ripple in reality follows.

Everyone's back to normal, as far as wardrobe issues are concerned. No one the wiser. Well, except me since she left me out of the time loop... and maybe Blix, who's literally rolling on the floor laughing his little head off. Sam is red-faced trying not to laugh. Sierra looks pissed, but not too much. She's not amused about what happened, though since no one will remember seeing her, I think she'll let it go. Ashley seems a little embarrassed. Okay, that's just strange. Ash is *more* embarrassed being out in public wearing cartoon panties and a training bra than she was spending two days completely naked after we crawled out of the morgue?

Okay, after I think that over for a moment, it does kinda make sense. Random strangers seeing us outside with no clothes would assume something bad has happened to us and think we need help. Someone seeing us walk around in cartoon print panties would probably either laugh or wonder what the hell was wrong with us. There's something else I don't understand. Both Ashley and I have worn two-piece swimsuits that showed more skin than the granny panties Sophia conjured... yet why was that not at all embarrassing? What secret power does underwear—especially goofy underwear —hold?

Uh oh. Am I mistaken or did Sophia just completely alter reality by thinking about it?

Oof. Things are going to get... interesting, aren't they?

Sophia flits out onto stage again and totally smashes her routine. I mean, she's no professional ballerina, nor does she want to be, but for an eleven-year-old in dance class, she does a phenomenal job.

Dad beams with pride.

The look on Sophia's face right before she whisks herself off stage is reassuring. It's more a 'whew, that's over with' and not a 'that was awesome, I want to do that again.' Good. My little confidence boost didn't alter the course of her life. She's not going to pursue a career in dance. This is merely her hobby.

Hmm. Wonder what she's going to end up doing. Not exactly easy to make a living as a mage these days. Oh well, another forty minutes or so of theater and then we get to go home for the night.

CHAPTER 42
EVEN IN DEATH

SATURDAY AFTERNOON

Well, made it to Saturday without any major catastrophes.

So far as I've noticed, the vampire apocalypse has not occurred. We're still in hiding. There's been nothing on the news regarding a takeover of the world by the undead and mortals being forced into serfdom. Probably a good sign. Soph's been trying to find the two remaining fragments of that creature that dispersed out of her bedroom, to no avail.

It gets me wondering if Eveline had something to do with it. Since she is no longer able to process the fact that Sophia exists, is that making it harder to find this energy?

Things have been quiet all week.

Dad, of course, could not resist the urge to embarrass the hell out of Sophia. Yes, we told him what happened at the theater. He walked out into the living room last night wearing He-Man boxers and a bathrobe. Sam found it hilarious. Sierra couldn't look at him. Sophia blushed. Naturally, Sam tried to convince Sophia to go out into the world, perhaps the mall, and look for people being jerks and zap them into cartoon underpants.

Mom played the bad guy there. She forbid Sophia from using magic for the random underpantification of total strangers, no matter how rude or annoying they were. Not that Sophia would have dared to.

Anyway, it's Saturday afternoon and we're at Uncle Hank's wake. Just like Uncle Hank to be a pain in everyone's ass by having his wake in the middle of the weekend. Ugh. What do I really care about weekends anymore? Another few months, and I'll set college aside. Then, every day will be a weekend for me. Ash and I will enjoy a permanent summer vacation. No responsibilities... well at least not the mundane ones like a job. Still have the 'working for Mr. Wolent' thing to worry about, but that's hardly a nine-to-five.

There are a surprising number of people here. At least thirty. A few glance in my direction when I enter, their expressions mostly a 'who the heck is that?' Obviously, my parents, grandparents, and siblings don't look at me wondering who I am.

I am late for reasons out of my control. Naturally, the 'rents couldn't tell anyone my body won't wake up until 2:30 in the afternoon because I'm a vampire now. I think the excuse we agreed on was something like I couldn't get away from my job or school. Dammit. Which one was it? Argh. Maybe they didn't even offer a reason other than 'unavoidable commitment.'

Ashley and I walk into the funeral home hoping no one asks me why I showed up two hours after the rest of my family. Yeah, I dressed nice. I'm wearing a black dress, dark stockings, shiny black heels. Okay, so they're kitten heels, but still. I'm trying. No one wants to see me doing an impression of a drunken ostrich trying to dance on roller skates, so I did not buy 'real' high heels. Ash's dress is similar, black and respectful.

Much to my shock, Sierra is wearing a black dress, stockings, and flats. It is not surprising to see Sophia in a dress, generally speaking.

A *black* one though, is bizarre. Pretty sure that dress got purchased yesterday. Now there's a paradox. Which is more weird? Sierra loves black clothes, hates dresses. Sophia hates black clothes, loves dresses. Hmm.

Sam's got a cute little suit on. The Littles are mostly sitting off to one side hanging out with some nieces and nephews we don't see very often.

Chloe is not here, nor is she in the Tahoe. She's at home. Mrs. Carter is watching her.

Dad's parents are seated near him. It's so weird hearing other people call Grandma and Grandpa 'Gloria and Ken.' Like whoa. They have real names. Mind blown. Mom's parents, Grandma and Grandpa Sheridan, are with them as well. My brain totally can't handle hearing them addressed as 'Mary' or 'Mike' as other people I've never met before wander by to offer their condolences.

Uncle Ricky, Mom's little brother, is here with his girlfriend. I think her name is Alyssa. Wang? Yang? Something like that. She seems nice. Much like she was at Thanksgiving dinner, though, she seems completely out of place and vibing like she wants to get the heck out of here as soon as possible. Yeah, she's very shy and doesn't like being in a room full of strangers.

I'm kind of mentally out of it at the moment since I did my best to wake up as early as possible. Had some help, though. Ashley and I got dressed up last night before sunrise knocked us out. Dad, I think, wrapped us in blankets and carried us out to Mom's Tahoe. We've been sleeping in the SUV in the parking lot of the funeral home for probably two hours.

There's something simultaneously appropriate and ever so wrong about my family driving us to a funeral home while we are *dead* asleep in the back of the truck. Dad didn't want me driving here after waking up this early. I'm grateful for that.

I woke up first. It took a bit of nudging and insistent prodding for Ashley to stir. She sat up with one eye closed, one open, looking like a character in the morning-after-the-big-party scene in a college comedy film.

The promise of the interior of the home being dark and free of sunlight gave us enough motivation to crawl out of the truck and hotfoot it across the parking lot. Yes, my sun tolerance has significantly improved since I first turned vamp. However, that doesn't mean that being outside a few minutes before I normally wake up is comfortable.

Inside, though? It's nice. The funeral home is cozy and dark enough for me to come online in the viewing room. Now that we're indoors, Ashley no longer needs to lean against me to avoid falling over. She still looks ready to fall asleep again, but she's managing to stand on her own power.

Uncle Hank lay in repose in a casket at the far end of the room, inside a small curtained alcove. He looks peaceful, but still somehow annoyed. I can practically hear him grumbling about how stiff the cushioning is in the casket and complaining that it was made in China.

Oh wait, I'm not imagining that.

Uncle Hank *is* bitching about the Chinese manufacturing monopoly.

His ghost stands off in the back left corner, pacing and muttering. He is angry because his casket was legit made in China and he wants to complain about it to someone but can't.

I let out a soft sigh. "Even in death he can't stop complaining."

"What?" Ashley looks over at me, spots him, then sighs. "Oh. Right."

My voice is far too quiet for anyone else to pick up on. Everyone, that is, except Uncle Hank.

He looks in my direction, then makes a weird face for a few seconds before casting his gaze over everyone else and back to me. I've already made the mistake of eye contact, so he's figured out I can see him.

Hank walks over. "Sarah? You can see me?"

Ashley pretends not to see him.

My instinct to say 'unfortunately' doesn't survive the disapproving glare of Follows Rules Girl. Yeah, I might think it but this *is* the poor guy's funeral. Seems wrong to be rude to him. "Yeah."

He again looks me over as if he's deciding if my outfit is 'suitably feminine.'

I'm really trying hard not to say something nasty.

"I see your mother finally got through to Sierra. She's dressed properly." He grumbles. "Should get her to one of them head docs, make sure nothing's going wrong in that noggin of hers. Maybe a minister, too."

Fight it, Sarah. Do not go into attack mode. He's already dead. He can't hurt anyone. "Sierra is just tomboyish. She doesn't like frilly stuff. She's not a lesbian, or she'd be wearing a suit like Sam." Okay, yeah, I know some lesbians go super fem. I'm just trying to grind Hank's gears here.

He scowls at me, then makes a snorting kind of huff as if to approve the fact Sam is wearing 'proper boy clothes' here and not showing up in another pink faerie dress. I guess the guy totally doesn't understand spiteful protest. Does he really think Sam wore the dress at Thanksgiving because he likes dresses? Maybe it doesn't help that my brother is still only ten and hasn't aged out of the 'cute' phase of boyhood. Now that his hair is longish, he could probably be mistaken for a girl if he had a dress on since he's got kind of a 'pretty' face for a boy and big eyes. His hair isn't draped to the shoulders long, merely this big brown orb of fluffiness.

"Sarah?" asks Hank after a long sour-faced pause.

"Hmm?" I glance over at him.

"Why are you the only one here who can see me?"

"I'm not. Sophia can probably see you."

Ashley squeezes my arm in a thank you for not throwing her under the bus. Or should I say throwing her under the hearse?

"She hasn't acted like it." He folds his arms.

"She's super gentle and sensitive. You are mean and crass. All the times she's ever seen you, you've been angry and mean and cruel to someone or some group. She's probably afraid of letting you know she can see you because she's scared of you."

He exhales out his nose. "Why do you look different?"

"Probably because you don't usually see me wearing a dress."

"No, I mean..." He gestures at me. "You kinda have this... glow about you. You are emitting light. Ainsley, too."

"Oh, for crying out loud. I am not sparkling," I snap. "And her name is Ashley."

Two guys I don't know in the back row of seats twist around to look at me.

I 'encourage' them to pay no attention to me. They shift around to face forward and resume talking about football.

Hank is clueless at my half joke. "You ain't sparkling. It's almost like there's a light shining on you that doesn't exist for anyone else. That friend of yours, too. Since I'm a ghost now, am I able to see that you're lesbians?"

Ashley grumbles. "I'm not a lesbian. I'm bi." She pauses. "Crap."

Hank leans back, eyebrow up. "Ainsley can see me, too?"

"Her. Name. Is. Ashley." I glare at him.

Ash nudges me in a 'don't even bother' gesture.

"No, Hank. We are not lesbians," I whisper.

"Then why are you marked?" He pokes an icy finger into my chest.

I pinch the bridge of my nose, totally understanding how Mom can get headaches from dealing with stupidity at work. "Guess there's no harm in telling you since you're dead now."

"So, help me, if he ends up haunting us..." Ashley smirks.

I look around to check for eavesdroppers. Finding no one close enough to be a risk, I lean toward Hank and whisper, "We're vampires."

He blinks. "Are you serious?"

"Are you a ghost?" I roll my eyes. "That's why you can see spirit energy on us. We're halfway between alive and dead. Remember that whole mess about my boyfriend attacking me? Yeah, well... I didn't actually survive that."

"Oh, thank the Almighty," mutters Hank.

I gawk at him. "Wait, being an undead bothers you *less* than the idea I might have been a lesbian?" Unbelievable. I shake my head. "Even dead, you're still a jackass."

My comment doesn't seem to bother him at all. He also doesn't show any signs of being shocked or sad that his great grandniece is undead, which means at some point I was briefly dead-dead. Not one question about if I'm okay, or what happened, or anything. He knows Scott attacked me. I remember one of the first things he said to me at Thanksgiving was 'they got the bastard.' Nope, none of that. He's merely relieved I'm not gay.

Sigh.

Ashley's pissed. She's doing a really good job holding herself back. Can't really start screaming at a ghost in public without all the mortals thinking you've cracked.

"Sarah," says Hank after a few minutes of silence. "Why am I still standing here and not in Heaven?"

"Gee, I freaking wonder," mutters Ashley.

I want to say 'either it's because Heaven is not real... or they have a 'no assholes' policy. Somehow, I manage not to. After a moment trying to think of some way to respond to him, I shrug. "You were probably too preoccupied wondering if anyone was going to talk badly about you at the funeral, so you couldn't get away."

"Have you ever even thought about the fact that Heaven might not really even exist?" Ashley glares at him.

The look on Uncle Hank's face is about what I'd expect to see on a priest if the band Gwar in full costume barged into the church and started knocking the plaster off the walls with loud music. Especially that one guy with the giant fake penis waving around.

Before he can go off on Ashley for having the audacity to question his beliefs, I say, "Hank... you are probably stuck here because you had to know what people were going to say about you. Or maybe you're just too damn stubborn. If you feel some kind of pull tugging at you to go somewhere, follow it."

He regards me for a long moment, shifting his jaw side to side. "You know how this crap works?"

"Not really. I'm not dead." I neaten my hair. "I'm outside the rules right now. Didn't get to see what happens after death because I was only officially dead for about two seconds. I have seen ghosts. Don't really know that much. Some of them stay around because they want to. Most people who die don't end up as ghosts. No clue why. And I have no damn idea where they go when they go somewhere."

"Into the machinery," adds Ashley without looking at him. "Your soul gets sucked backward through the inner workings of a cosmic sorting machine and then spat back out somewhere else years or decades from now."

He stares at her, fidgeting. "Your friend seems to know."

"She reads some crazy books." I chuckle.

We're quiet for a few minutes. More people I don't recognize come in, head over to the casket to pay their respects, and either walk right back out or take a seat.

"Hmm." Hank scratches his head. "This ghost deal isn't too bad. I'm not in constant pain anymore."

Sigh. Oh sure, he has to find something to say that makes me feel bad for him despite his attitude. "That's nice."

"Didn't expect to see so many people at the wake." Hank raises both eyebrows, seeming impressed.

Yeah, sure. You've been such a dick to so many people for so long, it's amazing anyone you're not blood related to bothered to show up. Again, I stop myself. Not going to turn into Aunt Hank. Being miserable to him will only make me feel bad. No point 'loading up with negative energy' or whatever like that girl Claire from my high school class would say. She's big into crystals and stuff. Yeah, kind of a space cadet. People used to call her 'Luna.'

"What happens now?" asks Hank.

"Umm. We sit around here for a while, then go home. Tomorrow, there's a funeral and they put your body in the ground," I say.

He frowns at me. "I meant as a ghost. Am I stuck here?"

"That's up to you." I look right at him. "I'm sorry you spent the last years of your life living alone in a care facility. At some point, you need to accept the truth that the reason it happened to you is because you are so antagonistic about everything. It sucks, but even the nicest people—like Grandma Sheridan—have their limits. No one is required to put up with super toxic people, even family. I mean, doesn't it mean anything to you that Grandma Sheridan was okay with you going to a home? The woman of endless patience and kindness reached her wits' end dealing with you."

Hank grumbles, then almost looks down as if feeling a tad bit guilty.

I'm probably reading too much into his expression, but here's hoping.

"Look," I say, "My parents and siblings know the truth about me. The grandparents and everyone else do not. However, if you want me to say anything to them, I will consider it. If, and only if, it is either nice, an apology, or a farewell. I will not pass along gripes, insults, politics, condescension, or anything whatsoever about that casket being manufactured in China."

That buys me almost ten full minutes of silence.

Uncle Hank glances off to the left, making a face of surprise at something I can't see. He shifts his attention back to me. "Would you tell Gloria I never meant all those things I said about her not cooking or keeping house well enough. I guess I was just stuck on my own misery. Didn't really mean to take it out on her. Let her know I think I hear Pookie calling me."

"First dog you had?" Ashley leans forward to look past me at the empty part of the room that seems to be holding his attention. Based on her non-reaction, she doesn't see anything there, either.

Uncle Hank gives her a blank look, as if the urge to be annoyed crashed into his strange newfound regret. "My wife. Pookie was her nickname."

"Okay. I'll tell her." I pause a second. "Anything else?"

He makes a series of faces, then half shrugs.

Damn. Too much to ask that he apologize to Ashley for implying anyone in the LGBTQ community is worse than being an undead creature. Guess that's too baked into his personality. If the Universe has a sense of poetic irony, I hope Uncle Hank reincarnates as a gay minority liberal. I say 'minority' because it's really hard to tell which group he hates the most. He probably won't. And even if he does, it's not like it would be satisfying payback since he wouldn't remember this life to be 'horrified' at becoming everything he used to deride.

Whatever. Maybe if Ashley is right and reincarnation is a thing, he won't screw it up as much the next time around.

CHAPTER 43
WARNING

THE FOLLOWING THURSDAY

Most of a week of peace is an amazing thing.

Grandma Sheridan took his relayed apology in stride, sorta. She mostly seemed to assume that was just me trying to make her feel better, until I said 'Pookie.' That unnerved her a little bit. Hopefully, playing it off that I am still close to being a kid enough to catch a fleeting glimpse of ghosts worked. Either way, the apology seemed to both surprise her and make her sad. Knowing Grandma, she's now feeling guilty for putting him in a home these past eight or so years.

So yeah, a week of peace since the funeral. Another amazing thing was playing out in the snow with Chloe. You know what's really weird and cool? Flying off to a remote part of the woods with no witnesses and spending a couple hours running around barefoot in snow. After the initial squealing subsided and we adjusted to the temperature, it was just... strange. Cool, but weird. Almost felt like fake snow since it had no noticeable temperature at that point.

We totally got our slacker on big time. Video games, anime

movies, manga episodes, you name it. Oh, I did some homework, too. Blah. Might as well put in some effort. In other happy news, the upstairs bathtub has been used repeatedly without anyone ending up getting yeeted into inconvenient and embarrassing places with only soap suds for clothes. Pretty sure the tub is once again ours.

It's still enchanted. Exactly what it does, I have no clue. Guess someone doesn't burn a ruby worth hundreds of thousands of dollars on a spell and make a temporary item, right?

Blix wanders into my room while Ashley and I are rewatching *Robotech*. It's old anime, like it came out when Dad was in high school. Still, it's cool. The imp jumps up to stand on the edge of my bed next to me, seeming pleased with himself. He holds out his hand expectantly.

Ashley makes a face at me like there's a 'pimp wants his money' joke at the tip of her brain, but she won't say it out loud with Chloe in the room.

I expected this and I am ready for him. I reach under my pillow and pull out three PlayStation games, still in their shrink wrap, and hand them over. Blix looks over the cases, nods approvingly and again offers his hand.

This time, I shake.

He nods, emits a pleased chirp, and walks out.

"What did I just witness?" asks Ashley, a hint of a chuckle in her voice.

"Oh, just some Karen karma." I lace my fingers together.

"Hah!" Ashley laughs. "Nice. Hope she didn't get hurt."

"I doubt it. However, the fewer details I know, the better, in case I get interrogated." I make a goofy face at her.

"Ach!," says a disembodied voice in the middle of my room. "Sarah, *Du musst schnell mit mir kommen!*"

"Gesundheit," deadpans Ashley.

"Ich niese nicht! Ich versuche dich zu warnen."

I look toward the origin point of the voice.

Klaus, the ghost, fades into view. He looks fairly normal now.

White shirt, dark pants, some manner of shoes. His outfit is kind of ageless. I'm sure it's something he might've worn back in the 1940s, but it doesn't look entirely old now. At least it's not any sort of military uniform.

"Oh, hey Klaus." I wave. "How are you doing?"

He pauses. "Oh. I am doing vell, zhank you. It is much roomier out here zhan the lamp or zat phone."

"Cool. Happy to help." I smile. "So, umm, what did you say before?"

"*Du musst schnell mit mir kommen.*" Klaus waves like he wants me to follow him. "*Beeil dich. Es bleibt nicht mehr viel Zeit.*"

"Not a damn clue what you said." I blink. "Neither one of us speaks German."

"I know a little German." Ashley nods. "He's a circus midget from Bavaria."

I facepalm. "Ouch."

"Ach." Klaus paces. "I try again, slower. I am sorry. When I get excited or nervous it is difficult to speak English. You need to come with me."

"Ugh." I look down at myself, loafing in bed in only a long T-shirt. "Why does this sound like it's going to require pants?"

"You should vear something," says Klaus. "At least put on some shoes."

Ashley sits up and pauses the cartoon. "What she is really asking is: do we need to leave the house and how serious is this thing that's got you upset?"

Klaus stops pacing. "Yes, you vill need to go outside. Zhe other vampires are doing a stupid thing. They have located their bad guy and are trying to vake him up."

"Morons," says Chloe from the floor. "Are you going to go slap the shit out of some idiots?"

"That is a distinct possibility." I hop off the bed and head toward my closet.

Once there, I pull my long shirt off, wad it up, and throw it onto my computer chair. Yeah, so what. Klaus is in the room, but ghosts are ghosts. They're going to be anywhere. Good chance every person on Earth has been seen naked by ghosts more than once in their life. Guessing ghosts probably stop caring after a few decades. Seeing people nude probably loses the thrill after a long enough time.

Klaus turns away from me, which I appreciate.

It only takes me about forty seconds to get completely dressed from my 'won't care too much if this gets destroyed' section of the closet. Ashley rushes over, tosses her nightie, and throws on a more practical outfit than she usually likes. That is to say, she didn't choose a cute dress. T-shirt, sweater, and jeans for her. Stuff she can move and probably fight in, though she's not really that much of a fighter. We both opt for canvas sneakers. They're cheap and replaceable.

"I knew it, I knew it, I knew it," I mutter while grabbing my katana and running out into the basement, then pulling a hard ninety-degree right turn toward the stairs, following Klaus.

He glides up and goes through the door to the kitchen without opening it. I fly after him, since it's much faster than running up the stairs. This has the unfortunate side effect of being completely silent.

Mom screams and nearly throws a bowl of snack crackers over her head as I fling the door open a bit too hard and rush into the kitchen. "Good grief, Sarah!"

"Sorry. In a hurry. Wasn't trying to jump scare you." I grab the sliding glass door and yank it open. "Can you guys watch Chloe, please?"

Ashley winces. "Sorry."

"Where are you two going?" Mom presses a hand into her chest, as if that might slow her heart down.

"Trying to stop the vampire apocalypse." I rush outside.

"Again?" yells Mom. "Didn't you already do that? Aren't you past your one-apocalypse a month quota?"

"Same idiots, new night." Ashley hops out behind me. "Sorry, Mom. We've really got to hurry."

"Well for crying out loud, try not to let the world get destroyed." Mom leans out onto the deck and looks up at me as I'm flying off. "And you're not even wearing a coat!"

"I know... don't want it to get destroyed."

Mom's sigh floats up from below.

I zoom into the air doing my best to chase Klaus who is annoyingly fast. Go figure, having an almost-zero total mass cuts down a whole lot on air resistance. The ghost flies generally toward downtown Seattle, waving at us to hurry up. We keep flying right past it. Seems like he's heading for Bainbridge Island. Not long after it becomes obvious that is exactly where he's going, I realize we have a white spot following us in the distance.

A partial roll to the side lets me look down past my sneakers... at Chloe.

Oh, for eff's freaking sake. Have I created a monster?

I wave at her to catch up. Kiddo pours on speed and pulls up between me and Ashley.

"Wow, you're not gonna take me home?" She blinks.

Grr. "I really should, but you're already here and there's no time. In the future, when I am going to do something dangerous, you are to stay home with Mom and Dad? Got it?"

"Ooookay." She sighs.

"Unless you specifically ask if you can go and I say yes." I take her hand and give her an affectionate squeeze. "I don't want you to get hurt. And I really don't want any other vampires around here starting to think of you as a risk."

Chloe nods. "Okay. Sorry. You didn't tell me not to go with you tonight."

"You didn't ask, either." Ashley tickles her.

"Umm. Yeah. That was kind of on purpose." Chloe sticks out her tongue. "I figured you'd say no, and I really wanted to watch you slap the shit out of some idiots."

"Hurry up!" shouts Klaus. "We are almost out of time!"

I dive after him. "Chloe, if there is a fight, you are to stay hidden."

She nods.

Grr. Should I punish her for sneaking after us tonight or let it slide and hope she listens for the future? Damn. I am way too lenient, aren't I? Maybe it's a good thing I'm not going to have kids of my own. I'm not responsible enough to be a mom.

Hey, cut me *some* slack. I'm only eighteen. I'm not prepared to be a parent. Well, nineteen technically, but yeah. Eighteen forever.

CHAPTER 44
THE DARWIN AWARDS

THURSDAY, LATER

K laus zooms toward the southwestern-ish area of Bainbridge Island.

I haven't been here too much, so I don't know what the exact spot is called, only that from the air it looks like an enormous swath of forest covering most of the southwest quarter of the island. He seems to head for the thickest part of the woods, a bit west and north of some residential areas. Far enough to be an irritating hike from civilization.

We swoop down out of the sky into the trees, landing amid a spread of old gravestones. This isn't an active cemetery. This is the kind of graveyard people see in YouTube videos where ghost hunters go to long forgotten places. None of the tombstones are intact. All are at least cracked. Most have fallen over. Some are more like small obelisks than traditional tombstones. Many aren't much more than cinderblock sized stones embedded in the ground with someone's name and dates on them. Everything is covered in moss and well into the process of being reclaimed by the forest.

"Whoa. This place is creepy," whispers Chloe.

Is that regret in her voice? She sounds a little scared.

Klaus, arm pointed ahead, runs into the trees, not caring if he passes through them.

I, being solid of body and not possessing the ability to pass through objects, weave around them as best I can.

The ghost leads us into the forest away from the spread of old graves. Maybe sixty or ninety (something like that) feet away from where we landed, we reach a crumbling mausoleum tomb type building. It's the size of a tiny house or a massive, elaborate garden shed. The stone door has already been crowbarred off and lay in chunks on the ground.

Voices whisper inside. I recognize Natasha at least. That's probably Seth, too. They seem to be debating the instructions Topher gave them insofar as how to 'open this thing.'

I'm so tempted to barge in there, shout something like, 'you freaking morons' and then start swinging my katana around. Honestly, just like Chloe should have stayed home, I really should call this in and have Mr. Wolent send backup. No idea what's going on in there. I might be getting in over my head. Also, I really don't want to be the one who has to kill anyone, especially perma-kill vampires. That's kind of a big deal.

Scott doesn't count. Not only was it extremely satisfying to end him for good, he was not a full vampire, merely a partially sentient creature barely aware of his own existence and enslaved to relentlessly obey whatever his primal ID demanded without the ability to think about anything at more than the most rudimentary level. Kinda like Kanye West, but undead.

I pull my phone out.

Screen's blank.

I tap it.

Nothing.

I push and hold the power button... nothing.

"Crap. I must've forgotten to charge my phone." I look at Ashley while stuffing it back in my pocket. "Ash, you have *the number* in your contacts, right?"

"Yeah." She pulls her phone out of her belt clip, then fusses with it. "Dammit. Mine's dead too."

"I don't have a phone. I'm only seven," says Chloe. "Who would I even call?"

"Hurry!" rasps Klaus, sorta whispering as if he's worried about being overheard.

Well, the idiots inside the crypt are vampires. They probably *could* hear him.

Oh, screw it. I pull the katana out of its sheath so it's ready in case I need it. There's no time to fly to Wolent's manor and ask for backup in person. It probably won't matter either way at this point how dangerous it is in there. If those idiots succeed, Rabanus Vesperus is going to devour all of us.

I almost tell Chloe to fly home by herself hoping she escapes his wrath—if we fail. The urge to do so is at the tip of my brain but it's not making it to my mouth. My senses are too preoccupied at the realization this crypt is throwing off serious power. It's kinda like being at a big electrical substation where ten gazillion volts are coursing around inside a metal box as big as my house... only with more doom and fear involved.

Like some sort of brain-dead idiot from a B-grade horror movie, I mindlessly walk over to the mausoleum and go inside. Dammit. Chloe. Get out of here. Why can't I say that out loud? Am I too scared? Am I trying too hard to be stealthy? Is some strange external sense telling me not to worry about her, that she'll be just fine and I need to hurry the hell up and stop these idiots?

The crypt interior has shelf space for sixteen coffins, eight per side in two stacks of four. None of the shelves are occupied. A hole in the floor that appears quite recently broken open reveals a damn stone stairway that has likely been completely covered for a very long time. Pale stone dust and small bits of rock chipped away from the former floor litter the much darker stone stairs.

I descend into the not-dark, katana at the ready.

The ominous dread saturating the air gets stronger and stronger with each step. Oddly, it's not making me feel like I'm advancing toward certain death. It's a strange mixture of raw power and reverence, like I'm entering some place that ought to be sacred or some such thing. Wonder if this is a Nisqually spirit mound or something along those lines? Nah, can't be. The design of this building is too European.

I reach the bottom of the stairs and find myself at the end of a long, rectangular chamber. The half I'm in is empty and plain. In front of me at the opposite end, Natasha, Seth, Robbie, and Topher appear to be trying to make sense of writing etched into the walls.

A big stone crypt box sits on a stone table near Team Idiot. Ornate carvings resembling a hooded grim reaper with black crow wings cover it. At least forty different little Angels of Death decorate that box. Dozens more larger versions of the same figure adorn the walls around it the distant half of the room.

Carved writing and grooves that appear to be simply decorative on the sarcophagus emit a pale whitish glow. It's so faint only a vampire's light-sensitive eyes would see it, but it is definitely there.

The sense of raw power emanating from the sarcophagus is breathtaking and not necessarily in a good way. I'm shaking in my sneakers. Feels like I'm a mouse finally realizing a cat has snuck up on it, two tenths of a second before the fangs pierce my neck.

I glance at my sword. Damn. Natasha's crew aren't the only idiots in the room. A fight in here is a seriously bad idea. Destroying a vampire in this chamber is exactly the wrong thing to do, even though, at this point... I'm obligated to perma-kill all of them. Wolent's order said that if Natasha's people even get close to opening this thing, their existence is forfeit. Gonna need one hell of a lawyer to convince anyone that standing in the same room with the vampire equivalent of a world-ending nuclear bomb isn't 'getting close.'

By rights, I should really proceed directly to the stabby-stabby bits and leave their dismembered remains out where the sun can get them. Wolent, Paolo, and Stefano would expect any society vampire to do that considering the destruction order. Okay, perhaps not Wolent as much. He might not expect *me* to go full on executioner. He would expect me to at least do my best to disable the condemned vampires and call in someone with a less developed sense of guilt to finish them off.

However, in this particular case, following orders is effectively doing exactly the thing we are trying to prevent. Whether or not these vampires have given up their right to exist—at least within any area that Mr. Wolent has influence—doing the deed *right here* is a serious mistake. Even if they are not perfectly of a mindset to will-ingly give themselves as a sacrifice as a specific step in opening the seal on that sarcophagus, who knows how much leeway we've got with ancient magic.

Destroying someone who is willing to open it, even if they aren't intentionally sacrificing their unlife might also count. I don't know. It might not, but that's not a chance I'm willing to take. My logic is sound. I will totally have that discussion with Mr. Wolent if he ever grills me about why I didn't simply start chopping heads off as soon as I walked in here.

"Man," whispers Ashley. "We should really have shotguns for this shit."

Her comment catches me so off guard, I blurt a laugh.

Topher squeaks and jumps, clutching his heart.

Natasha screams, dropping the little notepad she'd been refer-ring to while studying the wall.

Robbie spins to face us. For an instant, he looks terrified. Then he realizes it's not an army of Wolent's leg-breakers, merely me and Ashley. We're even less intimidating than Nancy Drew. He probably thinks I look ridiculous holding a katana. I know it's silly. Also, that works to my advantage. Almost no one would expect me to actually know how to fight with a sword. It doesn't take long for Robbie to stop being scared of two girls who look like high school sophomores that snuck out of the house past their bedtime.

"What the heck are you two doing here?" Robbie rests his hand on the gun tucked in the front of his pants.

The almost manic look in his eyes could either be from the overwhelming power filling this chamber... or him thinking that he can't let either one of us leave here alive to tell Wolent they found the box. Maybe he's not thinking about killing us, but he's definitely at least thinking they need to kidnap us or something and prevent us from going anywhere until they open the box.

Once Rabanus is set free, they no longer have to worry about anything Mr. Wolent says or wants—or so they hope.

And yeah, this is me making assumptions. Educated assumptions, yes, but still assumptions.

Dare I tell them about the whole willing sacrifice deal? It might scare them off doing this. Not too many vampires are fanatical to the point they would give up their immortality for anything. Natasha is nutty enough to 'sacrifice' one of her people against their will. Might not count. Same thing as me killing them while they are trying to open it. Might be an issue, might not. Too many variables and the consequences for being wrong are severe.

Nah. I'm not going to tell them about that... unless I absolutely have to. Seems like a dumb idea to give these morons the keys to the box they're trying to open.

"What are we doing here?" I ask, taking a step closer and putting my sword back in its scabbard. Maybe sheathing the katana will calm the three of them down. "What I'm doing here is trying to stop a bunch of Darwin Award winners from deleting themselves off the Earth."

Natasha waves dismissively at me. "Robbie, just put those two to sleep. Once we free him, it won't matter what that jackass in Seattle thinks."

A sudden, deafening *bang* fills the chamber.

Robbie's groin area explodes in a puff of smoke, blood, and fleshy bits. Two small puffs of dust appear on the floor and ceiling in time with a spark atop the sarcophagus and Topher grabbing his chest before falling.

The gunshot is so damn loud in this entirely stone room, the sensation of sound waves sending ripples across my brain is almost noticeable. Ringing follows. Natasha, Topher, Ashley, and I all clamp our hands over our ears and squirm in pain. I briefly catch sight of Chloe sneaking away from Robbie with her hands over her ears and a 'that was a freaking mistake' expression.

Robbie emits a squeaking gasp, doubles over, and slaps face-first into the ground in a flying ostrich pose.

A moment or so later, I regain the ability to hear.

"Ouch," says Ashley. "Didn't anyone ever tell you it's really freaking stupid to put a gun in your pants like that?"

Robbie howls in agony.

"Shit, that was loud as fuck." Natasha wiggles her fingers in her ears. "Dammit."

"I'm hit," whines Topher from out of my sight behind the sarcophagus.

"*You're* hit?" wails Robbie, rolling back and forth on the floor. "There's a hole in my dick and my balls are freaking *gone!*"

Natasha rolls her eyes and makes a grabbing gesture at her belt. Whatever she reached for is apparently not there anymore, as she seems surprised and looks down at herself. "Son of a bitch..." She turns around. "Where the frick is my gun?"

Seth's doing this odd little dance with his legs crossed. Must be sympathetic pain since he doesn't seem to have been hit by the rico-chet. "Try to relax, man. It'll grow back."

"I knoooow," shouts Robbie. "But it freaking hurts!"

"Hmm?" Ashley lightly jumps as if something snuck up on her and poked her in the leg. She looks down, then raises her hand holding a little, boxy submachine gun. "Oh, neat."

"Hey!" yells Natasha, looking at her belt, then Ashley, then back and forth twice more. "How the hell did you do that?"

"Ancient Jedi magic." Ashley holds the gun sorta off to the side, not pointing it at anyone. She's also not touching the trigger. "Calm down. Not gonna shoot anyone. Just don't wanna be shot."

"Aaaaargh!" wails Robbie, still rocking side to side.

Something pokes me in the leg.

I look down.

Chloe offers me a Glock.

I don't want a gun. But I want Chloe holding a gun much less than I want a gun, so I take it.

It's Robbie's.

And crap. Apparently, kiddo is an exceptional pickpocket. Right. I knew that. If Charles Dickens ever wrote a book about adorable impoverished Victorian child street-waif vampires who resort to stealing to survive, she could be his main character.

"Grr. Why are you constantly getting in the way?" shouts Natasha, while jabbing her finger at me. "You're an annoying little bitch, you know that?"

"I try." I shrug. "Look, that stuff I said before about this guy being apocalyptic? I'm not bullshitting you. If he wakes up, he's going to consume dozens of vampires. Basically, anyone in easy reach when he comes to is going to be breakfast. You, me, Topher, Seth, Robbie and his detached balls..."

"Fuck you," wails Robbie.

"Sorry, man. I don't think you're able to follow through on that offer at the moment." Ashley frowns.

"Oof. Below the belt." Seth cringes.

Grumbling about 'those annoying schoolgirls,' Natasha reaches down and hauls Topher back to his feet. He's got a bullet embedded in his right pectoral area. The wound is so shallow, half the bullet is sticking out of him. I don't think it even broke through his shirt.

Natasha looks at this, then blinks at him. "Seriously? That's barely a goddamned paper cut."

"It was hot." Topher brushes his hand at the bullet, knocking it out of a small divot in his skin. "It burned."

Robbie screams in agony again. Okay, I'm almost starting to feel bad for him, even if he was about to try shooting me.

I say try because there's a chance I might have gotten to him before he could knock me out with a bullet. Shooting a static target at a gun range is a lot different than trying to draw, aim, and fire at a screaming girl with a sword coming for your head. I'd like to say there's a better than fifty-fifty chance he'd have missed.

"What I really need you idiots to understand..." I push the button to drop the magazine out of the Glock, then rack the slide to eject the round from the chamber. Oof. Robbie loaded hollow-point rounds. Ouch. "Is that your plan is not accurate. You have bad information, and you are so damned fixated on what you want to be the truth, you aren't stopping to double check that it actually *is* the truth. Opening this sarcophagus is not going to reinvent society to put vampires in charge. You are going to be setting off what's basically a low-budget apocalypse movie."

Seth folds his arms. "Why low-budget?"

I raise an eyebrow. "Have you ever seen a genre mash-up combining a world ending apocalypse with something else—like vampires—that *wasn't* only available on cable TV at two in the morning?"

"Okay, good point." Seth scratches his cheek and nods.

"Argh! What the hell is wrong with you?" Natasha scowls at him.

"I mean, she's right." Seth gestures at me. "Nuclear apoc movie with zombies or vampires is totally a B movie idea."

Natasha hits herself in the forehead so hard the slap is probably audible outside.

Robbie starts hyperventilating instead of screaming. He grabs himself in both hands, goes red in the face, and shudders.

"What the hell is wrong with him now?" asks Topher.

"Phase three of vampire injury." I hold up three fingers. "First, there's pain. Then, there's a small window of nothing at all. Phase three, healing, is often accompanied by extreme itching."

"Gaaaah!" yells Robbie, convulsing. "Feels like a million termites are eating my nutsack."

Seth winces. He reaches into his green Army jacket, pulls out a handgun, and aims at Robbie's forehead.

Natasha grabs his arm. "What the hell are you doing?"

"He doesn't need to feel or remember that," says Seth.

"Might not want to do that." I cringe. "If any of you die in here, it might set off the end of reality."

Seth glances at me. "Shooting a vampire in the head won't kill him."

"Normally, that is true." I nod. "But we're right next to a freaking *glowing* sarcophagus. We don't know if it will siphon off his life energy. In this room, anything close to death might be permanent."

"I don't freaking care," rasps Robbie in between clenched-jaw screaming. "Do it!"

Seth hesitates, looking at me. "I dunno, 'Tash. That kid really seems to believe it's a mistake to open this thing. What if she's right and it's a vampire nuke?"

"Topher has been researching this for months." Natasha gestures at him with both hands. "Are you saying our expert here, who is all about research and information, is wrong?"

Robbie moans.

"I'm not saying he's wrong." I look at Topher. "I'm saying Remi Durand, who's been around for like seven hundred freaking years, is saying he's wrong. There are all sorts of stories across Europe about how bad an idea it is to wake this guy up."

"And you trust his word?" Topher raises an eyebrow.

"Yeah, I am trusting his word. But I guess it's no more reliable than something someone else wrote in a book you read." I try to put my hands on my hips, but can't. Got a gun in one hand and a sword in the other, so I just succeed in looking like a clueless dork who's baffled that she has arms. "Why do you trust stuff in a book? Just because it's written down doesn't mean it's infallible."

Ashley leans toward me. "Umm, didn't you guys already have this exact conversation?"

"Maybe. Uhh." I scratch my temple with my middle finger—not as a gesture. It's just awkward to scratch while holding a gun. "Didn't work last time. Figured I'd try again since now these guys have definitely set off Wolent's destruction order."

Natasha glares at me. "That isn't much motivation for us to consider what you're saying. If the ancient one isn't going to help us achieve our goals, and is instead going to destroy us... we're screwed either way. Either Wolent's people do it or"—she gestures at the crypt—"he does."

"Do you guys even know his name?" I ask.

Topher makes a face like I'd expect Sierra would if someone pantsed her at school: sheer paralytic terror followed seconds later by murderous rage. Dude's glaring at me like he'd have shot me if he had gun on him.

"Sorry... did I say something offensive?" I tilt my head at him.

"He doesn't know." Ashley laughs. "He's mad because you hit him in his weakness."

Topher grabs the open edges of his beige suit jacket and gives them a sharp tug. He seems to be attempting to reclaim dignity as if we'd just hit him with the most witheringly humiliating insult known to humanity... like Dad telling someone they look like someone who would try to play games on a Mac.

"Okay..." I shift my gaze to Natasha. "So, you are willing to risk destroying society over some rumors your guy found in some old books, and he doesn't even know the name of the specific elder that's in the box? It could be anything from Count Dracula, to the first vampire ever made, to Elvis Freaking Presley."

"Or Jimmy Hoffa," says Ashley.

"Someone kill me," mutters Robbie. "I'm not sure what's worse. The million ants chewing on my balls or this argument."

"I'm completely sure that Elvis Presley is not in the sarcophagus." Topher puts his nose in the air.

"Are you?" Ashley blinks.

"She's just being stupid." Natasha scowls.

"Yeah, Elvis is unalive and well in southern Cali," says Seth. "Least, that's the last I heard."

I fidget. "Okay, I just kinda said that. You're saying Elvis really is a vampire?"

"Yeah." Seth nods. "Almost every celebrity who suffers a sudden, mysterious death is. Especially if they're young at the time. Not *all* of them, but a lot. Immortality is the final thing they can buy."

"Makes sense." I'm really tired of holding this Glock, so I throw it to/at Robbie. "Here. Do yourself a favor and get a holster. Don't stuff it in your pants again."

"Especially a Glock." Seth shakes his head. "That trigger safety is really touchy."

"Can I have mine back, too?" Natasha looks at Ashley, putting on a fake sweet voice.

"Umm, not yet. I think you're going to shoot us." Ashley smiles cheesily.

Natasha grumbles and stomps toward us.

I pull the katana and point it at her. "Don't. We're still talking."

"I'm done bullshitting." Natasha sprouts claws. "Painless bullet to the head or claw time. Your choice. Give me my goddamned Mac."

"Oh, you're a Mac user?" I cringe. "That's unfortunate."

"No, you dumb bitch. Not a computer, a Mac freaking ten. My gun." Natasha points a clawed finger at Ashley. "Hand it over or I'm going to shred both of you."

Damn. So much for avoiding involuntary nudity tonight. I shift my weight into a combat stance, throwing some power into reflexes. "I'm not done explaining to you why what you're doing is a bad idea."

She lunges at me, reaching to slash at my face and throat.

I jump backward, swiping my sword in an upward circular slash that cuts off both her hands, right on the upswing, left on the downstroke.

All her bracelets and stuff fall to the floor.

Natasha stares at her arms, her expression more than a little surprised. Since she's a vampire, the blood isn't spraying out of her arms, merely kinda pooling on the flat spots where her wrists end.

"And what have we learned?" asks Ashley in a sweet voice. "Don't get into a sword fight when you've only got tiny little claws."

Natasha doesn't react.

"Ooh, she's got nothing to say," fake-whispers Ashley. "I think you uhh, stumped her."

The severed right hand on the floor twists itself into a middle finger.

"Oh. My. Gawd," I mutter. "That was horrible."

Seth seems to be trying not to laugh.

Despite no longer having claws, Natasha leans menacingly toward me.

I point the sword at her face. "Back up and calm down. Uhh, you can pick your hands up if you want."

"With fucking what?" yells Natasha. "You stupid bitch."

"Seth?" I glance at him. "You wanna help her out?"

"Yeah." Ashley smiles. "Give her a hand... or two."

I hang my head and sigh.

"I'm gonna kill her," mutters Natasha.

Seth puts his gun back in his underarm holster and hurries over to grab Natasha before she can charge at Ash. Though he keeps a wary eye on me, he picks Natasha's hands up and backs off with her beside him.

"Just hold them in place. They'll stick in a few minutes." I lower my blade but keep it ready.

Seth seems a little awkwardly uncomfortable holding onto severed body parts, but he does his best to position them properly when Natasha holds her arms up.

I shift my attention partially to Topher. "Now, the name of this vampire you're trying to wake up is Rabanus Vesperus. He was alive in the time of the Roman Empire. He's over two thousand years old, and has no idea what the modern world is like. Breaking the spell keeping him in there is going to plunge the entire world into a dark age where mortals scurry around in the dark hiding from vampires. Technology will disappear. All those fun things that keep us from being bored to hell like movies, television, video games, all of that will go away. You think he's going to do what you want, but it's going to be way, way worse. The only good thing for you is you won't exist to see the shitstorm you set off because you guys will be the first ones he consumes."

Natasha, Seth, and Topher stand there making blank faces at me. Topher mouths 'Rabanus Vesperus' a few times, seemingly drawing a blank—then makes an *oh shit* face.

Robbie uncurls and lies flat on the floor. "Holy shit it stopped..."

He hastily opens his belt, seemingly intent on checking to see how the repairs are going.

"Robbie," I say. "Do not take your pants off."

"What?" He shifts his stare to me. "Little girl never saw one before?"

I fold my arms. "You could say that."

Chloe appears between me and Ashley. "These bozos are stupid as fuck."

Robbie clamps his hands over his pants. "What the hell is a kid doing here?"

"Is that really a kid?" Seth raises an eyebrow. "She's older than she looks, right?"

"No." Ashley shakes her head. "She's from New Jersey."

"Oh," says Natasha and Seth at the same time.

Topher raises an eyebrow at me. He still looks terrified. "Why do you have a child with you? You aren't planning to, erm... bite her, are you?"

"Nah. She's one of us." I pat Chloe on the head.

"Natasha, dear..." Topher hurries over to her. "If that truly is Rabanus Vesperus in there, I am afraid this girl—as annoying as she is—is correct. We do not want to open this. I was unable to make sense of the glyphic writing on the walls in here, but I *have* stumbled across information about this ancient. I, umm... was unaware that he was the one occupying this particular sarcophagus. It is true that the legends claim the only way to release him is willing vampire sacrifices. Perhaps a dozen or more."

"I thought you said vampires can't feed from other vampires no matter how old they are." Natasha glares at him.

"Umm." Topher scratches his head. "As far as I know that is true. My knowledge of this elder, Rabanus, is that he was once involved in a generational war among our kind. He would certainly see us as his enemies being that we are not as old as him. I doubt he would seek to consume us, though he would surely destroy us."

Dammit. So much for keeping that whole willing sacrifice thing a secret. Fortunately, it seems this changes her mind. For freaking once, this stupid woman looks actually worried.

"How the hell does she know his name if you couldn't find it?" asks Robbie.

Topher shifts his gaze to me. "Not a bad question."

"Magical divination," I say. "Scrying. I know some mystics."

"Cool." Seth nods. "That sounds trippy."

"Magic..." Topher frowns, then fidgets.

"Is it bullshit?" asks Natasha.

Topher waves randomly. "I do not understand magic but I have come across enough information in old journals and records to make me not immediately dismiss such stories. The odds of this being true are great enough for us to consider the girl is probably correct. Now that she's mentioned the name, things I was unable to make sense of are sliding into place. I'm mostly convinced this is him."

"Which means we do not open it?" Seth raises both eyebrows.

"Indeed." Topher exhales hard. "I am afraid this has been a vast waste of time."

"So... umm..." Natasha stands there, arms out to either side while Seth keeps her hands from falling off. "What are you going to do about that destruction order? Did you come here to finish us off?"

"No. If that was my mission, the fight would be over by now." I tap my foot. "I came here trying to stop you guys from being seriously freaking stupid *without* anyone having to die permanently."

"Aren't you tired of hiding, though?" Natasha attempts to wiggle one of her fingers, which almost responds.

"No, not really... and even if I was, popping this guy out of his box is not going to change that. It's going to make the world an infinitely crappier place to live in. He'll devour everyone near him and then go on a rampage."

"Like she said..." Ashley nudges me. "B-movie apocalypse stuff. Real bad."

"I'm only seven and even I'm not that stupid," mutters Chloe. "Ending the world is bad."

"This is definitely a bad idea." Topher shakes his head. "We should leave."

Natasha looks down. Swear her face reminds me of a kid who thought they were getting an iPad for a gift and got an eye pad, as in a small bandage. Also, any parent that pranks their kid like that is an absolute jerk... unless they immediately follow it up by giving them a real iPad.

"Hey." I step toward her. "Don't you think vampires like Arthur Wolent would love it if vampires were out, about, and in charge? Men like him spend decades thinking about things like cost-benefit analysis and how to increase their own power. He's figured out that it's much easier to operate from the shadows. I think you would be happier if you just got used to staying off mortals' radar and enjoyed existence as much as you can... before you do something stupid enough to be deleted from the undead gene pool."

"We're already screwed." She sighs. "Once you tell your boss you found us here, we're done."

"Well..." I fidget. "Even if I don't *tell* him, he's going to know. I'm not that old. He can read my thoughts. However, if you really and truly have given up on opening this sarcophagus, he might change his mind. The destruction order wasn't because you have ideas about vampires going out into the open. It's because you were about to poke a nuclear bomb and destroy us all."

"Yeah, that would do it." Seth winces.

Natasha manages to wiggle her finger. "Damn itches."

"Doesn't it!?" yells Robbie with a manic face. "Will you please get that kid out of here so I can check my shit?"

I point. "Crawl behind the crypt."

Robbie looks over, shrugs, then drags himself out of sight. A moment later, he cheers, his voice echoing over the chamber. "Woo-hoo. Back in business, baby."

Why do some guys act like their entire reason for existence is their junk? Never will understand that. Boys are like the Death Star if the 'instantly destroy this star station button' was mounted right on the outside middle front of the thing. Such a bad design.

"All right." Natasha gingerly closes her left hand and opens it, wincing. "I swear I'm not interested in opening this crypt anymore. Whatever name that was seems to have scared the shit out of Topher. That's good enough for me."

Ashley reaches over and sets the Mac-10 in Natasha's left hand, which doesn't move that much. Looks like she's trying to get one of Sam's GI-Joe figures to hold a gun. If she's doing that, her emotional read on the woman must be good.

Chloe steps forward and holds up all of Natasha's bracelets. "Here. You dropped these."

Natasha peers down at her. "Thanks, kid. Uhh... my hands aren't working too well at the moment."

Chloe reaches over and stuffs the bracelets into one of the big outer pockets on Seth's jacket.

"That works," says Natasha.

Robbie grabs the top of the sarcophagus and pulls himself upright. He's still walking with a bit of a limp, but he manages to get over to us.

Natasha shakes her head at him, calling him an idiot with a stare.

"Okay, go on." I put the katana back in its scabbard. "I will tell

Mr. Wolent that you are finally convinced opening this sarcophagus is a bad idea."

She glances back at the crypt one final time, then sighs and walks up the stairs, still holding her hands out and up like she's protecting wet nail polish.

The three guys scurry after her.

Ashley exhales. "Well, that went better than expected."

I look down at my completely intact clothes. "Sure did. Not going to complain. I am curious about one thing, though."

"What's that?" Ashley smiles.

"Did Robbie shoot himself in the dick or did something nefarious go on?"

Chloe clasps her hands innocently in front of herself. "He was gonna shoot you guys. I might've poked the trigger. Sorry. I didn't think it was gonna be that loud."

Heh. I ruffle her hair. "It's okay. You're not in trouble."

She gives me this wide-eyed 'really? I'm not!?' stare.

"Don't do that to a mortal, though. Okay? No matter how stupid they are." I pat her shoulder.

"Okay. Don't have to. Mortals we can just derp." She makes a silly face.

"So, umm." Ashley fidgets. "Are we done here?"

I glance at the sarcophagus. "Umm. I think so. What else could we possibly do?"

CHAPTER 45
VAMPIRES OF MASS DESTRUCTION

THURSDAY NIGHT

We stand there looking at the glowing crypt for a moment.

This thing totally looks like it belongs in Skyrim... or some sort of apocalyptic 'angels and demons' game like *Hellgate: London*, something where mysticism and modern day collide. Natasha and her people broke through the floor to reveal this chamber. I'm not equipped to do anything about that right this second... but it's probably not a bad idea to repair it.

"We should probably zoom over to Mr. Wolent's place and give him an update." I gesture at the stairs. "Maybe he can arrange to have this fixed."

"Speaking of Mr. Wolent." Ashley bites her lip. "Are we going to get in trouble for not destroying the idiots?"

"I really don't think so." I rest my sword on the floor and lean on it like a cane. "It's not like we could kill them in here anyway, remember."

"Oh, yeah. True." She fake wipes sweat from her forehead. "So, what now? Are we just going to leave this nuclear bomb sitting here?"

A good point. Unfortunately, I left my cement mixer and work crew in my other pants. "I'm not sure what we really *can* do... other than talk to Mr. W and see if he can send some people to fix this place up so no one realizes this chamber is here."

"Ooh." Ashley snaps her fingers. "We could bring Sophia here. Maybe she could like teleport the crypt out into the ocean or even send it to the Moon."

Chloe laughs. "She'd totally do that."

"Yeah... except for one problem." I turn in place, looking around the chamber. "She'd never make it within 500 yards of this place."

"Huh?" Ashley scrunches her nose. "Why?"

I wave randomly at the room. "Don't you feel that energy radiating off that sarcophagus? This whole area is saturated in it. Soph would freak out and probably faint if she didn't nope out and run away."

"Oh. True." Ashley grimace smiles.

"Besides..." I move toward the stairs, eager to get out of here. "You know how we wake up if something threatens us? I don't want to risk her accidentally setting him off if he somehow senses she's about to launch him to the Moon."

"Eep!" Ashley covers her mouth. "Oh, I never thought of that."

"Hmm..." I pause halfway up the stairs. "Maybe we could get her to do some magic on the outer door so it's like *super* locked or something."

She nods. "That's an idea."

"Locking the door would be quite sufficient," says a deep, male voice seemingly from everywhere.

It's like being the only person in a concert hall and someone's talking over the stereo system.

Ashley shrieks at the jump scare and does this crazy uncoordinated attempt at a kung-fu thing. Either that or she flailed her arms trying to not lose her balance.

I just kinda froze in place.

Chloe makes a face at us, as if to ask why we're being stupid.

"Uh oh. Did we just end the world?" I whisper.

"I must convey my thanks for removing those insufferable fools from my presence," says the everywhere-voice. "Their endless prattle was enough to drive an immortal to insanity."

Eyes closed, I swallow hard and force myself to turn around and look, fully expecting to see the sarcophagus opening. Never thought blowing a vampire's testicles off would count as the key to an ancient ritual intended to trap a great force of evil in a box.

I'm shocked to see it still closed. The lid isn't even cracked open a tiny bit.

"Umm… Rabanus?" I whisper.

"Indeed," says the voice.

He sounds so freaking normal—only a slight trace of an undefinable European accent—I'm kinda not believing it's really him.

"I am Rabanus Vesperus, young one."

"Umm." I look around at the ceiling, searching for speakers. Someone's playing a major prank. Uh oh. There are no speakers. "Why can I understand you? Shouldn't you be speaking Ancient Roman or something?"

"My body has rested for ages. My mind has not. I am familiar with your modern language."

"Why are you guys freaking out?" asks Chloe.

"You don't hear that?" Ashley scoops kiddo up and clings to her, like a giant child needing a teddy bear for protection.

"No."

"My voice is a mental projection," says Rabanus. "It did not seem necessary to alarm the tiny one."

Oh wow. Umm. So, this ancient vampire nuclear bomb doesn't want to scare Chloe. That seems… unexpected.

A sense of smiling comes from… somewhere.

"You told that fool in glasses his books were not trustworthy." A dry chuckle scrapes across my mind. "So, too are the legends and fables your French king has heard. None of it is truth. I sleep to sleep, not to awake one day and destroy. The irritating fool is correct in that we cannot feed from our own kind."

Ashley and I exchange a glance. She seems to relax a bit.

"Oh wow. So, you're not a nuclear bomb." I sigh in relief so hard I nearly fall over. "That's really good to know."

"You have my gratitude for removing those fools from my presence," says Rabanus. "I would appreciate it if you might repair this place, so no further fools disturb me. If and when I do decide to stir, I have no plans to rampage nor upend the natural order of things. Even in my time, our kind kept ourselves out of mortal minds. Even the smallest mice are a deadly adversary in large enough numbers. You would do well to remember this."

I nod in no particular direction. "Yeah. I'd believe it. Okay. Umm. Wow. So, I've spent the past few weeks freaking out over a nothing burger. I'd be mad but, honestly, I'm happy. No end of the world."

Ashley looks about ready to start laughing.

"All right. Umm, sorry to disturb you. Gonna leave now. Will figure something out for the repairs."

The mental voice emits a brief grunt of acknowledgement.

Whew. I'm not even sure what the heck to say to Wolent. I'm just going to go to his manor and stare at him. Let him watch for himself.

He'd never believe me otherwise.

CHAPTER 46
THE HUNT: PART TWO

Well, as I expected, Wolent was a little stunned.

Finding out we have a 2200-year-old vampire sleeping but not sleeping in the area came as a bit of a shock. After reading my mind as to the events of what went on at Bainbridge Island, Wolent has rescinded the destruction order for Natasha and her people. There is no 'nuclear threat' so to speak, so no reason to be that harsh on them. I think he's more upset that whatever people Paolo and Stefano sent to monitor that group lost track of them and allowed them to reach the tomb.

It also now makes sense why the Shadows didn't get involved. Rabanus was not, after all, an apocalyptic threat. Whatever strange ability they have to 'just know things' would not have alerted them to this situation.

Friday was pretty cool and normal. It's amazing how much more fun unlife is when I don't have the end of the world hanging over me. Early on Friday, Ash and I double-dated. I had Hunter, she sorta got back with a guy she dated in junior year. When I say 'got back with,' they're not dating... just a booty call. The old joke about flipping a coin, heads for guys tails for girls, got made about a dozen times.

We went out to dinner, caught a concert, then split up for the sex part. Ashley went to her mom's house with Chris so neither the Littles nor Chloe could walk in on them. I think that's his name... and I went to Hunter's. Unlike me and Hunter, I think Ashley had a snack during their lovemaking session.

Ash and I met back at home a little after one in the morning. Like shifting gears in a 1987 Mustang without a clutch, we went from marathon sex with our boyfriends (sorta) to watching anime like thirteen-year-olds.

It really is nice not having to worry about messing up a job from Wolent that ends up destroying all of society. I haven't been this happy and carefree in a really long time.

So, that was Friday.

Saturday is much less crazy. Christmas is next week, after all. I did finally go and get Sophia a proper crystal ball. Crazy how expensive those things can be. They had one that was over ten grand. I did *not* get that one. Mom would've fainted if I brought that into the house. Stupid thing was like three feet in diameter. It might've broken the floor in her bedroom. I got her a less ostentatious ten-inch one. Rose pink. I'm sure she'll adore it.

Now I only need to keep it a secret for a few more days. Next Wednesday...

Speaking of Sophia, she walks into my room at 5:14 p.m. holding the 'ghost trap', wearing her backpack, and looking ready to go kick something's ass. Or collect something's ass, more like.

"Found one?" I ask.

"Yep." Sophia nods. "Can we go to the mall?"

"The mall?" I blink. "It's at the mall? Now?"

"Yeah." She sighs. "It's going to be there for about another thirty-one minutes, then it's gonna jump again. I figured out why it's so hard to find them."

"Why is that?" Ashley levitates off the bed in the same pose she's sitting, and glides over to the wardrobe cabinet.

"Because they are blinking in and out of existence." Sophia flails her arms. "They appear somewhere, then disappear into the something for days or hours and come back. I have to look for it and get lucky that I'm looking for it when it's actually here."

"Disappear to the something?" I blink. "What the hell does that mean?"

"It's a big word I don't know how to say." Sophia pulls her phone out of her backpack and walks over, showing me the screen.

Among a bunch of typed notes about planar boundaries and magical theory, she points at the phrase 'interstitial space.'

"Interstitial space."

"In-ter-stish-al," says Sophia.

"I think it means a place between other places." Ashley pulls a dress on over her head.

Sophia rolls her eyes. "I know what it means, just not how to pronounce it."

"Reader problem." I chuckle.

"Okay. To the mall we go."

"It's almost dinner time." Chloe peers over at us from the floor. "Mom won't let you out of the house."

Sophia holds up her hand. "I already talked to Mom. She said we can go chase the essence fragment now because it's so temporary and hard to find... but we have to get home in fifteen minutes."

"Fifteen minutes?" I blink. "It will take us at least five to fly there... if we haul major ass."

"Then we better get going." Ashley steps into her Uggs and scurries for the door.

I scramble out of my 'comfy house loungewear' (also known as a long T-shirt) and throw on the first things worthy of going outside in I get my hands on: a blue dress, leggings, fuzzy socks, and also Uggs. Damn. This outfit is not great for fighting—or flying. Flying is why leggings are involved. If I have a wardrobe malfunction while landing (dresses love to flap upward) no one will see anything they wouldn't see in a yoga class.

Granted, if someone actually sees me landing, whether or not my bare ass or underwear is exposed is a minor detail. I'm going to need to erase memories. Flying is kind of one of those 'not supposed to happen' things the normies can't know about.

We hurry upstairs. I pause in the kitchen long enough to wheedle an extra ten minutes out of Mom, because travel time. That still only leaves us fifteen minutes at the mall. Hopefully, this is enough.

Once out on the back deck, Sophia jumps on my back. I grab her arms for extra safety, and leap into the air. Chloe's following because, of course, she is. No big deal now. This is not a dangerous job and it's not even six at night. No one would give a little kid a second glance for being awake at this hour. We look totally normal, except for not having winter coats on. Well, Sophia has her coat. The rest of us don't.

Oops. Rushing.

It's also snowing a bit.

So, yeah. By the time we get to the mall, we're wet.

To escape being noticed flying at a crowded mall, I decide to land on the roof and 'break in' via a not really locked to me door. We scurry down a stairwell to the ground floor, invisible to security cameras on the way.

Sophia does a little magic to dry us off, then she pulls out that copier lens thing.

We navigate the maintenance passages behind the stores before deciding to enter a door at random. This brings us into the back room of a clothing store specializing in expensive tiny things that only Korean girls—or my family—could possibly fit into. None of the five people working here pay any attention to us as we walk out of their back room and head into the mall.

Nice, Ash.

Once we're out in the mall concourse, Sophia holds up the magic lens and hurries off to the left. Three minutes later, we stop at the entrance to a kitchenware store. Hundreds of knives and other sharp things hang on the walls.

A glowing orb of faint peach-colored energy drifts around near the back.

"Oh hell no." Ashley shivers. "That's bad."

"Why the heck is that thing hanging out in a knife shop?" I whisper. "What about Sophia in any way likes knives?"

Sophia fidgets. "I don't. Guess my theory about it being attracted to places I like was wrong."

"Oh, it knows we're coming for it." Ashley rubs her cheek. "It wants weapons. Soph likes the mall, right?"

"I do." She smiles.

"Knife store just happens to be in the mall. It's ready for war." Ashley almost hides behind me.

Sophia pulls her mittens off and stuffs them in her pockets. "It's not going to go crazy like the one at the school did."

Whoa. Sophia sounds a bit like Seirra there for a second. Not a hint of nervousness in her voice.

Chloe takes the 'ghost trap' from her. "Like last time?"

"Basically, like last time but much easier." Sophia tilts her head to the left, then the right like a boxer cracking their neck before a fight.

No, her neck does not crack or make any sound.

Kiddo wanders into the knife shop, fearlessly. She pretends not to notice the orb and makes her way over to where it floats. Right as she reaches it, the orb wobbles, spins, then zooms toward us, racing toward the mall outside the kitchen shop.

Sophia holds up her hand in a 'stop' gesture. The orb abruptly slams to a halt as if it had hit a wall. She makes a pushing gesture, causing the orb to drift back toward Chloe. The thing shudders, wobbling side to side. Some of the knives on the wall shake and rattle.

The guy behind the desk looks up, muttering to himself, wondering if we're experiencing an earthquake.

Chloe hits the button on the 'ghost trap' Dad made, opening the doors. A faint pinkish glow shines out from inside it, no doubt the bastard orb we caught at the school.

Sophia swipes her hand downward. Orb two plummets straight down into the trap, which snaps shut. It wobbles, fumes, and emits smoke for a few seconds. The clerk and some customers don't seem to notice it—or Chloe.

"Wow." I whistle. "That seemed easy."

"Yeah." Sophia examines her fingernails. "It is kinda easy now that I figured out what I'm doing... and Eveline isn't messing with me, helping the stupid things."

"Nice." Ashley nods.

Chloe wanders over to us, holding up the trap on the wire like she went fishing and got her first real catch.

"Great." Sophia exhales. "Just one more... I have to hurry up and fix this before Christmas."

I look at her. "Why? Is there some sort of winter equinox thing going on with magic?"

"No." She flails her arms at me, full of urgency and worry. "I don't want Santa to be mad at me."

I chuckle. "You know it's Mom and Dad, right?"

Ashley gasps and covers Chloe's ears.

Kiddo doesn't react. Her awful parents never bothered telling her about the Santa thing, nor did they really do much in terms of giving her gifts for Christmas. It feels more cruel to tell Sophia Santa is an idea more than a being than it is to say the same thing to Chloe.

"Sare?" Sophia tilts her head at me, causing her pink wool hat to flop over sideways. Yes, it has a little embroidered unicorn on the rim. "Well, I mean... vampires are real. So are leprechauns and dryads and trolls and stuff. Just saying. There might really be a Santa out there."

I chuckle. "Fair point."

"Oh, wait." Sophia biffs herself in the forehead. "Hang on. I'm being dumb."

"No, you're not. Nothing wrong with hoping there's a Santa. Even if you are eleven years old." I whistle innocently.

"No, not about that." Sophia narrows her eyes. "Let's go somewhere remote with no witnesses."

"Uh oh. You did it now, Sare." Ashley elbows me. "You've offended the Santa Mafia. She's been ordered to take you out."

"No." Sophia rolls her eyes. "I need to do magic stuff. I'm being really stupid about this orb thing."

"Can it wait for after dinner?" I ask.

Sophia opens her mouth, pauses, then sighs. "Yeah. It can. You're right. Mom wants us home."

CHAPTER 47
FULLY OPERATIONAL

SATURDAY NIGHT

S oon after dinner, we head out into the world yet again.

Not going too far, though. The woods behind our house are enough. Sam and his friends go in there all the time to play and it's plenty removed from immediate view that we could do just about anything paranormal and not risk exposure. Sure, anything seriously loud would get noticed. However, it takes time for people to come investigate strange sounds. We'd have more than enough time to get out of there and leave someone talking about the crazy stuff they heard on some fringe YouTube paranormal video.

So, the whole lot of us—me, Ashley, the Littles, and Chloe march out into the mini-forest.

Sierra's bringing her sword, just in case. I'm pretty sure she's not expecting to need it as much as she's taking advantage of any excuse to carry it around. Those opportunities don't happen very often, after all.

With copious amounts of crunching and snapping twigs, we make our way into the trees. Eventually, we can't see our house anymore nor any neighbors' places. Even though civilization is a mere ten-ish-minute walk in any direction, we can pretend we're far out in the middle of nowhere here.

"This work?" I ask. "You just need privacy, right? Not like you're going to do something that will contaminate the place we live?"

"Nope." Sophia laughs. "This is fine."

While Soph wanders back and forth creating a small circle with sticks, rocks, and some salt she's appropriated from Mom's kitchen, the rest of us stand there watching. Got a feeling Max the hellhound isn't too far behind us either.

"Why did you say you were being dumb?" asks Ashley after about eight minutes of no one talking.

"Because." Sophia looks over her circle. "That should be good. Umm, because I captured a piece of it already. I didn't need to spend days trying to find more." She pats the 'ghost trap.' "I can use the pieces I have to force the rest of it to come to me... instead of chasing it."

"Oh." I shrug. "Sounds good."

Sophia sets the ghost trap down in the middle of her circle, takes four steps back, then concentrates. The trap wobbles and rumbles briefly. We all watch in rapt fascination as a series of small peach-colored lights appear out of thin air and orbit in lazy circles around the area.

"Creature formed of magic," whispers Sophia, "in parts of three, I command you now, come back to me."

Sierra cringes, then whispers, "Does magic have to rhyme?"

Sophia glances sideways at her. "No. But it sounds cool."

It's really hard to laugh at Sierra's 'no... no it does not sound cool' stare.

"If it works, it's cool." Sam shrugs. "Doesn't matter what it sounds like."

Ashley thinks it sounds cool. Me? Neither lame nor cool. Yeah, Dad's joke is so totally true. In order to make my siblings, my parents divided my soul into three parts: the super girly, the tomboy, and the pragmatist. Put all three of the Littles together and it's me.

A faint screaming noise akin to firing Blix out of a cannon arises in the distance growing rapidly louder until one of those orbs rockets into view and slams into the ghost trap. If coalescences of magical energy could leave claw marks like a cat trying to resist being dragged into a carrier, there would be a really long rip in reality from here to wherever that thing came from.

Flickering light blasts upward from the *Ghostbusters* inspired trap, flaring to painful brightness for a split second before it collapses in on itself, turning once more into the red-skinned goblin-shaped creature with a whole mess of long tentacles sticking out of its back.

Now, the magical abomination is *not* stuck waist deep in the floor. It stands on huge misshapen feet, which means the creature is about ten feet tall and freaking *towering* over us. It also does *not* look very happy to see us.

Sophia, in flagrant disregard to being Sophia, stares defiantly at the thing. Not even a whimper from her.

"Great..." Sierra raises her sword in both hands. "You put the stupid thing back together. Now what?"

"Now," says Sophia, "We destroy it."

"Uh oh." Sam blinks. "Something broke Soph. She wants to kill."

Sophia points at it. "That is not a real creature. It was never alive. It is not alive. It is simply a gathering of magical energy imperson-ating a giant red goblin."

Said giant red goblin raises its fist and tries to smash my little sister.

I dive at her, grabbing Sophia and zooming her out of the way as a fist bigger than my chest divots the ground where she'd been.

The *whump* of it hitting is enough to knock Sam into a stumble and send Chloe scrambling for a hiding spot.

Growling, the giant creature tries to grab Sierra with its back tentacles. Thankfully, she is seriously fast and leaps out of the way, making it look easy.

I drop Sophia on her feet, sprout my claws, and put myself between her and this giant monster. "Any words of advice before I fling myself at it?"

"Yeah." Sophia takes three steps to the right, so I am no longer between her and the creature. "I have a *word* of advice."

The giant goblin thing faces her, raising one eyebrow as if it can't wait to hear what she's going to say. Its expression totally says 'oh, really little child, what are you going to do?'

Sophia widens her stance and raises her hands up over her head, then yells, "*Fireball!*"

A basketball-sized orb of seriously intense bright flames appears between her hands. Sophia hurls it forward with a cute little grunt of exertion.

The fiery whoosh drowns out Sam yelling as the pyroclastic orb zooms into the creature's huge gut.

I think he said, "Hit the deck" or something along those lines.

Next thing I know, a massive explosion flings me off my feet. I catch myself with my ability to fly before I slam into anything painful, like a tree, then reorient myself upright while continuing to slide several feet backward under a painfully hot wind, my boots plowing clear trails in the undergrowth.

When the billowing cloud of orange heat dissipates a second or two later, nothing remains of the enormous creature but a pelting of small chunks of fleshy, meaty bits that smell vaguely of overcooked steak.

Sophia still stands where she had been before, close-ish to the epicenter of the blast. Everyone else is at least ten feet farther away and picking themselves up off the forest floor. A rumbling echo continues into the distance from the explosion. Sophia is unburnt and unmoved by the blast, though she is covered in fleshy, meaty chunks like everyone else.

"Holy hell," whispers Ashley.

"She blew the absolute shit out of it." Sierra blinks.

"Eww," says Chloe. "I'm covered in goo."

As are we all.

"Oh, this is disgusting." Ashley looks down at herself, spattered with little meatball sized bits of smoking flesh as well as some manner of dark red goop.

"Is it destroyed?" asks Sierra.

"Yep." Sophia nods.

"We should get the hell out of here before someone comes running to see what just exploded." Sam plucks a wad of meat off his chest and flings it aside. "This smells disturbingly like someone let Dad near the grill again."

"Good plan." I nod.

Sophia waves her hand around over her head.

Sierra flinches.

The gore leaps off us, gathers into a floating mass less than one fifth of the size of the original creature, and then flops to the ground. She waves sharply at it in a 'get out of here' gesture. The meat bits and goo glow bright pink, then disintegrate to nothingness.

"Neat," says Ashley.

Sophia shrugs. "That's normal. Conjurations always disintegrate when the magic ends. I just sped it up a little."

Sierra walks over to me and whispers, "Did something kidnap Sophia and replace her with an almost perfect but not quite right doppelganger?"

Sophia laughs. "No, I'm me. Just... now that I know that stupid Eveline was messing with me this whole time... I don't feel like a failure at magic anymore."

"She cast a freaking *fireball*," whispers Ashley in awe. "That is freaking amazing."

Amazing is one word for it. Holy crap. Mom is going to lose her mind when she finds this out.

"Uh oh." Sam whistles. "Soph is now fully operational."

"Eep!" I fake cringe.

"Ha ha." Sophia rolls her eyes.

"*Someone* has been doing some extra reading in the Tome of F Knowledge, haven't they?" Ashley wags her eyebrows.

Sophia grinds the toe of her boot into the dirt. "Maybe."

"Guess that F stands for fireball." Sam chuckles.

A distant siren approaches.

"C'mon, you guys. We gotta get out of here." I hurry toward home with the Littles, Ashley, and Chloe right behind me.

Yeah, holy cow. Sophia is 'fully operational' indeed.

Look out world. We're in trouble.

fin